The *Silvae* of Statius

The *Silvae* of Statius

*Translated with Notes and
Introduction by*

Betty Rose Nagle

Indiana University Press
Bloomington • Indianapolis

This book is a publication of

Indiana University Press
601 North Morton Street
Bloomington, IN 47404-3797 USA

http://iupress.indiana.edu

Telephone orders 800-842-6796
Fax orders 812-855-7931
Orders by e-mail iuporder@indiana.edu

© 2004 by Betty Rose Nagle

Manufactured in the United States of America

Library of Congress Cataloging-in-Publication Data

Statius, P. Papinius (Publius Papinius)
[Silvae. English]
The Silvae of Statius / translated with notes and introduction by Betty Rose Nagle.
   p. cm.
Includes bibliographical references.
ISBN 0-253-34387-9 (cloth : alk. paper) — ISBN 0-253-21667-2 (pbk. : alk. paper)
1. Occasional verse, Latin—Translations into English.
2. Rome—History—Domitian, 81–96—Poetry. I. Nagle, Betty Rose. II. Title.
PA6697.E5S5 2004
871'.01—dc22

                         2003017927

1 2 3 4 5 09 08 07 06 05 04

for Barbara A. Johnson

longi tu sola laboris conscia

CONTENTS

Acknowledgments

Part of this work was made possible by a sabbatical and a leave of absence from Indiana University. Christine Hansen and Carole Newlands generously read and commented on an early draft of some of the poems. My editor, Mike Lundell, solicited my submission of a prospectus after hearing from my colleague Cynthia Bannon about a reading I gave for my department in fall 2000. My colleague Eleanor Leach kindly requested a packet of some of the poems to use in her graduate Latin survey class, thus giving them a test run by one of their intended audiences. A version of 2.5 ("Melior's Parrot Is Dead!") appeared in the *Cells* issue (2001) of *Two Lines: A Journal of Translation,* pp. 151–59. A version of 5.4 ("An Insomniac's Prayer") first appeared in *Metamorphoses: The Journal of the Five-College Faculty Seminar on Literary Translation* 11.2 (Fall 2003). My copyeditor, Alice Falk, and an anonymous reader both helped me avoid a variety of inaccuracies and infelicities. Shackleton Bailey's Loeb edition of the *Silvae* appeared after I had completed the manuscript of this book, but the same anonymous reader helpfully called my attention to particularly interesting points where his Latin text agrees or disagrees with what I have chosen to translate.

I am grateful for all this support and encouragement. Yet, while Barbara Johnson was not literally "the sole witness of my long toil," I benefited more than words can express not just from her insightful advice as a critic, but especially from her loving support as a partner.

The *Silvae* of Statius

Introduction

The Life and Works of Statius

Publius Papinius Statius lived from roughly the mid-40s to the mid-90s CE. Born in Naples of Greek extraction, he was the son of a professional poet and teacher. Except for a brief mention in Juvenal's Seventh Satire, our information about Statius comes exclusively from his own works, especially *Silvae* 5.3. One of the longest of the *Silvae* (nearly 300 lines), this poem laments the death of Statius' father, memorializes his career, and celebrates the influence he had on his son. His poetic performances met with great success in the competitions which were part of public festivals at that time. Some of these, such as Naples' own Augustalia, had recently been established in Italy to honor the emperors, but they were modeled on the long-flourishing Greek festivals at Nemea, Pythia, and Isthmia (the Olympics did not include such contests). There has even survived an inscription at Eleusis honoring Statius' father.[1] Professional poets traveled an established circuit of competitions, much as professional tennis players and golfers do now. Statius himself competed successfully at the Augustalia, and at the Alban Games established by the Emperor Domitian. Two features of these traditional Greek poetry contests influenced the *Silvae*. Poems in praise of public figures, composed in dactylic hexameters, were a part of the competitions, as were contests in impromptu performance.[2]

When Statius was in his teens, his father moved the family to Rome to continue a teaching career in the world capital. There the older poet instructed future members of the ruling elite, including perhaps the Emperor Domitian (if he is the future pontifex maximus to whom *Silvae* 5.3.178–80/240–43 alludes).[3] Statius continued to live in Rome (or at his villa in the nearby Alban Hills—a gift from Domitian, as was its connection to the aqueduct that also served the emperor's own Alban villa, 3.1.61–63/92–94) until returning to Naples toward the end of his life. These two cities form the axis of his life and poetic career—Naples, the cultural capital of Greek southern Italy, and Rome, the center of imperial power and influence. Around the Bay of Naples were also the luxury villas which had long served as retreats from public life for the ruling elite. By Statius' time, when the aristocracy found involvement in government much more dangerous and far less rewarding under the Empire than it had been under the Republic, many retired permanently; they "cultivated their own gardens," in Epicurean parlance, devoting their energies to art, literature, and philosophy. The *Silvae* aim a spotlight on the ethos and culture of such men and their families, celebrating and commemorating both those involved in government and those leading lives of cultured detachment around the Bay of Naples or on the outskirts of Rome. Statius himself may have felt a tension between the attractions of the two cities. Even while visiting a friend's villa near Sorrento, he is eager to get back to Rome (2.2.11–12/14–16). Conversely, in a poem persuading his wife to retire with him to Naples, he presents it as a better Rome (3.5.81–112/115–59).[4]

Statius was a contemporary of the Emperor Domitian, last in the Flavian dynasty (which consisted of Vespasian and his two sons, Titus, the very popular elder brother, and Domitian, the autocratic younger brother who was feared rather than loved by his subjects), during whose reign (81–96 CE) he composed all of his surviving works. In 92 he published the *Thebaid*, an epic on the war fought between the sons of Oedipus for the throne of Thebes. Far from treating an obscure subject, this was actually a work of topical interest. For the Romans, civil war—metaphorically war between brothers—had plagued them ever since the founder Romulus had murdered his twin, Remus. The Flavians had come to power (as had Augustus and the Julio-Claudians) after a period of civil war, and the dynasty was marked by contention between the two brothers; the younger one had ruled briefly in his own right while his father and elder brother were in the Near East capturing Jerusalem, and then had brooded over the postponement of his ambitions during the reigns first of Vespasian and then Titus. With his epic *Thebaid,* Statius staked his claim to be the great Virgil's successor. Like the *Aeneid,* the *Thebaid* contains twelve books; and like Virgil, Statius composed his epic very slowly (taking twelve years, he claimed) and gave public recitations from the work in progress. Two lost works were also composed during that period. According to Juvenal 7.87, Statius composed a pantomime libretto for the dancer Paris (executed in 83). Only a four-line fragment survives from a work on Domitian's German campaign, presumably the one which he performed successfully at the Alban Games of March 90 (*Silvae* 4.2.65–67/93–97).[5]

In 93, soon after the completion of the *Thebaid*, he published a collection of occasional poems—the first three books of the *Silvae*. In these poems Statius wove together the Greek and Roman strands of his cultural heritage. The cultivation and celebration of friends had long been a theme in Roman poetry. As already noted, hexameter poetry in praise of public figures formed a category in the Greek-inspired festival poetic competitions in which Statius' father and he himself had participated. So did impromptu poetic composition, a factor which may help to explain Statius' frequent claim in the *Silvae* that he had quickly improvised a given poem soon after the occasion which inspired it. Another volume of *Silvae* (the fourth book) came out in 95, and a fifth book appeared posthumously. At his death, Statius also left behind his unfinished *Achilleid,* an epic treatment of the life of Achilles, of which he had composed little more than the first book.

In the same year as his victory at the Alban Games, Statius failed to win in the competition at the Capitoline Games, also established by Domitian. Perhaps for this reason, but allegedly because of his health, Statius returned to Naples; in *Silvae* 3.5 he makes the case for retiring there to his wife, the widow of another poet and mother of Statius' stepdaughter, his only child. There is no evidence for the date of his death, but it is conventionally given as 96, the year of Domitian's assassination.

The Silvae

Traditionally, the *Silvae* have been categorized as "occasional" poetry—that is, poetry which responds to specific events, such as birthdays, weddings, appointments to public office, departures for and returns from trips abroad, and the like. Occasional poetry tends to be disparaged as a minor genre, yet the quality of any poem certainly depends not on the occasion but on the poet; some so-called occasional poems far transcend and outlive their limited topicality. It had long been a tradition in Roman poetry to celebrate and memorialize such occasions in the lives of one's patrons and friends. To this Roman tradition Statius adds the strain of panegyric from the Greek poetry contests in which he and his father both participated. Whatever specific occasion prompted the poem, Statius uses it as an opportunity to praise its addressee. Hence, the *Silvae* have more recently come to be called "praise poetry."[6]

The first four books of the *Silvae* consist of twenty-seven poems arranged by the author. Each has a prose preface addressed to the book's dedicatee, which serves as a table of contents and also allows Statius to articulate his poetic principles, especially concerning the ostensibly improvised nature of the compositions; the latter undertaking emerges in the guise of anticipating possible criticism for his perpetuating spontaneous effusions whose timeliness has already faded. The posthumous fifth book contains four complete poems and a fragment; the brief prose letter attached to it probably was not intended by Statius as a preface.

By far the majority of the poems are composed in dactylic hexameter, the meter traditional for the praise poetry performed at Greek festivals and, of course, the meter par excellence of ancient epic. A few other poems are written in hendecasyllables. This is a swifter and less formal meter; hence Statius uses it for the two Saturnalia poems (1.6, 4.9), as well as for a poem celebrating the rapid construction of a new highway (4.3). A poem in honor of the epic poet Lucan (2.7) would seem to demand hexameters, but Statius explains his choice of hendecasyllables as a way to avoid comparison with Lucan's own epic lines (2.pref.24–26). Inexplicably, this meter also seems to have a closural function for Statius: three of the poems in hendecasyllables come at the end of a book, and the fourth (4.3) ends a group of three in honor of Domitian.[7] Finally, there are two poems in lyric meters, each written in a different form of Horatian ode (4.5, 4.7), perhaps as a compliment to the literary taste of the addressees.[8] An ancient poet's choice of metrical form reveals much about the nature of the subject and the poet's attitude toward it, because certain forms were long-established as appropriate for certain subjects. Granted that hexameters were the form traditional for Greek competitive praise poetry, hexameters by the author of the already-famous epic *Thebaid* must surely also have had epic implications for their readers. Statius' choice of the meter of epic for these supposedly improvised occasional poems, then, marks them as serious works intended to keep the memory of their subjects alive for posterity.

The title of the collection *Silvae* literally means "Forests," but the word has several metaphorical meanings of literary-critical significance.[9] *Silvae* can be improvisations or sketches, which suits Statius' insistence in the prefaces on speedy composition (and on the role of extemporaneous performance at contests). From the mixed nature of trees in a forest (as opposed to an orchard), *Silvae* can be a miscellany, and the name therefore is appropriate for the variety of poems in the collection. The implications of neither "improvisation" nor "miscellany," however, should suggest any carelessness or randomness on Statius' part in selecting and arranging the poems in each book. Scholars have noted patterns of arrangement as elaborate as those found in Augustan poetry books. The title of David Bright's *Elaborate Disarray: The Nature of Statius' "Silvae"* (1980)—a work that appeared early in the revival of literary interest in these poems—reveals its concern with structure and arrangement, as does the subtitle of Stephen Newmyer's *The "Silvae" of Statius: Structure and Theme* (1979). More recently, Carole Newlands has discussed the artful arrangement of books 1 and 3.[10] And finally, from the nature of the wood from a forest as the raw material for construction comes the sense of *Silvae* as "rough drafts," the material on which more polished compositions can be based (cf. Quintilian 10.3.17). The poet Lucan, whose birth *Silvae* 2.7 commemorates, gave a collection of his that title, but it has not survived and we have no idea of what the contents were like. Yet another possibility is that the title of the *Silvae* alludes to Virgil's *Eclogues*, specifically the line *si canimus silvas, silvae sint consule dignae!* (4.3; "If we sing about forests, let them be forests worthy of a consul!"). Perhaps the *Silvae* are intended as Statius' answer to the *Eclogues*, as his *Thebaid* answers the *Aeneid*.[11]

Overall the *Silvae*, with their combination of Greek praise poetry and the Roman poetry of friendship, represent "something new in Latin literature,"[12] and within the collection are several more specific innovations. Statius was the first Roman poet to devote entire poems to descriptions of works of art or architecture.[13] Greek and Latin poetry had long included descriptions of works of art (e.g., the Shield of Achilles in the *Iliad*); the technical term for such a description is *ecphrasis*. The objects described in the *Silvae* range from a colossal equestrian statue of Domitian (1.1) to a statuette of Hercules (4.6). They include the baths of Etruscus (1.5) and the villas of Vopiscus (1.3) and Pollius (2.2), Violentilla's Roman town house (part of 1.2), the temple to Hercules rebuilt by Pollius on the shore near his villa (3.1), and the emperor's palace (4.2). An engineering project—Domitian's new highway—is described in 4.3. Statius was the first to write long descriptive poems about villas; according to Newlands, this new genre of his influenced comparable poems on English country homes, beginning in the seventeenth century with Ben Jonson's "To Penshurst."[14] Both baths and road construction were novel subjects for poetry.[15] Finally, Newlands asserts, Statius was the first to deal extensively with the relationship between a poet and the imperial court.[16] Contrast Statius' approach with that of the Augustan poets and their well-known posture of refusal (*recusatio*); they declined to write on lofty imperial themes, claiming that they were incapable of taking on such a grand task.

Thus the *Silvae* open an unprecedented literary window onto the material culture of the period. In his ecphrases of public and private buildings, Statius praises the splendor and magnificence of imported marbles, gilded ceilings, mosaic floors, precious metals (e.g., the silver fixtures of Etruscus' bath). He also praises feats of design and construction, such as Vopiscus' villa on two sides of a river, with its water piped into every bedroom, and Pollius' villa high on a cliff, with its covered portico providing access from the sea, various rooms oriented for different views, and imported works of art. The *Silvae*, according to Zoja Pavlovskis, are "the first poetry in Latin literature to celebrate openly the amenities made possible by the Empire's abundant wealth."[17] Statius' attitude toward wealth and luxury forms a strong contrast with typical Roman moralizing, such as that expressed by Horace. It is not wealth per se which Statius praises, to be sure, but the lifestyle it enables its possessors to lead (sometimes, paradoxically, characterized by Epicurean simplicity) and the taste with which they make use of their wealth. For this reason Statius even praises lavishly extravagant expressions of grief (e.g., Melior's desire to burn all of his wealth on Glaucias' tomb, 2.1.162–63/223–25, and Abascantus' erection of a temple-like tomb for Priscilla, with statues depicting her in the guise of various deities, 5.1.225–33/304–15).

For the kinds of occasions Statius treats in the *Silvae*, late Greek rhetorical handbooks meticulously prescribe the topics to include and the order for their inclusion. Some scholars, therefore—Alex Hardie most recently—have stressed the supposed influence of this epideictic ("display") rhetoric on the *Silvae*.[18] Since training in rhetoric formed the basis of an elite Roman male's education, doubtless something like those rules for epideictic genres (*genethliacon* = birthday poem, *propempticon* = bon voyage poem, and so on) existed in Statius' time, though perhaps not in such prescriptive detail. Surely his addressees and other readers would have been familiar with the basic requirements for each genre.

In fact, this familiarity on the part of his audience allows Statius to use the generic categories and their "rules" in creative and original ways. In book 2, for example, there are two consolations to men whose favorite young slave has died (2.1, 2.6). Anyone who reads these two poems, along with the four other consolations contained in the *Silvae* (3.3, 5.1, 5.3, 5.5), will notice the common themes and motifs, some of which surely must arise from the situation itself and not from any rhetorical prescriptions for its treatment. In book 2, however, Statius consoles Melior for the death of his parrot, using the same themes and motifs for a pet as he employs for a young slave. *Silvae* 2.4 is reminiscent of Ovid's lament for a dead parrot (*Amores* 2.6, which similarly appears in a collection that also contains a serious lament for a person—the poet Tibullus, mourned in *Amores* 3.9), as well as of Catullus' famous poem 3 on a dead sparrow. These poems on dead pet birds by Catullus and Ovid are in turn part of a long tradition in ancient literature of poems about animals, living and dead. It is this poetic tradition which influences Statius in *Silvae* 2.4 at least as much as any rhetorical prescriptions do. The first poem in book 5 of the *Silvae* is a consolation, too, but one addressed to the deceased, and one including much praise not only for her but also for her husband.

Statius also makes creative use of the rhetorical categories of the "thanksgiving poem" (*eucharisticon*) and the "birthday poem" (*genethliacon*). Two of the *Silvae* respond explicitly to dinner invitations. *Silvae* 4.2 begins as thanks to the emperor for a banquet, but really uses the occasion for a lavish description of the palace. The point of departure for 4.6 is a dinner shared with Vindex, but the real subject is a description of the host's statuette of Hercules. A third poem is apparently the result of a dinner invitation; Statius implies in the preface to book 1 that he performed or presented his description of Etruscus' baths (1.5) during a break at dinner. There is no *genethliacon* per se in the *Silvae;* the birth of a child is the point of departure for 4.7 and 4.8, but the poems' true aim is to congratulate the father. Because 2.7 is paradoxically a birthday poem for someone long dead, it combines topics appropriate for a consolation, too.[19] The poem about Melior's peculiarly shaped tree is revealed only near the end (2.3.62–63/76–77) to be a birthday present; in connection with this birthday theme, the very end (76–77/96–98) refers to the fund Melior established for the Poets' Society to commemorate the birthday of his friend Blaesus.[20] While 3.2 is a fairly straightforward bon voyage (*propempticon*) for Maecius Celer, who is departing for his military post in Syria, 5.2 begins as a bon voyage to Crispinus, who is leaving for Tuscany, but evolves, by way of wondering where he will travel when he is appointed military tribune, into congratulations for that appointment.

Indeed, Statius is far more indebted to his poetic predecessors than to the rhetoricians. Not only in the lament for Melior's parrot but in several other *Silvae* does the influence of Catullus appear. Statius' marriage poem in hexameters (1.2) owes a debt to Catullus 62 and 64. The poem jokingly critical of Plotius Grypus' Saturnalia present (4.9) echoes some of Catullus' "horror" about Calvus' gift (poem 14), and the injunction against a hendecasyllabic poem from Grypus in return may echo the competitive versifying in Catullus 50.[21] The poem on Earinus' lock of hair (3.4) of course recalls Catullus 66, the translation of Callimachus' "Lock of Berenice."[22] To Horace, Statius owes the metrical form of 4.5 (Alcaic ode) and 4.7 (Sapphic ode), as well as the use in 4.4 of hexameter for a verse epistle.[23] Horace's *Satires* 2.3 and 2.7 are the "literary paradigm" for a Saturnalia poem.[24] Some of Statius' Epicurean themes, too, recall Horace, though his praise of luxury and of luxurious villas is set in opposition to the simplicity Horace prizes.[25]

As one would expect from the epic successor of Virgil, that poet's influence is pervasive. A typical reminiscence occurs at the beginning of the description of Domitian's palace as *tectum augustum, ingens, non centum insigne columnis, / sed quantae superos caelumque Atlante remisso / sustentare queant* (4.2.18–20/ 25–28: "The house is huge, majestic; not a hundred / columns distinguish it, but just as many / as could keep gods and heaven standing up / if Atlas took a rest"). This recalls (but outdoes) Latinus' palace, *tectum augustum ingens centum sublime columnis* (*Aeneid* 7.170; "a building majestic, huge, lofty with one hundred columns"). As Hardie observes, the *Silvae* are epic in diction, phraseology, tone, and devices; this aspect of the *Silvae* he attributes to the tradition of "Greek praise in the epic style," such as Theocritus' *Idylls* for the Ptolemies.[26] Quite true—but this "epic style" is also that of the poet of the *Thebaid* and *Achilleid*. Critics in the Renaissance remarked on the epic *granditas* of the *Silvae*,[27] a quality not limited to the hexameter poems. For example, Newlands speaks of a "tension" created by the presence of epic machinery in a hendecasyllabic Saturnalia poem (1.6).[28] In fact, despite Hardie's claim that Statius' "epic style" originated in Greek praise poetry, one could argue that his use of the epic form for topical subjects is, if not inappropriate, at least paradoxical and perhaps used for creative effect. There is a fundamental incongruity in using the form associated with immortalizing "kings and battles" to commemorate dinner parties, country homes, and bath buildings.

Statius' style in the *Silvae* is one of verbal and conceptual wit, as English poets from the Elizabethans to the Augustans understood that term.[29] Thus D. A. Slater suggested that Alexander Pope would have been well-suited to translate the poems.[30] A prominent aspect of Statius' wit is his fondness for antithesis and paradox, a fondness to which the titles of some scholarly works even pay homage—for example, Bright's *Elaborate Disarray* (1980) and D. W. T. C. Vessey's "Transience Preserved" (1986). While Harm-Jan van Dam overstates the case in asserting that each poem has "some leading paradox as the central idea," it is easy to see this pattern in 2.1, the consolation for the death of Melior's Glaucias, with its core paradox of the (ex-) slave who is a son and related paradoxes such as the adoptive father whose grief exceeds that of the natural parents.[31]

A succinct example occurs when Venus tells Earinus, as she is about to deliver him to the emperor in Rome: *Palatino famulus deberis amori* (3.4.38/58; lit., "you, a slave, ought to go to a Palatine love"); the paradox is emphasized by the juxtaposition of the antithetical words *Palatino* ("Palatine," i.e., "imperial") and *famulus* (slave). Even more rhetorically elaborate is Statius' description of the Hercules statuette as "small in size, in impact, huge" (*parvusque videri / sentirique ingens*, 37–38/48; more literally, "small to be seen, to be felt,

8

huge"). In this phrase, the effect is amplified by chiasmus (the word arrangement *abba*: here, adjective infinitive infinitive adjective). A few lines later a similar paradox is emphasized by the words juxtaposed in a one-line sentence: *dant spatium tam magna brevi mendacia formae* (4.6.43/55; "This big [*magna*] impression gives its small [*brevi*] size heft"). Elsewhere, in the letter to Vitorius Marcellus, Statius comments that with the arrival of summer, Rome's population has left town: *ardua iam densae rarescunt moenia Romae* (4.4.14/17; "towering Rome's thick crowds are getting sparse," or, more literally, "now the high walls of crowded Rome thin out"). He again juxtaposes opposites, here at the middle of the line: *densae* (crowded) and *rarescunt* (thin out).

Another aspect of Statius' wit is his fondness for puns on proper names. He puns, for example, on the name of Felix (the adjective *felix,* which means "happy, prosperous, productive," appears in the Latin of *Silvae* 2.2 at lines 23, 107, 122); and, if Pollius' wife Polla is in fact Lucan's widow Polla Argentaria (*argentarius* means "banker"), he puns on her name when he uses banking terminology (2.2.151–53/194–97).[32] Elsewhere, he puns on Melior ("Better") by addressing him in the preface to book 2 as *vir optime* (best man); he puns twice on the superlative in Vibius Maximus' name, declaring *Maximo carmen tenuare tempto* (4.7.9/9; "For Maximus I try a slighter song"; more literally, "for the Greatest I am trying to thin out my song") and referring to Vibius' child as *Maximus alter* (32/32; lit., "another Greatest"). The meaning of Septimius he connects to the "seven" (*septem*) hills of Rome: *quis non in omni vertice Romuli / reptasse dulcem Septimium putet?* (4.5.33–34/33–34; "Who would not think that sweet Septimius / had toddled over Rome's septuple hills?" or, literally, "had crawled on every peak of Romulus"). Similarly, Statius hints at the meaning of Ursus ("Bear") in the phrase *hominem gemis . . . / . . . hominem, Urse, tuum* (2.6.14–15/22–24; lit., "you lament a person, your person, Ursus"), emphasizing the pun by juxtaposing the words *hominem* and *Urse.*

Other wordplay is bilingual. Usually Statius gives the Greek and supplies a Latin translation: for example, *Erato iucunda* (1.2.49/65; lit., "the delightful Lovely One"); *pelago circumflua Nesis* (2.2.78/99–100; since Nesis means "island," of course it is—as the literal translation here explains—"flowed around by the sea"); *omen . . . Euploea carinis* (3.1.149/213; Euploea, lit. "a fair voyage," "augurs well for ships," or more literally, is "a good omen for ships"). Sometimes, however, he leaves it to the reader to supply the Greek equivalent. The phrase *pigra oblivio vitae* (1.4.57/86; lit., "a sluggish forgetfulness of life") alludes to the Greek medical term for Rutilius Gallicus' condition—*lethargia* or *lethargos.* Likewise, the phrase *immemorem . . . amnem* (5.2.96/140; lit., "the unmindful river") is a periphrasis for Lethe, the river whose Greek name means "forgetfulness."[33] Roman poets and their readers all knew Greek well enough to devise and appreciate such puns, but it is also likely that the Greek heritage of Statius—born in Naples to a Greek father who taught Greek literature—contributed to his particular delight in them.

Exaggeration, the form of conceptual wit known as *hyperbole,* abounds in the *Silvae*—as one would expect in poems of praise, especially in those addressed to the emperor. For instance, Domitian's colossal equestrian statue has used up all the copper from the famous mines at Temese for the rider's breastplate alone (1.1.41–42/64–66), just as his arch over the river Vulturnus has used up all the Ligurian marble (4.3.99/124). Likewise, the emperor's palace is so vast that it vaults the very heavens; but huge as it is, its owner dwarfs it (4.2.23–25/32–35). His eunuch cupbearer is lovelier than those mythical paragons Endymion, Attis, Narcissus, and Hylas—than all but Domitian himself (3.4.40–45/61–70). Also, Crispinus' commission by Domitian as military tribune is equivalent to Mars having given him the sword and put the helmet on his head (5.2.178–80/253–56). This sort of exaggeration has appalled some critics, especially those writing before Domitian's image had been somewhat rehabilitated. Critics who take it literally have dismissed it as flattery or understood it as a faithful vision of official ideology.[34] More recently, many critics have interpreted Statius' praise of the emperor as "subversive" or at least intentionally ambiguous.[35]

I myself incline instead toward Michael Dewar's understanding of praise that is so egregiously hyperbolic: Statius is playing by the rules of a game understood by all, and neither his addressee nor the rest of his audience would have taken him literally; if the alternatives are sincerity or subversion, then the praise "is 'sincere' in the sense that it is intended as a compliment."[36] Indeed, the poet's ingenuity is part of the compliment. As K. M. Coleman puts it, "the deserts of the *laudandus* [praisee] were less relevant than the virtuosity of the *laudator* [praiser]."[37] Hyperbole is not reserved exclusively for the emperor. For instance, the duties of Abascantus involve communicating no fewer messages than Mercury or Iris carries (5.1.101–104/135–39). Elsewhere, Crispinus at drill on horseback is mistaken by Statius for Mars (5.2.113–17/165–70). The river between the two halves of Vopiscus' villa could lure Diana away from Lake Nemi (1.3.76/109–10). Venus would prefer to have been born from the depths of Etruscus' baths (1.5.54/72–73). The covered portico zigzagging up the cliff to Pollius' villa is as big as a city (2.2.31/39–40). One of the Sirens hurries to hear Pollius' song, sweeter than hers (2.2.116–17/150–51), and Pollius is wealthier than Midas, Croesus, and the kings of Persia and Troy (121–22/158–60).

In Statius' descriptions of marble, mosaics, and precious metals, their shine is a prominent feature, and words for "shine" (e.g., the verb *niteo,* the adjective *nitidus,* and the noun *nitor*) become thematic. As Hubert Cancik observes, "For Statius, splendor is one of the most important aesthetic categories."[38] People shine as well: Earinus' hair (3.4.8/13), cheeks (65/101–102), and shoulders (87/131) all do, and Nemesis "added a gleam" (2.6.74–75/107–108) to the eyes of Ursus' slave Philetos just before she made him sicken and die. In the case of people, however, sometimes the "shine" is metaphorical, since *nitor* comes to mean "elegance"; hence *nitidi Melioris* (2.3.1/2) is "polished (lit., 'elegant') Mellor."[39] Prominent also in the descriptions are contrasts of light and dark, shade, shadow, and reflections.[40] Statius describes the sunlight streaming into Vopiscus' villa, reflected by the floor mosaics (1.3.53–56/77–81), as well as the shadow of leaves on the water below (18–19/27–29). A striking instance of such a contrast is the reflection at sunset of Pollius' Sorrentine villa floating on the waters of the Tuscan Sea (2.2.48–49/59–60; "as weary day and darkening mountain shadows / now fall, the mansion floats on waves of glass"). Statius' praise for the splendor and the technological marvels he describes incorporates his reactions of awe and amazement at what he sees; a related theme is that of human control of nature—what Pavlovskis calls "genuine joy in man's subjugation of nature"[41]—as is found in Pollius and his Sorrentine villa, or Domitian and his highway.

The lines of the *Silvae* are frequently and richly ornamented with patterned arrangements of nouns and adjectives. We have already seen one such pattern, chiasmus, in 4.6: the Hercules statuette "small in size, in impact, huge" (37–38/48). Whereas the order of words in chiasmus is *abba,* the pattern *abab* is called *synchesis,* or interlocked order. An instance occurs at the beginning of Statius' lament for his father, when he claims to be suffering from writer's block and asks *quis . . . / frigida damnatae praeduxit nubila menti?* (5.3.12–13/16–17; lit., "who . . . / has drawn chilly clouds [*frigida . . . nubila*] in front of my doomed mind [*damnatae . . . menti*]?"). This is also an example of a "golden line": a pair of adjectives at one end, a pair of nouns at the other, with a verb in between; here the two adjectives come first. Some other lines are not quite "golden," because they contain an extra word. Such a "quasi-golden" line begins the poem for Stella's wedding (1.2): *unde sacro Latii sonuerunt carmine montes?* ("Whence [*unde,* the extra word] have the hills of Rome [*Latii . . . montes*] resounded with holy song [*sacro . . . carmine*]?"). The two noun phrases—*sacro . . . carmine* and *Latii . . . montes*—occur in the same, hence interlocked, order (adjective noun, adjective noun).

Statius regularly expresses an idea twice in succession, along the lines of Isaiah's "unto us a child is born, unto us a son is given." This figure of *reduplicatio*—the restatement of essentially the same idea in a different way—is characteristic of Ovid and it demonstrates his virtuosity (as it does for Statius, who uses the figure less frequently). For example, Coleman notes four instances in her commentary on *Silvae* 4.3.[42] Part of the first stage of the construction of Domitian's highway is *alto / egestu penitus cavare terras* (to "hollow out the earth far down with deep excavation," 41–42; trans. Coleman [1988]). The next stage involves filling in the roadbed *ne nutent sola, ne maligna sedes / det pressis dubium cubile saxis* ("so that the earth shall not wobble nor the spiteful ground provide a treacherous bed for the weight of the stones," 45–46; trans. Coleman); here, the first short expression of purpose is expanded for a line and a half. Likewise, a brief statement is elaborated at 52–53: *illi saxa ligant opusque texunt / cocto pulvere sordidoque tofo* ("others bind together the slabs and interweave the work with baked dust and dirty tufa"; trans. Coleman). Finally, the river Vulturnus thanks Domitian for keeping him from being *pulvereum gravemque caeno* ("in a dirty state and laden with mud," 88; trans. Coleman).

That reduplicatio is being employed may be a matter of interpretation. For example, another instance may occur earlier in 4.3, when Statius mentions one of Domitian's laws: *quis* [sc. *legibus*] *fortem vetat interire sexum / et censor prohibet mares adultos / pulchrae supplicium timere formae* (13–15/17–20; lit., "by which [laws] he forbids the strong sex to be ruined, and as censor keeps grown males from fearing the punishment of their lovely beauty"). Coleman, however, distinguishes between the edict in general (13) and its specific application to postadolescents.[43] Likewise, in 3.4, Venus hitches up her swan chariot and immediately arrives in Rome: *iam Latii montes veterisque penates / Evandri* (47–48/74–75; lit., "already [here are] the Latin hills and the home of old Evander"). Is that reduplicatio, or is the general (the hills of Rome) followed by the more specific (the Palatine)? Two other instances are more clearcut. Venus brings Earinus to Domitian, because she knows his taste, having played a role at Domitian's wedding: *ipsaque taedas / iunxerat et plena dederat conubia dextra* (3.4.53–54/84–85; lit., "she herself had joined the torches and had given wedlock with a full right hand"). In a final example, *ducat nubila Iuppiter per orbem / et latis pluvias minetur agris* (1.6.25–26/26–27), the clauses "let Jupiter bring his clouds throughout the world" and "let him threaten the wide fields with rain" are both variations on the idea "let Jupiter control precipitation."

A feature related to reduplicatio is Statius' wide repertoire of synonyms. Possibly the most striking example occurs at the beginning of 3.2, a poem addressed to Maecius Celer as he sails off to his post in Syria. In the first seven lines there are six different words for "sea" (*ponti*, 2; *fretum*, 3; *unda*, 4; *profundo*, 5; *alto*, 6; *aequora*, 7). Then in line 14 a circumlocution refers to the sea as *regni . . . secundi* ("the second realm," an allusion to the division of jurisdictions between Jupiter, Neptune, and Hades), and in 17 appears yet another synonym, *sinus*.

Another aspect of Statius' diction frequently remarked on by scholars is his tendency to stretch the meanings of words. He employs them in ways that are new, different from previous ("normal") Latin usage, and even artificial, idiosyncratic, and ultimately difficult to understand.[44] Like Ovid, too, he invents new words. One such neologism is the compound adjective *fluctivagus* (? 1 95/129, 3.1.84/122, "wave-wandering"— or, as I translate it to capture its novelty, "wave-faring"). Statius' heritage may be a factor in his neologizing, since many of his linguistic innovations are based on Greek.[45] Compound adjectives appear frequently; for example, Statius has more different compounds with *-fer* than any of his predecessors aside from Ovid.[46] Compounds in *-fer* and *-ger* ("-bearing" or "-laden") have an epic flavor, and so contribute to the epic tone of these poems of praise.

An element especially reminiscent of Ovid is Statius' use of mythological vignettes. The gods have speaking roles or play some other part in a number of the *Silvae*. The novelty here, as Hanna Szelest has observed, is that Statius involves gods and other mythological figures in the lives of his real-life addressees.[47] This interaction between the two worlds of myth and real life is one of the most striking innovations in the *Silvae*. Apollo and Asclepius come to Rome to cure Rutilius Gallicus (1.4), and Asclepius journeys there to castrate Earinus (3.4). Venus and Cupid play matchmaker between Stella and Violentilla in 1.2, and Venus acts as *pronuba*, a sort of matron of honor. Interestingly, Venus also serves as a matchmaker, and even perhaps by implication as *pronuba*, in 3.4, when she brings Earinus from Pergamum and presents him to Domitian in Rome (45–56/71–88). She tells the boy *ego isti / quem meruit formae dominum dabo* (34–35/53–54; lit., "I will give that beauty the master it has deserved"), adding, *Palatino famulus deberis amori* (38/58; lit., "a slave, you are owed to a Palatine love"). She dresses him, arranges his hair, and adorns him with jewelry before presenting him to Domitian. She knows what the emperor likes since she played a role in his wedding (53–54/83–85). Janus is another god with a prominent role; his speech (4.1.17–43/25–66) makes up the bulk of the poem celebrating Domitian's inauguration as consul on 1 January 95. The chief Muse, Calliope, makes a prediction when Lucan is born (2.7.41–104/51–130), as does the Cumaean Sibyl (the mouthpiece of Apollo) when she addresses Domitian at the end of 4.3 (124–63/154–207). Earlier in 4.3 the river-god Vulturnus, whose river the emperor's highway project has tamed and bridged, expresses praise and gratitude (72–94/89–118). Hercules comes down to help in the construction of the temple Pollius is building for him (3.1); he had requested a larger shrine, and thanks Pollius at the end when it is completed. The poem about the peculiarly shaped plane tree on Atedius Melior's estate in Rome (2.3) creates a myth involving Pan's pursuit of a nymph on the property and Diana's rescue of her; the outline of this tale recalls a number of similar ones in Ovid's *Metamorphoses*. Briefer vignettes have sea nymphs coming on shore to pick some of Pollius' grapes (2.2.100–103/127–31), Anio swimming at night in his own river near Vopiscus' villa (1.3.70–74/100–105), and sea nymphs rigging Celer's ship and sea gods escorting it (3.2.25–41/ 31–52). In addition to these longer passages, hardly a line goes by without a characteristically Roman allusion to mythology. A subcategory of these briefer allusions contains those that occur in similes, one of the epic features of the *Silvae,* in which comparisons are regularly made not with a single mythological reference but often with three or four at a time, piling up the effect (e.g., 3.4.40–44/61–68, where Earinus is described as lovelier than four mythical beauties, or 4.2.46–56/64–80, where Domitian dining is likened to Mars, Pollux, Bacchus, Hercules, or rather, Jupiter).

The *Silvae* reflect much that is traditional—Greek praise poetry and poetic contests; Greek rhetorical categories and prescriptions; and Roman poetry, including Catullus, Horace, Ovid, and especially Virgil. Nonetheless, much of what Statius does in these poems is creative and original, from memorializing such objects as a new bath or a new highway to coining new words and radically extending the meaning of old ones.

The Addressees

Statius' addressees represent a socially diverse group of individuals ranging from freedmen on up to the Emperor Domitian himself. In part this diversity reflects the increasing social mobility of the times, arising from the acquisition of wealth and power by those who were not traditional Roman aristocrats. It is also one of the features which makes the *Silvae* such a valuable source of information for social and cultural studies of the Flavian era. One could divide Statius' addressees into those involved in the imperial Roman government and those who lead quiet private lives. Or, one could divide them into those living in or near Rome and those living around the Bay of Naples. Those with roles in government include the emperor, of course, to whom are addressed more poems than any other individual, as well as aristocrats and freedmen involved in the government. Ruurd Nauta categorizes them (aside from the emperor) as "senatorial careerists, equestrians ambitious for their offspring, wealthy gentlemen of leisure, or freedmen heads of the great Palatine bureaux," noting that "about half of his addressees did not pursue a political career."[48] In the case of those actively involved in government, Statius includes details of their political activity, sometimes at such length that they constitute "an extensive career review."[49] For example, *Silvae* 1.4 addresses the Urban Prefect Rutilius Gallicus on the occasion of his recovery from a serious illness. The urban prefect was the emperor's deputy in Rome, and consequently held the second most important position in the Empire. The god Apollo sketches a résumé of Gallicus' career for his son Asclepius while they are en route to the prefect's sickbed (1.4.67–93/100–144). The aristocrat Arruntius Stella receives a poem from Statius to honor his marriage; although this is a private occasion, not directly related to his public career, Statius puts what amounts to a "career review" in the mouth of the goddess Venus (1.2.174–81/231–42), as she recommends Stella to his bride.

Because the imperial bureaucracy of departments (Nauta's "great Palatine bureaux") headed by powerful freedmen arose as an extension of the emperor's personal household, it was not really a form of civil service analogous to modern governmental bureaucracies. Yet to some extent it did provide continuity between emperors, and there did develop patterns of typical careers for imperial freedmen comparable to those for the equestrian and senatorial classes.[50] The *Silvae* inform us about the careers of two such freedmen bureaucrats. The consolation to Claudius Etruscus for the death of his father (3.3) includes an account of a career (63–105/82–137) which began under Tiberius, continued through the reigns of Caligula and Claudius, and culminated under Domitian with the position of *libertus a rationibus* (freedman in charge of accounts); a survey of his duties takes twenty lines (85–105/112–37). Andrew Wallace-Hadrill regards the existence of a "quasi-public" career path for freedmen as "implicit" in 3.3.[51] Likewise, the consolation to Abascantus for the death of his wife Priscilla (5.1) tells about his career as *libertus ab epistulis* (freedman in charge of correspondence) under Domitian; more than twenty lines treat the numerous responsibilities of his post (83–107/112–43). These poems also include evidence about the precarious nature of such careers in a system in which one man monopolized power and patronage. When Claudius Etruscus' father was eighty years old (3.3.146/189), he fell from favor and was exiled, but the emperor permitted his recall shortly before his death at ninety (154–67/200–217).[52] Personal favor was all-important; thus part of 5.1 depicts Priscilla lobbying the emperor on behalf of her husband's appointment (71–75/94–98). That Claudius Etruscus, the equestrian son of an ex-slave who had himself been granted equestrian rank, had the wealth and taste to design his own baths (the subject of 1.5) gives us some idea of the extent of social mobility. Another imperial freedman, Earinus, the emperor's eunuch wine steward, receives a poem to accompany the lock of hair he is sending in a bejeweled golden box to Asclepius at Pergamum; a reference in the preface to book 3 indicates that Earinus had commissioned the poem.

Many, if not all, of the poems addressed to those pursuing a public career give evidence for the emperor's role in their advancement, attesting to his monopoly of power and influence.[33] Thus, Stella's prospects for an early consulship and for celebrating the Dacian triumph depend on Domitian's continuing favor (1.2.174–81/231–42), as Venus hopes parenthetically: *sic indulgentia pergat / praesidis Ausonii* (174–75/232–33; lit., "so may the Ausonian guardian's favor continue"). The bon voyage to Maecius Celer departing for Syria to serve as a legionary legate concludes with Statius imagining the young man's return from service when the emperor recalls him for "greater things" (3.2.127/164). The emperor has extended the duties of Vitorius Marcellus, currently a praetor, by appointing him as *curator viae Latinae*,[54] and, Statius prays, may in the future appoint him to some military command (4.4.56–64/71–81), if "the Latin leader's divine power continues thus" (. . . *Latiniique ducis sic numina pergent*, 57; compare the phrasing in 1.2.174–75, quoted above). Plotius Grypus' responsibilities, a special command for provisioning the army,[55] are those which the emperor gave him (*dedit*, 4.9.18) and put him in charge of (*praefecit*, 19). Finally, it is Domitian who has inaugurated Crispinus' career by appointing him military tribune, at the conclusion of 5.2 (173–77/245–52).

Turning from those addressees active in public life to those living in retirement, we find Manlius Vopiscus at Tivoli; Pollius Felix at Sorrento, and his son-in-law Julius Menecrates at Naples; and Atedius Melior, Novius Vindex, and Claudius Etruscus at Rome. These men are praised for their interests in literature, art, and philosophy. Both Vopiscus (1.3) and Pollius (2.2) are lauded for their pursuit of Epicurean *quies*. The pleasures of Vopiscus' villa are so lacking in extravagance (*luxuque carentes / deliciae*, 1.3.92–93/136) that Statius claims that Epicurus would have preferred them had he left Athens (93–94/137–38). Pollius' villa is even presented as a reflection of his Epicureanism.[56] He mastered nature to build it, and from its heights and those of his own mind (*celsa . . . mentis ab arce*, 2.2.131/172) calmly surveys the surrounding turmoil, in an echo of the opening of the second book of Lucretius. Both Vopiscus and Pollius are called "eloquent" (*facundi . . . Vopisci*, 1.3.1/1; *placidi facundia Polli*, 2.2.9/8); both write poetry in a variety of forms (1.3.99–104/146–52; 2.2.112–15/144–49), some of it on Epicurean themes; and both have art collections in their villas (1.3.47–51/68–74; 2.2.63–72/79–90). Pollius' collection specifically contains statues of leaders, prophets, and sages whom he emulates (2.2.69–72/86–90).

Like Vopiscus, Vindex has an art collection which contains works by the old masters (1.3.47/68; 4.6.22–30/30–39); he is praised for his connoisseurship in particular (22–24/30–33). Unlike the previous owners of the Hercules statuette by Lysippus (Alexander, Hannibal, Sulla), Vindex can celebrate that hero in poetry (99–108/130–42), since his art collection is what holds his attention when he is not composing verse (30–31/39–41), and the statuette's sculptor would prefer no one else's approval (108–109/142–44). The meal he provides Statius, with its literate conversation and lack of the usual decadent cuisine (5–16/7–21), sounds quite Epicurean. Like Vindex (1–4/1–5), Melior lives in Rome (on the Caelian Hill, 2.3.14 16/16 19, paradoxically *secrete palam*, 69/85: lit., "by yourself, publicly" or "withdrawn from the world, [but] openly");[57] he scorns his wealth and does not horde it (70–71/87–89; cf. Pollius' wife Polla at 2.2.151–54/194–97). And also like Vindex, who is praised for being, among other things, a loyal friend (4.6.92–95/120–25), Melior's character is lauded (2.3.64–71/78–89); his loyalty to a friend is revealed in the mention of a fund that he has established for an annual celebration of his friend Blaesus' birthday (76–77/96–98). Like Pollius, Claudius Etruscus is praised for constructing a building which reflects his character; Statius commends him for baths which are the product of his *nitenti / ingenio curaque* (1.5.63–64/88–89; "brilliant cleverness and careful thought," trans. Mozley [(1928) 1982]). In another poem (3.3), Etruscus' filial devotion (*pietas*) become thematic in the consolation for his father's death. Finally, Statius praises both Vopiscus (1.pref.23–25) and Melior (2.pref.2–3) for their literary interests and critical judgment.

Julius Menecrates, on the other hand, exemplifies those whom Nauta categorizes as equestrians concerned for their children's careers. In 4.8 Statius congratulates him on the birth of a second son, his third child. Earlier Domitian had granted him the *ius trium liberorum* (the right of three children),[58] and Statius plays with the idea that this honorary grant had been an omen that Menecrates would in fact have three children (20–22/29–32). The poem concludes with the thought that Menecrates' daughter is equipped to marry into a patrician family, while his sons will enter the Senate when they come of age—contingent, of course, on the emperor's continued goodwill (59–62/82–87). Also included among Statius' addressees are two women: Polla Argentaria, the widow of the poet Lucan (2.7) and perhaps also the wife of Pollius, and Priscilla, the late wife of Abascantus (5.1). Violentilla, Stella's bride, is addressed briefly in 1.2, as is Polla, the wife of Pollius (who may also be Lucan's widow), in 2.2.[59]

It is best to refer to the figures above as Statius' "addressees" rather than his "patrons" or "friends." Moreover, attempts to distinguish between the latter two terms can be misleading: in the heyday of literary patronage at Rome, with circles of poets and other intellectuals gathered around aristocrats such as Scipio or Messalla or Maecenas, poets used the language of friendship for the relationships with those we refer to as their "patrons." Nor were ancient and modern uses of the terms the same; "friend" and "friendship" had more formal connotations among the Romans.[60] The *Silvae* make clear to readers that Statius was on much closer terms with some of his addressees (especially, for example, Pollius) than others. In the preface to book 3, Statius tells Pollius that his planned return to Naples is a withdrawal not so much to his homeland as to his friend (23–25). In part because of the blurred distinction between "patron" and "friend," Statius very rarely indicates whether a poem was written on his own initiative or was commissioned. Requests to write a poem are explicitly mentioned regarding 2.7 in memory of Lucan, commissioned by his widow (at the beginning of the poem itself, and in the preface to book 2), and 3.4, Earinus' lock (in the preface to Book 3). Some of the invitations to dinner or to visit villas may have been intended to provide the occasion for a poem, perhaps one composed then and there. Statius says Etruscus "received" (*recepit*) his bath poem during a lull at dinner (1.pref.29–30), and in the now-missing ending of the preface to book 1 he may have spoken of performing 1.6 at the Saturnalia entertainments it describes (1.pref.31–32).[61] It is possible that Statius came to the emperor's banquet prepared to recite 4.2.[62]

So far as "publication" of the *Silvae* goes, it would be better to use some other term—such as "circulation," "communication," or "presentation"[63]—to avoid any anachronistic connotations. Peter White discusses the ways in which poems were "primarily communicated," including recitation, impromptu performance, and the presentation of a private copy; he characterizes published books "only as the last and least important means of presenting poems to patrons."[64] Statius appears to have performed at least some of the *Silvae* for an audience which included the addressee. This is somewhat analogous to reading from a work in progress, as he did with the *Thebaid*—with great popular success, according to Juvenal's Seventh Satire (82–86)[65]—and as he implies he will do with the *Achilleid* (*Silvae* 5.2.160–63/228–32). He then sent individual poems to their addressees; the copy itself and the praise it contained were both an honor. Later, according to the prefaces, he selected and arranged poems into books, with a dedicatory epistle as a preface; further honor accrued to that addressee (Stella for book 1, Melior for book 2, Pollius for book 3, and Marcellus for book 4).

Some of the same individuals are addressed and some of the same occasions treated by Statius' contemporary, the epigrammatist Martial, whose works are another valuable source for life in the Flavian period.[66] There is a significant difference in tone: Martial is more glib and familiar, while Statius is more serious and elevated, due in part perhaps to a difference in social class—

Martial was equestrian while Statius seems not to have been[67]—and also to dif-
ferences in degree of familiarity with the addressee. The most important factor, however, probably is the difference between the genres of epic and epigram. Statius himself alludes to this generic difference, when he says of his
poems about Atedius Melior's tree and parrot that they were "written as it were
in place of epigrams" (*quasi epigrammatis loco scriptos,* 2.pref.15–16). In this
way he calls attention to his treatment in epic manner of topics which would
seem to invite epigrammatic treatment instead. This difference in genre also
accounts for Martial's brevity. Many of Martial's epigrams satirize the vices of
his time and deal with Roman low life; in that respect, he presents a wider
spectrum of society than does Statius. Like Statius, however, Martial treated
the marriage of Stella and Violentilla (6.21); the death of Melior's favorite,
Glaucias (6.28–29); the baths of Claudius Etruscus (6.42) and the death of his
father (7.40); the anniversary of Lucan's birthday for Polla Argentaria
(7.21–23); Earinus' dedication of a lock of hair (9.16–17); and Vindex's statuette of Hercules (9.43–44). He also treats occasions which Statius mentions
without devoting an entire poem to them: Melior's establishment of a fund for
the Poets' Society to commemorate the birthday of his friend Blaesus (8.38; cf.
Silvae 2.3.76–77/96–98) and the recall of Etruscus' father from exile (6.83; cf.
Silvae 3.3.164–67/213–17).

The socially diverse group made up of Statius' addressees includes those
who are extremely involved in public life (e.g., Rutilius Gallicus, the urban
prefect at Rome) and those who are completely detached from it (e.g., Pollius
Felix in his villa on the Bay of Naples). But the individual to whom more
poems (five) are addressed than to any other belongs in a class by himself—
the Emperor Domitian.

Domitian's Image in the Silvae

The Emperor Domitian's image as "an isolated, paranoid, and secretive ruler"
derives in part from the bias of senatorial authors such as Pliny and Tacitus;
yet even his defenders among historians who have recently reassessed the man
and his reign concede that he was autocratic and oppressive.[68] Certain autocratic features of his reign cannot be denied: he was attended by twenty-four
lictors, as Roman dictators had been; and he was censor (an office whose duties included the supervision of morals) for life without a colleague, unlike any
of his imperial predecessors or successors. Suetonius' *Life* of him points to the
deterioration of his behavior (*Domitian* 3), with his cruelty increasing because
of fear, his greed because of financial necessity. Miriam Griffin shows how in-

terrelated these developments were: fear and insecurity led to overspending on popular entertainment, building projects, and military pay raises, which in turn led to financial need and hence rapacity.[69] According to Suetonius (*Domitian* 10), the situation deteriorated still further after Saturninus' mutiny in Germany in 89. The so-called reign of terror was typified by informants, treason trials, and confiscations of property based on trumped-up charges. The first three books of the *Silvae* were published in 93, which may have been an especially bad year, as Domitian expelled philosophers from the city, held treason trials, and executed or exiled senators.[70] Fear of the emperor's displeasure may have motivated Statius' return to Naples, and may in part explain why some of Statius' addressees did not pursue a public career or even live at Rome.

Domitian's insecurity was based in his position as a member of a dynasty which had emerged from civil war after the last member of the previous dynasty (Nero) had been assassinated. Indeed, his fears were realized when his own assassination ended the Flavian dynasty. The principle of inherited succession was well-established by the end of the Julio-Claudian dynasty; Tacitus reports one of Vespasian's associates encouraging him to claim the throne because, unlike his rivals in the civil war of 69, he had two sons on whom to found a dynasty (*Historiae* 2.77). But Domitian's only son died long before his own succession. This lack of an heir provoked anxiety in both Domitian and his subjects. To counter this fundamental insecurity Domitian presented an image of military success—although in fact, unlike his father and brother, he was not a talented general—and an identity as a living god.[71]

To further his image of military success, Domitian went on campaign in person four times, received twenty-three *salutationes* (acclamations for victories won by him personally or by generals fighting under his auspices), more even than Augustus during his forty-year reign; he celebrated between two and four triumphs instead of one—as, for example, his father had done.[72] References to Domitian's military exploits appear throughout the *Silvae;* the very first image of the emperor is of course the colossal equestrian statue in 1.1. A good illustration of passing references to these martial accomplishments occurs in the consolation to Etruscus for the death of his father. Remarking that the father's exile did not last long (3.3.164/213–14), Statius addresses the emperor as *Germanice* (165/214), and says that this brevity is no surprise in view of the mercy Domitian showed the Chatti, Dacians, Marcomanni, and Sarmatians (167–71/218–23). As he does in 3.3, Statius refers to the emperor frequently as *Germanicus* (Conqueror of Germany), the title he adopted in the fall of 83 after his triumph over the Chatti; coins issued by Domitian illustrate his fondness for it.[73] Statius also refers to the emperor as *Caesar,* long a part of imperial titulature, and as *dux* ("leader" or, more specifically, "general"). Statius' variations in how he referred to the emperor were dictated in part by metrical necessity; that is, the terms are not metrically interchangeable. In the prose prefaces to books 3 and 4, however, where Statius is unconstrained by metrical requirements, he refers to Domitian as *Germanicus noster.* At the end of 4.3, the Cumaean Sibyl promises Domitian that he will conquer even more extensively (154–57/194–98), and that he will ride into battle but not in triumph (158–59/198–201), stressing, as did the emperor himself, his personal participation in the field and implying a suitable modesty about further triumphs which Domitian does not in fact seem to have had. Statius himself alludes to an occasion when the emperor supposedly refused a triumph (3.3.171/222–23), but in 4.1, the god Janus predicts a hyperbolic thousand additional triumphs (39–42/57–63).

By far the most important element in Domitian's ideology, however, was his identity as a living god. Emperors (and their family members) were routinely deified after death. Near the end of 1.1 Statius refers to the members of the Flavian dynasty so deified—Domitian's son, brother, father, and sister—whom he claims come down to embrace and kiss their kinsman represented on the equestrian colossus (94–98/145–49). Several times he refers to the temple Domitian built for this deified clan, once calling it a "Flavian heaven" (4.3.19/25), and elsewhere saying that the emperor "put his own stars [i.e., deified family members] in another heaven" (5.1.241/326). But Domitian was the first emperor to present himself as a god on earth. In the consolation for Abascantus, Statius refers to the *deus qui flectit habenas / orbis et humanos propior Iove digerit actus* (5.1.37–38/48–50; lit., "the god who wields the reins of the world and, nearer than Jupiter, arranges human affairs"). Elsewhere (5.2.170/241), he calls Domitian *proximus ille deus* (lit., "that closest god"), who looks out on Rome from nearby Alba and who fills Crispinus' house with the news of his appointment as tribune (168–71/240–43). In yet another passage Statius recalls how Priscilla lobbied on her husband's behalf, worshiping the *mitem genium domini praesentis* (5.1.74/98; lit., "the gentle [or 'merciful'] spirit of the present master [or 'lord']). A *deus praesens* is a "god present (among us)"—or, as Kenneth Scott puts it, "an epiphany."[74] The phrase *domini praesentis* further alludes to Domitian's title as *dominus et deus* (Master and God). Domitian appears to have encouraged Romans to employ this title: if he did not explicitly mandate its use, neither did he discourage it, as previous so-called good emperors had.[75] At the banquet to which Domitian invited him and which Vessey interprets as a sacrament,[76] Statius refers to "the [or 'my' or 'our'] master's table" (*domina . . . mensa,* 4.2.6/8).

In several other ways Statius alludes to Domitian's divinity. On the day of his inauguration as consul for the seventeenth time, he is said to shine along with the moon and stars—in fact, to outshine the Morning Star (4.1.3–4/4–6). When Statius sees the emperor in person at a banquet, he claims that Domitian has to dim the radiance (*radios,* lit. "rays") of his face (4.2.42–44/60–62) in the presence of mortals. This assertion alludes to the ancient belief that the gods' full glory could be lethal, and that gods in disguise on earth could still be recognized by a sort of glowing aura. More specifically, it is a reference to the "radiate crown," an important part of the emperor cult and a feature of ancient ruler cults long before Domitian.[77] Coincidentally, Domitian had a ruddy (i.e., glowing) complexion (Suetonius *Domitian* 18.1), which was variously interpreted by ancient authors as a modest blush, an angry flush, or a sign of impudence.[78]

The *Silvae* also hint at Domitian's more-than-human status in several predictions of an impossibly long life. Janus predicts three and four times the seventeen consulships he has already held (4.1.36–37/52–54); "three and four times" may be only a figure of speech, but if taken literally, Domitian's life span would be an additional fifty-one to sixty-eight years. Elsewhere comes a prayer that he live "two and three times" longer than his father, who died at the age of seventy (4.2.58–59/83–84). The Cumaean Sibyl prophesies that under his reign his new road will become older than the Appian, which dates back several centuries (4.3.162–63/205–207). It may be worth noting that some of these predictions for an extremely long life are not expressed by Statius directly but are put in the mouth of others (albeit authoritative others, Janus and the Sibyl). Furthermore, not only will Domitian live a very long time (i.e., approximating divine immortality), he will remain forever young (i.e., like the ageless gods). At the end of 5.1, Statius depicts the Fates ratifying Priscilla's prayer for her widower Abascantus to become an old man while the emperor remains young (258–62/347–53).

Like a god, Domitian has immense power, which Statius at times seems to regard as virtually limitless. When Priscilla is on her deathbed, Abascantus prays to *magni . . . exorabile numen / Caesaris* (5.1.164–65/219–20; lit., "mighty Caesar's divine power, which can be influenced by prayer"). Statius then asks rhetorically, "Is there anything he may not do?" (*estne quod illi / non liceat,* 165–66/221–22), and exclaims about how much longer mortals would live if setting the limits of life were under the emperor's jurisdiction (166–68/222–24). Similarly, the Sibyl imagines the improved conditions on earth if he drove the sun chariot (4.3.136, 137–38/170, 172–74), he who is *Natura melior potentiorque* (135/171; lit., "better and more powerful than Nature").

Like Augustus, Domitian was associated with the god Jupiter;[79] but in Domitian's case, the connection was personal—that god supposedly protected him from Vitellian soldiers fighting on the Capitol during the civil war of 69

(Tacitus *Historiae* 3.74). Hence, when Statius blames his defeat at the Capitoline Games in 90 on *saevum ingratumque . . . / . . . Iovem* (3.5.32–33/44–47; lit., "cruel and ungrateful Jupiter"), he means both the god and by implication the emperor who founded these games in his protector's honor. The poem about Domitian's cupbearer, Earinus, compares him favorably to Ganymede (3.4.12–15/18–23) and refers to his master as *Iuppiter Ausonius* (18/27; lit., "an Ausonian [i.e., Italian, or Roman] Jupiter"). At the climax of Statius' recollection of his dinner at the palace, where he "seemed to recline amid the stars with Jupiter" (*mediis videor discumbere in astris / cum Iove,* 4.2.10–11/14–15), he compares the emperor to Mars, Pollux, Bacchus, and Hercules (46–51/64–72) before concluding that the only adequate comparison is to Jupiter (*dux superum,* 55/77; lit., "leader of those [gods] above") during a visit to the Ethiopians as he is serenaded by Apollo and the Muses (53–56/75–80). Book 1 begins with the poem about the colossal equestrian statue of the emperor; in the book's preface, Statius alludes to the identification of Domitian with Jupiter by citing the proverb *a Iove principium* (1.pref.16–18; "from Jupiter must one begin") as he states that this poem comes first. As gifts of food rain down on the audience of Domitian's Saturnalia entertainment, Statius concedes to Jupiter control of the rain, provided that *these* showers come from *our* Jupiter (1.6.25–27/26–28).

Other elements of Domitian's policy and ideology appear throughout the *Silvae*—the public games he celebrated, the building projects he undertook, and even specific legislation. There are several references to the Secular Games (the *ludi saeculares,* the "New Age Jubilee," as I call them) celebrated early in 88, during a period of crisis in Domitian's reign; they are mentioned in 1.4, for example, because Rutilius Gallicus, as urban prefect, played a role in organizing them. The first emperor, Augustus, had held them in 17 BCE when his reign was well established. The Secular Games supposedly commemorated the end of one cycle of time and the beginning of another. Thus, for both Augustus and Domitian, their celebration allowed the current reign to be represented as a new Golden Age at a time useful for the emperor's public image. Statius even asserts that Domitian's reign is superior to the original Golden Age (1.6.39–42/42–45). Several times, including at the beginning of 1.4, Statius refers to the return to earth of Justice, the last of the gods to leave at the end of the Golden Age. Similarly, he connects the return of *Pietas* ("Duty," "Devotion," or even "Righteousness") to earth with Domitian's censorship (5.2.91–92/133–35). Besides celebrating the Secular Games, Domitian introduced new games. Beginning in 86 the Capitoline Games in honor of Jupiter were celebrated every four years at Rome; in 88, the annual Alban Games were first celebrated near the emperor's estate in the Alban Hills, in honor of Minerva, his special patron. Statius repeatedly mentions the glory of his own victory in the Alban poetry contest of 90 and the disappointment of failing to win in the Capitoline Games later that same year. The last poem in book 1 describes the elaborate Saturnalia entertainments of 89; lavish public games were part of Domitian's effort to win popular favor.

Domitian's building projects included a temple for the deified members of his family, as mentioned above, and the restoration in 82 of the temple of Capitoline Jupiter, damaged during the civil war of 69 and again by fire in 80. Rebuilding that temple was part of the imperial Jovian ideology, but for Domitian it also had personal significance as the place where Jupiter supposedly saved him from soldiers of an opposing faction during the civil war of 69. At the end of 4.3 the Sibyl prophesies that Domitian will reign "as long as . . . the Tarpeian father of the reborn hall [i.e., Jupiter] thunders" (*donec . . . renatae / Tarpeius pater intonabit aulae,* 160–61/203–204); near the beginning of that poem, Statius refers to the emperor as he "who returns the Thunderer to the Capitol" (*qui reddit Capitolio Tonantem,* 16/21). Statius concludes his first Saturnalia poem by asserting that the festival will continue "as long as the Capitol you restore to the world remains" (*dumque terris / quod reddis Capitolium manebit,* 1.6.101–102/114–16). At the end of 3.4, Statius has the eunuch freedman Earinus pray that his master "rejoice [to see] the Tarpeian temple [i.e., the temple of Capitoline Jupiter] grow old with him" (*gaudeat . . . secum Tarpeia senescere templa,* 105/156–58). Not all of the emperor's construction projects were so closely tied to ideology. Statius devotes a whole poem (4.3) to Domitian's new highway, which improved the route between Rome and Naples by providing a shortcut and draining marshy ground.

The emperor's position as censor reflects his (perhaps puritanical) concern for his subjects' morality. In that capacity Domitian enforced the Augustan-era law criminalizing adultery, sometimes with political motives. Young Crispinus is praised (5.2.98–106/143–55) for defending, while still a novice orator, a friend falsely accused. Twice Statius praises the emperor's law against castration—once, ironically, in the poem to Domitian's own eunuch (3.4.73–77/ 109–15), right after a brief narrative of the castration itself (65–71/101–107). Elsewhere (4.3.13–15/17–20) the law is included in a list of imperial legislation, where it is preceded by praise for the vine edict (11–12/14–16), which reduced the land in Italy devoted to growing grapes for wine, thereby freeing land to raise grain.

The image of Domitian in the *Silvae* corresponds to the one the emperor wished to project, so far as we can tell from other evidence. In this respect he is not so different from the rest of Statius' addressees. Surely the poet has presented all of them as they wished to be seen—Etruscus, clever designer of a bath; Pollius, cultured Epicurean above it all in his cliff-top villa near Naples; Vindex, art connoisseur. In the emperor's case, to be sure, everything is on a grander scale: *his* statue is an equestrian colossus; *his* building project is an improved highway; the office *he* holds makes him responsible for the whole world.

The Text of the Silvae

I have used Edward Courtney's Oxford Classical Text edition ([1990] 1992) of the *Silvae;* departures from it are listed in appendix 2, and most are discussed in appendix 3. For a long time the state of the text was quite vexed. Slater begins the preface to his 1908 prose translation by explaining why his is the first English translation of the poems:

> In the first place, the text has until recent years been perpetually changing. Even now it can hardly be regarded as settled. . . . [But now t]here is . . . no longer quite the same difficulty that [the Renaissance humanist] Politian felt when he declared "si quis Papinium pergat excutere, nullum fore inquirendi; vixque absoluto superiore statim scrupum alium occurrere" ["if anyone should persist in examining Papinius, there would be no end to investigation; scarcely has the previous worry been settled, when another one immediately turns up"; my trans.].[80]

Writing in 1983, M. D. Reeve declined to judge which of the recent editions was the best, on the grounds that "scholars will argue till doomsday about what Statius could and could not have written."[81] The problem is in part caused by the precarious survival of the *Silvae* from antiquity. No ancient literature has survived continuously from the time of its origin; the earliest manuscript of most works may be no more recent than the tenth century, or even later (one exception is Virgil: there are extant fourth-century manuscripts of the *Aeneid*). In other words, a whole millennium of copying has intervened, and copying is a process much prone to error. Some authors and works survive in numerous manuscripts, and textual scholars are able to reconstruct a "family tree" (*stemma*) indicating the relationship between them. Determining which manuscripts provide independent evidence enables editors to compare them and assess which reading is most likely correct.

One of the *Silvae* (2.7) appears in a tenth-century anthology, but the earliest manuscript of all the poems dates from the fifteenth century; it was discovered in a library in Madrid in 1879 but not recognized for what it was until 1899. The history of this manuscript, which scholars refer to as M (Matritensis 3678), is as follows. In 1417–18 the Renaissance humanist Poggio Bracciolini found a manuscript in a library near Lake Constance, had a copy made by a local copyist (whose work was so unsatisfactory that Poggio called him *ignorantissimus omnium viventium,* "the most ignorant of all men alive"), and arranged to have it delivered to another humanist in Florence. The exemplar from which M was copied then disappeared, so we do not know its age. A number of Italian copies were made from M, none of which therefore provides any independent evidence about the text. In 1494 another humanist, Angelo Poliziano (whose name is anglicized as "Politian"), thought he had rediscovered the exemplar of M; he entered marginal notes based on information from it in his copy of the first edition of 1472 (his annotated copy still survives). After much debate, scholars seem to have agreed that what Politian found was indeed the exemplar.[82] Even when an ancient work survives only in the descendants of a single manuscript, textual scholars are still able to improve the text with conjectures (i.e., emendations), based on knowledge about typical scribal errors, the handwriting of scribes in different places and periods, Latin usage in general, and the author's practice in particular. Reviews of Courtney's edition praised his willingness to emend, unlike his more conservative recent predecessors, who preferred to accept obvious corruptions in M.[83] The difficulty of Statius' style—its so-called artificiality—has made textual criticism particularly complicated, since he so often deviates from "normal" usage.[84]

The manuscripts of the *Silvae* provide titles for the individual poems. Since such titles are lacking in the works of earlier ancient poets, scholars have debated whether they are an innovation on Statius' part or were supplied later.[85] That Statius' own prose prefaces provide in effect a table of contents, with titles of a sort, would seem to make further labeling redundant; in fact, the existing titles often simply repeat the ones implied in those prefaces and could therefore be derived from them. The posthumous book 5 begins with a letter to Abascantus, but unlike the other prefatory letters it lacks of table of contents; thus some scholars have argued that titles were supplied for the poems in this book first, and then by analogy for those in the preceding books. Because book 5 is posthumous, Statius is unlikely to have given the poems those titles; besides, if Statius had provided a title for 5.3, surely it would have been "Lament for *My* Father" rather than "Lament for *His* Father" (*Epicedion ad patrem suum*). The inclusion of addressees' full names in the titles could indicate not that Statius himself provided them but that they were added fairly soon after his death. Because these titles are most likely not Statius' own, I have sometimes taken the liberty of giving a poem my own title: for example, "Insomniac's Prayer" instead of "Sleep" (5.4) and "Melior's Parrot Is Dead" instead of "The Same Man's Parrot." For a full list comparing my titles with the those in the Latin manuscript, see appendix 1.

Translator's Remarks

"Statius is not much read these days and should be better known and more widely enjoyed," says David Slavitt in the preface to *Broken Columns* (which includes his version of Statius' *Achilleid*).[86] Statius was popular and successful in his own time, and in the Middle Ages writers like Dante praised him highly, but nowadays the *Silvae* cannot be truly enjoyed and appreciated in English translation. While prospective readers of Statius' other works have recent verse translations available,[87] the latest English version of the *Silvae* is D. R. Shackleton Bailey's 2003 version for the Loeb Classical Library, a prose crib to accompany the Latin text on facing pages. This is a significant improvement, both in text and translation, over its predecessor in the Loeb series, but its fairly literal prose is no more successful in capturing the spirit of the original than was J. H. Mozley's 1928 version. Shackleton Bailey's is only the third English translation of the whole collection; the first was D. A. Slater's prose version (1908), published only a few decades after the discovery of the manuscript known as M. Scattered versions of individual selections from the collection have also appeared, such as those by W. G. Shepherd in the Penguin anthology *Poets of the Early Empire*.[88]

In this first complete translation of the *Silvae* into English verse I have most often used blank verse, or unrhymed iambic pentameter; the majority of the poems are written in dactylic hexameter, and blank verse was introduced into English to translate part of the *Aeneid* and has been associated with epic ever since. For the hendecasyllabic poems, I have used a much looser form, tetrameters; some are entirely iambic, some entirely trochaic, and others a mix. For the two odes in book 4, each in a different Horatian strophe, I have used the so-called Horatian ode: two iambic pentameter lines followed by two tetrameter lines. In order to read my verse metrically the reader needs to keep two things in mind. First, I occasionally elide without any orthographic indication; thus sometimes "the" must be read as "th'," "heaven" as "heav'n," "power" as "pow'r," and so on. Second, in the case of proper names such as "Theseus," I sometimes treat "eus" as two syllables, and sometimes run the vowels together as one (this license, called *synizesis*, was taken by Roman poets themselves).

In the odes I have tried to translate line for line, in order to preserve the four-line strophes as a sense unit. My versions of the hexameter and hendecasyllabic poems, however, are significantly longer than the originals. It is a truism that Latin, whether verse or prose, is far more succinct than English, and therefore an English translation will usually be longer than the original. My translations are longer not only because of this inherent difference, but also because of my choice of verse form. Blank verse has ten syllables in a line, or at most eleven (it is possible to end with an extra, unstressed syllable, or with a stressed eleventh syllable if an anapest is substituted for the final iamb). In contrast, the dactylic hexameter line varies between thirteen and seventeen syllables. In addition, explanatory material I have included as part of the translation itself contributes to the greater number of lines. Finally, in the *Silvae* very few sentences do not end at the close of a line. Therefore, in virtually every case where a run-on line does occur, I have preserved it, since its rarity suggests that Statius reserved it for particular effect.

In some cases, I have decided to preserve Statius' word order rather than his syntax; it is not always possible to keep both, given that English relies far more on word order to convey meaning than Latin does. I have sacrificed syntax when the order of words seemed especially important—when, for example, it was important to keep the first word first, or to retain a juxtaposition of two words. Sometimes this has meant changing the original from active voice to passive, or vice versa. An example occurs at the beginning of 4.2, in which the first word of the poem is a key to the theme. The subject of 4.2 is an imperial banquet, and the first word is "royal" (*regia*).[89] Hence my translation:

> Royal banquets at Dido's court of Carthage
> are praised by him who brought the great Aeneas
> to Roman soil. (1–3)

A more literal version would be something like "Royal banquets . . . he praises who . . ."

This translation aims to be a readable version which will capture Statius' wit and convey the allusiveness so typical of Roman authors. As in my translation of Ovid's *Fasti*,[90] I have endeavored to gloss most of the poet's references and allusions within the translation itself. This technique derives from my conception of translation as bringing the author to the reader, rather than the reverse. A translated poem should be, above all, a poem in its own right. Readers' enjoyment is thwarted rather than facilitated by more than a sprinkling of foot- or (worse yet) endnotes. To reduce the number of endnotes, I have collected my discussion of textual matters in an appendix, where those who are interested may consult them, and those who are not may ignore them. When a word in the translation is followed by an asterisk instead of a note number, interested readers will find the passage discussed in appendix 3. Sometimes, instead of supplying internal glosses, I adapt what Statius has written to suggest the presence of an allusion without supplying all the details; an example of this approach follows.

In his lament for a friend's dead parrot (*Silvae* 2.4), Statius alludes to the belief that swans sing an especially beautiful song just before their death. Mozley's version of lines 9–10 is adequate: "Let the well-known tale of Phaethon give place: 'tis not only swans that sing their coming deaths." His footnote, however ("Because the death-song of swans is referred to in it"), adds nothing that readers cannot infer for themselves. Statius' allusion to "the general public's tale about Phaethon" (*Phaethontia vulgi / fabula*) is quite dense: as Phaethon's borrowed sun chariot crashed to earth, it scorched a lake proverbial in antiquity for its swans; and, in another story, Cygnus, a relative of Phaethon's, was transformed into a swan. Shackleton Bailey's footnote by contrast is informative, citing the relevant lines in the Phaethon episode of Ovid's *Metamorphoses*. (Incidentally, Slater's version here—"Oh, tell no more the oft-told tale of Phaethon's sisters"—is simply wrong: those weeping sisters became not swans but the trees from whose resinous "tears" amber derives.) To convey the sense of an allusion to a commonplace I have rendered these lines as

> The "swan-song" is a tired cliché—they're not
> the only ones who sing before they die. (2.4.12–13)

Elsewhere, in the "Insomniac's Prayer" (*Silvae* 5.4), the speaker compares his wakefulness to that of Argus, the guard Juno posted to keep his many eyes on Jupiter's beloved Io while she was in heifer form; after the monster's death, Juno used his eyes to decorate her peacock's tail. This is my version:

> I've had enough. Oh, for the thousand eyes
> that Juno's bird-to-be kept open wide—
> in shifts, of course, and never all on guard. (5.4.15–17)

Compare Mozley's Loeb version (lines 11–13 of the original): "Ah! How may I endure? Not if I had the thousand eyes of sacred Argus which he kept but in alternate watchfulness, nor ever waked in all his frame at once." Mozley explains this reference by footnoting "sacred" with the comment "as being sent by Juno." Shackleton Bailey also translates *sacer* as "sacred," but explains by noting that Argus was "[p]rotected by Juno." Contemporary readers might well fail to identify Argus, but my reference to "Juno's bird-to-be" substitutes an allusion which is still recognizable as such (I do not say, for instance, "Juno's peacock"), but which, given the "thousand eyes," they are more likely to understand and appreciate.

I have quite often translated the ancient names for places and peoples with the modern equivalent, especially if they are well known (e.g., Sorrento, Tivoli). In some cases this may be jarring to those more familiar with the ancient names: for example, "Balkan mountains" for "Dalmatian" ones (*Dalmatae montes*, 4.7.14/14), "Slavic winters" for "Sarmatian" (*Sarmaticasque hiemes*, 5.1.128/172), "Hungarian peaks" for "Pannonia's ridgetops" (*iuga Pannoniae*, 5.2.135/195), and beasts "from Russian steppes, Saharan dunes" for ones that are "Scythian" and "Libyan" ([sc. *feras*] *Scythicas Libycasque*, 2.5.28/33). There are some inconsistencies in my practice; for example, the "Balkan mountains" mentioned at 4.3.174 are *not* "Dalmatian" but "Thracian," since *Haemus* (4.3.138) was a mountain in Thrace. Also, I sometimes use the ancient, not the modern, names; for example, in 3.3 there are "Dalmatian peaks" (118), *not* "Balkan" ones (the original is *Dalmatico . . . monte*, 3.3.90), and "Sarmatian nomads" (222), *not* "Slavic" ones (*vagosque / Sauromatas*, 170–71; lit., "wandering Sarmatians"). One should note here that Statius himself refers to peoples and places in a variety of ways. At the end of this book readers will find a glossary of proper names, which also serves to supplement the notes. For instance, to find out the identity of "Juno's bird-to-be," look up "Juno," where the entry identifies her bird as the peacock.

I have often even tried to avoid Roman terms for institutions and material objects. I frequently render *signa* as "banners" rather than the more usual "standards." Often *lictor* is not "lictor" but "bodyguard" or "marshal," and the *fasces* carried by these "marshals" become "maces." The Centumviral (literally, "hundred-man," a reference to the jury pool) Court, I have rendered as "Probate Court," even though it also had jurisdiction over other kinds of cases. As mentioned earlier, "New Age Jubilee" is my version of the *ludi saeculares,* or "Secular Games." Finally, I have rendered Domitian's title *Germanicus* as "Germany's Victor," to remind the reader of the triumphal associations which explain the emperor's fondness for this title.

Although a wide range of synonyms is one feature of Statius' style, Latin in general has a relatively small vocabulary, so repeated use of the same word is not necessarily significant. The more frequent its appearance, however, or the more unusual or powerful the word, the more likely it is that the repetition *is* meaningful. I have usually tried to preserve cases of meaningful repetition in my translation. In the poem about Claudius Etruscus' splendid new bath building (1.5), not surprisingly forms of the verb *niteo* (to shine) and the adjective *nitidus* (shining) appear often (four times in 65 lines: *nitidis,* 12; *nitet,* 36; *nitentibus,* 49; and *nitenti,* 63). In the first three cases I have rendered Statius' Latin with the same English word: "gleaming stone" (17); "gleam" (49; "the only gleam," *sola nitet*); "gleam" (65–66; "in basins / that gleam," *labrisque nitentibus*). In the final instance, English idiom required me to use "shine" rather than "gleam": "your creativity shines here" (88–89, *nitenti / ingenio*). It is unfortunate that this final metaphorical case does not reflect the earlier literal ones, since that does seem to be Statius' witty point—Etruscus' creativity in designing and constructing this building shines in all the shining materials out of which it is made.

In another poem for Etruscus, the consolation for his father's death (3.3), forms of the noun *pietas* and the related adjective *pius* naturally occur frequently (ten times in 216 lines: 1, 7, 31, 36, 85, 137, 155, 173, 191, 204). In every case I have translated *pietas* as "devotion" ("Devotion, . . . god / supremely high," 1–2 = *summa deum, Pietas,* 1; "sad Etruscus' / devotion," 225–26 = *maesti pietas . . . Etrusci,* 173; and so on), and *pius* as "devoted" ("devoted grief," 8 = *pios fletus,* 7; "devoted groans," 39 = *pio gemitu,* 31; "devoted clouds [of incense]," 47 = *pia nubila,* 36; and so on), or "with devotion" ("with devotion groan," 178 = *pius ingemis,* 137). In this same poem I have preserved a subtler repetition because the context seems to make it significant. Statius begins by addressing the personified deity *Pietas: summa deum, Pietas . . .* , which I translate as "Devotion, . . . god / supremely high . . ." (1/1–2). The poet later addresses the emperor as *summe ducum,* which I translate as "Leader supremely high" (155/201); also, in the original and in my translation both these phrases occur at the beginning of a line (i.e., an emphatic position). Finally, in 3.3 two forms of the word *dominus* ("master" or "lord") occur only eight lines apart (*domini,* 103; *domino,* 110). These both refer to Domitian, and I have rendered them emphatically as "Lord and Master" as a nod to Domitian's title *dominus et deus* ("master and god" or "lord and master"): "the gold to make our Lord / and Master's paneled ceilings glitter" (134–35) and "new subjects loyal to your Lord and Master" (144).

In the *Silvae,* as in all Latin poetry, alliteration is a notable feature. In Stella's wedding poem, an instance of alliteration in *ll*—*veLLere, quo SteLLae ViolentiLLaeque professus:* (1.2.25)—is followed by one in *c* (and *qu,* a related sound): *Clamaretur hymen. Cedant CuraeQUe metusQUe, / Cessent mendaCes obliQUi Carminis astus* (26–27/34–36; lit., "let the wedding song be shouted. Let both cares and worries withdraw, let the lying tricks of an indirect poem [or 'poetic innuendo'] desist"). Soon thereafter comes a line with alliteration in *t: Tu Tamen aTToniTus, quamvis daTa copia TanTae / nocTis* (31/41–43; lit., "nevertheless you, dumbstruck, although access to so great a night had been granted"). Some of Statius' alliterative patterns are more elaborate. In the consolation to Melior, we find *et SituS in thalaMiS et MaeSta Silentia MenSiS* (2.1.68/89; lit., "there is neglect [or 'mildew'] in the bedrooms, and sad silences at table"). Besides the simple alliteration in *s* and *m,* there is a repetition of *si-m* (*SIlentia . . . Maesta SIlentia Mensis*), and internal rhyme in *-en-* (*silENtia mENsis*). In my translation, I have been able only to a limited degree to suggest this aspect of Statius' style.

Two features of Latin poetry not peculiar to Statius can be confusing to readers. First, in narrative there can be sudden shifts in tense, from past to present. Grammarians call that use of the present "historical," and its effect is to make the story more vivid. We often do the same thing ourselves in telling a joke or anecdote. Since I have usually retained Statius' tenses, the reader must be alert for these shifts. Second, grammatical person can change; Statius may, for instance, in the same poem speak to his addressee in the second person, and speak about him in the third. There can even be sudden changes of addressee—most confusingly in 2.1. The formal addressee of the poem is Melior, but Statius also often addresses the dead boy, Glaucias. Similarly, in 3.3 Statius sometimes addresses Etruscus' dead father in the consolation directed overall to Etruscus himself.

Sometimes the addressee is neither the subject nor the recipient of the poem, as when Statius addresses the river Hebrus at the beginning of his lament for his own father (5.3.17/22). All these apostrophes reflect a speaker's increased emotional intensity. Some of them I retain in my translation, and some I transpose into the third person. For instance, when Statius describes his writer's block at the beginning of 5.3, he claims that the Muses are standing around dumbstruck:

> Their chief herself has propped her head
> against her silent lyre, just as she stood
> beside the Hebrus when son Orpheus died. (20–22)

Here Statius actually addresses the river Hebrus, down which Orpheus' head floated, still singing after death; a literal translation would be "just as she stood beside *you, Hebrus*" (my emphasis; in Latin, *qualis . . . / adstitit, Hebre, tibi,* 16–17). Later in the same poem, Statius claims that his grief for a father who died in his prime may even exceed that of a mother for her son, a wife for her young husband (5.3.64–71/84–91). In defense of this position, he says that Erigone did not mourn less for her father than Andromache for her infant son:

> why no, the former choked her final groans
> by hanging, but after great Hector's death,
> *your* shame was being a Greek husband's slave. (102–104; emphasis added)

Here I have retained Statius' apostrophe to Andromache (78–79 in the original). Note that here Statius speaks of Erigone in the third person and then suddenly inserts a second-person address to Andromache, surely puzzling to a reader who had not been alerted to expect such a shift.

From time to time in my translation, I have used the signs editors use to indicate either uncertainty about or alteration of the text. Sometimes a word or phrase which cannot possibly be what Statius wrote resists the best efforts of textual scholars to emend it. Editors indicate these "torments" (*cruces,* lit. "crosses") by putting the disputed material within obeli: for example, *Ascanius miseramque †patri flagrabat† Elissam* (5.2.120). When I do the best I can with one of these difficult spots, I preserve the obeli: in this case, "and used to make that wretch †burn for his father†" (174). If an editor judges that something in the original (a word, phrase, line, or more) is missing, he or she indicates a *lacuna* (gap) with asterisks; in supplying a best guess at what has been lost (or at least suggesting something roughly like what is missing), he or she indicates such additions with angled brackets: < >. I usually indicate cruces, lacunas, and supplements with the appropriate editorial signs. For example, the asterisks in line 246 of my translation of 1.2 correspond to the ones after line 183 of Courtney's text. Again, in line 75 of my translation of 3.2, "nor will I leave, save when your hull <departs>," "<departs>" reflects *<cedente>* in line 60 of the original (*ibo, nec egrediar nisi iam <cedente> carina*). Sometimes, however, my signs do not correspond to Courtney's. Not infrequently, I have indicated a supplement where Courtney's asterisks indicate a lacuna. This is because I have chosen to adopt a supplement, sometimes another scholar's and sometimes Courtney's own, published elsewhere; these matters are discussed in appendix 3.

Throughout this translation I am indebted to the work of commentators and previous translators. Of the latter, I have referred to Slater (1908), Mozley ([1928] 1982), and the French translation of H. J. Izaac, which Henri Frère revised after Izaac's death and included with his text and notes in the two-volume Les Belles Lettres edition (1944). As noted earlier, the new Loeb edition/ translation by Shackleton Bailey (2003) appeared too late for me to consult it during the preparation of my translation. I have relied on Friedrich Vollmer's commentary ([1898] 1971) for all the poems. For book 2 van Dam (1984) was indispensable, as was Coleman (1988) for book 4. For *Silvae* 1.1 and 1.4, I also made use of the book-length commentaries devoted to those single poems by John Geyssen (1996) and John Henderson (1998), respectively. Finally, I have drawn not only on Courtney's edition but also on his series of articles that were, in effect, preliminary studies.[91]

Book 1

Preface

Greetings from Statius to his friend Stella!

A long time and a great deal have I wavered, Stella, you fine young man, quite as distinguished in my kind of literary pursuits as you wished to be—should I collect these poems, which poured out of me with a sudden feverish intensity and a certain delight in making haste, and publish them myself, even though <they flew> forth from my breast one at a time.*[1] Well, yes, why <should I> burden myself with this authorized edition <at the same time> as I am still afraid for my *Thebaid*, although it has left me?* But we read Virgil's *Gnat* and even acknowledge Homer's *Battle of the Frogs*, nor has there been any illustrious poet who hasn't composed some prelude to his major works in a more relaxed style. Besides, isn't it even too late to hold them back, since you in whose honor they have been dedicated surely have them? Of course, in the eyes of other people, much of the indulgence given them at first has naturally disappeared, since they've lost the only charm they had—speed. Well, yes, none of them dragged on longer than two days, some even poured out in a single day. How afraid I am that the very lines also prove that fact about themselves!

The first poem has an unimpeachable witness, because one must, as the saying goes, "begin with Jupiter." These hundred lines which I composed, "On the Colossal Equestrian Statue," I was bold to hand over to our most gracious Emperor the very day after that monument had been dedicated. "You could," someone will object, "have also seen it beforehand." You will answer that person, my dearest Stella, you who know that the "Wedding Poem" which you commissioned was written in two days (boldly, by gosh, and yet it has three hundred hexameters). But perhaps you will lie for a fellow-poet. Of course, Manilius Vopiscus, a very learned man and one in particular who rescues from neglect literature that is now all but disappearing, is in the habit of boasting voluntarily on my behalf that I wrote my description of his "Villa at Tivoli" in a single day. Next comes the poem dedicated to Rutilius Gallicus during his "Recuperation"; about it I say nothing lest I appear to be taking the opportunity to lie because the witness has died. Instead, the testimony of Claudius Etruscus is <at hand>, who got his "Bath" poem from me during a lull at dinner.* At the end is the "First of December"—its speedy composition in any case is credible; well, yes, <while sitting in the arena itself, I publicly recited my description of> that very happy night of unprecedented delights for the people. . . .*

Domitian's Colossal Equestrian Statue (*Silvae* 1.1)

What massive structure stands, made twice as big
by its colossal statue, holding Rome's
Forum in its embrace? The finished work—
did it float down from heaven? Or rather did
this portrait leave the Cyclopes exhausted   5
after Sicilian foundries gave it form?
Or did Minerva's hands portray for us
the very way you held the reins just now,
Germany's Victor, when the sight of you
surprised the Rhine and Dacians' towering home?   10
Go on, let old tradition² be amazed
by Homer's Horse well-known from ages past.
Its timber, cut from mountain forests, shrank
the holy peaks of Dindymon and Ida.
This Roman horse could not have fit in Troy   15
despite its ruptured walls, nor could those flocks
of boys combined with unwed maidens lead it,

nor could Aeneas himself, nor great Hector.
Besides, that Trojan Horse inflicted harm
and held ferocious Greeks in its embrace,   20
while this one's gentle rider sanctions it.
It does one good to watch his face, which bears
the marks of war and tranquil peace combined.
Don't think that it exaggerates the truth.
His graceful features are just right, and just   25
right too his dignity. No higher does
the Thracian steed of Mars bear him with pride
in his great weight; after the battle's done,
it rushes quickly, steaming, toward the Strymon;
its mighty breath speeds on the river's flow.   30
    The work's location's just right too. In front,
war-weary Caesar's temple doors swing open,
tribute from his adopted son to one
who set the precedent that showed our future
Emperor-Gods the path that leads to heaven.   35
He learns from your expression how much gentler
you are in war, not being prone to rage
and mayhem even against foreign foes.
You trusted Chatti and Dacians to keep
the peace. If you'd been Caesar's general,   40
Pompey the Great—the lesser man—and Cato
would both have given in on Caesar's terms.
And so, on both its sides basilicas
keep watch—the Julian here, Aemilian there
(the towering royal hall of warrior Paullus).   45
Your father's temple, Concord's too, bestow
indulgent looks upon your statue's back.
While you yourself—your head up high and swathed
in limpid air—beam down upon their temples,
and seem to look and see if renovation   50
allows your palace to rise, lovelier still,
and scorn old fires; to see if Vesta's flame
from Troy keeps silent watch, and she approves
her acolytes again, now that their scandal's
stood up to all the scrutiny it received.   55
Your statue's right hand brings a halt to conflict;
your left Minerva lightly rests upon

the way that Phidias posed Athena's "Victory";
she stretches out Medusa's severed neck,
as if with spurs she makes the horse fire up.   60
No other site on earth, however choice,
is sweeter to the goddess, Father Zeus,
even if you yourself were holding her.
Your chest is such that it can roll away
the world's troubles; Temese's famous mines   65
gave all their ore for it and then gave out.
A riding cloak hangs down your back; your side,
untroubled, has its sword at rest, as big
a blade as that with which the great Orion
threatens and frightens stars on winter nights.   70

    And so, the steed mimics its rider's spirit
and bearing, fiercely holds its head up high,
threatening to bolt. Its bristling mane stands stiff
along its neck, its shoulders strain with life.
Its widespread flanks will stand up to the force   75
of such big spurs. Instead of empty turf,
of ground and nothing else, the hoof of bronze
grinds the locks of the captive Rhine-god's hair.
The sight of this bronze horse would frighten witless
Arion, horse a fake Medusa caused   80
to throw its driver, yet it nearly won;
Cyllarus, horse that Leda's Twins take turns
to ride, beholds the horse with fear and trembling
(the Gemini's shrine stands nearby). This horse
will never change its master's reining hands,   85
will serve forever only that one star.

    The ground can scarcely stand up; saddled with
so great a weight, the earth beneath it pants.
It labors, not with steel or bronze, but godhead,
although an everlasting platform bears it   90
that could support a piled-up mountain peak,
so tough it could endure the bruises worn
where Atlas kneels while holding up the heavens.

    No long delays dragged on. The presence there
of the god in person does the laborers good.   95
The young men set to work, amazed by strength
they do not usually have. A towering crane

creaks from the strain, a steady crash goes up,
pervades the city's seven hilly peaks,
and tops the shifting drone of mighty Rome.   100
    A legendary pool, a hallowed chasm,
commemorates its guardian spirit's name.
Curtius himself had heard the sound of bronze
struck countless times, the Forum made to bellow
by savage beating. Then he lifts the weathered face   105
hallowed by time, the head that's owed respect,
that earned its oak wreath saving comrades' lives.
At first he feared the horse's mighty bearing,
the light it flashed (horse bigger than the one
that he once rode into the lake); he quaked,   110
submerged his towering neck thrice in the pool,
but soon rejoiced to see the world's protector:
"Greetings, scion and sire of mighty gods,
the power I'd heard of from afar. How blessed
my lake is now, how much respect now owed,   115
since I've been given the chance to know you near
at hand and from my close location watch
your deathless radiance. Only once was I
the source and origin of Rome's salvation;
but you have mastered wars for father Jove,   120
you tamed the Rhine's battles and you subdued
Saturninus' atrocious insurrection,
you broke the stubborn Dacians' mountain home
to terms by lengthy war. If you'd been born
in my era, I'd not have dared, and you'd   125
have tried to dive deep in the lake, but Rome
would then have held your reins to hold you back."
    That horse should step aside, the one located
across from Roman Aphrodite's temple,
standing in Caesar's Forum. This, they say,   130
is the work you were bold to cast, Lysippus,
horse of the greatest Macedonian general.
But soon it was amazed to turn its head
and find its rider's face was Caesar's now.
Scrutinize closely 'til your eyes are tired,   135
from what a height this horse looks down on Caesar's.
Who's got so little taste he wouldn't say,

when he has seen them both, the horses are
as different as the men who're riding them!
    This work quakes not at rains that winter brings,   140
nor fiery branching bolts from Jove, nor ranks
of winds from Aeolus' prison, nor the years
that intervene. This still will stand, while earth
and heaven exist, while Rome sees light of day.
Here in the still of night, when earthly things   145
find favor with the gods who star the sky,
your crowd will leave the heavens, slip down to kiss you
and embrace. Son, brother and father both,
and sister—all those stars 'round just one neck!
    Enjoy forever tribute from the People   150
and great Senate. Apelles' pigments wish
they could have painted you, and old Athenian
Phidias would have hoped to set a likeness
of you inside a new temple of Zeus.
And mild-mannered Taranto would prefer   155
your face in its piazza where Lysippus
put a colossal Zeus, and rugged Rhodes
would choose your eyes, that mimic fiery stars,
and scorn its own Colossus, sun-god Phoebus.
Stay fixed in place and love the earth; in shrines   160
we consecrate to you, reside in person.
May heaven's halls not yet bring you delight,
but may you see with joy this gift be given
its incense offered it by your descendants.

For the Wedding of Stella and Violentilla (*Silvae* 1.2)

    Whence ring the hills of Rome with holy song?
For whom, Apollo, do you stir your pick
anew, and lean your fluent ivory lyre
against a shoulder brushed by flowing locks?
Behold, a long way off, Muses move out   5
from song-filled Helicon. They shake nine torches,
the flame required to formalize a marriage;
from springs of song they bring the ritual water.
Among them, looking bold, Elegy nears,

and standing taller she inspires the Muses,   10
bustling around (her couplet's shorter leg
has lengthened into epic for this song).³
A tenth new Muse is what she longs to seem,
and mixed among them even fools the sisters.⁴
Venus herself, our founding hero's mother,   15
has played the role of leading in the bride,
her modest eyes downcast, and sweetly blushing;
herself prepares the marriage bed and rites,
and veils her godhead, dressed in Roman style,
tones down her hair, her face, her cheeks, in hopes   20
of being less impressive than the bride.
I know the reason for the rites today,
Stella, you're what this chorus celebrates,
yes, you (open your door to it); for you,
Apollo, Bacchus, and the wingèd god   25
who haunts Arcadia's shady mountain peaks
come bringing wreaths. Neither sweet Love nor Grace
desists from sprinkling you with countless flowers
and aromatic clouds, as you embrace
your longed-for spouse's snow-white limbs.   30
Your brow now catches roses, lilies now
with violets, fends them from your lady's face.
　　And so the day is here, wrapped by the Fates
in white for luck, to shout the marriage song,
Stella's and Violentilla's. Cares and worries—   35
let them depart; let satire's lies desist;
gossip, keep still. That free and easy love
accepts conditions, lets itself be bridled.
Common gossip is spent, townsfolk have seen
kisses that had been talked about so long.   40
But Stella, you are thunderstruck and still
you hope, though given access to a night
so great, and fear for prayers a kindly power
already answered. Drop your sighs, dear bard,
drop them, she's yours. You may now come and go   45
across the threshold as you like, you need
not watch your step; nowhere a doorman now,
or modesty's rules. Sate at last embraces
you've courted (they have come to pass) and likewise

recall to mind the long hard nights you spent.   50
Your prize has surely made it all worthwhile,
had Juno set you Herculean labors,
or Fate assigned Underworld freaks to fight,
or you were caught in tides from Clashing Rocks.
Your bride is worth the fatal chariot race   55
Oenomaus set for his daughter's suitors,
who quaked to hear his snorting team behind them.
Not if you'd judged instead of thoughtless Paris,
or kindly Dawn took you and left Tithonus,
would you have got a prize the likes of this.   60
      But what has caused this unexpected bliss,
the poet's marriage bed? Right here with me,
while doors and hallways seethe with crowding guests,
and many high officials' bodyguards
knock with their maces, here, sweet Muse of Love,   65
instruct. There's time to have a fitting talk;
the poet's cultured house knows how to listen.
One time, in Venus' chamber on the Milky Way,
the kindly goddess chanced to be in bed
when night had just been driven off, relaxed   70
from Thracian lover Mars' rough embrace.
Around her headboard and her pillow press
a troop of dainty Loves, awaiting orders,
where she may bid them light their fires, which hearts
to sting, whether to rage on land or sea,   75
whether she wants to stir up other gods,
or still to persecute the Thunderer.
As yet she has no fixed resolve in mind,
she lies exhausted on the sheets where once
her Lemnian husband's net witnessed her sin,   80
then crept and caught her in that guilty bed.
And here, a boy amid the wingèd troop,
whose torch has the most flame, whose touch, though light,
has never missed a shot, makes this sweet speech
with dainty voice (his quivered brethren hushed):   85
"Mother, you know my right hand never slacks
when on campaign for you; whichever one
of men or gods you have assigned to me
gets burned. But just this once agree to let

yourself be moved by tears and pleading oaths,   90
the vows and prayers of men, mother who bore me,
for we aren't made out of hard flint, this crowd
of us is yours. There's a splendid young man,
born from a noble Roman line; at birth,
Nobility acknowledged him with joy   95
and right away, predicting Stella's beauty,
conferred a nickname from our stellar sky.
This man I once (for your delight) stuck full
of arrowheads, callously made him shake.
Although much courted as a son-in-law,   100
that man I have defeated, tamed, and bade
to wear a captive's yoke for his great lady
and keep his hopes alive throughout long years.
But her I spared (for so you always bade)
and lightly grazed with torch and clumsy bowshot.   105
After that thunderbolt, I can attest
how great a flame the anguished youth resists,
how much he bears my weight by night and day:
I've never leaned harder on anyone,
Mother, and gouged him with repeated wounds.   110
I've also seen Hippomenes desire
to race on Atalanta's heartless track,
but he was not so pale into the homestretch.
And I have seen Leander's arms compete
with oars; I've praised his hands and often lit   115
his swim across the strait; the heat which made
those cruel waves grow warm was less than Stella's.
Young man, you've gone beyond the loves of old.
I was myself astonished you endured
against such tides; I fortified your will,   120
my feathers dried your tears. How often did
Apollo lodge complaints because I made
his poet grieve so much! Now, Mother, grant
the marriage he desires. This friend of ours
and loyal standard-bearer could recount   125
the toils of epic warriors, famous deeds
of men, and battlefields awash in blood,
but he devotes his instrument to you,
prefers to walk the gentle poet's path,

and weaves your myrtle in his laurel wreath.   130
He traces back the stumbles young men make,
his own and others' wounds. Goodness, how much
he has respect, Mother, for love's great power—
he mourned a dead pet dove, your sacred bird!"
He'd finished; from his mother's dainty neck   135
he fondly hung; his feathers warmed her breast.
She answers, doesn't look annoyed at him:
    "A mighty prayer indeed, and rarely granted
even to men I've thought well of myself,
the Muses' young man craves. This girl of his,   140
just as she fell from womb to earth, I picked
her up myself, and took her to my breast,
marveled at her outstanding grace and beauty,
rivaled by family rank and fame ancestral.
I never stopped adorning neck and cheeks,   145
stroking her hair to smooth it out, my son,
with scented oil. A sweet version of me,
she shot up tall. From far away regard
her head, lofty and dignified, her hair
piled high. Gauge how she rises high above   150
her fellows, as Diana looms above
her nymphs, as I stand out from Nereids.
And she is also fit to rise with me
from azure waves, to ride with me my seashell;
if she could climb to heaven's flaming halls,   155
and come inside our house, you Loves yourselves
might very well mistake this girl for me.
This girl I've blessed with lavish riches—
her mind outdoes such wealth—so I complain
that luxury goods are gone: mulberry bushes   160
in China now are stripped of silk cocoons
too much; the amber tears are gone from trees
that do not weep enough for brother Phaethon;
and too few woolens now are turning purple
from shellfish pulp, and ice from ancient snows   165
now rarely hardens into crystal gems.
For her I told Hermus and Tagus Rivers
to run with gold silt (but that's not enough
for ornaments); for her I told sea gods

and all sea nymphs to seek out pearls to string.   170
If you had seen this girl, Apollo, still
would Daphne roam the Vale of Tempe, free
from care; if she'd been spotted on the shore
of Naxos, near the bed where Theseus lay,
when he had left, deserting Ariadne,   175
the god who saved her would have bolted too.
If Juno's protests hadn't changed my mind,
then heaven's ruler would have donned false horns
or feathers for this girl, on her he would
have fallen as a stream of real gold.   180
But she will be bestowed on that young man
whom you, my son, my greatest source of power,
desire her for, although she often says,
from grief, she will not bear a second yoke
of marriage. I've already felt her yield,   185
grow warm in turn for him." With that, she stirred
her star-bright limbs, went out through the grand doorway
of her chamber, and called her team of swans.
Love hitched them up, then takes his jeweled seat
and drives his joyful mother through the clouds.   190
And soon the Tiber's Roman citadel
appears. The bride's tall house opens to show   ·
the splendid rooms inside; the swans rejoiced
and beat the brilliant threshold with their wings.
    Fit for a goddess is this residence,   195
and not too mean for heaven's shining stars.
Here is Numidian marble, Phrygian too,
and here the hard Laconian stone is green,
here's wavy onyx, veins that match the deep,
mountains of shining purple stone, the envy   200
of Spartan porphyry, Tyre's dyers, too.
Rooftops are perched on countless columns, beams
Dalmatian gold completely sheathes are blazing.
A cool that's shed by ancient trees keeps out
the rays of sun; clear waters live in stone,   205
and nature doesn't keep her seasons here—
the Dog is chill, the winter solstice, warm—
the house changes the year and tones it down.
    She leaps for joy, protective Venus does,

when she has seen her great protégée's home,   210
as if she'd reached her favorite spots—the isle
of Paphos, Cyprus' homes, Sicily's temple.
She then addressed the girl herself, stretched out
alone in bed: "For how much longer will
your modest empty bed keep wasting time,   215
dearest to me of all Italian girls?
What end to faithful, virtuous ways? Will you
never yield to a husband's yoke? There soon
will come a grimmer time of life. Employ
your beauty, put your fleeting gifts to work.   220
Not for this have I given you such grace,
a proud expression, and my very essence,
so you might live out years of widowhood,
as if you were not dear to me. Enough
and more, that you have scorned your former suitors.   225
Yes, but this one, who's yours in every drop
of blood, marvels at you, loves you alone
among them all; he doesn't lack for looks
or family line; besides, what youths, what girls
in Rome, don't know by heart his cultured verse?   230
His consul's bodyguard of twelve you'll see
before his time (may such support keep coming
from Rome's Protector); now for sure already
he's on the board that supervises cults
of foreign gods, consults the Sibyl's Books   235
of prophecies; and soon his country's Father,
whose will it's right for me to know beforehand,
will show that youth support for curule office
with purple robe and ivory chair as signs
of rank, and grant—an even greater honor—   240
the right to celebrate with spoils and laurels
the recent victory won against the Dacians.

    So come, unite in marriage, free your youth
from idleness. What nations and what hearts
have I not wed with my uniting torch,   245
* * * * * * * * * * * * * * * * * * * *?
Bird flocks and cattle, wild beasts packs, have not
refused my will. I set the very heavens free
to wed the earth when clouds thin out with rain.

Thus too the cosmic cycle is renewed.   250
From whence would come Troy's splendor, new at Rome,
and he who snatched his gods from flaming Troy,
without my union to a Trojan mate?
And whence would Tiber multiply my offspring?
Who would have built walls on the seven hills,   255
the Roman Empire's head, had I forbidden
my Mars' seduction by a Roman priestess?"
    This charming speech inspires respect, unspoken,
for marriage. Now there come to mind again
the man's presents and pleas, tearful laments   260
all night on her doorstep, her name in code—
"Étoile"—that bard had used in song through all
of Rome, "Étoile" before the banquet starts,
at night "Étoile," "Étoile" at dawn, much more
than Hercules bereft had called the name   265
of Hylas lost. And now she gladly starts
to change her mind, to think herself too hard.
    Best wishes for your marriage, most serene
of Latin bards, because you have traversed
a rugged route and undergone hard toil,   270
and made it into port. In just that way
Alpheus, river runaway from Greece,
ablaze with passion for a distant nymph,
had hauled his stream unsalted through the brine;
at last he reaches this Sicilian spring   275
and tastes with panting mouth his Arethusa,
who marvels at his sweet freshwater kiss
and can't believe her husband came by sea.
    What a day you got then, a glorious gift
from heaven, eager Stella! How your heart   280
leapt at your answered prayer, when wedded bliss
had found your lady's favor! Then you seemed
to reach and roam the shining vault of heaven.
That Trojan didn't jump so much for joy
on Sparta's shore when Helen reached his ship,   285
and Tempe didn't see Peleus like this
when Thetis neared Thessalian land and Centaur
Chiron reared up to gaze. How long the stars
delay! How slow dawn seems to a groom's prayer!

But when from afar, Leto's son, the father   290
of bards, and Bacchus, Semele's child, became
aware that Stella's marriage bed was ready,
Delos and Nysa both rouse speeding troops.
Apollo's Lycian mountains ring for him,
and chilly Thymbra's sheltered shade, and you,   295
Parnassus; Bacchus hears Pangaean mountains
reverberate, Ismarus, and the Naxos shore
where once the god and Ariadne wed.
And then they entered cherished doors, and brought
their song-filled friend, from here a lyre and pick,   300
a dappled hide and sacred rod from there;
a laurel wreath upon his raptured brow
one sets, and one, a Cretan ivy crown.
    Scarcely is day out of the starting gate,
and now the signs are right for marriage, now   305
each house boils over as the festive train
processes on the route between the two.
Doorways are green with garlands, torches flare
at points along the way, a crowded slice
of Rome's vast population shares the joy.   310
Every elected office, all the ones
marshals attend, is coming to the door;
every toga with stripes of curule rank
rubs up against the rowdy common folk.
On this side knights are struggling through the crowd,   315
on that, a mix of skirts and bands of youths.
Blessèd is what the crowd calls both of them,
but more envy the man. For some time now
the marriage god has slouched against a doorpost,
wanting to sing a virgin song to charm   320
the bard. Juno bestows the awesome bond,
the wedding torch of Concord doubles it.
That was the day, night's for the groom to sing,
at least what's right to know. Ilia lay
like this beside the stream when duped by sleep   325
before Mars came; Lavinia's snow-white face
flushed not so red when Turnus gazed at her;
Claudia faced the people not so proudly
when she had moved the Mother's foundered ship

and this ordeal proved her a virgin still. 330
 And now we need to vie in different kinds
of verse, you fellow-acolytes who tend
the Muses' rites; let the enraptured squadron
go with fillets and ivy in their hair,
each one empowered by his rejoicing lyre. 335
Especially you who steal the final foot
from epic grandeur, present songs that suit
this happy wedding feast. To praise this day
the famous elegists would all have bustled:
Philetas, with his hometown Cos applauding; 340
hoary Callimachus; Propertius, famed
for his poetic Tuscan grotto; Ovid,
happy despite his exile's Black Sea *Sorrows*;
Tibullus, whom a glowing hearth made rich.
 No single love indeed, or simple motive 345
compels my song: with you, Stella, I share
a common Muse; we often rave possessed
alike, take allied drafts from cultured streams.
But you, dear bride, at birth my Naples first
took to her breast, and you, sweet pride and joy, 350
toddled on native soil of mine. Let Cumae
be exalted, Sebethus burst his banks
with pride in you, its lovely protégée;
don't let the Lucrine nymphs be satisfied
more by their landmark sulphur caves, nor Sarno 355
at Pompeii, by his river's peace and quiet.
 Say, come, be quick with brilliant progeny,
to steer Rome's laws and camps, to toy with verse.
Let good Diana speed the month for birth,
and let Lucina spare the mother, please, 360
and, child, you spare her too, so you don't harm
her firm breasts and don't harm her tender womb;
when nature shapes your face within that nook,
from father take much of his charming grace,
from mother, more. But you, fairest of Romans, 365
now at last belong to a worthy husband.
Foster the bonds long sought. Thus may you lose
no loveliness, your face long bloom with youth,
and may that beauty thus be slow to age.

Manilius Vopiscus' Villa at Tivoli (*Silvae* 1.3)

Seeing fluent Vopiscus' icy place
at Tivoli, twin wings that have been grafted
on Anio's stream, getting acquainted with
the dealings back and forth between the banks
that act as partners, villas each competing   5
for all their master's time—if someone's had
this chance, then he's not felt the feverish bark
of the Dog Star, nor Leo's heavy glare
(Hercules skinned that lion in Nemea's grove).
That's how wintry the building is, and that's how   10
unnatural chill blunts the sun; the house
doesn't roast at Olympics time of year.
Pleasure's very own dainty hand—it seems—
drew up the plans along with you, Vopiscus
*   15
Venus then anointed the roof with scents
from Cyprus, brushed her hair over it, leaving
her charm's seductive traces in the dwelling,
and kept her wingèd sons from taking theirs.
O day that must be long recalled! Delights   20
that come to mind once more, and eyesight wearied
from seeing so many wonderful things!
How gentle is the land's inherent temper!
What beauty found in places richly blessed
before man's artful touch! Nowhere has Nature   25
indulged herself so lavishly. Tall groves
bend over swiftly moving streams; deceptive
reflections answer leafy boughs; along
the river's length the same dark image flits.
The Anio himself—his deference   30
is wonderful—foam-white downstream and up,
here drops his swollen rage and rocky rumbling,
as if loath to disturb tranquil Vopiscus'
days spent with Muses, slumbers filled with song.
The shores each feel at home; the river parts   35
the building very gently; both the banks
are in the mansion's keeping—no complaints

because the stream outside gets in its way.
Now let tradition boast the narrow stretch
of Hellespont Leander dared to cross,   40
outswimming dolphins to his rendezvous.
Here peace and quiet last forever, here
no storms have jurisdiction, nowhere are
the waters troubled. Here one's voice and vision
(and hands, almost) can reach across, just as   15
the tide that floods Euripus' channel widens
Euboea's narrow space from shore; just as
from Italy's heel Reggio sees Messina,
Sicilian town across the straits that part them.
    What should I sing of first, what in between?   50
And then at what conclusion hold my peace?
Should I express wonder at gilded beams,
or Moorish citrus wood for all the doorposts,
or shining marble shot with colored veins,
or water piped to flow through all the bedrooms?⁵   55
Sight draws me here, and here, my mind. Am I
to tell of awe-inspiring ancient groves
of trees? The hall that sees the stream below,
or the one looking back on silent woods,
where peace and quiet is kept safe, where night   60
is still and undisturbed by stormy winds
or rumbling noise that undoes restful sleep?⁶
Or baths, amid fumes on their grassy base,
the fire installed on chilly banks, where pipes
connect the river to the steaming furnace,   65
and make it laugh because the nymphs are panting,
despite their source of water so nearby?
I've seen the work of ancient masters' hands,
metal diversely shaped and brought to life.
It's quite a task, recalling all the figures   70
of gold, or ivory, gemstones fit for rings,
or studies for colossal full-scale works
the artist's hand had played around with first
in silver or in less expensive bronze.
While my gaze roamed around and I was guiding   75
my vision everywhere, I found I'd trod
on riches unaware. The brilliance flooding

down from on high, and tiles reflecting light
that gleamed, revealed the ground. The floor delights
in many artful colors: novel figures   80
outdo the unswept floor motif. My steps
grew timid. Why show wonder now at huge
* *

at separate wings with three-part dining rooms?
Why show wonder because the central court   85
preserves you, tree, that rise up through the roof
and doorposts into limpid air? This master
won't let you feel the blows of savage axes.
And maybe, unbeknownst to you, Vopiscus,
a Naiad slippery wet, or Hamadryad,   90
owes you for years that have not been cut short.
Why mention dinners served on either bank,
bright-shining pools, or springs deep in the stream?
Or you, the Marcian Aqueduct, who slip
across the river way below its surface,   95
speeding along through boldly laid lead pipe.
(This means that Alpheus, which flows from Elis
under Ionian waves to Etna's harbor,
isn't the only such sweet water channel.)
Anio himself leaves his source in a cave   100
right there, and under nighttime's friendly cover,
strips off his blue-gray cloak, and sprawls, chest down,
now here, now there, on springy moss, or hurls
his huge self into pools, and swimming, slaps
the glassy water. That's the shade Tiburnus,   105
Tivoli's founder, reclines in, and that's
the place Albula, spirit of mineral lakes,
longs to submerge her sulphur-reeking hair.
This residence could make Diana part
with Nemi and Egeria there her servant,   110
could make that chilly Spartan mountain lose
its nymphs and make Pan leave Arcadian woods.
From Palestrina Fortune's Sisters too
would move to Tivoli, if oracles
enough were not supplied by Hercules.   115
Why should I praise Phaeacian orchards, trees
that Homer sings about, which bear two crops

a year and never reach out empty branches?
Let Telegonus' acres (he who founded
Tusculo) step aside; let the Laurentian   120
ones of Turnus take second place, resorts
at Baiae, Formiae's shore (realm of Homer's
Laestrygonians). And let take second place
Circe's treacherous isle on glassy waves
where Ithacan "wolves" briefly howled; the high   125
and mighty citadel of Tarracina;
the resting place that Trojan's gentle nursemaid
owes to her charge. Let also step aside
Anzio's shore—your place will call you back
at bleak midwinter's cloudy solstice time   130
when hours of daylight are already short.
      Here, to be sure, Epicurean habits
of yours rehearse and practice weighty matters,
pursuing here productive peace and quiet,
serious excellence with brow serene,   135
the glow of health, pleasure that lacks indulgence.
Your school's old founder would prefer it here,
if he'd abandoned Athens and his garden.
It's well worth heading here, even through storms
that plague Aegean winter sailing season,   140
when captains fear the stars' forecast of rain,
and even if your ship would have to sail
around the cape of Greece and make a course
through Sicily's seething straits. It's worth that trip,
so why look down on pleasure near to home?   145
The local fauns enjoy your music here,
and Hercules himself, and Tivoli's
founder, Catillus, theme of greater poets,
whether you mean to strive with lyre like Pindar's,
or take it up for high heroic purpose,   150
or stir up spiteful satire's black corrosion,
or shine up letters with your usual polish.
Midas' riches and wealth of Persian kings
ought to be yours—blessed be your spirit's riches.
Across well-watered fields of yours should speed   155
the Hermus River, banks all tawny yellow
with gold, and Tagus with its glittering silt.

Come often here like this, for leisure time
to think and write; like this, I pray, your heart
be cleansed of every cloud, while you outstrip   160
the age of Nestor at his long life's end.

Rutilius Gallicus Has Recovered! (*Silvae* 1.4)

You do exist, hurrah, you gods above,
and Fate does not relentlessly spin out
one's thread. Lady Justice has kind regard
for righteous men, and reconciled to Jove
(who banished Saturn's Golden Age), returns   5
to earth—the stars he doubted that he would,
Gallicus sees again. Germany's Victor,
to heaven you are dear, dear to its gods
(who would say you are not?): Fortune has blushed
to strip your empire of so great a servant.   10
Right next to you those shoulders stand once more
<to share your load of cares, able to hold>*
an immense weight: they shed the doomed old age
Fate spun, revived and good for years to come.
Therefore the eager cohorts who revere   15
their urban prefect's flag, the laws which flee
to shelter at your breast and to complain
about chaotic courts, the cities dressed
in togas everywhere which bring complaints
from far away and beg your just decision—   20
let them compete in joy, let Roman hills
resound with sevenfold roars,* and let be stilled
the buzz of rumors that he's getting worse.
Why yes, he does remain alive, and life
will long remain for him at whose command   25
are guards that gently keep Rome unafraid,
and our new age will not have laid such blame
on fate, nor will the just repeated rites
of Jubilee have been somehow at fault.
But it will not be Phoebus I exhort,   30
although my lyre's pick is mute without him,
nor Helicon's ladies, and as a tenth,

Minerva, neither Mercury nor Bacchus,
gentle sons of Arcadia and Thebes.
Come here yourself, serve up new strength and spirit,   35
you who will be my theme; for not so greatly
without an expertise divine, have you
bestowed abundant gems of rhetoric
upon the Roman bar, on Probate Court,
insightful judgment. Though the enraptured Muse   40
of Pimpla's spring keeps out a poet's thirst,
and though Pirene's well of secret lore
is not bestowed, my preference is the flood
taken from your wellspring in lavish drafts,
either when unconstrained by meter's form   45
you undertake plain words arranged as prose,
or when your charming fluency is reined
within the narrow ring* my art prescribes.
Wherefore, if we give back her gifts to Ceres,
to Bacchus, wine; if, though she's rich in prey,   50
Diana still receives the skins of beasts
in every shrine; as Mars gets captured arms;
come now, Gallicus—just because you have
more eloquence, a style that overflows
with grandeur—come, do not reject the reverence   55
of my more modest lyre. Stars gird the moon,
into the sea have tumbled lesser streams.
     What prize for virtue has been granted you
by Rome's concern and love! What tear-filled eyes
I noticed, both elite and common folk   60
unused to feeling grief for those in power!
The blessèd Senate was not so afraid
when royal Numa passed away, nor were
his lofty fellow knights, when Pompey did,
nor when their hero Brutus did, Rome's women.   65
Here is the reason for that—you are loath
to hear a prisoner's grimly clanking chains;
you spare the lash and do not go as far
as your exalted power says you may,
but largely shed* the strength that arms provide;   70
you treat as worthy pleas from lowly folk;
in court you render verdicts but don't shove

top officials aside, and so you temper
your sword with judge's robes. This is the path
one takes to deep affection, this the way   75
respect relies on being mixed with love.
Besides, the grave relentlessness of fate
itself made everyone afraid, the sudden
onset of danger, violent decline
with no respite. And that was not the fault   80
of age (your seventh decade just had started),
but stressful work, a robust mind's command
over the body, anxious wakefulness
on his Emperor's behalf (how sweet a task)—
from this there crept deep in his weary limbs   85
deceptive calm, inert unconsciousness.
  Apollo then, the god whose holy name denotes
groves high on Alpine peaks, looks back, alas
long unconcerned for this great son of Turin.
He left <the dark forest at last, grief-struck,   90
broke off delay>,* and said, "Hither with me,
my son the Healer, hither gladly go:
it is allowed (so we must seize the chance)
to give a mighty man rebirth. Let's go,
and hold that spindle still, which strains to snap   95
his life's thread now. Fear not a deadly blast
of smoky lightning. This time Jove himself
will praise your healing arts; the life I save
is not a common one, nor born without the will
of heaven. I'll give a very brief account   100
while we approach his house. His family gets
their own good name from him, on them redounds
nobility of his, his stock is not obscure,
but is outdone by his ensuing brilliance,
has gladly yielded to its great descendant.   105
At first like them he showed his excellence
in time of peace—a great and shining light
in court; soon, trained in countless army camps
everywhere, under western skies and eastern,
<on open tracts of sea and widespread lands>*   110
he kept his oath and served his full enlistment,
but could not even then retire in peace

to rest his strength and unbuckle his sword.
This man robust Galatia dared assault
with war (as they did me that time at Delphi);   115
nine harvests long Pamphylia was afraid,
the fierce Pannonians too, and, shocking source
of parting shots, Armenia, whose river
Araxes now endures a Roman bridge.
Why cite once more the honor guard of two   120
he had as judge at Rome, his doubled term
in charge of Asian courts? That province would
have liked him for itself three times or four,
but then elections called him back, that year
desired to get his name, to have him hold   125
the consul's chair, vouchsafed to him not once,
but twice. Why praise the wondrous willingness
of Africa to pay the tribute rate,
a triumph's worth of revenue sent home
in time of peace, such wealth not even he   130
who levied it had dared expect to get?⁷
Why exalt this with song which cannot match
what's praised? For this revenge on Hannibal,
Lake Trasimene's shores, the Alps, the souls
of Cannae's dead rejoiced and first of all   135
the mutilated* ghost of Regulus
laid claim in person to this glorious tribute.
There isn't time to reveal northern battles,
the Rhine in revolt, pleas the German prophet
Veleda made when captured, nor the fresh   140
and very great distinction, Gallicus,
that in your trust the City's care was put,
so great a ruler's choice, while Dacians died,
to take the reins, at no surprise to Fortune.
If what I'm saying seems worthwhile, my son,   145
we'll steal this man away from hateful Jove
who rules below. Rome's celebrated Father
asks and deserves this favor; not in vain
did you Jubilee choirboys in robes
of purple sing your recent hymn for me.   150
Whatever herbs the health-producing cave
of hybrid Chiron holds, and what your shrine

at Pergamum keeps stored, or cures the sands
of blessèd Epidaurus bring to life,
flowering dittany's aid, which Crete brings forth   155
beneath Mount Ida's shade, and froth that flows
from serpents' mouths—I will myself combine
my healing touch with every helpful balm
experts have gleaned from Arabs' fragrant fields,
or shepherds plucked from rich Thessalian grassland."   160
    His speech was done. They find the body now
inertly sprawled, the spirit battling on,
and each one girds himself in doctor's style
and both together gladly give advice
and take it 'til with diverse drugs they broke   165
the deadly bane, dread haze of harmful sleep.
The man himself assists the gods, his strength
prevails against disease, forestalls the aid
they bring. No swifter did Achilles' skill
restore Telephus, nor Machaon's salve   170
close up the gashes Menelaus feared.
    What room amid the crowds of high and low
for worried prayers of mine? And yet I call
to witness both the lofty stars and you,
divine patron of bards, what fear I had   175
each day, each night; glued to the door I kept
a constant watch on everything, now on guard
for sounds, and now for sights, the way a dinghy
towed in the wake of some enormous hull
when a storm rages, gets its tiny share   180
of frenzied waves, rolls in the same south wind.
    Now spin white threads with joy, you sister Fates,
spin lucky threads; let no one calculate
the length of life he has already spent:
today he is reborn. Gallicus, you   185
deserve to pass by Trojan Priam's age,
the Sibyl's years, many as grains of sand,
decrepit Nestor's. Could my poor man's pinch
of incense now make any sacrifice
as you deserve? Not if Umbria's vales   190
should empty out their lovely pastureland
of all those snow-white bulls, would that suffice

for me to do enough. Amid that kind
of tribute, still the gods have often been
well-pleased with grain poured on a piece of sod,   195
sprinkled with just a scanty bit of salt.

The Baths of Claudius Etruscus (*Silvae* 1.5)

It's not Helicon's gate my lyre, possessed,
pounds with its weighty pick; it's not the Muses
I call upon, powers I've often wearied.
Apollo, you, and Bacchus, you as well,
are both excused from singing in this choir,   5
and you, Arcadia's wingèd god, keep still
your tuneful creature's shell; this song of mine
demands ensembles of another sort.
Our lady water-nymphs, the flashing lord
of fire, still tired and red from Etna's forge—   10
to have lured them will be enough. Put down
destructive arms awhile, my Theban epic;
I want to fool around for my dear friend.
Pour cup after cup, boy, but take no trouble
to count; fire up my dawdling lyre. Away   15
with Toil and Trouble, while I sing the baths
that bloom with gleaming stone, while frisky Clio,
my history's Muse, no fillets in her hair,
nor modest ivy, plays for my Etruscus.
Come, verdant nymphs, and turn your limpid faces   20
toward me, and bind your hair, that's clear as glass,
with tender ivy; wear no clothes at all,
the way you rise from your deep springs to tease
the smitten Satyrs with the sight of you.
But you whose sin disgraced your waters' glory,   25
it's no delight to rouse; get far away
from here, Salmacis' spring that cheats a man
of maleness, and Oenone's stream dried up,
bereft from grief for Paris lost, and one
who took Hercules' protégé as loot.   30
You nymphs of Latium and Rome's seven hills,
whose waters make the Tiber rise anew,

whom Anio's falls delight, and Aqua Virgo,
that's going to welcome bathers where it's piped,
and Aqua Marcia, bringing chilly melt   35
from Marsian snows, and in whose towering bulk
the wandering water grows and is conveyed
suspended in midair on countless arches—
yours is the work we're nearing, yours the house
my gentle verse reveals. No richer grotto   40
has ever been your home. Venus herself
guided her husband's hands, showed him the craft,
and, lest a common flame burn in his forge,
lit it herself with wingèd Love's own torch.

No entry here for Thasos marble, white   45
with spots, Carystos, white with waves of green;[8]
onyx is far away, and sadly mourns,
and serpentine, kept out of here, complains:
the only gleam in here's a mountain quarried
from tawny Berber marble, also one   50
that would make Tyre's and Sidon's purple weep
with envy; only stone which Attis stained
himself in Synnas' cave with shining blood.
There's barely room for Spartan stripes of green
to vary Synnadite. The doorsteps aren't   55
neglected, out blaze vaults, the ceilings shine
with living forms in varied glass. Struck dumb
at such rich wealth, the fire that circulates
to heat the rooms is sparing with its power.
So much daylight is everywhere—the sun   60
bores through the roof with all its rays, relentless,
but then is burned by heat that's not its own.
Nothing is common there, you'll nowhere note
the usual brass, lucky water's piped
through silver, spills on silver, stands in basins   65
that gleam; amazed by pleasure, it declines
to leave (the constant level makes it seem).
In snow-white banks there lives a sky-blue stream,
clear all the way up from the depths below—
whom would it not persuade to leave the heat,   70
head for the cooling pool, and take off clothes
which limit movement so? Here's the blue deep

Venus would choose to be her place of birth,
here you would better see yourself, Narcissus,
and here would swift Diana gladly bathe,   75
no matter if Actaeon caught her by surprise.
Why go on to mention the wooden court
that's laid over the floor, that's going to hear
the crack of balls, where feeble fire roams
around the room while ductwork underneath   80
is circulating clouds of wispy steam?
Not if a guest had newly come from Baiae's shores
where he had seen Domitian's villa, would
he scorn such things (if little things with great
may be compared), neither would anyone   85
who just had been in Nero's Baths refuse
to sweat again in here. Bravo, my boy,
your creativity shines here, and all
the pains you took. May this new bath grow old
along with you, and may your father's luck   90
now better learn from this to be reborn.

Domitian's Saturnalia Celebration (*Silvae* 1.6)

Father Phoebus, stern Minerva,
festive Muses, go far from here:
I'll call you back for New Year's Day.
Saturn unshackled, let him come,
December, belly big with wine,   5
shameless Wit and joking Laughter,
while I recount this happy day,
our joyful Emperor's drunken feast.*
Scarcely was Dawn rousing sunrise,
when treats rained down from where they hung: 10
the morning breeze shook off this dew.
The first-class hazelnuts which fall
from fertile groves on Black Sea shores,
and dates from hills in Palestine,
plums which devout Damascus grows,   15
figs which sultry Caunos* fully ripens,
fall for free as lavish booty.

61

Gingerbread men, honeyed cheese puffs,
Umbrian fruit not yet quite ripe,
and wine cakes, all were falling down,   20
and dates as if from unseen palms.
April showers don't flood the land
so much from cloud-filled stormy skies
as winter's cloudless hail has bruised
the crowded Colosseum stands.   25
Let Jupiter above bring clouds
and threaten rain, provided showers
like these come down from our own Jove.
    But look, there comes through all the stands,
with striking looks and lovely garb,   30
a crowd big as the seated one.
These bring bread and pure white napkins,
and quite exquisite banquet fare;
those lavish wine that leaves one weak:
so many Ganymedes, you'd think.   35
The dress circle (a better class
and sterner), folks in business suits,
both are nourished at once by you,
and since you feed such multitudes,
o happy man, the market price   40
of daily bread is moot for now.
Come, Ancient Past, and now compare
the old-time Golden Age of Jove:
not so freely did wine flow then,
nor did harvest time come early.   45
A single table feeds all kinds,
children, women, common folk, knights,
Senate: holiday license lets
respectful attitudes relax.
You even shared this common feast   50
along with us (which god could be
invited here, which could accept?).
Now all can boast, both rich and poor,
that they have dined with our Leader.
    Amid noise and novel excess,   55
the fun of watching flies right by:
the sex untrained in using swords

62

stands up and, shameless, fights like men!
You'd think Amazons were waging
heated battles on Black Sea shores.   60
Here boldly goes a line of dwarfs;
Nature finished them all at once,
short and balled up tight in a knot.
They deal out blows and fight up close,
threatening death (with those hands of theirs!).   65
Mars laughs and bloodstained Valor too;
the cranes, the Pygmies' ancient foe,
about to fall on scattered prey,
marvel at these fiercer fighters.
    Now as evening shadows draw nigh,   70
what a turmoil the tossing out
of gifts and coupons brings about!
Here come the easy girls for sale,
here one can recognize all kinds
of acts on stage which please the eye   75
or win applause for expertise.
Here buxom belly dancers clap,
there the castanets are clacking,
Syrian jugglers make noise there,
here are actors, and tricks by those   80
who trade sulphur for broken glass.[9]
    And meanwhile endless clouds of birds
fall from the sky in sudden flight,
flamingos plucked from holy Nile,
pheasants from shivering Black Sea shores,   85
and guinea fowl the Berber nomads
catch when the humid south wind blows.
There aren't people to grab them all;
and yet stuffed pockets still rejoice
as new bonanzas are prepared.   90
They raise countless voices to heaven
praising their Prince's Saturn-fest,
and call "Master" with sweet goodwill:
that's the one forbidden license
when slaves are masters for a day.   95
    Deep blue night was just approaching,
when down a flaming wheel descends

midfield among the thick shadows,
outshining Ariadne's Crown.
Heaven lights up with fire, letting   100
dark night take no license at all.
Lazy Rest flees, and slothful Sleep
sees these things and goes out of town.
These shows, this joking given license,
this dinner feast, food free of cost,   105
rivers of lavish wine, who could
write a poem about it all?
Now I falter, drunk on the wine,
<good Leader, you have freely poured>,*
and drag myself to tardy sleep.   110
    How far through time this day will go!
Immortal, it won't fade with age,
while these hills and Old Man Tiber
exist, while your Rome stands, while what
you have rebuilt for all the world   115
up on the Capitol remains.

Book 2

Preface

Greetings from Statius to his friend Melior!

Such is both our delightful friendship, Melior, you very fine man, no less so-
phisticated in literary taste than in every social situation, and the very character of the literary works I am delivering to you, that this whole book of mine
relates to you even without a prefatory letter. For it starts with our Glaucias
(†I fell in love with him when I gave him a hug at your house†), whose charming boyhood—so often the lot of those doomed to die young—†you no longer
have†. The fresh wound of his loss, as you know, I accompanied with a "Consolation" so hastily that I have had to apologize to your feelings for the speed
of my composition. And I am not now boasting to you about what you know,
but I am pointing this out to the rest lest anyone critique the poem with too
sharp a pencil;[1] it was written by one dismayed and given to one in pain, since
a late consolation is practically superfluous. The next poem, my friend Pollius'
"Villa at Sorrento," I should have expressed more carefully, if only in homage
to his own eloquence, but my friend has forgiven me. Certainly the light
poems on your "Tree," Melior, and your "Parrot," you know were written as if
they were epigrams. The same fluency of style was called for by the "Tame
Lion" laid low in the arena; I delivered that poem immediately to our highly

exalted Emperor before either the lion or it had gone cold.[2] My "Consolation" for the loss of his slave-boy written for our mutual friend Ursus, in addition to what I owed him personally, I have also gladly included in this book, because that young man, very open-hearted and quite learned without idly wasting his time, will credit you for the homage he gets from this one. The volume closes with "A Birthday Poem for Lucan"; when his widow Polla Argentaria and I happened †to consider† how to commemorate the day, that rarest of wives wanted it written and billed to her account. Proof of my greatest possible respect for so great an author is the fact that I was afraid to express my praise for him in hexameters.

If these poems, such as they are, dearest Melior, don't displease you, you may bring them to public attention; otherwise, return them to me.

Lament for Glaucias, Melior's Favorite (*Silvae* 2.1)

This consolation for your foster son,
taken too early, Melior, is thoughtless.
How can I start here where his ashes still
show sparks of life? This piteous wound which sliced
your veins yet gapes, that great blow's slippery path.   5
Already I address the healing words
of song relentlessly, while you prefer
beating of breasts and loud lament, and hate
my lyre, and turn deaf ears away from it.
My song is out of season; sooner would   10
tigers and lions, robbed of offspring, listen.
Not if the Sirens' song should waft to you,
or else that lyre the trees and beasts could heed,
would your crazed groans be soothed. Deranged grief sticks in
your breast; your heart howls at the slightest touch.   15
No one forbids it—glut yourself with woe,
master the aching pain by letting it
run free. Now is your joy in weeping sated,
and now, worn out, do you no longer scorn
my friendly prayers? Now may I sing? Behold,   20
my face is bathed in tears as I compose
this very song, sad drops blot out the words.
The fact is, I myself along with you
led out the grim procession's solemn rites,

the boy's atrocious bier, watched by the City;   25
I saw the cruel accursèd incense heaped,
the spirit wailing over its own corpse.
As you outdid the groans that fathers make,
the arms that mothers bruise, as you embraced
the pyre and were resolved to gulp down flames,   30
I barely held you back, although I shared
your feelings, and by holding, gave offense.
And now, alas, a luckless bard, I've loosed
my ribboned band and wreath of laurel leaves,
my brow's distinctive mark, reversed my harp³   35
and beat my breast with you; but you,* I pray,
if I have felt a partnership in grief,
and so deserve it, calmly let me be
your pain's allied companion: fathers listened
to me, right when the shock had blasted them;   40
for mothers prostrate near a pyre I've sung
my solace, for devoted sons as well,
including me when I collapsed and groaned
beside a kindred fire, the loss (o Nature)
of what a father! I don't sternly bar   45
you from your grieving, just combine your groans
with mine and so together let us weep.
       For some time now, as I have sought a way
to start, rightly belovèd boy, that suits
your merits, I've been torn. This way your age,   50
that's poised upon life's threshold, and your beauty
take me away, I'm taken off that way
by your precocious self-restraint and sense
of shame, discretion riper than your age.
Where is your pale complexion's rosy blush,   55
the starry eyes that beam like heavenly orbs,
the modest brow's controlled restraint, the locks
that freely flow above, a fringe of soft
and lovely hair? Wherever is the mouth
that sweetly pleads, the lips, in mid-embrace   60
fragrant as springtime flowers, the blend of tears
and smiles, the voice, a honeyed blend
at which a snake would set aside its hiss,
and cruel stepmothers gladly serve the speaker.

Your real assets I don't inflate at all.   65
Alas, that milk-white throat and arms, the neck
that never lacked its master's leaning weight!
Where is the prospect, not remote, of manhood
to come, that badge of honor, bearded cheeks,
your hope and frequent prayer?⁴ All that reduced   70
to ashes by one grievous, hateful hour
and day. For us, remembering is what's left.

    Who will cheerfully soothe your heart with chats
you're fond of, who'll relax your secret cares?
When angry bile inflames you to an outburst   75
at your slaves, who will calm you down, and turn
your focus from your blazing wrath to him?
Who'll snatch some food you've started eating, wine
you've sipped, right from your mouth, and so disrupt
the entire meal by such a darling theft?   80
Who'll lie upon your bedspread, interrupt
your early morning sleep with whispers, slow
your going out with tight embraces, call
you back for kisses right from the door itself?
When you come in again, who'll be right there   85
to meet you, jump to reach your face and hands,
and throw his little arms around your shoulders?
Your home is dumb* and still, your house, forsaken;
the rooms molder, the table mourns in silence.

    What wonder your devoted foster father   90
showed his respects for you with funeral rites
that were so grand? You were your master's haven
of rest from age, his darling you were now,
and now delicious care within his breast.
No foreign auction block paraded you;   95
mixed in for sale with pert Egyptian baggage
you weren't sold as a child, and didn't try,
with studied pranks and practiced words, to find
yourself a master, slowly getting one.
Here is your home and here your place of birth;   100
your parents long were dear to your master's house,
were freed to bring you joy, to stop complaints
about your birth. But right out of the womb
your master took you off and held you up,

elated; as your very first cries hailed   105
the stars, he made you his, if not by birth,
by his design; he hugged you to his breast
and carried you, and deemed himself your sire.
Parents are sacrosanct; it's Nature's role
to sanctify these first relationships   110
throughout the world—begging their pardon, please,
and asking Nature that she let me do it,
it's right for me to say that not all things
are bound by ties of blood and family line,
often freshly adopted links grow in   115
closer than kindred ties; siring a child
lets fate decide, happiness has a say
in choosing one. That's how the Centaur Chiron,
half a wild beast but sweet to young Achilles,
outdid the hero's father back at home,   120
nor did an older Peleus escort his son
to war at Troy—the tutor Phoenix
stuck alongside his brilliant foster son.
From afar King Evander hoped to see
his son's return in triumph with Aeneas;   125
the loyal squire Acoetes watched him fight;
and while the wingèd hero's sire, far off
in shining heaven, failed to help at all,
wave-faring⁵ Dictys cared for Perseus.
Why cite mothers outdone in love by nurses?   130
And why cite you, crawling safe at the breast
of Ino your aunt, Bacchus, after Juno
tricked your mother and got her turned to ashes?
Ilia reigned in husband Tiber's stream
without a worry for son Romulus,   135
who wearied Acca when she carried him.
I've seen myself how grafted twigs grow taller
on trees that aren't their own; your thoughts and feelings
had made you that boy's father long before
either his character or beauty did;   140
and yet, those sounds he made, the words confined
to babbling still, the incoherent wails,
a tearful baby's cries, you loved them all.
    A flower that's going to die at the first breeze

stands out in fields of grass, shamelessly tall;   145
so had that growing boy ahead of time
outdone his fellows, confident in stride
and looks, and left his age quite far behind.
If he stood, hunched for wrestlers' chaining holds,[6]
you'd think a Spartan mother gave him birth   150
(Apollo would exchange his Hyacinthus
for him right off, and Hercules would trade
his Hylas); or, if he was running through
fluent Menander's Attic plays, and wore
a charming cloak,[7] Comedy's frisky Muse   155
would take delight, and praise his tone, and crush
his lovely hair with garlands made of roses;
if he declaimed the old blind poet's toils
at Troy, Ulysses' luck and slow return,
the way he understood the meaning stunned   160
even his father, even those who taught him.
　　The fatal Spinner's inauspicious hand
had to have touched his cradle; Envy cuddled
the boy and hugged him in her lap, took care of
his fuzzy cheeks and thick luxuriant hair,   165
and taught those skills, those words of his inspired
for which we beat our breasts. His years had just
begun to match Hercules' dozen labors
as he shot up, but childhood still was near;
and yet he had a sturdy stride by now,   170
and measurements too much for his attire—
his garb seemed to be growing small on him.
What fabrics then for you, what garments then
did your indulgent master not make haste
to get for you? Loath to confine your chest   175
with small cloaks, or bind it in skimpy tunics,
he always chose, not shapeless folds of cloth,
but clothing made to fit your size, and dressed you
now in a scarlet cloak, and now in folds
like grass, and now in sweetly rosy purple;   180
he then enjoyed setting your hands ablaze
with fiery gems; no crowd of escorts failed,
no presents; what your modest beauty lacked
was just the toga freeborn children wear.

But then luck changed. Suddenly hostile Fate   185
lifted her hands. Goddess, where do you harshly
stretch out your savage nails? Are you not moved
by beauty, moved as well by piteous youth?
This boy Procne could not have torn to pieces
the brutal way she did her son to spite   190
her husband, nor could that cruel witch from Colchis
have steeled herself for savage wrath against him,
even if Jason's second wife had borne him.
Grim Athamas, who killed his son while mad,
would turn his crazy bow and spare this boy;   195
although he hated even Hector's ashes
and cast his son down from a tower at Troy,
Ulysses would have wept to kill this boy.
        The crisis came, his eyes were icy now
and dull, and now the nether Juno grasps   200
a lock of hair to cut and free his soul.
The Fates were weighing down his feeble years,
and yet it's you he sees with dying eyes,
whispers your name with failing tongue, blows out
every last bit of breath from emptied lungs   205
for you to catch, remembers only you,
and hears you only, calling him; for you,
he moves his lips, his last words are for you
as he forbids your groans, consoles your pain.
Yet thank you, Fate, because a lingering death   210
did not eat away at his boyish beauty
as he lay ill, and he'll approach the shades
intact, his body wholly unimpaired,
just as he was. Why should I speak about
the funeral liturgy, the lavish gifts   215
the flames received, the body set ablaze
with mournful opulence, the fact a mound
of purple rugs enlarged your gloomy pyre,
the fact that choice Cilician saffron bathed
the hair which soon would blaze, and Indian spice,   220
and perfumed oils that came from everywhere,
Arabian myrrh, Egyptian cinnamon,
and balm of Gilead? Melior longs
to bring everything lavishly, to set

his whole net worth on fire, loathing the wealth 225
you'd left forlorn, but fire begrudges you
the gifts that flames too skimpy fail to take.
    A shudder shakes my heart, from how you were,
near the pyre when the corpse was set on top;
Melior, once so tranquil, I began 230
to feel afraid. Were you that man who'd been
cheerful and well-disposed to look upon?
Whence comes the violent frenzy, brutal hands
that beat your breast, and wild, disheveled hair?
Now you sprawl on the ground and turn away 235
from hateful daylight, now you grimly rend
your clothes and breast alike, and close dear eyes,
taste icy lips. His sire and mournful mother
were there as he lay dead, but stunned, watched you.
What wonder? All the city folk in crowds 240
that went ahead of you bewailed the outrage;
the Mulvian Bridge used the Flaminian Way
to get them over Tiber and out of town.
The child, whose death was undeserved, received
the groans his youth and beauty did deserve 245
as he was given up to gloomy flames.
That is how Ino's son Palaemon lay
beneath his mother, seeming dead, when cast
adrift and washed ashore at Corinth's harbor,
just so the greedy fire swallowed up 250
Opheltes, who'd been skinned alive by scales,
playing on grass in Lerna's snake-filled swamp.
    Fear not, and cease to dread what death forebodes.
Cerberus' triple mouth won't howl at him;
no Fury's fiery torch, no Fury's snakes 255
shooting up from her head will frighten him;
in fact, the greedy skiff's ferocious boatman
will land him closer in to barren banks
and blasted shores, so that the boy won't have
the chance to make a rough disembarkation. 260
    What happy news does Hermes, Guide of Souls,
bring me? Can such cruel times have any joy?
Your noble Blaesus' looks and lofty face
the boy had known at home; he often saw

you fasten new garlands around his portrait   265
and press the lifelike painting to your breast.
This man was roaming river Lethe's banks
among Romulus' line of Roman nobles;
the boy knew him on sight, approached in silence,
timid at first, and trailed along beside,   270
tugging his garment's hem, then followed †boldly†
because his bolder tugging wasn't spurned[8]—
the man believed he came from his own stock,
some late descendant, never known in life.
As soon as Blaesus realized this was   275
the darling link to his uncommon friend,
the boy who was his own death's consolation,
he lifts him up from the ground, fastens him
around his mighty neck, and in his arms
joyfully carries him for quite a while,   280
and offers mild Elysium's gifts to him,
the barren branches, songless birds,
and flowers pale and blighted in the bud.
And he does not forbid remembering you,
but fondly blends his feelings with the boy's   285
and shares his love for you and yours for him.
    The end—death took him off. So why not now
allay your wounds, the head long sunk in grief,
lift up. All things are dead or going to die,
as you observe. Both nights and days pass on,   290
and stars, and earth's firm structure does no good.
For man's a mortal race—when folk are doomed
to fall, who'd weep the loss? Warfare lays claim
to these, the sea, to those; these are destroyed
by passion, those by crazed and cruel desire,   295
not to mention disease; the frozen maw
of winter waits for these, for those the Dog
with restless, deadly heat, for these the fall,
pale gray, with jaws that bring the stormy rains.
Whatever's been born, fears the end. We all   300
will go, will go away; the countless shades
all have their number drawn by Hades' judge.
    But he for whom we groan blessedly flees
the reach of men and gods, uncertain chance,

the unforeseen and slippery spots in life,   305
and is exempt from fate. He did not ask
to die, nor did he fear or flee. The worried folk
are we, the wretches, we, who are unsure
whence comes our final day, what end our life
will have, from which direction looms the bolt,   310
what cloud may crack with doom. Are you not swayed
by thoughts like these? But you'll be gladly swayed.
　　Be present here, released from that dark threshold,
Glaucias (wholly guiltless souls aren't barred
by ferryman or rigid deadbolt's watchdog)—   315
you are the only one who has the knack
of getting any wish from Melior—
and soothe his heart yourself, yourself forbid
his eyes to drip, fill blissful nights with words
of comfort and your lifelike countenance;   320
say you're not dead, and keep on asking him,
as you can do, to look out for the sister
left forsaken, your wretched parents too.

Pollius Felix's Villa at Sorrento (*Silvae* 2.2)

　　Between the Sirens' namesake, Cape Sorrento,
and cliffs above the Tuscan Sea that bear
Minerva's massive temple, stands a villa
that keeps a lofty watch on Naples' bay,
where hillside vineyards dear to Bacchus bask,   5
unseared by envy for vintage Falerno.
Here from across my native bay I once
was fetched by tranquil Pollius' eloquence
and stylish Polla's youthful charm. By now
had contest-circuit athletes headed off   10
from Naples' newest games to those that honor
victory at Actium. Pale dust had settled
on my hometown arena's idle calm.
Welcome summons, despite my longing then
to turn my steps onto the route to Rome,   15
the Appian Way, famous queen of highways.
A detour worth my while. A tranquil bay

of crescent water breaks through cliffs that rise
at either end. The scene is set by Nature—
unbroken beach between the cliffside leads   20
through overhanging rocks to land behind.
The first attraction of the scene—a steaming pair
of domes, the baths where water sweet and fresh
encounters bitter brine (as did that nymph
who plunged from spring to sea, avoiding rape).   25
There nimble troops of Tritons long to bathe,
and wet-haired, sea-green nymphs. In front, on duty,
the swelling ocean's dark-blue ruler guards
the blameless hearth. With friendly foam he sprays
a shrine of Hercules, guardian hero   30
of fertile fields. Happy the harbor is
that has a pair of deities like these:
one keeps the land, while one impedes the waves.
The sea's calm is a marvel. Weary waters
here set aside their frenzy; winds, once-crazed,   35
abate their blasts with greater mercy here.
Here storms are not so bold to rush. The sea,
unflustered, shows the very same restraint
its master does. From here a colonnade,
a city's size, goes slanting slowly up,   40
and tames the rugged heights with lengthy roof.
Where bright sun used to mix with darkening dust,
an unattractive wilderness of path,
it's now a pleasure going, like the route
that leads to Corinth's top by covered walkway,   45
from down by Dionysus' temple there.
     If I could drink the Muses' fountains dry,
and fathom Phoebus' chaste Castalian springs
that Pollius' urn has roiled by dipping deeper,[9]
then still my verse would fail to match the villa's   50
scenic splendors, enhanced in countless ways.
The chain of sights almost outdid my eyes;
the guided tour almost outdid my feet.
A horde of things! What first to marvel at—
the villa's genius or its master's own?   55
This room beholds the first faint rays of dawn,
while that one holds back sunset's fading gleam,

and will not part with now-exhausted light;
as weary day and darkening mountain shadows
now fall, the mansion floats on waves of glass.   60
These rooms rumble with pounding surf, while those
don't know the ocean's roar and like the quiet.
On this scene Nature smiles, while vanquished there,
she yields to her improver's plans for uses
she did not know, but has grown tame to learn.   65
The level ground you see was once a hill,
and wildlife haunted halls you enter now.
You see tall trees where land did not exist;
its owner whipped these mountains into shape,
and made it tame and glad to follow him.   70
The rocks are harnessed now, behold a cliff
pick up and move when master says it must.
So now, dear Pollius, you've outdone the poet
who sang a dolphin into carrying him,
or strummed a city out of Theban stones,   75
or mourned the second time he lost his wife
by drumming up an audience of trees.
You, too, move stones, trees also follow you.
        Why bother to report old masters' works
in paint and bronze? The ones Apelles' palette   80
was glad to bring to life; the marvels polished
by Phidias' hands before his masterpiece,
Olympian Zeus; whatever Myron's skill
or Polyclitus' drill made come alive;
the bronze alloy from Corinth's flaming fall,   85
worth more than gold, in busts of kings and poets,
of ancient sages, ones that you take care
to follow. These your very heart can feel,
the heart of one carefree, composed and calm,
courageous, being always your own man.   90
Why go over the thousand vantage points
and changing vistas? Each room has its own
delightful patch of sea all to itself,
and different windows each command a view,
across calm seas, of land that's theirs alone.   95
From here the view is Ischia, from there
Procida stands embossed upon the sea.

And here—the Cape that's named for Hector's squire,
Misenus; there the island Nisida
in isolation inhales sulphurous air.   100
And there, Cape Bonvoyage, felicitous
for ships, appears, while there we see jut out
Megalia Isle, that strikes the curling waves.
The "Meadowlands" of Pollius, far away
across the bay, glares at the mansion here,   105
distressed by where its master lies at ease.
And yet, one room stands out above them all,
one room, compelling you to look at Naples
straight out over the sea. And here are marbles,
taken from all the world's deep quarry pits: 110
Egyptian Syenite, a vein red-splashed,
and Synnadite, by Phrygian axes hewn,
where Cybele mourns blood once shed by Attis—
embroidery in stone, purple-spotted white.
From Sparta comes porphyry green as grass   115
but hard as granite; here from Berber sands,
a tawny yellow gleams. From islands come
the two-toned Chian, Thasian glitter-flecked,
Carystian, close match for sea-green waves.
Well done, my friend, that you so much esteem   120
and often haunt *objets* and places Greek.
And so, don't let your native Pozzuoli
begrudge our better use in Naples here
of you, our cultivated foster child.
   Why mention now the wealth of fields imposed   125
upon the sea, and wine-besotted hills?
In autumn when the grapes would soon be ripe,
a nymph has often climbed from sea to cliff,
and under night's concealing dark has brushed
her dripping face against a ripening vine,   130
and snatched away the hillside's luscious grapes.
The grapes so harvested have often scattered
in nearby waves, where mountain fauns have lunged
and longed to catch their Doris naked there.
   Felicitations, land that Felix owns   135
with Polla! Prosper for them all their years,
as long as Priam lived and Nestor too.

Noble to slave for masters such as these!
Don't be outdone in beauty by their place
at Tivoli, site shared with Hercules there,   140
or by their "Meadowlands" on Naples' bay.
Don't let Taranto charm them into making
more frequent trips to vineyards they have there.
When Pollius puts the Muses' craft to work
right here at this, his Villa Sorrentina,   145
he might expound his model, Epicurus,
or strike the epic lyre I play myself,
or weave unequal lines in couplet form,
or draw a sword of iambs, honed to cut.
From over here, a nimble Siren swoops   150
from rocky perch to songs that top her own,
while over there, a nodding helmet's crest
reveals Minerva moving with the beat.
Then tearing gales grow calm, the sea itself
is kept from drowning out his cultured lyre.   155
Attracted by its sound, the dolphins leap,
and stray beside the cliff to beg for more.
Live long, with wealth surpassing Midas' vaults
and Croesus' gold, with blessings far beyond
the crowns that Troy's and Persia's princes wore!   160
The risks of power will not misspend your time,
nor will the rabble's whim, nor courts of law,
nor army camps. Your spirit soars above
desires of every kind, and tames both hope
and fear, outraging Fortune by this proof   165
that you're immune to her. Your final hour
will not come swooping to surprise one caught
in hazard's whirl, but quite filled up with life,
and ready to depart, while we are cast
to chance, a worthless crowd, to passing goods   170
the ready slaves, and prey to endless hope.
Your mind, a lofty tower, looks down in scorn
on people straying far off course, and smiles
to see the common human pleasures there.
Time was when voters in two cities scrambled   175
to win your favor and carried you high
aloft throughout their towns. Citizens there

in Pozzuoli worshiped you, my Naples
adopted you here. You made lavish gifts
to both alike with fiery youthful pride   180
that comes of straying from what's really good.
But now that fog has cleared and you behold
the truth. Those storms still buffet other men;
your craft has made it safe to tranquil calm
within a harbor free of cares. Persist   185
like that, and never let your ship, once pensioned,
sail out into the storms that toss us still.
And Polla, you are, of all Roman women,
<the most cultivated, in intellect
your husband's match>.* You have a carefree heart,   190
a brow unchanged by giving angry looks,
a countenance that radiates with joy,
and pleasure worry-free and innocent.
For you no sterile money chest that chokes
the wealth it hides away, nor agonies   195
of risk from loans at greedy interest rates,
but wealth displayed, enjoyed with wise restraint.
With hearts which Harmony has joined so well,
and so well-schooled by that same force, my friends,
*   200
still heed those lessons in the lack of care.
The wholehearted mingling of wedding torches
has been for long united; hallowed love
preserves the terms of chaste affection's bond.
Survive through years of cycling time, surpassing   205
the fame now held by former married legends.

Melior's Peculiar Plane Tree (*Silvae* 2.3)

There stands a tree with shadows dark embracing
my polished Melior's pool of crystal water.
<Why> does its trunk bend right to water's surface,
then come up straight and tall once more,
as if it grew again from roots unseen   5
within the glassy pool where it resides?
Apollo's not for questions slight as this.

Explain it, nymphs; obliging fauns, inspire me.
    A band of nymphs was fleeing Pan, who chased
as if he wanted every one, but one   10
alone he really wants, named Pholoe.
Pursued through woods and streams, the nymph escapes
and flees those shaggy strides, those nasty horns.
Past martial Janus' grove in flight she skimmed,
past Cacus' gloomy turf, Quirinal fields,   15
until she reached the Caelian bosk. At last,
worn out by strain and effort where today
there stands the house, inviting and sincere,
of tranquil Melior, adjusting her robe
around her, down she lay beside the pool.   20
The goat-god quickly catches up, and sure
of consummation, now inflamed he steadies
his panting chest, now looms above his prey,
when look—Diana swiftly strides across
the seven hills, tracking Aventine deer.   25
Dismayed by what she saw, the goddess faced
her trusty comrades. "Will I never bar
this rude, repulsive goat from wanton raping?
Will my virginal troop grow ever smaller
in size?" Her speech was finished; next she drew   30
an arrow out and did not rifle it
with bending bow and normal arrow's whiz,
but with one hand she launched it—feathers first—
(they say) to tap the nymph's untimely sleep.
The nymph awoke, and seeing both the light   35
of day and brash assailant, quickly dove
into the pool, still wearing all her clothes,
to keep from showing any snow-white flesh.
Because she thought that Pan was right behind her,
she even wrapped herself in pond floor weeds.   40
What would the scoundrel do, suddenly cheated
of prey? The water was too deep for him.
He'd never learned to swim; his shaggy hide
would soon get waterlogged. He lay the blame
on everything—Diana had been heartless,   45
the pool was jealous, jealous too the arrow.
A newborn plane tree there close by the plants,

one that's destined to have a lanky trunk,
with countless arms and head that reaches skyward.
Around it mounding sand yet damp, he sprinkled   50
the water he craved just as much himself,
and charged it with the following task: "Long live
this tree, a striking pledge to mark my vow.
Bend down and bow toward the stony nymph's
hidden chamber, to love and lie upon   55
her water with your leaves. And don't—oh please—
deserve it though she may—let her be burned
alive by fiery sun nor scourged by hailstones.
One task remember: Strew your leaves upon
her waves and stir them up. Then long will I   60
attend to you and to our lady of this
lush site, and keep you safe for hale old age.
Jupiter's oak, Apollo's laurel, poplar
with two-toned leaves, will be astonished then,
as will my pine, when they have seen your boughs."   65
His speech complete, the god's old warmth is mirrored
as tree trunk bends to fertile pool and leans
with loving shade to penetrate the water.
It wants embraces too, but these the sprite
averts, nor will she let herself be stroked.   70
At last from waters below, straining skyward
it steadies itself, neatly lifting up
a trunk that seems to grow from roots below.
Diana's nymph despised the tree no more;
the pool that scorned its branches beckons them.   75
        This birthday gift of mine for you, though slight,
perhaps will live to reach a mighty age.
Your tranquil heart is home to charming grace,
and goodness, light of heart but not lightweight.
No quiet idleness is yours, not yours   80
illicit power pursued relentlessly.
You take a middle path, amid what's right
and what is pleasant too. Unstained in honor,
to turmoil you're a stranger, having found
a way to be not distant, but detached,   85
because you have disposed your time so well.
You show a ready scorn for all your wealth,

not hoarding in the dark the riches which,
by sharing, you ameliorate, dear Melior.
In blooming youth of character and mind,   90
persist in matching agèd Nestor's span,
outdoing years your father, years your mother
brought down with them to bliss in fields Elysian.
For them the Fates have made this intercession,
have interceded too for noble Blaesus.   95
His high renown will now escape the rot
of silence, since your memorial fund for him
will make it bloom again, forever green.

Melior's Parrot Is Dead (*Silvae* 2.4)

O parrot, paragon of birds, your lord
and master's fluent pet, of human speech
the clever mime, O parrot, what sudden fate
has shut your chattering off? Just yesterday
you came with us to dinner, piteous thing,   5
so soon to perish; we were there to see
as you went picking treats from favorite dishes,
as you went hopping, way past midnight, couch
to couch. You even greeted us, repeating
your practiced phrases. But, great songster, now   10
you dwell in Lethe's never-ending silence.
The "swan song" is a tired cliché—they're not
the only ones who sing before they die.
But what a cage you had, its golden dome
all bright on silver bars with ivory fittings!   15
Your beak would cause its squeaky door to rattle—
the hinges now creak out their own complaint.
That splendid cell is empty now, and gone
for good that slender structure's scolding squawks.
Here come the crowds of learnèd birds, endowed   20
by Nature with the glorious right to speak.
Apollo's bird should wail, the starling too,
who knows by heart the things that it's heard said,
and magpies too, a king's own human daughters,
until their contest lost on Mount Parnassus.   25

The partridge should, whose call's a singsong run,
and Philomel, with Thracian woe forlorn.
In unison make moan, and to the pyre
escort the kindred corpse, and, all of you,
come learn this piteous song, for pity's sake: 30
    "He's fallen, best and brightest of our tribe,
the parrot, emerald monarch of the East,
in looks not trumped by peacock's jeweled tail,
nor pheasant, bird that comes from chilly Phasis,
nor fowl in humid southern Guinea hunted.   35
Greeter of kings, who hailed great Caesar's name,
he was at times a sympathetic friend,
at times an entertaining tablemate,
repeating practiced phrases in reply
so readily. Whenever he was loose,   40
dear Melior, you never felt alone.
But not without display is he dispatched
to shades below. With spicy Eastern oils
the corpse is burned, while fine and dainty feathers
exhale the scent of myrrh from Arab lands   45
and Sicily's saffron. A lucky bird,
still spry—no agèd phoenix—mounts his pyre."

Death of a Tame Lion (*Silvae* 2.5)

    What good for you, that you have tamed the rage
you once displayed?* What good, that you've unlearned
your wicked lust for human blood, enduring
a puny master's claim to your respect?
What good, that you have learned to leave your cage   5
and then return to prison yet again,
to drop your fresh-caught prey and to let go
when hands were thrust between your loosened jaws?
    You've fallen, skillful bane of towering beasts,
not caught in nets by native hunting bands,   10
nor leaping over spears, inspiring dread,
nor falling for some gaping hidden pit.
A beast in flight has vanquished you. Ill-fated,
your cage stands open now, while, shut behind

their bolted doors, once-tranquil lions raged   15
that this atrocity had been allowed.
Then every mane went limp for shame to see
the corpse, and frowning wrinkled all their brows.
     The first blow toppled you—a shame unknown—
but you weren't crushed. Your courage still remained;   20
your valor rallied right in death's own midst,
your menace didn't all turn tail at once.
But like a badly wounded soldier, knowing
that death is sure, who charges where the foe
has been deployed, with sword upraised in menace   25
despite his failing grip, our lion stares
like that; staggering and stripped of noble bearing,
he pants and tries to catch both breath and foe.
     Though vanquished, be consoled for sudden death,
because both rich and poor, grief-struck, have moaned   30
as if a star of gladiator fights had died,
because among so many beasts whose death
was cheap—from Russian steppes, Saharan dunes,
from banks of river Rhine and Egypt's land—
our mighty Emperor was moved to see   35
the wasteful loss of just a single lion.

Consolation to Flavius Ursus
for the Loss of His Favorite Slave (*Silvae* 2.6)

     Too cruel is anyone who differentiates
reasons for shedding tears and puts a limit
on grief. A wretched thing it is for parents
to set on fire the young proofs of their love,
their children (what an outrage!) not yet full-grown;   5
hard, too, bewailing half a bed bereft
after a wife is taken young, and sad
groans for brothers, and wailing over sisters;
but you a lesser blow subdues,* it gets
inside your feelings deeper far, outdoes   10
much greater wounds. A slave, since Lady Luck
with her blind hand so mixes up the names
for things and doesn't know the hearts of men,

a slave is who you're groaning over, Ursus,
but one devoted, one whose loyalty   15
and love had earned these tears; his attitude
bestowed on him freedom greater than could
a whole family tree. Don't curb your weeping,
don't be ashamed; but let that pain of yours
snap off its reins, and if the gods are pleased   20
by such harsh things * * * * * * * * * * * * * *
* * * * * * * * * * you're groaning for a man
(alas, I stoke your grief myself), your man,
Ursus, who liked his pleasant servitude,
who felt no gloom, who of his own accord   25
mastered himself. Who, I ask, would rebuke
grief that's been given free rein for such a death?
The Parthian groans about a warhorse killed;
for loyal dogs Molossians weep; pet birds
have had a pyre; Silvia's stag had Virgil.   30
Suppose he weren't a slave? I've seen his manner
and noted it myself, of one who longed
for you alone as master: unexpected,
the pride on his face; though his blood was young,
his character was clear for all to see.   35
Much would young brides, both Greek and Roman, hope
and long to bear a child like this. No match[10]
was proud Theseus, fetched from the Labyrinth
safe by the clever Cretan's anxious thread,
no match was Paris fresh from herding flocks,   40
when he was going to see his Spartan love
and hurled reluctant ships out on the sea.
This is no lie, nor is imagination
leading me on the way it usually does:
I've seen and still I see how he outmatched[11]   45
the one avoiding war on virgins' shores
whom Thetis had concealed, her son Achilles;
outmatched Troilus, who fled around the walls
of Troy, built by his cruel father Phoebus,
until Achilles' spear caught up with him.   50
Unmatched were you, by far more handsome, see,
than all the boys and men, and less so only
than is your master! His beauty alone

surpasses yours as much as does the moon
outshine lesser lights, as much as the Star   55
of Evening overwhelms the other fires.
Your face had not a woman's kind of beauty,
your features had no softened grace, like those
the outlawed process causing suspect beauty
makes change their sex: a fierce and manly charm   60
was yours, a gaze not insolent, and eyes
with stern, attractive fire, the kind of looks
that young Arcadian warrior had at Thebes
when he was helmet-free, with simple locks
of bristling beauty, cheeks not yet hedged in   65
but gleaming with first bloom; a youth like that
Eurotas rears beside his Spartan stream,
like this a boy of young and tender age
comes to his first Olympic competition
and there commends his early years to Jove.   70
His frank and decent attitude, his ways
serenely balanced, sensibilities
mature beyond his young and tender age—
what poem could reveal? Often would he
rebuke a willing master, give him help,   75
support, profound advice; if you were glum
or cheerful, so was he, his own man, never,
he took his own expression from your face,
and so he's worthy of a fame surpassing
the ancient mythic models for devotion—   80
Achilles, that Thessalian Pylades,
and Theseus, king of Athens and its watchword
for loyalty. But let his praises stay
within the bounds his lot in life allows:
no more loyally did Eumaeus, sick   85
at heart, await Ulysses' slow return.
     What god, what chance picks wounds so grim? Why are
the hands of Fate so set on doing harm?
O how much braver, Ursus, would you be,
if stripped of property! If prosperous Locri   90
had belched Vesuvian fire, smoke and debris,
if rivers swamped Polenza's pastureland,
or if Lucanian Acir left its banks

or Tiber's force had rolled its waters high
on its right bank, you would, with brow unclouded,   95
endure the gods, or if their promised harvests
had been denied by life-sustaining Crete
and by Cyrene, and wherever else
bountiful Lady Luck comes back to you
with bosom well-endowed. But evil Envy,   100
expert in pain, eyed your heart's vital spot,
the path to hurting you. Now on the hinge*
of adult life, that handsomest of youths
attempted linking up a three-year span
with three Olympiads he'd lived so far.   105
Nemesis grimly watched with fierce expression
and first filled out his muscles, gave his eyes
a gleam, his stature raised unusually high,
alas, showing the wretch her fatal favor,
and then tortured herself by looking, gave   110
him envious looks, embraced him lying ill,
clapped him in chains of death, and showed no mercy,
clawing a face to pieces which she should
have held in awe. The fifth, critical, day
had almost passed, the Morning Star was just   115
saddling his horse: and now the cruel shores
of ruthless Charon, dreadful Acheron,
were what you saw, Philetos, one bewailed
by what a cry from master! No more cruelly
than he, would your mother have bruised her arms   120
black from beating them, if she had lived,
nor would your father have; surely your brother,
who did attend your funeral, blushed to see
himself outdone in grief. No mere slave's pyre
for this deceased: sweet-smelling Arab incense   125
the fire drained, Cilicia's saffron harvest,
cinnamon robbed from Egypt's phoenix, sap
oozing from Asian cardamom, and tears
his master wept. Only those did the pyre,
did the ashes completely drain. The fact   130
that vintage wine put out the hoary ashes,
that onyx polished smooth walled up the bones
within its precious lap, neither of these

details was more welcome to that poor shade
than groans. But even he says stop. Why yield   135
to grief, Ursus? Why nurse your loss, and love
your wound to spite yourself? That eloquence
of yours, well-known to those whom you defend
when they're hauled into court[12]—where is it now?
Why rack the darling shade with grief so cruel?   140
Although that special soul had earned your pain,
you've paid your debt. He meets the righteous dead,
enjoys Elysian peace, and there he finds
his parents, who are nobly born perhaps,
and there perchance in Lethe's silent bower   145
Avernal nymphs who mingle all around
disport with him, while Hades' wife and queen
takes note of him and steals a sidelong glance.
Pray set laments aside; the Fates, perhaps
the boy himself, will give you yet another   150
Philetos; gladly will he show this twin
the way to act, the manner to adopt,
and teach his double how to win your love.

On the Anniversary of Lucan's Birth (*Silvae* 2.7)

Lucan's birthday celebration
let everyone attend whose heart
poetic frenzy has spurred on,
who drinks the flying horse's spring
near Venus' shrine on Corinth's heights.   5
And you, the very powers in charge
of poetry's important role,
the lyre's inventor, Mercury,
you, the Maenads' spinner, Bacchus,
Phoebus and Parnassus' Sisters,   10
with joy put on new purple bands,
arrange your hair and let white robes
be draped around with fresh ivy.
Let poesy's streams profusely stray,
Helicon's forests, grow more lush—   15
if daylight comes through any gap,

let garlands fill the foliage in.
Let a hundred fragrant altars
stand in groves on Mount Parnassus,
a hundred Theban victims too,   20
bathed in Dirce, Cithaeron-grazed.
Lucan is who we sing about,
listen, keep auspicious silence;
for you this is a major feast,
keep an attentive silence, Muses,   25
while he who led your dancing steps
in two art forms, rhythm constrained
in poetry and freed in prose,
your Roman priest, is cherished now.
    A blessèd land, ah, too happy,   30
Cordova, you who see the Sun
come down on top of Ocean's waves
and hear his setting chariot's hiss,
you whose olive presses challenge
Athens, rich in her patron's gift: 35
Lucan is your claim on the world.
This is much more than giving it
those other Spaniards, Seneca
and sweetly charming Gallio.
Let Lucan's river Baetis flow   40
upstream and reach the stars, grander
than Homer's Meles; Mantua,
Virgil's home, don't challenge Baetis.
    Just born and sweetly babbling cries,
his first, while crawling on the ground,   45
Calliope acknowledged him
as hers and fondly took him up.
Then for the first time she relaxed,
set her mourning aside, threw off
her long sorrow for Orpheus: 50
"O child consecrated to song,
soon to surpass the older bards,
no streams nor packs of beasts nor trees
in Thrace will your lyre's music move,
but with expressive song you'll draw   55
the seven hills, Mars' own Tiber,

cultured knights and purple Senate.
The fall of Troy by night, the route
of slow Ulysses homeward bound,
Minerva's daring ship *Argo*—   60
let others follow rutted paths:
valued by Rome as one mindful
of Roman heritage, more boldly
will you unsheathe a togaed song.
First, while still at a tender age,   65
you'll amuse yourself with Hector
behind Achilles' chariot,
and mighty Priam's pleading gold,
and you'll reveal the Realm Below;
ungrateful Nero you will praise   70
to delighted theater crowds,
and bring them my own Orpheus.
You will address the subject of
a sinful despot's wicked fire
roaming the hills of Romulus.   75
Then your sweet discourse will give
Polla's virtue fame and glory.
Entering early manhood, soon
you will thunder on more nobly
about Philippi white with bones   80
of Roman dead, and Pharsalus,
where that godlike general's lightning
* * * * * * * * * * * * * * * * * * * *

Cato, weighty freedom fighter,
and great Pompey, the people's choice.   85
Egypt's crime you'll loyally mourn
and give Pompey a monument
taller than its bloodstained Pharos.[13]
These things you'll sing while a young man,
early in life before the age   90
when great Virgil composed his *Gnat*.
Let fierce Ennius' rough Muse give way,
cultured Lucretius' high madness,
both him who charted *Argo*'s course
and him who changes bodies' shape.   95
What's that? I will say even more.

Virgil's *Aeneid* will itself
be awed when you sing for Romans.
　　Not only will I give brilliance
to your works, but will consecrate　　　　　　　　　100
with marriage rites a cultured bride
fit to grace your genius, the kind
Venus and Juno would bestow
in beauty, candor, kindliness,
property, family, charm and grace;　　　　　　　　105
the wedding hymn outside your door
I will make ring in festive song.
　　Fates, too cruel and unrelenting!
Long life, never the great ones' lot!
Why, lofty things, are you exposed　　　　　　　　110
more to hazardous accidents?
Why is greatness, through cruel chance,
not permitted to reach old age?
Just this way does Alexander,
Ammon's son, whose star arose　　　　　　　　　　115
and set like lightning, lie confined
within the tomb Babylon brought him.
Just this way as Achilles fell,
shot by shaky Paris' hand, did
mother Thetis shudder with dread.　　　　　　　　120
Just this way I used to follow,
along the babbling Hebrus' banks,
Orpheus' still-unsilenced head.
Just in this way you too yourself,
a crazed tyrant's outrage, will be　　　　　　　　　125
ordered to enter Lethe's flood
while you sing of battles and give
comforting words in lofty style
to mighty tombs (o dreadful crime,
o dreadful), and will fall silent."　　　　　　　　　130
　　She spoke and with her brilliant pick
she scraped away the falling tears.
　　Fame's high-flying chariot may
have raised you through heaven's swift vault,
where the mightier souls arise,　　　　　　　　　　135
and you look down and laugh at tombs;

or else you're blessed and occupy
peaceful groves on Elysium's shore
rightfully opened up to you,
where Pharsalus' horde assembles,   140
and while you make a grand song ring,
Pompeys go with you, and Catos—
in any case, it's certain that
your great soul keeps you sacrosanct
and proud, so you know nothing of   145
Tartarus, but from far off you hear
sinners being flogged and look back
at Nero, pale from having seen
his mother's torches in pursuit—
be a shining presence and please,   150
since Polla calls, win just one day
from gods who reign over the Silent:
by custom this door lies open
for husbands coming back to wives.
Yours is not Troy's first Greek widow,   155
she does not clothe you in the guise
of some pretended deity,
out of control in Bacchic rites
meant to avoid another marriage.
You she cherishes, tends to you   160
firmly fixed in her heart's deep core.
And yet your features furnish her
cold comfort, that golden portrait
which brightly shines above her bed
and hovers over as she sleeps   165
without a care. Go far from here,
all Death: today a life was born.
Let bitter mourning yield, let tears,
now sweet, trickle down from your eyes,
and what your festive sorrow once   170
lamented, now let it adore.

Book 3

Preface

Greetings from Statius to his friend Pollius!
Dearest Pollius, most deserving of the Epicurean ideal of peace and quiet to which you cling so steadfastly, surely I don't have to prove at length the impetuosity of these poems to you; you know that many of them came to life suddenly in the bosom of your hospitality and you frequently were alarmed by the daring of my style; as often as I withdraw into the inner sanctum of your eloquence, I enter literature more deeply and am led by you into all the intricacies of these pursuits of ours. And so, with mind at ease, I send this third book of my *Silvae* to you. Of course, the second also had <you> to testify on its behalf, but this one has <you> as its advocate. For right on its doorstep is "Hercules at Sorrento"; when I had seen that temple consecrated on your beach, I immediately glorified it with these lines. The next poem was a "Bon Voyage" for Maecius Celer, a very illustrious young man, and one quite delightful to me; when he had been posted to the Syrian Legion by our most august Emperor, since I could not follow him, I accompanied him in this way. The devotion of Claudius Etruscus to me as well earned him some "Consolation" from these pursuits of mine, when he was mourning his elderly father with genuine tears (a very rare thing nowadays). Furthermore, Earinus, a

freedman of our Victor over Germany, knows how long I postponed his request, when he had asked me to write a dedication in verse for the "Locks of Hair" which he was sending along with a jeweled box and mirror to Asclepius at Pergamum. Last is a selection "To My Wife" with which I urge Claudia to retire with me to Naples. The style of this, to tell the truth, is conversational, and of course at ease, as one is with one's wife, and it aims at persuasion rather than aesthetic pleasure. Toward this poem in particular you will be well disposed, since you know that my chief goal in seeking this peace and quiet is you, and that I am retiring, not so much to my hometown, as to you. Best wishes.

Hercules' Temple at Pollius' Sorrentine Villa (*Silvae* 3.1)

Suspended for a year, your rites are now
restored by Pollius, who indicates
the reasons, Hercules, for this inertia—
that you are worshiped in a bigger shrine,
that you don't occupy, in poverty,   5
a seaside structure unadorned and fit
for wandering sailors to take shelter in,
but one whose doorposts shine, whose roof's held up
by columns made of marble brought from Greece.
It's like a new ascension up to heaven   10
after the flames on Oeta's heights, the pyre
you built yourself, had purged your mortal flesh.

I can't believe my eyes or trust my memory!
Were you the unsung watchman guarding over
that doorless shrine and tiny altar in it?   15
So why this brand-new hall and radiant gleam
unexpected for rustic Hercules?
The gods have fates, and places also have.
Swift act of devotion! The barren shore
was what one used to see until just now,   20
a sea-splashed mountain flank, and rocks grown shaggy
with briars, ground that would not gladly bear
the tread of any foot. Whatever stroke
of sudden luck enriched the rugged cliffs?
Has music's magic power brought these walls?   25

So Thebes was built when Amphion played his lyre,
and stones were charmed when Orpheus strummed and sang.
These labors stun the year itself, the months
in one brief cycling span are awed to see
a work that should have taken many years.   30
The god it was who brought and raised his stronghold:
he strained to clear out rocks that would not go
without a fight, and shoved away a mountain
with his huge chest—the sort of task you'd think
cruel Hera might inflict her stepson with.   35
    So come, be present here, and bring your spirit
to this, your temple's birthday celebration.
Free from indentured labor now, you dwell
in Argos, land your mortal kin once ruled,
and dance on taskmaster Eurystheus' grave,   40
or occupy your real father's throne,
the place in heaven that your valor won.
There Hebe puts her apron on and serves
you drafts of blessèd nectar, better than
did Ganymede, whose role she has usurped.   45
Your presence is required, not by the Hydra
that poisoned Lerna's swamp, nor peasant host
Molorchus, nor Nemea's dreadful lion,
nor caves where Thracian mares ate human flesh,
nor altars foully stained by Egypt's king,   50
but by a home that is felicitous,
ingenuous and innocent of guile,
a dwelling very fit to host the gods.
Lay down your savage bow, your quiver's ruthless
ranks, and your club drenched with the blood of kings,   55
and drop the foe that drapes your rugged shoulders.
For you the high and holy couch is here
with purple vines embroidered; figures carved
in relief roughen the frame's ivory surface.
Peacefully, gently, come, not wild with rage   60
nor cringing like a slave, the way we see
you act upon the tragic stage, but more
in comic style. For instance, as you were
in Auge's arms, all Bacchic frenzy spent,
and soaked with brother Dionysus' wine,   65

or when one night's illicit prowling stunned
King Thespius, fifty times your father-in-law.
For you these festive games are held, where youths
compete in wrestling, spar with safety gloves,
repeating contests every cycling year.   70
Upon your temple's roll of priests has been
recorded here Menecrates' grandson,
delighting the old man. He's little still,
and like you were when Hera sent a plague
of snakes to you, her stepson. First you squeezed   75
them to death, then were sad they wouldn't play.
      But how the temple rose so fast, come, Muse,
to whom we poets owe respect, and tell.
Our hero's bow will make an epic sound—
its string will imitate your lyre's twang.   80
      The time had come when scorching skies bore down
on earth; the Dog Star, struck by so much sun,
had fiercely set the panting fields on fire.
And now the day was here: Diana's grove,
(where runaways are royal priests) was smoking   85
with torches; Nemi's lake (it knows what happened
to Theseus' son) was gleaming with their light.
The goddess takes a holiday herself:
she garlands hounds who've earned a furlough, wipes
her arrows clean, and lets wild beasts go safe,   90
while all of Italy's hearths observe her day.
My Alban foothills place would have sufficed
to ease the heat and sooth away my cares
(the Emperor's gift to me was running water).
But I—no stranger to Sorrento—stayed   95
on cliffs, the Siren's namesake, eloquent
Pollius' home. I daily got to know
the peaceful habits of the man, and fresh
bouquets from Helicon, the virgin poems
he had not shown or read to anyone.   100
The same old rooms had got us down, and made
us feel too cramped indoors; we chanced to spend
Diana's day beside the sea-sprayed shore;
a spreading leafy tree kept off the sun.
The bright blue sky had vanished, giving way   105

to sudden clouds, as sodden south wind weighed
the fragile zephyrs down. Dark clouds appeared
at Carthage just like that, when Juno doomed
its tragic queen to wed the Trojan prince,
a marriage only howling nymphs attended.   110
We scatter; servants grab the festive meal
and wine bowl with its wreath of flowers. There's nowhere
to move the party, although countless homes
are settled high in joyful fields above
and many splendid roofs enrich the slopes.   115
But threatening clouds insist we shelter quite
close by, as does our confidence the heavens
will smile again despite the present gloom.
There stood a fragile hut—a hallowed temple
it called itself—whose tiny confines held   120
the lowly hearth of Hercules the great,
with scarcely room to fit wave-faring sailors
or those who search the deep for food. In here
we get our crowd together, here is packed
the banquet, costly couches, gathered servants,   125
and stylish Polla's charming entourage.
The shrine was cramped, there wasn't room indoors.
The god blushed red and smiled, and filled the heart
of his dear Pollius, hugged the man and coaxed:
"Are you the lavish builder whose largesse   130
has filled Pozzuoli, girlish Naples too?
The one who planted our hillside with lots
of rooftops, so many green groves, with lots
of lifelike bronze and marble portraiture,
so many faces lit with painted life?   135
That house of yours, that tract of land—they give
you pleasure now, but what were they before?
You paved a pathway over naked rock.
A trail was all that used to lead where now
your colonnade of well-spaced pillars rises   140
to keep your visitors from getting dusty.
Beside the curving shore your baths confined
the thermal spring within a twin-domed spa.
These structures tax my powers to count. For me
alone is Pollius poor and destitute?   145

And yet I enter cheerfully a home
like yours, and love the shore where you have made
me welcome. But, close by, my neighbor Juno
looks down and laughs in silence at my seat.
Bestow on me a temple fit to match   150
your other enterprises—ships would stop
without the need to pray for winds to blow.
I could invite the Olympian father here
to dine, a crowd of gods would be my guests,
my sister, from her temple high atop   155
Minerva's promontory there, would come.
Don't be alarmed because a solid knob
of spiteful mountain stiffly blocks your way
that countless ages never have worn down.
For I'll be there myself to help so great   160
an enterprise and smash the rugged guts
of earth against its will. Begin, be bold,
and trust in Hercules' encouragement.
Amphion's fortress won't have risen faster,
nor walls two gods had labored on at Troy."   165
Hercules spoke, and slipped from Pollius' mind.
        No time is lost before a plan is sketched,
and countless hands gathered. These are concerned
with hewing trees and raising beams, while those
are laying deep foundations. Clay is baked   170
to ward off winter cold and keep out frost,
while stone is slaked in kilns and crushed to lime.
But paramount among the labors is
to excavate by force opposing cliffs
and rock that won't submit to iron tools.   175
At this point Father Hercules himself
lays weapons down to sweat with sturdy ax
and clear away the unformed ground himself,
while evening shadows screen the brooding sky.
Wealthy Capri and verdant Tuore Grande   180
reverberate, and mighty crashes come
echoing back to land from out at sea.
Mount Etna does not make a sound so epic
when Cyclopes are forging thunderbolts;
no greater is the crash from caves on Lemnos   185

when fiery Vulcan hammers out a breastplate
and decks the virgin Pallas with his gifts.
The craftsmen are amazed by cliffs grown small
when they return at rosy light of dawn.

Another year has just begun to pant   190
with summer's heat. A richer Hercules
looks down upon the waves; his mighty stronghold
rivals stepmother Juno's nearby temple,
his shrine is worthy now to host his sister.
His contests' robust rites are being signaled   195
with peacetime fanfare now, and now with smoke
from altars burning on the sand. This homage
would be refused by neither Zeus (whose games
the Olympics are) nor shady Delphi's lord
(the Pythian ones are his). There's nothing tragic   200
about the venue. So, let these replace
the Isthmian Games and Nemean ones—those both
arose to mourn the cruel death of boys.
The boy who sacrifices here is more
felicitous—he's Pollius little grandson.   205
From pumice caverns sea-green nymphs leap out;
they aren't ashamed to perch on dripping rocks,
to hide and watch the naked wrestling matches.
Watching as well are Monte Barbaro,
bushy with vines Bacchus taught men to use,   210
and woods that garland Nisida, an isle
in isolation; tranquil "Meadowlands";
Cape Bonvoyage, that augurs well for ships;
Venus at Bauli near the Lucrine lake.
Cape Misenum, that Trojan bugler's tomb,   215
you'll learn the Greek fanfares played close to you;
Naples, site of imperial games, you smile
indulgently on Pollius' private rites,
their manly competition in the nude,
the miniatures of wreaths your victors win.   220
Come on, why don't you, gladly take a part
with your unbeaten strength in contests held
to honor you. Whatever your pleasure is,
to split the clouds with discus throws, or shoot

arrows that wingèd winds cannot outfly,   225
or use that strength to tie your wrestling foes
in knots the way you did that Libyan giant,
show favor to these rites. If you still have
those golden apples left from venturing west,
then put them in respected Polla's lap,   230
since she accepts such homage and deserves it.
If she'd regain her pleasing grace, her years
of tender youth, perhaps here too (forgive me
Hercules), you would be her lady's maid,
just like the role that Lydian queen assigned you.   235

    Inspired to joyful frenzy, I have brought
the newborn altar this, my birthday gift.
Now in the doorway he—I recognize
him speaking out the words of this pronouncement:
"A blessing on your zeal! Your labors here   240
were modeled on my own. Taming the stiff,
unbending crags and barren nature's shame—
disgraceful wilderness—you've turned the haunts
of beasts to better use, restoring gods
to view from shame and dim obscurity.   245
Now what reward am I to pay, what thanks
for kindness give? I'll hold your life-thread still,
make Clotho's spindle stretch it out (I know
the way to triumph over Death's hard heart).
I'll keep the mournful grief of loss away,   250
restore you, unimpaired, to ever green
old age. I'll let you watch your grandchildren
prolong their youth, 'til both are ripe for spouses,
and 'til their sassy flock of new descendants
now worms its way into grandfather's arms,   255
now races in a troop to be the first
to coax kisses from tranquil Polla's lips.
This temple's life will never have an end
appointed, so long as fiery heaven's
fabric will bear me up. My other haunts   260
will host me no more often—not Nemea,
not ancient Argos, nor my Tivoli home,
nor Cadiz where the sun beds down at night."

He spoke, and touched his altar's rising flame.
The silvery poplar leaves that wreathed his brow   265
shook with the nod that sealed the oath he swore
by Styx and by the Olympian father's bolts.

Bon Voyage, Maecius Celer! (*Silvae* 3.2)

    You gods, whose passion is to save bold ships
and calm the windy ocean's cruel dangers,
spread out a gentle sea, serenely turn
your council to my prayers, and do not let
the placid waves drown out the one who pleads.   5
Weighty and special is the thing we give
to Neptune's depths, on loan to keep it safe
and then return; young Maecius is entrusted
to that uncertain deep as he prepares
to transport overseas the greater part   10
of my soul. Bring those lights that sailors welcome
and settle, Twins, on the yardarm; let sea
and sky be lit by you, but drive far off,
I pray, the cloudy star of sister Helen
of Troy, and banish it from all of heaven.   15
You, too, sea nymphs, Nereus' azure troop,
to whom this second kingdom's glory fell
by lot, the great sea's "stars," if I may call
you that, rise up from foamy Ocean's caves
of glassy green, compete in tranquil swimming   20
to throng the bay of Baiae and its shores
that teem with tepid waves, and try to find
the tall vessel which noble Celer, son
of valiant Rome, is glad to climb aboard.
You will not have to try for long to find it;   25
she's now the first to bring across the sea
her heavy cargo, this year's grain from Egypt,
to Pozzuoli; first to hail Capri,
and sprinkle drops of Egypt's wine from starboard,
an offering to the Tuscan Sea's Minerva.   30
Loosely circle both sides, divide the tasks,
and you, pull taut the mast's hemp bonds, while you,

rig the topsails; you, spread bellying sails
to the West Wind; let some put back the thwarts,[1]
and some let down the curving vessel's rudder;   35
let there be those who test and balance oars,*
and who tie up the boat that trails astern,
those who dive deep and haul up anchor cable;
let this one here control the tide, let it
turn and flow east; let not a one of you   40
blue-gray sisters be left without a duty.
Let Proteus with his many changing shapes
and Triton with his double one, swim on
ahead from here, and Glaucus too, who lost
his human loins to sudden transformation,   45
whose fond tail fin still strikes Anthedon's coast
as often as he glides to native shores.
But you, Palaemon, first before them all,
with goddess mother Ino, nod approval,
if my passion is making your Thebes known,   50
and if I sing with no less worthy lyre,
of its inspired musician Amphion.
Let father Aeolus, whose prison breaks
the winds, who is obeyed by sundry blasts,
breezes over the whole world's oceans, storms,   55
and rainy clouds, let him impose on other winds
a tighter mountain barricade, let West Wind
alone have access to the sky, alone
drive ships and skim above the tops of waves,
constantly on the sea 'til Celer's sails,   60
unharmed by any whirling hurricane,
convey him to Egypt to hold in trust.
     They heard. West Wind himself summons the craft
and chides the dawdling crew. Behold, my heart
already sinks with frightened chill, I can't   65
hold back, although the omen makes me shudder,
the tears poised at the corners of my eyes.
And now a crewman has untied the rope,
parted the craft from land, and cast the gangplank
into the sea (bad luck to use it twice);[2]   70
the cruel captain's prolonged shout from the stern
scatters embraces, severs faithful kisses—

on your dear neck I may not dally long.
Yet I will go ashore last of the crowd,
nor will I leave, save when your hull <departs>.   75
    What bold creative thinker made the sea
a novel, isolated kind of highway
for us poor creatures, banished loyal sons
of solid ground to the waves, made them go
into the yawning ocean? No more rash   80
was that exploit which joined to Ossa's peak
chilly Mount Pelion, and doubly crushed
with rocky crests a panting Mount Olympus.
Was it so very little, crossing swamps
and putting narrow rivers under bridges?   85
Into the void we go, and everywhere
we flee our native lands, shut up inside
skimpy timber and brass, exposed and bare.
Thence came the winds' fury and outraged storms,
heaven's roars and more bolts from Thunderer.   90
Before the age of ships, the oceans lazed
in languid sleep, Thetis did not delight
in spewing foam, nor clouds in spattering waves
with rain. Billows boiled at the sight of ships
and storms rose against man. Then Pleiades   95
and Goat grew cloudy, then Orion worsened.
    I have a right to complain. See, the ship
speeds off, driven through fickle waves, and slowly
becoming smaller, bests the eyes which keep
it long in sight; its slender beams embrace   100
so many fears, and carry you, who are
above the rest, Celer, visible sign
of my affection. Now with what emotion
can I endure the hours of sleep, endure
the days? Who will report to me, afraid   105
of everything, if the Lucanian Sea
has sent you past its raging coast with waves
that ease your way, whether whirling Charybdis
surges, or Scylla seethes, that monstrous maiden,
the one who plunders deep Sicilian waters,   110
what is the impulsive Adriatic's mood
as you speed by, are Cretan waters calm,

what sort of breeze conveys you over Ocean,
which smiled upon Europa's theft by bull?
But I deserve to complain. Why, when you   115
were heading for your post, did I not go
as tireless comrade even to the Indies
unknown, or bare Crimean steppes? I'd stand
beside the martial banners of my chief,
whether you wielded arms or reins, or made   120
rulings in courts martial,³ and your achievements
I could not share, but surely would admire.
If Phoenix once, revered by great Achilles,
came to Ilium and the shores of Troy,
although unwarlike and not bound at all   125
by Agamemnon's rage, why is my love
so indolent? My faithful feelings will
never be far from you, and I will follow
your spreading sails with my far-reaching prayers.

    Isis, one time a cow in Argive stables,   130
now Egypt's queen, power of the sweltering East,
welcome this ship with your loud-rattling sistrum;
this excellent young man, on whom Rome's Leader
bestowed the Syrian Legion's troops and banners,
bring him serenely through your temple doors,   135
your hallowed ports and cities. Let him learn,
with your protection, whence the marshy Nile
has boundless fruitfulness, why do its waters
subside and its banks dam the flood with silt
built up by swallows, why Memphis is jealous,   140
or why Canopus' shore plays with abandon
despite its Spartan namesake, why Anubis,
like Hades' watchdog, guards Egyptian altars,
why lowly beasts are equal to great gods,
what sacrificial altar the long-lived phoenix   145
strews as his pyre-to-be, what fields does Apis,
the sacred bull revered by trembling shepherds,
deign to graze, or in what stream does he plunge.
Bring him as well to Alexander's tomb
where that city's founder endures, embalmed   150
in honey, and the palace plagued with asps
where Cleopatra plunged in poison's charms and,

Rome's foe at Actium, escaped Rome's chains.
Escort him all the way to his command
and Syrian post, then hand the young man over,   155
goddess, into the care of Roman Mars.
Nor will he be a stranger; as a boy
he sweated in those fields, noted as yet
for just his tunic's wider stripe of rank,
but bold already then at nimbly wheeling   160
cavalry squads and putting Eastern arrows
to shame by his long javelin throws.
    That day will come, on which the Emperor,
intending greater things for you, will bid
you leave, discharged from service on that front,   165
but will I stand again upon this shore,
observe the immense waves, and ask for winds
to blow the other way, from east to west?
O then with what great pride, with what proud lyre,
will I bestir my pick for answered prayers,   170
when you wrap me around your mighty neck, and
lift me on your shoulders, when first you lean
upon my breast, fresh from the ship, and share
the chats you have saved up, and taking turns,
we tell about the intervening years: 175
you, the raging Euphrates, royal Bactra,
the hallowed wealth of ancient Babylon,
and Zeugma, route for troops that bring Rome's peace,
how* sweet are thriving Idumaea's groves,
which dye makes costly Tyre grow red, and which,   180
the purple double-dyed in Sidon's vats,
where one first finds rich twigs with resin buds
that sweat the glistening balm of Gilead;
but I, what tombs I gave the vanquished Argives,
what lines conclude my long hard work on Thebes.   185

Consolation to Claudius Etruscus (*Silvae* 3.3)

    Devotion, power most dear to heaven and god
supremely high, who rarely now regards
this desecrated world—be present here

with fillets in your hair and snow-white cloak,
just as you were when still you lived on earth   5
among a golden race of simple folk
before the wicked drove you off; attend
these touching rites and see devoted grief,
applaud Etruscus' tears and wipe them dry.
Who'd see him burst his lungs with endless wails,   10
embrace the pyre and lie among the ashes,
without supposing that a young wife's corpse
were mourned, or else a son's new-bearded cheeks
the flames now took? A father is the cause
of all his tears. Attend these holy rites,   15
both gods and men. Away, away from here
you wicked ones who nurse a secret sin
and find a weary father's old age long,
who feel the guilt of having struck their mother
and fear strict treatment from the Judge below: 20
the pure and innocent I call. See him
gently cradle and hold the agèd face,
sprinkle his father's hallowed old gray head
with tears, and catch his last chill breath with love;
his sire's years went swiftly, thinks the son   25
(amazing loyalty!), the gloomy Sisters
have been in haste to cut the fatal thread.
Let tranquil shades exult on Lethe's banks,
rejoice, Elysian dwellings, offer garlands,
let festal altars cheer your ghostly groves.   30
A happy shade, ah, very happy, comes,
whose son laments. Far off be hissing hair
of Furies, far, the triple-headed guard,
and let the lengthy road lie open wide
for such outstanding shades. Let him approach   35
the silent lord's terrible throne, give thanks
for one last time and anxiously request
for his young son as many years as his.
   Blessings upon devoted groans! I'll comfort
your worthy grief and further consecrate   40
in memory of your agèd father gifts
from Helicon. You, flood the pyre, Etruscus,
with lavish Eastern balm, you, flood it now

with grand harvests—Cilician ones of saffron,
and Arabs' incense. Let the fire take off   45
your whole inheritance; mound up your gifts
on ashes that will send devoted clouds
of smoke to shining heaven: my gifts aren't meant
to burn, your grief will last for years to come,
displayed by me. For not unknown to me   50
is weeping for a father, just like you
I hurled myself right at the fire and groaned.
That day convinces me to check your loss
with song: laments once mine, I now bring you.
    Your line, tranquil old man, was surely not   55
a noble one, a pedigree come down
from distant kin; huge fortune made up
for birth and hid your parents' flaw. And yet,
no common masters did you bear, but those
the East and West alike are subject to.   60
That's no disgrace to you, for what exists
on earth or in the heavens except on terms
it must obey? In turn all things are ruled,
and dominate in turn. Every land
has rulers. Lucky Rome prevails and dominates   65
those rulers' crowns. The power to rein her in
is granted emperors who are soon subject
to gods, but even gods obey these terms.
The swiftly dancing stars are also slaves,
the wandering moon's a slave, nor does the sun   70
retrace its route so many times unbidden,
and (if it's right comparing lowly things
with those most high) even Hercules bore
a cruel king's dread terms; nor was the pipe
Apollo played while herding sheep ashamed   75
because the god was subject to a mortal.
    Besides, you did not cross to Latin shores
from savage ones—your native soil was Smyrna;
you drank from Meles' source, that awesome spring
near Homer's birth, from Hermus' golden stream   80
where Bacchus goes to gild his horns with silt.
Next, your career flourished, your status grew
from different posts; always to walk near gods,

always to serve right at the Emperor's side
and stick close to those hallowed secrets—that   85
was your assignment. First, Tiberius' courts
opened to you when scarcely did your face
show manhood's changes (since your youthful years
were trumped by so much talent, here, unsought,
your freedom comes), nor did the next successor,   90
ruthless and dogged by Furies, send you off.
So next, his callow comrade all the way
to Britain's frosty north, you bore a tyrant
dreadful in speech and looks, who brutalized
his own people—your lot was like the men   95
who tame fierce beasts, who sink their hands in mouths
that know the taste of blood, and then command
them to let go and live no more on prey.
Claudius then, old but not yet dispatched
to the star-studded firmament, promoted   100
you for merit to special tasks, and passed
you on to serve his brother's* grandson next.
What †god-fearing† man ever was allowed
to be in service* to so many shrines,
so many altars? Wingèd Mercury   105
is messenger for Jove most high, and Juno
has power over rainbow-trailing Iris;
obedient Triton waits for Neptune's orders;
you have properly born unscathed the yoke
of emperors, so often changed, and happy   110
has been your skiff in all of life's deep waters.
　　　Now lofty Fortune's aura came full stride
in your devoted house; a single man
is now entrusted with the Empire's Treasury,
administering its wealth, the revenue   115
produced by all the great world's population—
whatever gold-filled pits in Spain disgorge,
whatever glitters on Dalmatian peaks,
what's gleaned from African crops, what's threshed
on floors along the sultry river Nile,   120
and what pearl divers pick from Red Sea beds,
the flocks well-tended on Tarentine streams,
crystals like ice and Moorish citrus wood,

esteemed Indian tusks; a single servant
receives and has control of what comes in   125
from North and violent East and cloudy South;
sooner could you count up the winter raindrops
or forest leaves. Alert and keen of wit,
that man controlled the flow of all expenses—
demands, however great, of Roman spears   130
under all foreign skies, of City wards
for doles of grain, of temples, aqueducts,
breakwaters for the port of Rome, the far-flung
system of roads, the gold to make our Lord
and Master's paneled ceilings glitter, ore   135
to melt in crackling fire and cast as busts
of gods, or else to mint as Roman coins.
    Therefore you had scant rest, all thought of pleasure
banished, and skimpy meals, never a loss
of concentration caused by drinking wine   140
too deeply, yet the ties of marriage were
dear to your heart—binding your mind with links
of love, joining in happy wedlock, siring
new subjects loyal to your Lord and Master.
Who would not know his wife Etrusca's birth   145
and striking beauty? Never did I see her
with my own eyes, of course, and yet her portrait
reflects exquisite charm, the equal of
her renown, and her sons reveal that grace
in features which are just the same as hers.   150
Not common was her birth; loyally did
her brother hold the highest civil office
and take command of Roman swords and banners
when madness first drove savage Dacians on
and doomed that race to a great Roman triumph.   155
So, whatever the father's bloodline lacked,
the mother made up for—the house rejoiced
to see an obscure branch brighten its prospects
by marriage ties. Living proof of their love
was not far off. Indeed Lucina came   160
twice to assist at births, fruitfully easing
difficult labors with her own light touch.
Ah, happy woman, if a lengthy life,

if Fate's life-thread had justly let you see
your sons' faces, their lushly bearded cheeks.   165
But those joys failed, broken off in your prime,
the hand of Fate cut your years at their peak,
just as the lilies droop their pale-green stems,
as thriving roses die in the first breeze,
or the spring violet faints in fresh green fields.   170
Around that corpse you Cupid bowmen flew,
her bier anointed with your mother's balm,
endlessly tore and strewed your hair and feathers
upon the fire, and heaped a pyre of quivers.
What funeral gifts or what laments, Etruscus,   175
did you offer your mother's pyre then,
when now you deem your father's death untimely
and with devotion groan for his long years!
    That man was honored by Vespasian too,
who's shared his glorious sons with earth and stars   180
and now rules heavenly courts; he gladly gave
that man a role in the Judaean triumph,
a worthy place in the procession's line
(his humble birth was no hindrance at all).
The same one moved him from the people's grandstand   185
down to the knights' reserved section, changed
his status, stripped the iron freedman's ring
from his left hand and matched his sons' high rank.
For twice eight five-year spans the years flowed by
propitiously, without a cloud his life   190
progressed; how generous for his sons' enjoyment
he was, willing to spend beyond his means,
his son Etruscus' customary splendor
derived from that resource bears witness still.
His noble manners came from your support,   195
if you indeed always held him in check
with fond embraces, never father's orders;
his brother too was gladly quite disposed
to yield before his brother's firstborn status.
    What thanks for their father's resurrection,   200
Leader supremely high, do these young men
repay to you, or what devoted vows?

Did age, slowed by decrepitude, worn out
by public life, make some mistake, or Fortune,
fond of him for so long, choose to retreat?   205
The shocked old man shuddered in fear of blows
from blasts to come, but you, Domitian, were
content to warn with just a lightning flash
and gentle storm; although his colleague left
Italian fields behind and crossed rough seas,   210
he was ordered to leave for pleasant shores
where Greeks had colonized Campania's coast,
and was no exile, but a guest. Not long
did you, Germany's Victor, make him wait;
then you unbarred entrance to Rome again,   215
eased his sorrow, and set his prostrate household
upright. No wonder, most tranquil of leaders,
since this is the same clemency which gave
the conquered Chatti sparing terms of peace,
let Dacians keep their mountain, and just now   220
after dreadful wars with the Marcomani
and with Sarmatian nomads, did not think
that their defeat deserved a Roman triumph.
      And now his days are at an end, the Fates'
relentless skein runs out. Here sad Etruscus'   225
devotion asks me for a song the likes
of which neither the Sirens' cliff can manage,
nor can a swan which knows its death is sure,
nor cruel Tereus' wife. Alas, I've seen
him wearying his arms with such great blows,   230
and sprawled with face bent down to kiss the corpse!
His friends and servants scarcely held him back,
the blaze scarcely drove him away. He groaned
just as Theseus did along the shore
back home when lying sails misled his father.   235
Then with tremendous groans and face befouled,
he spoke to still-warm ashes: "Why do you,
most loyal father, leave us just as Fortune
is coming back? Our great Protector's powers,
the short-lived wrath of gods, we've now appeased,   240
but you will not enjoy the use of such

a gift; robbed of it, off you run, ungrateful,
to the shades; one may not divert the Fates,
appease the savage power of Lethe's stream.
Happy was he to whom the flames at Troy   245
deferred and let him pass when his great shoulders
carried his father off, and Scipio,
who at a tender age rescued his sire
from cruel Carthaginians; happy too
Etruscan Lausus' rash devotion was!   250
So then, could that Thessalian wife redeem
her spouse from death, or could that suppliant
from Thrace conquer pitiless Styx with song
for his lost wife? By how much would it be
better if one could do this for a father!   255
You won't be carried off completely though,
nor will I let your ashes go too far;
here I will keep your shade, here in the house.
You will keep watch as master of this hearth,
what's yours will all obey you; duly junior   260
to you and always following behind,
I'll give your hallowed spirit constant food
and drink, your image I'll revere; for me,
polished marble and expert lines of paint
will represent your likeness; now both ivory   265
and tawny gold will reproduce your features.
And from that source I'll ask your course of conduct
and long life's measuring stick to speak to me
devoted words in dreams that bring advice."
This speech his father hears with joyful pleasure,   270
descends slowly to pitiless shades, and takes
along the words to tell his dear Etrusca.
      A final greeting, most gentle of fathers,
a last farewell, old man: while your son lives,
you never will endure the Underworld   275
in sadness, nor your mournful tomb's neglect.
Always will altars smell of fragrant flowers,
always your happy urn will drink perfume
and tears, a greater tribute still. This man
will give your spirit hallowed offerings,   280
and build a monument on your own land.

My song as well he dedicates to you
(model devotion gets its just deserts),
glad that he gave you this monument too.

Farewell to Earinus' Lock of Hair (*Silvae* 3.4)

Go, lock of hair; I wish for you a safe
and speedy voyage; go, recline at ease
inside your golden box with jeweled wreath.
Go, and Venus, Cythera's gentle goddess,
will calm the southern headwinds, grant a crossing   5
full speed ahead, perhaps will even get
you off the frightening ship, and bring you over
above the waves on her own seashell craft.
        Accept a much-praised lock, Asclepius,
Apollo's youthful son. Accept with joy   10
and show your unshorn father. Let him judge
that which the Emperor's boy presents, and think
the sweetly shining locks are brother Bacchus'.
And maybe, though it's never fallen yet,
he'll even cut his crowning glory short,   15
and shut it up inside another box
of gold to offer it to you himself.
        Pergamum, you are much more blessed than Ida,
mountain of pines, although she prides herself
on clouds that covered Ganymede's abduction   20
(of course it's true she gave the gods above
the one that Juno always frowns to see,
whose touch she spurns, whose wine she scorns to drink).
But you, favored by gods, distinguished for
Earinus, your handsome foster son,   25
you've sent a table steward here to Latium
whom our Italian "Jove" and Rome's own "Juno"
alike behold with brow that's tranquil still,
and both approve. Nor would there be so much
delight for Lord and Master of the world   30
unless the gods had planned and willed it so.
        The story goes that golden Venus drove
her swans from Sicily's Mount Eryx, steered

for groves of hers on Cyprus, then she entered
the town of Pergamum. There sick folks find   35
their great mediator and advocate,
the gentle god Asclepius, who halts
their hastening doom and spends the night
among the snakes that bring good health for them.
And here the boy, with beauty like a star   40
of bright and dazzling magnitude, is playing
in front of that god's shrine, when Venus spots him.
At first his looks surprise and fool her some—
she thinks he's from her tribe of Cupid sons—
but that one hasn't got a bow, nor does   45
a feathered shadow dim his gleaming shoulders.
Amazed by the boy's grace and charm, she asks,
beholding both his face and hair, "Will you
go off to some Italian fortress-town
and Venus not do anything about it?   50
Will you endure a shoddy house, the yoke
of common servitude? Heaven forbid!
I'll give to that beauty of yours the master
which it deserves. Come on now, boy, and come
with me. Through starry skies by wingèd chariot   55
I'll bring Rome's Leader this tremendous gift.
No ordinary owner waits for you,
but loving bondage as a palace slave.
I've never seen, never, I say, a thing
so sweet beneath the sky's whole dome, nor given   60
it birth myself. For you the Moon's belovèd
will gladly step aside, as also will
Cybele's darling Phrygian boy; so too
the one whose meaningless reflection wore
him out with love that bore no fruit. You'd be   65
that water nymph's choice; she'd have grabbed the urn
you brought and pulled you with it in her pool,
harder than when she nabbed Hercules' squire.
You're ahead of them all, boy; only he
is handsomer to whom I'm giving you."   70
Just so she spoke, then lifts him up with her
into the light breeze and says to take
a seat in her two-swan chariot rig.

In no time, here's the Palatine, the site
of ancient King Evander's Roman home.   75
With massive new construction projects there
the world's renowned Father, Germany's Victor,
improves it, raising it to match the stars.
Already then are worries close at hand
for Venus: What's the hairstyle best for him?   80
What clothes will make his rosy cheeks light up?
Which gold becomes his fingers? Which, his neck?
She knew our Leader's godlike expert eye,
since she herself had joined his wedding torches,
and granted him a spouse with lavish gifts.   85
Just so she fixes Earinus' hair,
on him she drapes a purple cloak, bestows
on him her radiant fire. The previous favorites
and flocks of servants step aside. This new one
carries to our great Leader heavy cups   90
of finest fluorspar and crystal ware.
The server's fair white hands outshine the cups,
and Bacchus gets a new increased appeal.
        You're dear to gods above (and gods on earth),
the boy who's been selected first to taste   95
respected wines, to touch the mighty hand
so often which the Getes would like to know,
with which Armenians, Persians, Indians want
to be in touch. Yours is a lucky star,
and gods have blessed you much and favored you.   100
And once, lest first beard's fuzz should mar your cheeks,
and dim your beauty's shine, Pergamum's god
himself forsook its heights to cross the sea.
Apollo's youthful son—but no one else—
was authorized to soften up the boy.   105
His gentle method changed the body's sex—
but nothing else. Yet worry gnaws at Venus
because she fears the boy will be in pain.
Our Leader's lovely mercy had not yet
begun to keep all males intact from birth.   110
It's wicked now to crush a person's sex
and alter him; Nature, delighted, sees
only what she herself has given birth.

Misguided laws no longer make a slave
mother fear the burden of bearing sons.   115
A young man now, if you'd been later born,
with shadowed cheeks, with body grown and strong,
like others you'd have sent, to your delight,
Asclepius' temple not this gift alone.
But now your locks must sail to native shores   120
without the trimmings from your first beard's growth.
This lock was soaked with lots of spicy oil
by Venus; this the kindly Graces combed
with three right hands. For this the purple hair
that guarded Nisus' realm 'til it and he   125
were cut will step aside, as will the one
wrathful Achilles let grow long to save
for giving thanks when he got home, but cut
to honor dead Patroclus' pyre instead.
As soon as it has been resolved to clip   130
the snow-white brow, expose the shoulders' shine,
dainty Cupids come rushing up in person
along with mother Venus. They undo
his hair and put a silken barber's towel
over his chest, then using scissors made   135
by crisscrossed arrows, cut the hair and put
the lock inside the box of gold and jewels.
Their mother herself traps it as it falls
and treats it once again with mystic oils.
Then from the crowd of Cupids, one, who chanced   140
to bring in upraised hands a first-class mirror
of jeweled gold, says, "Let us give this, too.
No gift will be more welcome to your hometown god,
the gold itself will thus have more effect.*
Just fix your gaze and leave your face right here   145
forever." Saying this, he shuts away
the mirror with the image trapped inside.
     But Earinus, boy a breed apart,
stretched out his hands to heaven. "Please, in return
for gifts from me, O mankind's gentle guardian,   150
restore our Lord and Master's lengthy youth.
If I deserve it, keep him safe, preserve him
for the world's sake. With me the stars make this

request, and this request is land's and sea's,
that he may pass through years of mythic length.   155
May he rejoice when building projects age
along with him, the Palace he improved,
Tarpeian Jove's temple restored by him."
And after Earinus prayed like this,
a marvel stunned the town—the altar stirred.   160

To My Wife (*Silvae* 3.5)

Why are you sad by day, and why, my wife,
all through the nights we share in partnership,
heave troubled sighs of worried sleeplessness?
I do not fear your promise to be faithful
has been infringed, or that another love   5
is in your heart; slander's arrows cannot
be loosed at you (too bad if, hearing this,
Nemesis looks dissatisfied), they cannot be. Even if I'd been snatched away
from native shores and served a score of years,   10
wandering through war and through the ocean's waves,
you'd drive a thousand suitors off, untouched,
not by contriving to unweave the fabric
you had not finished yet, but openly
without deceit, and having armed yourself,   15
you'd have denied the marriage bed to them.
Yet say, whence comes this altered, cloudy look?
Can it be that you criticize my moving
back home in broken health and settling down
to spend my old age in my native land?   20
Why is this grim to you? Surely no lust
is lodged in your heart, nor do conflicts waged
at Rome's frenzied race track hold charms for you,
nor crowds at raucous shows enter your thoughts,
but virtue, sheltered quiet, never shabby   25
delights.[4]
        Which waters, furthermore, am I
snatching you through to come as my companion?
Although, even if I were going to

the icy North to stay, or out beyond
the misty ocean of far Western Thule,   30
or seven-mouthed Nile's unreachable source,
you would urge on the trip. In fact, it's you,
whom kindly Venus doubtless joined to me
by lot in years of flowering youth and keeps
into old age, it's you, whose wound transfixed   35
me first, untouched by marriage, roaming still
as young men do, it's you, whose reins I took
with glad responsiveness, and once the bit
was in my teeth, I have continued champing
and do not mean to change. With all your heart   40
you embraced me, when my anointed locks
wore the Alban prize, the Emperor's wreath
of hallowed gold; from you my garland got
breathless kisses; when Jupiter denied
my lyre the Capitoline prize, you shared   45
defeat and you too grieved the cruel god's
ingratitude; my songs' first rushing words,
whole nights of whispered composition,
your sleepless ears picked up; and you alone
witnessed my long labor, and with your years   50
of married life, my Theban epic grew.
How you behaved when I was nearly snatched
away to Stygian shade a while ago
and heard already Lethe's stream at hand—
that I observed and kept my eyes wide open   55
even when they already sank in death!
Clearly the Fates extended my spent span
only because they pitied you, and gods
above, despite their power, were afraid
of your reproaches. After things like that   60
do you delay traveling as my companion
a closer route to that attractive bay?
Ah, where is that well-known fidelity,
often put to the test, with which you match
the heroines of old, both Greek and Roman?   65
Penelope would have happily made
her home in Troy (for what can frighten those
who love?), if her Ulysses had allowed;

118

other Greek wives complained at being left—
Aegiale and Meliboea did,   70
and she, the war's first widow, driven mad
by so cruelly beating her breast from grief.
No less than these you know fidelity
and dedication. Surely that is how
you miss your late first husband's ashes still,   75
that's how you have embraced his last remains
and beat your breast with mighty blows of grief
each year for him, another poet-spouse,
although you now are mine. No differently
do you devote attention to your daughter: 80
That is what your maternal love is like,
that's how your daughter never leaves your heart,
secured deep in your mind by night and day
your keep her. Not so much do mother birds,
swallows and halcyons, embrace their nests,   85
surround these springtime homes, and warm their darlings.
And now that girl is keeping you in Rome
because, alone and husbandless, she still
wastes lovely youth in barren idleness.
But marriage will come, come torches and all;   90
her beauty's merits and her mind's deserve it.
Whether she clasps a lyre and makes it throb,
or with her father's voice, produces notes
the Muses ought to learn and modulates
my songs, or spreads pale arms in graceful motion,   95
talent is topped by virtue, skill by restraint.
Will it not shame those fickle boys, the Cupids,
nor shame you, Venus, that this glorious beauty
is idling? Not only Rome is fruitful
in matchmaking and lighting festive torches: 100
my country too can give you sons-in-law.
The firestorm from dread Vesuvius
has not so greatly drained those fearful towns
of their citizens: they still stand and thrive
with people. Here are Cumae's buildings, founded   105
with Phoebus' patronage, and Baiae's shores,
host to the world, and Pozzuoli's harbors,
and there Capua's walls which mimic regions

of mighty Rome, also founded by Trojans;
my Naples also, too cramped for its natives   110
and yet not sparse in immigrants, once called
Parthenope, that Siren who was brought
across the sea and whom Apollo showed
this gentle soil with Venus' dove as guide.
    This is the site (for savage Thrace is not   115
my native soil, nor is North Africa)
to which I struggle now to get you moved,
tempered by gentle winter and cool summer,
bathed by a peaceful sea's lethargic waves.
These places have untroubled peace, a life   120
of idle leisure, quiet undisturbed
at all, and sleep that lasts the whole night through.
No frenzied courts or laws unsheathed for quarrels;
these people's rights derive from custom only,
fair treatment comes without a judge's power.   125
Why should I praise the places' splendid settings
and their improvements—temples, porticoes
which countless columns demarcate, the bulk
of twin theaters, open-air and roofed,
games second to Capitoline alone,   130
why praise †the shore, and the freedom like that
Menander celebrates†,[5] produced by blending
Roman honor with Greek lack of restraint?
No dearth of varied life's diversions here,
whether it pleases you to go and see   135
geyser-filled Baiae's most seductive shores,
or prophet Sibyl's site of inspiration,
the hilltop noted for a Trojan oar,
Bacchic Monte Barbaro's soaking vineyards,
or Capri, home to Teleboean settlers,   140
whose lighthouse rivals the night-wandering moon
and lifts its beam to please the frightened sailors,
Sorrento's hills, dear for their wine god's bite
(this place my Pollius enhances more
than other residents), the lake with salts   145
in healing currents, Stabiae reborn.
Should I recount for you the thousand dear,
belovèd friends of mine I have back home?

But this is enough, it's enough to say:
wife, she bore me for you, and bound me tightly   150
to share long years in partnership with you.
Does she not well deserve to be regarded
as one who bore and nurtured both of us?
But I'm ungrateful, adding further points
and having doubts about your character: 155
you'll go, my dearest wife, you'll even go
there first. Without me, you will find that chief
of rivers, Tiber, shabby, and so too
the walls founded by well-armed Romulus.

Book 4

Preface

Greetings from Statius to his friend Marcellus!
I have come up with a book, my dearest Marcellus, to dedicate to you, devoted
friend. Of course, I believe that none of my little works has begun without in-
voking the divine power of our very great Emperor, but this book has three
<selections in praise of him put at the front. So you see that you could not be
more honored>* than that the fourth selection concerns homage to you.

    First, however, I have glorified the "Seventeenth Consulship" of our Vic-
tor over Germany. Second, I have offered him "Thanksgiving" for the honor of
inviting me to an official court banquet of his. Third, I have marveled at how
the "Domitian Highway" has removed the very burdensome delay experienced
on the sandy old route. Thanks also to this service, the "Letter" I'm writing to
you for this book will arrive sooner from Naples. Next is an "Ode to Septimius
Severus," a young man, as you know, among the most distinguished members
of the equestrian class. Of course, he is also your fellow-student, but aside from
that relationship, a dear and very close friend of mine. Well then, I can even
charge to your account the poem about our mutual friend Vindex's statuette,
"Hercules at Table"; he deserves this honor because of his relationship with me
and because of his literary interests. I have testified enough about my esteem

for Vibius Maximus for both his excellence and his eloquence by going public with my letter to him about the publication of my *Thebaid*. But now as well there is an "Ode" asking him to return sooner from Dalmatia. Adjacent to it is a selection for my fellow-townsman Julius Menecrates, an illustrious young man and the son-in-law of my friend Pollius. I offer him "Congratulations" because he has honored our Naples by official recognition for the number of his children. To Plotius Grypus, a young man of the senatorial class, I will deliver a more suitable little work some other time, but meanwhile I have included in this volume the "Tetrameters" which we laughed over on the Saturnalia.

So why more poems in the fourth book of the *Silvae* than in the previous ones? To keep those who have censured me, so I hear, for publishing this kind of composition from thinking they have accomplished anything. In the first place, it is redundant to advise against a fait accompli. Next, I had given many of these poems to my Lord Caesar, and how much more considerable a thing is that than publishing them? But is practicing for fun not allowed? "In private," someone says. Yet onlookers are allowed at both a sparring match and bayonet practice.[1] Last of all, whoever reads something of mine with prejudice, immediately declares his opposition. So why should I comply with his advice? In short, obviously I am the one who is making a display of himself; let my critic keep still and enjoy it. Anyhow, this book will have you to defend it, Marcellus. And if you agree, enough said. If not, we will both be censured. Best wishes.

On Domitian's Inauguration as Consul
for the Seventeenth Time (1 January 95 CE) (*Silvae* 4.1)

With joy the consul's purple toga joins
the Emperor's other twice eight times in office;
Germany's Victor starts a special year,
he rises with its first new sun, with stars
in multitudes, and shines, brighter himself   5
and bigger than the Morning Star at dawn.
Let Latin laws rejoice, and jump for joy
you high officials' chairs; with greater pride
let Rome's septuple ridges scrape the sky,
and let Evander's Palatine exult   10
the most of all—up to the Palace there
have climbed new marshal's maces, back has come
this doubly guarded consulship;* its prayers
answered, the Senate house is glad it has

prevailed against the Emperor's modesty.   15
Measureless time's most mighty renovator,
his spirits raised, lifts both his faces up,
and offers thanks from both his shrine's two doors,
Janus himself, whom you have linked to Peace,
who's close to him,[2] and ordered that he end   20
all wars and swear an oath, like you, to keep
the newest Forum's laws. Behold, he lifts
in prayer the hands in front and those behind,
and with his double voice predicts these things:
　　"Greetings, great father of the universe,   25
ready with me to restart time again,
always in this the month that's named for me
your Rome keeps yearning to observe you just
this way. This is a fitting birth for time,
a new year's fitting entrance. While in office,   30
bestow unending joy; around your shoulders
let that intensely purple toga drape,
the robe that your Minerva rushed to make.
Do you observe the temples' different glow,
the higher altar flame, and how my season's   35
wintery stars themselves warm up for you?
Your habits, kindly one, bring joy to troops
of knights, the people's tribes, and senators
in purple stripes; on everyone in office
this consul sheds his light. What previous year,   40
pray tell, ever had such a thing as this?
Come tell me, mighty Rome, and, ancient Past,
with me count through the consuls; don't review
the rolls for minor cases, only ones
my Emperor thinks are worth his while outdoing.   45
Three times and ten consul of Rome as years
slipped by, Augustus only later proved
that he deserved it; you, though young, have passed
your forebears by. How often you refuse
and you reject the Senate's wish! And yet   50
you'll bend, allow this day. A longer chain
of consulships awaits, and blessèd Rome
will triple, yea, quadruple all the ones
you've held so far. With me you're going to found

another age; a hundred years from now   55
you will repeat the New Age Jubilee.³
You'll carry off a thousand battle trophies;
so just allow the triumph celebrations.
Still there is Bactra, still there's Babylon
to saddle with new tax; not yet do sprays   60
of laurel from an Indian victory triumph
rest in Jupiter's lap, not yet do Arabs,
nor do Chinese, petition Rome for favors,
not yet does every year have you in office,
the ten months you have not renamed now yearn   65
to get the honor of new ones from you."
    So Janus spoke, and closed his doors in peace.
The gods then all appeared, and gave good signs
from joyful heaven; a lengthy prime of life
for you, great king, was ratified by Jove,   70
who guaranteed your years would match his own.

Thanks to Domitian
for a Banquet Invitation (*Silvae* 4.2)

    Royal banquets at Dido's court of Carthage
are praised by him who brought the great Aeneas
to Roman soil; feasts Alcinous hosted
are shown in song that will survive by him
who wore Ulysses out with so much sea.   5
But I, to whom the Emperor's given a meal
with its divine new joys—the first time now—
and whom he let sit at the Master's table,*
what instrument should I employ to laud
this boon, and what thanksgiving offer good   10
enough? Not if the place of Homer's birth
and Virgil's, both alike, should tie a wreath
of fragrant laurel 'round my joyful head,
would I say worthy things. Amid the stars
with Jove I seem to take my place at table   15
and drink what Ganymede has served to me,
the gods' own wine. I've let fruitless years pass;
this day's my first, my life's threshold is here.

125

And you, the world's ruler, the subject globe's
great father, you, men's hope and gods' concern,   20
it's you I look at from my seat? Is it
allowed to watch this face up close, allowed
amid the food and drink, and is it right
not to stand up and show respect for you?
   The house is huge, majestic; not a hundred   25
columns distinguish it, but just as many
as could keep gods and heaven standing up
if Atlas took a rest. It stuns its neighbor,
Thunderer's royal hall; because your place
is in a seat like his, the gods are glad   30
(so do not hasten your ascent to heaven).
So great a massive structure opens up,
a spacious hall more boundless than a plain
extends and vaults much sky in its embrace:
only its master dwarfs it. Mighty godhead   35
fills the household and weighs it down.* The stones
in there are rivals, trying to outshine
the rest—whole mountains of African marble
and Phrygian, tons of Aswan granite, stone
from Chios, rock that rivals blue-gray sea,   40
and plain white Luna, only good enough
to hold up columns made of colored stone.
The view up high is distant; bleary-eyed
you'd barely catch a glimpse of ceiling's zenith,
would think that was panels of gilded sky.   45
When the Emperor has bade Rome's leading men
and ranks in knights' dress uniforms to take
their places here all at a thousand tables,
Ceres, with skirt hitched up, and Bacchus toil
to do enough. The agent sent by Ceres   50
with grain for all mankind circled around
like this in fruitful flight, like this the One
Who Loosens Cares shaded the once bare hills
and sober fields beneath grape-bearing vines.
   But my desire had not the time to scan   55
the choice cuisine, nor Moorish timber slabs
on Indian ivory legs the size of columns,
nor squads of well-drilled slaves, but only him,

just him, with features calm and cloudless grandeur;
he dimmed his radiant beams, and humbly dipped   60
his fortune's flag, yet from his face there shone
the rank he tried to hide. A look like that
savages, tribes unknown, would know on sight.
No differently, when Mars has turned his team
of horses loose, does he lie down at ease   65
in Rhodope's icy vale; just so does Pollux rest
his oily limbs, relaxed from Spartan boxing.
Just so beside the Ganges Bacchus lies
as Indian maenads loudly howl his name.
Just so, when earnest Hercules returned   70
from all those dreaded tasks did he rejoice
to spread his lion skin and stretch out on it.
What puny things I say, Germany's Victor,
I have not matched your countenance as yet:
looking like that on one more of his trips   75
to Ethiopian feasts at Ocean's end,
the gods' own leader, countenance relaxed
from drinking divine nectar, bids the Muses
give a private performance, tells Apollo
to celebrate his victory over Giants.   80
        For you may gods approve (since people say
they often heed what lesser beings ask)
that you surpass—two times or three—
your father's own old age. May you dispatch
the duly deified to stars above   85
and build new shrines for gods,⁴ but keep
your earthly home. May you inaugurate
a new year often, often greet its god
Janus to start your latest term as consul,
often repeat Jove's Games in four-year cycles.   90
This day on which you've given a blessèd meal
to me, your table's rites divine, has dawned
for me just like the one so long ago
beneath the Alban Hills, when first I sang
your German lines and next your Dacian war,   95
at Games for your Minerva; then on me
you set the victor's olive wreath of gold.

Domitian's Highway (*Silvae* 4.3)

What dreadful noise of heavy steel
on hard stone has filled up the coast
that flanks the paved Appian Way?
Surely Punic squads aren't making
that noise, nor does their foreign chief   5
restlessly rock Campanian fields
with his treacherous kind of war,
nor does Nero cut through the shoals
and tunnel through mountains, to drain
filthy swampland through his canal.   10
Rather, this is the work of one
who has hemmed in the Gates of War
with new courts and the righteous laws
by which he gave chaste Ceres back
sober acres so long denied   15
for growing grain instead of vines,
by which he keeps the stronger sex
from ruin and, as Censor, stops
full-grown men from fearing torture
because of their handsome good looks,   20
who gave Thunderer's temple back
and restored Peace to her own home,
and who ordains there always be
a temple for his father's clan,
a starry vaulted Flavian heaven.   25
His subjects' sluggish journeys weighed
on this man's mind, their every trip
held up despite the level plains,
so he removes the long detour,
and paves the sand with solid stone,   30
glad the Cumaean Sibyl's home,
Monte Barbaro's lake district,
and Baiae's hot springs are thus moved
nearer the seven hills of Rome.
Here a traveler once was slow   35
even driving a two-wheeled gig,
and he would sway perched up where pole

and axle cross, the spiteful ground
would suck wheels in, and Latin folk
dreaded getting seasick on land.   40
No trip was brisk, but sticky ruts
hindered and slowed the journey down,
while the drooping draft horse crept on
protesting too much weight to pull.
What used to waste a solid day,   45
now is scarcely a two-hour trip.
No wings of birds stretched through the air
nor ships' hulls will go more swiftly.
  The first task here is starting work
on trenches, cutting out a track,   50
and digging deep within the ground;
soon, it is putting other fill
back in the ditches drained of soil,
where the road's humped back will nestle,
so the ground will not keep swaying,   55
so the spiteful site won't provide
an unstable bed for pavement
when it bears the weight of traffic;
then, it's holding the roadway tight
with blocks rammed down to shore both sides   60
and frequent posts to mark the curbs.[5]
So many hands work all at once!
Some strip mountains by felling woods,
some smooth the blocks and beams with tools,
other mortar the stones in tight   65
with lime from kilns and dark tufa.
These handle draining thirsty pools
and channel smaller streams far off.
These hands could tunnel Mount Athos,
as Xerxes did and, with a bridge   70
that does not just float on pontoons,
block groaning Helle's mournful sea.
Through their canal (a short distance
had not the gods vetoed passage)
Corinth's Isthmus and sea would mix.   75
  The shore and moving timber swarm,
a long crash goes up through cities

along the route, a faint echo
from either end, both south and north,
rebounds to Monte Barbaro   80
from vine-clad Monte Massico.
The noise amazed peaceful Cumae,
Liternum's slough, and slow Savo.
      A sandy head of dripping hair
tangled[6] with tender marsh grasses   85
Vulturnus raises, leaning back
against the Emperor's massive bridge,
and hoarsely lets the words spill out:
"My plains' gracious benefactor,
I have flooded valleys roadless,   90
I knew nothing about living
within my banks, but you laid down
the law and made me straighten up.
That muddy menace I once was
hardly endured hesitant[7] ships,   95
but now I bear a bridge which lets
traffic traverse and trample me;
my habit once had been ripping
the soil away and rolling trees
(what a disgrace!), but I have now   100
begun to be a real river.
Yet I offer you thanksgiving,
and value this bondage so much
because I have deferred to you
under your reign, at your command,   105
and this inscription will record
you are my sovereign power supreme
and everlasting conqueror.
Now you keep me in happy bounds,
don't permit me to be filthy,   110
and dredge my barren silt's disgrace
so that I do not sink weighed down
with sand and muck when I enter
the sea (the way Bagrada crawls
in silent banks through Punic fields),   115
but I will race and sparkle so,
that my limpid stream can challenge

the calm sea and nearby Liris."
    The river spoke; meanwhile a stretch
of pavement rose above its back.   120
Its lucky entrance is an arch
big as the bow which belts the clouds,
where the Emperor's spoils of war
and all of Luna's marble shine.
There the speedy traveler turns,   125
there the Appian Way is sad
because it's being left behind.
Then does the trip become more swift
and eager, then the team itself
takes pleasure in the quicker pace,   130
as when rowers' arms are weary,
and breezes first fan the canvas.
So then, all you Eastern nations
who keep good faith with Rome's Father,
travel here by the easy route,   135
come more quickly, spoils from the East.
Nothing stops or slows the zealous.
He who left the Tiber at dawn,
at dusk may sail the Lucrine Lake.
    But what woman do I perceive,   140
white of hair and headbands too,
here at the fresh road's farthest end
where the site of ancient Cumae
is pointed out by Phoebus' temple?
Do my eyes deceive me, or does   145
the Sibyl, from her hallowed cave,
bring the Euboean laurels forth?
    Let us defer to her, my lyre,
put away your music for now:
a holier prophet starts—be still.   150
See how she rolls her head and raves,
possessed, over the whole new road.
Then she makes this revelation:
"I have often said, there will come
(wait in patience, plains and river),   155
there will come with heaven's good will
one who is destined to improve

your foul woods and your fetid swamps
with lofty bridges and a road.
Lo, this man is divine, this man   160
Jupiter orders to command
our happy world on his behalf;
no worthier man has claimed these reins
since Aeneas, with my guidance,
greedily seeking what would come   165
made his way to prescient groves,
then left Avernus' realm behind.
This man is good at bringing peace,
in time of war he must be feared.
if this man steered Sun's fiery wheels—   170
better than Nature is, and stronger—
India would not suffer drought,
springs would gush in Sahara's sands,
and Balkan mountains would grow warm.

    Hail to you, the ruler of men   175
and sire of gods foreseen by me,
you whose coming I recorded.
Do not now scan those words of mine
written down in moldering scrolls
which priests consult with ritual prayers;   180
rather, listen while I chant them
in your presence as you deserve.
I have seen the long succession
of years you'll live in thriving vigor
which the kindly Sisters still weave: 185
a long line of generations
remains for you, outliving sons
and great-great-grandsons, you will spend
such years of everlasting youth
as Nestor reached in peace, they say,   190
as Tithonus' old age totals,
many as I asked from Phoebus.
The snowy North swears allegiance,
soon the East will grant great triumphs.
Where Hercules and Bacchus roamed,   195
south of the sun's own fiery path[8]
you'll reach the Nile's source and the snows

of Mount Atlas, and being blessed
by all the honors heaped on you,
you will ride off into battle   200
but decline to ride in triumph,
so long as Vesta's flame still burns
and the Capitoline Father
thunders from his reborn temple,
until, while you still reign, this road   205
may reach old age more full of years
than is the ancient Appian Way."

A Letter to Vitorius Marcellus (*Silvae* 4.4)

Run through the fields near Naples, letter of mine,
do not be slow, and start your trip from where
the famous Appian Road's offshoot grows,
its firm foundation sunk in soft sea sand;
and when you've swiftly entered Rome, head straight   5
for the right bank of sandy yellow Tiber,
the Tuscan side that dams the Naval Basin's⁹
deep waters, where garden homes¹⁰ fringe the shallows.
There you will see Marcellus, who excels
in both his looks and spirit—you will know him   10
because his lofty height makes him stand out.
At first convey the customary "Greetings,"
but once inside, be sure to say in verse:
        "Now the land and the swiftly turning sky
are languid from the flight of rainy spring,   15
the Dog Star's barking makes the heavens burn,
towering Rome's thick crowds are getting sparse.
Of these, Praeneste's shrine is shielding some,
and some, Diana's icy grove at Nemi,
shivering Algidus, or Tusculan shade;   20
these aim for Tivoli's woods, Anio's cool.
And you as well—what milder region now
draws you away from City noise? What change
of air lets you elude the summer sun?
What of Gallus, your principal concern,   25
your dearest friend, and dear to me as well?
I don't know which should get the most esteem,

his excellence of character or temperament.
Does he now summer on Latin shores, or now
resort again to quarry-filled Carrara,   30
his Tuscan home? But if he's sticking close
to you, I'm not far off when you two chat.
I'm sure of that, since both my ears are burning.[11]
But you, while too much sun's in Leo's mane,
and makes it fiercely blaze, do strip your heart   35
of cares and steal yourself from constant toil.
Even the Parthian shuts his quiver's lid,
unstrings his bow; even a charioteer,
after Olympic toils, cools down his steeds
in Alpheus' stream; even my lyre grows weary   40
and slackens; timely rest fires up and feeds
one's strength, and leisure time makes merit grow.
Just so, after he'd sung about Briseis,
Achilles came more fiercely still and burst
on Hector, once he'd set his pick aside.   45
And you as well, the silent, idle hours
resorted to a while will set aflame;
you'll spring back fresh for customary actions.
Now surely Roman statutes don't stir up
disputes, the lazy time of year's at peace,   50
harvest's return has sent the courts away,
no mob of those whom you defend, or clients
who have complaints to file, are calling now
from your front porch for you to come outside.
The Probate Court's presiding spear[12] is idle,   55
that place where now your very widespread fame
for soaring eloquence stands out already,
and fluent speech transcends your youthful age.
Lucky in his concerns is one whose heart
no poet's peaceful laurel wreath entwines,   60
whose temperament thrives and whose spirit girds
itself for great adventures and endures
whatever comes; my life of leisure I console
with song, the fleeting joys of fickle fame
are what I seek. Behold, pursuing rest   65
on Naples' genial shore, a Siren's place
of refuge once, with idle thumb I strike

my slender strings, and sitting on the threshold
of Virgil's monument, I take new heart
and sing before my mighty master's tomb.   70
But you, if Fate bestows a long career
(I pray it does), and if the Emperor's power
continues thus (your zeal has worshiped him
before the Thunderer, and he is stitching
another task onto your current post,[13]   75
and charges you to supervise repairs
of the whole stretch of the slanting[14] Latin Road),
perhaps you'll go to harness Roman troops
and guard the Rhine or shores of murky Thule,
the Danube's banks, the terrifying pass   80
at Caspian Gates. Of course your worthy merit
lies not in powers of eloquence alone:
your frame is fit for war, your mighty* arms,
the kind that can support a breastplate's heft.
If you should train to go into the field   85
as infantry, above the ranks your helmet
will sway, or if you'll manage jingling reins,
a high-strung horse will be your slave. I sing
the deeds of others while I slide downhill
into old age: handsome in fitting gear   90
you will yourself do things to sing about,
great examples to train your little Geta;
his warrior great-grandfather now already
demands* worthy actions from him, and gives
the chance to learn of triumphs right at home.   95
Come now, arise—a boy against a man—
and overtake your father, you who are blessed
by mother's bloodline, father's worthy merit.
The blessèd Senate's purple breast now hugs
and nurtures you; it gladly guarantees   100
that you will hold all of the highest posts.
    These things I'm telling you, Marcellus, here
on the bay where Vesuvius sends up
the signs of shattered rage, billowing fire
that rival flames from Sicily's volcano.   105
It's strange but true! Will coming generations,
when crops return, when wasteland's green again,

believe that cities and whole populations
lie crushed below, that fields their forebears farmed
vanished in floods of lava?* Still the peak   110
makes deadly threats. Far may that doom be
from your own town, that madness from your mountains.
    Now if perhaps you ask what tapestry
my Muses have begun my Theban epic,
its toilsome voyage now complete, has furled   115
its canvas in the haven it had hoped for,
and on Parnassus' ridges in the woods
of Helicon, has offered festal flames
incense and innards from a virgin heifer,
and hung my headband on a votive tree.   120
Another style of band now occupies
my idle head: Troy—of course—is my effort,
and great Achilles, but the Lord Who Holds
the Bow calls me to go another way
and points it out—the even greater wars   125
of Rome's Emperor. Desire has drawn me there
for some time now, while I've been drawn away
by fear. Will I shoulder that massive bulk
or will its mighty weight subdue my neck?
Speak, Marcellus, will I endure? Or should   130
a ship that's used to smaller waves not yet
be trusted to a stormy ocean's perils?
    And now, farewell, and please forbid esteem
for this deeply devoted bard to leave
your heart. For Hercules <will not outdo>*   135
your friendly heart's support; to you will yield
loyal Theseus' fame, and his as well
who dragged and mangled Priam's son at Troy.
as consolation for his slaughtered friend."

Horatian Ode to Septimius Severus (Silvae 4.5)

Richly blessed with my little farm's rewards
where Alba tends old Trojan hearths, I greet
    forceful and fluent Severus,
      without my lyre's usual song.

Now savage winter has retreated North,   5
eclipsed by suns up higher in the sky,
    now the sea and land are beaming,
      because zephyrs broke the North Wind.

Now every tree is coiffed with yearly leaves
for spring, and now are heard renewed laments   10
    of birds, their unfamiliar song,
      which they composed in winter's hush.

My frugal land and ever-wakeful hearth,
and ceiling dark with soot from much firelight,
    give me comfort, wine too, from jugs   15
      where Bacchus just had been a-boil.

No thousand fleecy flocks are bleating here,
nor does a heifer low for her sweet love,
    and when their master sings alone,
      my mute fields call back in response.   20

But I have loved this country best, second
only to my hometown; here my poems
    won the Queen of Battles' fond prize,
      a wreath of gold for Alban Games,

when you, my comrade, strove with all your heart   25
and cheered me on during the sweet ordeal;
    thus Castor shook with every thud
      when brother Pollux boxed that king.

Did Lepcis, off the beaten path, bear you
on far African shoals? Then soon those sands   30
    will bear prolific Indian crops
      and outproduce sweet Arab spice!

Who would not think that sweet Septimius
had toddled over Rome's septuple hills?[15]
    Who'd say he did not nurse from springs   35
      at Rome after he'd left Lepcis' breast?

No wonder you have merit: right at birth
you entered Rome's harbor, knowing nothing
    about African shoals, and swam
    Tiber's stream as his foster child.   40

While little, with those pledged to Senate rank,
you grew, content with <narrow> purple's gleam,
    but prompted to pursue vast toil
    as one of nature's noblemen.

You neither speak nor look Punic, you think   45
like us: you are Italian, yes, Italian.
    So, in the corps of knights at Rome
    are some who make Africa proud.[16]

Yours is a cheerful voice amid the buzz
in court, but eloquence that's not for sale;   50
    the sword of speech stays sheathed in peace
    except when drawn at friends' behest.

And yet the peaceful countryside delights
you more, now your father's farm at Veii,
    leafy Hernican highlands now,   55
    and now good old-fashioned Cures.

Here you will put more down in words set free
from meter's rules, but when you sometimes think
    of me, play on your lyre again,
    discreetly hidden in a grotto.   60

Vindex's Statuette, "Hercules at Table"[17] (*Silvae* 4.6)

    As luck would have it, I was wasting time
relaxed from cares, from inspiration's grip
released, wandering the Pens' extensive grounds
as daylight died, when I was snatched to dine
with gracious Vindex. This has slipped inside   5
the deepest corners of my mind and stays
as food for thought; for we did not devour

the belly's playthings, cuisine sought from West
to East, and wines rivaling the Archives' age.
Poor souls, who love to know how pheasant differs   10
from Thracian winter crane, which goose has got
the biggest liver, why the Tuscan boar
is choicer than Umbria's, on which seaweed
slippery oysters recline at gentler ease.
Genuine passion, conversation sought   15
from Helicon's midst, merry jokes—these things
made us devour the whole long winter's night
and banish gentle sleep, 'til Castor's Twin
looked out from his Elysian home and rose
(his mate, the Evening Star, had traded places),[18]   20
and Dawn smiled at the sight of last night's table.
A night so fine, I wish it lasted twice
that long, as Hercules' conception did!
A night the calendar should mark with pearls,
that should be long recalled, that's going to have   25
an everlasting spirit all its own.
A thousand bronze and ancient ivory figures,
waxes whose bodies gave the false impression
that they would speak—I came to know them all
by heart right there. For who will ever rival   30
the eye of Vindex, recognizing styles
of ancient masters, making attributions
of statues which the sculptors left unsigned?
Bronzes that clever Myron stayed up late
to toil on, marbles that Praxiteles,   35
working hard with his drill, made come alive,
ivory polished by Phidias' thumb, that which
the forge of Polyclitus bade draw breath—
Vindex will show you; that is this man's hobby,
of course, every time he sheds his lyre;   40
this passion calls him from the Muses' grotto.
        Of all these works, Amphitryon's son the hero,
that upright table's guardian spirit, stole
my heart but could not sate my gazing eyes:
such great dignity's in the work, confined   45
in narrow bounds is majesty. A god,
a god has let himself be seen by you,

Lysippus, small in size, in impact, huge;
the marvel is, its height's inside a foot,
yet you will want to shout, if you have cast   50
your gaze over its limbs: "This is the chest
that crushed the lion's rampage, these the arms
that used to bear the lethal club, that broke
the *Argo's* oars just by rowing so hard."
This big impression gives its small size heft.   55
What sense of due proportion, what control
was in the clever artist's hand, what skill
and care in shaping table ornaments,
and, equally, conceiving huge colossi!
A thing like that no primal Cretan smith   60
would make for sport from a scant lump of ore,
nor Brontes, whose brute strength shapes lightning bolts,
nor he who crafts the gods' own polished arms.
No scowling likeness, out of place at feasts
where guests relax, but just the mellow look   65
Molorchus' humble cottage marveled at
after the hero drank a cup or two,
and just the way Athena's priestess knew him
when she conceived a child; just the way, too,
when he'd shot up to heaven in sparks from Oeta,   70
though Juno scowled, he gladly drank his nectar.
A gentle look, as if his heart rejoiced,
cheers up the table's mood. This hand holds up
an enervating cup of brother Bacchus,
that one doesn't forget the club; his seat   75
is rough, a rock the Nemean hide adorns.

    A fitting fate this relic had. The king
of Macedon once kept its awesome power
on his glad table, carried it along,
his comrade all day through, was pleased to grip it   80
with the hand which had just taken a crown
or granted one, had toppled mighty cities.
From this he always sought the heart to fight
the morrow's battles, this he always told
triumphant tales of glorious battle lines,   85
if he had robbed Bacchus of Indian captives,
or forced an entrance into Babylon

with his spear's might, or crushed with war the lands
and liberty of Greece; from the great train
of deeds that won him praise, he only tried,   90
they say, because it was the hero's home,
to justify the fact he'd conquered Thebes.[19]
When Fate was breaking off that man's great deeds,
while he was drinking fatal wine, weighed down
by now with death's dark cloud, his feared two portents,   95
dining at what would be his final table—
his dear god's altered looks and sweating bronze.
 Soon a leader from Carthage came to own
this wondrous ornament; the stalwart god
was honored with libations poured by one   100
whose hand was always brutal, proud and false
his sword—Hannibal. Drenched in Roman blood,
with dreadful plans to burn the city's buildings,
he earned the god's hatred; despite the feasts,
despite the wine, it grieved the god to go   105
as that abominable camp's companion,
especially when a stronghold he had founded
was torched with wicked flames, Saguntum's homes
and shrines besmirched without good cause, and madness
loosed of mass suicide for honor's sake.[20]   110
 The Punic leader died—this noble bronze
no common house acquired. Banquets that Sulla
gave were adorned by it, a statue used
always to enter celebrated households,
and lucky in its owners' pedigrees.   115
 And now, if gods take care to know the way
of human hearts, although no royal court
surrounds you here, heroic one from Tiryns—
your owner's mind's upright and innocent
of wrong, the loyalty of olden days   120
is his that makes of friendship, once begun,
an everlasting bond. As still the late
Vestinus knows, in youth's first flower the match
of great forebears; our Vindex breathes him day
and night, and lives embraced by that dear shade.   125
So here you have a joyful peace and quiet,
Hercules, god most stalwart; you don't see

the violent conflicts of war, but the lyre,
fillets, and laurel passionate for song.
For you this man will hymn your deeds' remembrance,   130
how greatly you alarmed the royal houses
of Troy and Thrace, how greatly, Stymphalus
snow-clad, how greatly, rainy Erymanthus;
the things Spain's cattle baron bore from you,
the things that godless king of Egypt bore.   135
This man will harmonize the gates of hell
you stormed and plundered, girls you left in tears
for what you stole from western isle and Black Sea shore.
Never could you be honored by the king
of Macedon, or savage Hannibal,   140
nor Sulla's voice of terror, as the verse
of Vindex does. And surely you, Lysippus,
this work's creator, would prefer to win
approval from the eyes of no one else.

Horatian Ode to Vibius Maximus (*Silvae* 4.7)

Long have you helped me race an epic course,
my brave Erato, now postpone that toil
    as you confine your mighty work
    to wheeling 'round a smaller ring,

and you, the lyric circle's sovereign lord,   5
grant me brief use of this new instrument,
    if I have sanctified your Thebes,
    Pindar, in Latin verse of mine.

For Maximus I try a slighter song;[21]
now must I take a virgin myrtle wreath,   10
    now has the †greater† stream run dry,*
    and I must drink a purer one.

When will they send you back here to sweet Latium,
those Balkan mountains where a miner sees
    the Realm Below and then comes back   15
    pale as the gold he has dug up?

Look here, I was born in a closer place,
yet I'm not kept from Rome by charming ports
    at idle Baiae, or the Cape
    where Hector's wartime bugler lies.   20

My Muse is paralyzed without you here,
slower than usual comes my lord Apollo,
    and look, my new Achilles poem
    is stuck just past the starting gate.

Indeed, with you as its loyal adviser,   25
my *Thebaid*, racked by so much revision,
    tries out with daring lyre the joys
    Mantuan Virgil's fame brought him.

But I forgive your slow return—you've given
your empty house a child to foster it.   30
    O happy day! There comes to us,
    look here, another Maximus.

Childlessness must be shunned with every effort,
a hostile legatee prays hard for that,
    seeking (oh no, it's a disgrace!)   35
    an early death for his best friend;

when childlessness is buried, no one weeps,
the heir seizes the house, greedily stands
    looming over the spoils of death,
    and even counts the pyre's expense.   40

Long may this noble infant's life endure,
and through a path that few obstacles block,
    let his nature grow like father's,
    grandfather's deeds let his outdo.

From you, your little one will hear recalled   45
the Syrian campaign, in which you served
    as wing commander there out East,
    a sign that Castor favored you;

from him, how he followed that scorching bolt,
our Emperor invincible, and gave   50
    to nomad Slavs[22] those bitter terms,
    having a single sky for life.

But your skills let the boy learn first, the ones
employed when you survey the world's long life,
    reproducing Sallust's crisp works   55
    and those of Padua's favorite son.

Congratulations to Julius Menecrates on the Birth of His Third Child (*Silvae* 4.8)

    Open the gods' doors wide, Naples, and fill
their wool-decked shrines with clouds of Arab incense
and victims' entrails throbbing still; for lo,
noble Menecrates' line now increases
with a third child. The city's noble mob   5
of leading families grows and comforts her
for losses caused by crazed Vesuvius.
Let not secluded Naples only throng
the festal altars; Pozzuoli, too,
fellow-harbor[23] and land its gentle founder   10
loved, and Sorrento dear to wine-soaked Bacchus—
shore where grandfather built a seaside villa[24]—
with garlands let them gird the altars too;
his horde of grandchildren crowds 'round and strives
to mirror features like grandfather's own.   15
Their uncle, too, who saw distinguished service
in North Africa, let rejoice, and Polla,
who deems these stepgrandchildren hers by blood
and lifts them to her kindly breast. Bless you,
young man, for giving your deserving city   20
such shining lights. Lo, how the sweet commotion
sounds through a house so many masters fill
with shouts. Let Envy, dark and grim, withdraw
far off, and turn her green eyes* somewhere else:
old age and honor due to lifelong virtue   25
these children have had guaranteed to them

by Fate's white thread and words of prophecy
their city's god Apollo has inspired.
    And so the fact His Greatest Majesty,
Father of Rome, had granted you the rights—   30
so joyous—due fathers of three, that was
a sign. So often has Lucina come
and entered in this righteous home, invoked
for one more birth. Fruitful like this, I pray
your house remains, this blessing never changed.   35
Bless you, because your offspring has increased
by sturdy males more often, but a girl
born to a father when he's young should make
him joyful too (fitter for daring, they;
but sooner from her will grandchildren come).   40
Your daughter is like fair-skinned Helen, worthy
of mother Leda's Spartan wrestling bouts
when still she crawled between the Twins, her brothers;
like a clear night sky's appearance is
when two bright stars have brought their luster close   45
beside the moon that beams between the pair.
    But I'm aggrieved, young man so rare, a grievance
that will not ease; I'm getting angry too,
as much as those who love are ever angry.
So great a joy—should I have found it out   50
through common gossip? Your third baby wailed;
nary a letter came at once with news
in mighty haste, to bid me mound the altars
with festal flames, to wreathe my lyre with greens,
the doorway deck, bring out a smoky jug   55
of Alban wine, and mark the day with song,
but slow and idle, now at last I sing
my best wishes? Yours is the blame, and yours
is this disgrace. Prolonging my complaint
of course won't do; for lo, your merry horde   60
surrounds and guards their father. Whom, with troops
like these, are you not sure to overcome?
    Gods of my city, whom Euboean settlers
brought to Italian shores across the sea
with mighty portents—you, Apollo, leader   65
of colonists from far away, whose guiding dove

is perched in stone on blest Eumelus' shoulder,
who turns his head and fondly worships it;[25]
Athenian Ceres, you whose breathless race
we converts always run with torches waved,   70
keeping our secret vow to you in silence;
and you, the Twins, sons of Leda, whose place
of birth in Sparta has not worshiped more,
nor has your most important Spartan shrine:
preserve this household's people for their country.   75
Let them be ones who use their eloquence
and wealth to help a city worn with age
and frequent hardships, and keep its name green.
For them, let father model tranquil ways,
grandfather, splendor shared, and both of them,   80
zealous pursuit of virtue's loveliness.
Indeed, both wealth and birth will let this girl
enter a noble house when first she weds;
these boys, right when they reach maturity—
provided the unvanquished Emperor's power   85
is with good men, disposed to intercede—
will find the Senate opens to their knock.

Teasing Tetrameters to Plotius Grypus (*Silvae* 4.9)

Surely it's a joke, dear Grypus,
that for my little book you sent
a little booklet in return.
This still can seem a witty thing,
if you send me something else next;   5
for if you keep joking, Grypus,
it's no joke. Look, let's count the cost.
Mine had a scarlet dust jacket,
brand-new paper, a fancy knob
at *both* ends of the winding rod;   10
all this cost me, leaving aside
my own labor, a ten-*as* piece.
You are giving one gnawed by worms
and mildewed, paper like what drips
African olive brine, or keeps   15

the Nile's incense or pepper fresh,
or bakes mackerel from Istanbul.
The words inside aren't even yours,
speeches thundered in all Rome's courts
as a young attorney, before[26]   20
the Emperor had you supervise
his commissariat, put you
in charge of where to stay the night
on all his junkets far and wide,
but the yawn-inducing remarks   25
of old Brutus, off of the shelf
of some poor bookseller, purchased
for more or less an *as* issued
by Caligula, now worthless—
that's yours. Was there a total lack   30
of freedman's caps pieced from used cloaks,
handkerchiefs, or yellowed napkins,
rolls of paper, or dates, or figs?
Nowhere to find a clump of prunes
and figs stored in a cone-shaped jar?   35
Nor dry lamp wicks, nor skins unpeeled
from onions? Not even some eggs,
not smoother grits nor coarse oatmeal?[27]
Nowhere those damp nomadic homes,
the curved shells of African snails?   40
No heavy bacon, or gamy ham?
No salami, no bologna,
no table salt, bitters, or cheese,
nor cakes of green washing soda,
or raisin wine, boiled from the skins,   45
nor dessert wine, cloudy and sweet?
How little would it cost to give
smelly candles, a pocket knife,
or thin tablets of note paper?
Weren't you allowed, I ask, to give   50
grapes preserved in jars sealed with pitch,
platters thrown by Cumae's potters,
or else one set of dinnerware
(I did not say, of dinner "wear,"
so why shudder?), white cups and plates?   55

But like an honest businessman
whose scales are right, you do not cheat
but give me just the same weight back.
What if I came very early,
breakfast half-digested, and belched*   60
morning greetings from me to you,
would you greet me in turn at home?
When you've treated me to a feast,
would you expect the same right then?
I'm angry, Grypus, but take care;   65
just don't be witty now, the way
you usually are, and send me back
tetrameters like these as well.

Book 5

Preface

Greetings from Statius to his friend Abascantus!
With complete enthusiasm should good examples be honored, since they are
in the public interest. The devotion which you render your Priscilla is an es-
sential part of your character and can endear you to anyone, especially a husband. For loving a wife while she is alive is a delight; when she has died, an
obligation. And yet I have jumped at this task not as one of the crowd, nor
only as if duty-bound. For Priscilla loved my wife, and by loving her, made her
more commendable to me; consequently, I am an ingrate if I pass over your
tears. Besides, I strive always to oblige every side of the imperial household to
the best of my modest abilities. For he who worships the gods in good faith
also loves their priests. But, although I have wanted a closer experience of your
friendship for a long time now, I would nevertheless prefer not to have found
an opportunity yet.

Lament for Priscilla, Wife of Abascantus (*Silvae* 5.1)

If my hands were clever at painting portraits,
or giving gold or ivory form to make

them come alive, this is the way, Priscilla,
I would devise a welcome consolation
for your husband. His outstanding devotion   5
deserves you back to ease his pain, your face
depicted in the pigments of Apelles
or sculpted into life by Phidias' hand:
That is the way he tries to rob the pyre
of your shade, carries on a mighty contest   10
with Death, exhausts the artists' careful pains,
and seeks to love you in all forms of art.
Mortal is tribute wrought by dextrous hands.
For you, a much-praised youth's most special wife,
I am attempting proper formal tribute,   15
long-lived, not destined to become obscure,
immortalized in song upon my lyre,
provided that Apollo favors me,
and he who always come to me united
with Apollo, the Emperor, approves: 20
no other monument will keep you better.
    It's late indeed to treat so great a pain,
when now the flying wheels of Phoebus spin
another year around, but when the blow
was fresh and still the newly wounded house   25
was wearing black <and everywhere laments
resounded, what path then for consolation>*
or access to his poor, sad ear? Then weeping,
rending garments, exhausting flocks of slaves,
outdoing their laments, raging at Fate   30
and unjust denizens of heaven in protest—
that was comfort. Were Orpheus there himself
to ease those groans, accompanied by woods
and streams, were all his aunts, the Muses, flanking
the singer, all Apollo's acolytes   35
and Bacchus', no songs of his at all,
no lyre heard by gods of pale Avernus
and Furies' snakes would have the power to soothe:
so great a grief reigned in his dumbstruck breast.
The scar is faded now, but flinches still   40
while I recite; from heavy eyes rain tears
for his wife. Still they have devoted tears?

Wondrous fidelity! More quickly did
Niobe drain her eyes for all those children,
more quickly will her mournful dew fail Dawn,   45
Tithonus' wife, or will Achilles' mother
tire of crashing her storms against his tomb.
Bless your feelings! They're noted by the god
who handles the world's reins, and nearer us
than Jove, arranges men's affairs; he sees   50
your mourning, and he gets a lesson here
about his worthy secretary's private life,
because you love a shade and venerate
her last remains. Here is passion most pure,
here is a love his Lord and Master ought   55
as Censor give his well-deserved approval.
    No wonder if long harmony has linked
you both with chains unbreakable, whose hearts
have merged together as a single blend.
She was married before, it's true, had wed   60
another husband, but she cherished you
as if you'd been teamed with a virgin bride,
embracing you with all her heart and soul,
just as the elm tree loves its lifelong partner
the vine, and with that shoot blends in its leaves,   65
and prays that autumn's harvest is a rich one,
and gladly wreathes itself in precious clusters.
Those women are extolled by praising forebears
and lovely beauty's gift, who lack the virtues
of character; possessed of praise that's sham,   70
they want for what is real: your birth was splendid,
blessèd was your appearance, much-desired
by husbands, yet greater distinction comes
from you yourself, knowing one bed alone,
arousing deep in your bones one single flame.   75
That love no Trojan rapist would have spoiled,
nor those Ithacan suitors, nor the brother
whose gold corrupted Atreus' pure wife.
If you bestowed the wealth of Babylon,
tons of Lydian treasure, the Indies' wealth   80
and power, Cathay's and Araby's, she'd choose
to die unsullied, poor but with her virtue

and pay the price of honor with her life.
And yet, hers was no constant grim expression,
nor a manner excessively severe, 85
but guileless, cheerful loyalty, a blend
of charm and virtue. Yet, if anxious fear
had summoned her to greater things, with joy
would she have taken on for her spouse's sake
armed bands, or fiery lightning, or the perils 90
out on the sea. Better it is that hardships
were not what proved the care you gave your marriage,
how pale you turned on your spouse's behalf.
But by the better route of prayer you won
divine support for your husband, while day 95
and night you importuned the gods and groveled
prostrate at every altar, while you begged
our ever-present Master's gentle spirit.
    You were heeded and Fortune stepped in kindly.
Yes, the devoted youth's diligent calm 100
was noticed, and his loyalty unscathed,
his breast girded for taking pains,
alert perceptions and a sober heart
fit for unraveling the many turns
of chance, these were noticed by him 105
who knows all the affairs of every subject
and so surrounds himself on every side
with secretaries he himself has screened.
No wonder: that man takes note of both East
and West, of what the South and wintry North 110
are doing, tests his plans for war and peace
and checks their rationale. That man has set
upon young Abascantus' †mane-brushed†[1] shoulders
a vast and massive bulk, a burden barely
manageable (no bureau in the Palace 115
has more to do)—dispatching far and wide
around the globe the Emperor's commands,
managing correspondence on the ways
and means of Empire; what reports of victory
come from the North, what news from rogue Euphrates, 120
what, from Ister's banks (its name upstream
is Danube), what from banners on the Rhine,

how much the last frontier has given up—
Britain, with tides resounding all around
(for all the spears which bear up joyful laurel   125
<show victorious eagles through lucky battles>,*
and not a lance is marked by shameful feathers).
Besides, when his Master awards commissions
to loyal officers, his tasks include
disclosing who is competent to lead   130
as chief centurion (a knight assigned
to infantry), who to command a cohort,
whom the more senior rank of tribune suits,
who is more fit to lead cavalry squads;
if I should count all his reports, no more   135
would wingèd Mercury with herald's staff
bring from the lofty stars, nor Juno's handmaid,
who plummets through the limpid air, an arc
of colors binding rainy sky, nor Rumor,
whose speeding course outstrips the day and brings   140
reports of your triumphs, Germany's Victor,
leaving the slow Arcadian god up near
the stars, and Thaumas' daughter, still midair.
  How you appeared to gods and men, Priscilla,
that kindly day your spouse received promotion   145
to great affairs! You just about outdid
his own great joy, pouring out your heart
and lying down to grovel eagerly
before the hallowed feet of him, your Master,
who well deserved such thanks. On Delphi's peak   150
the Pythia does not rejoice so much,
she whom the god from Delos put in charge of
his yawning mystic cave, nor she whom Bacchus
assigned the awesome right to troop the thyrsus
out in front, banner of his dumbstruck band.   155
Yet not therefore was her calm modesty
changed nor puffed up by this success: her spirit
kept on its course with unassuming manner
although good fortune grew. Concerned support
she showed her spouse's duties, she urged on   160
his labors and diverted them as well.
Moderate meals and sober drink she hands

to him herself, modeling this on their Master,[2]
as an Apulian frugal farmer's wife
or one weathered by Sabine sun, who sees   165
from stars already peeking out it's time
her husband finished work and got there soon,
hurries to get tables and couches set
and waits to hear the sound of plough's return.
I speak of minor things: with you she would   170
have gone as your comrade though icy North,
Slavic winters, the lower Danube's course,
and the Rhine's blanching cold, with you she would
have bravely steeled herself through all the turmoil,
and, if camp rules allowed, would gladly bear   175
a quiver, gladly use an Amazon shield
to guard her flank, provided she would see you
close to the lightning speed of the Emperor's horse
amid the dusty clouds of war, both hurling
weapons like those the god himself is wielding   180
and splashed with sweat that drips from *his* mighty spear.
    Enough of song about her life. Time now
to lay aside your laurel wreath, Apollo,
and doom my hair to mournful cypress leaves.
    Whatever god has bound Good Luck and Envy   185
with ties of hostile kinship? Who has bade
these ill-assorted goddesses to wage
a constant war? Has the one ever noticed
a house the other does not right away
nail with her evil eye and rout its joy?   190
Priscilla's household blossomed still unshaken
and cheerful, nothing mournful there; what fear
indeed could Fortune cause, faithless and fickle
though she may be, given the Emperor's favor?
Envious Fate found out a way, and illness   195
cruelly attacked the loyal hearth. Like that,
the spiteful South Wind blasts a vineyard full
of grapes, like that a field of grain, grown tall,
sickens and dies from too much rain, a breeze
blows envious storm clouds up like that   200
against a ship speeding before the wind.
Priscilla's extraordinary beauty

is plucked by Fate, just as a lofty pine,
the forest's pride, succumbs to lightning blasts
or roots already loose, and stripped of boughs   205
no longer whispers back to any breeze.
What good is modesty and pure devotion,
what good are gods revered? The somber nets
of death hemmed the poor woman all around,
the Fates' unyielding skein is stretched, the end   210
of her completed thread remains to snip.
No crowds of slaves, no healers' zealous art
helped her illness, yet all around her friends
are feigning hope; she notes her husband weeping.
That man now begs the inviolate stream   215
of Lethe down below in vain, now sheds
his anxious tears at every altar, marks
their doors and scours their thresholds with his breast,
now calls upon a power that *can* be moved
by prayer, the Emperor's. Alas the course   220
of Fate unyielding! Is there anything
forbidden *him*? What long delays could have
accrued to mortal lives, Father, if you
had power over all! Shut in the pit
of darkness, Death would groan, and idled Fates   225
would put their spinning down a longer while.
        But now her features sag, at last her eyes
lose focus, hearing is no longer sharp,
save only for her husband's well-known voice.
It's him alone her mind turns from the midst   230
of death to see, him whom she turns fixed eyes
to face and bravely folds in feeble arms;
she does not choose her last daylight to feast
her eyes upon, but her sweet husband's face.
Then, dying, she consoles her loving soul mate: 235
"That half of me which will live on, to whom
o how I wish I could bequeath the years
of which unyielding Fate robs me, please spare
your tears, don't beat your breast with savage blows,
do not torture your spouse's fleeing shade.   240
I leave our marriage, yes, and yet for me
to do this first preserves the proper order,

since I'm older; the time I've spent is dearer
than long old age. I have already seen
you bloom and shine, and seen you getting closer   245
and closer still to *his* exalted hand.
No longer do the Fates, do any gods
have power over you. My death takes that
away with me. So now, gladly proceed
along the path you have begun, and show   250
his holy person and *his* powerful spirit
your tireless love. As you yourself desire,
now give, I bid, a hundred pounds of gold
to the Capitoline temple to make
our holy Emperor's face forever shine[3]   255
and mark the love with which I worshiped him.
This way I will not have to see the Furies
nor Tartarus, the nastier place, but be
a blessèd one upon Elysian shores."
Slipping away, she spoke, embraced the body   260
allied to hers, without bitterness passed
her lingering breath into her husband's mouth,
and closed her eyes with his belovèd hand.
     But mighty grief inflamed the young man's heart,
and now he fills his emptied household full   265
of savage cries, now longs to draw his sword,
now he proceeds to high places (his friends
can barely hold him back), now with lips locked
on hers, he falls upon the one he's lost,
savagely stirs up pain sunk deep in his heart,   270
just as the Thracian bard, numb at the sight
of his dead wife, beside the river Strymon
set down his lyre and in a daze bewailed
her bitter funeral pyre without a song.
     That man of yours would even have cut short   275
his life—now scorned—so you would not approach
the void of Tartarus with no companion,
but he was kept from this by a mind loyal
to his Leader and one that would be heartened
by *his* divine assignments and by love   280
greater than for his wife. Who could compose
a song worthy of her funeral procession,

the gifts which that unfortunate cortège
offered her corpse? Crammed in that swarming length
what one whole spring gave Arabs and Cilicians   285
flowed by, flowering Sabaean frankincense,
the Indian crop for burning, incense robbed
from Palestine's temples, also the balm
of Gilead, threads of Corycian saffron,
and beads of myrrh, while she herself reclines   290
on high bolsters covered in Chinese silk
beneath the shade a purple canopy
provides. But all along that train they watch
her spouse alone, on him the eyes of Rome
are turned, as if he brought the pyre young sons: 295
that pain is on his face, his hair and eyes
have so much darkness. Her they call set free
by peaceful death and blessèd, him they wept for.
    There is a spot before you reach the City,
the mighty Appian highway's place of birth,   300
the place Cybele sets aside her groans
for Attis dead, is bathed in Italy's Almo,[4]
and thinks no more of native Phrygian streams.
Here your outstanding husband buried you,
Priscilla, gently swathed in purple cloth   305
(he could not bear a smoky, roaring pyre),
inside a rich rotunda. Longer life
has no more power to pluck away at you,
time's handiwork has no more power to harm:
such care your body got, such rich perfumes   310
your coffin, so revered, breathes out.[5] Transformed
into all kinds of statues, you took on
new form: in this bronze, Ceres, here in this,
the shining Cretan, Maia gleaming* there,
and in this marble, Venus, but with shame.   315
Those powers are not offended at taking on
your lovely features; crowds of slaves stand by,
whose habit is to serve; for ritual meals,
couches and tables constantly are kept
set up. That is her home, her home! Who would   320
call it a gloomy tomb? Rightly would one,
on seeing this devotion from her husband,

at once exclaim: "Here is, I realize,
the secretary of that One who just
set up a shrine for his immortal clan,   325
another heaven for those stars of his."
As, when a mighty ship sets sail anew
from Egypt's coast and now has fully rigged
the countless ropes on every side and raised
the sail-bedizened mast's broad arms, and plunged   330
into the sea-lanes, there on the same ocean
a humble launch claims its share of South Wind.
  Why does your heart now cherish boundless weeping,
most worthy youth, and stop long pain from leaving?
Are you afraid Priscilla quakes to hear   335
Cerberus' bark? For such devoted ones
he stays silent. Afraid the ferryman
may be too slow, or drive her off confused
from shore? He transports worthy souls at once
and kindly boards them on his gracious skiff.   340
Besides, whenever a shade comes whose praise
her loyal husband sings, then Hades' queen
commands that joyful torches be brought out
and ancient heroines leave hallowed grottoes,
disperse the gloom with rosy light, and strew   345
wreaths of Elysian flowers before that soul.
This is the way Priscilla meets the dead,
and there on your behalf petitions Fate
and intercedes with grim Avernus' rulers
that you may live a long full life, and leave   350
the Master who brings peace to all the world
while he's still young and you are old. Resolved,
the spinning Sisters swear to her request.

In Praise of Crispinus,
Son of Vettius Bolanus (*Silvae* 5.2)

  The wooded Tuscan countryside, the home
of Tages, first to read the will of gods
from signs, is my Crispinus' destination;
the trip is brief, the land is not remote,

and yet an inner gnawing rends my heart,   5
my sodden eyes blink out their welling tears,
as if I tracked a friend's departing sails
across Aegean storms, grew weary watching
his ship from cliffs high up, and now complained
because the far expanse outreached my sight.   10
       What if the glorious first experience
of military service[6] called you now,
the sweet inauguration, noble child,
of life in camp? With what great weeping would
my joy be pouring out, and what embraces   15
would I bestow! Still, must your kindred wish
for what will make them sad, when now your life
has only gone around the yearly cycle
twice eight times? But your mind is more mature
than your scant years, your age almost collapses   20
beneath the weight of what's too much for it.
It's no surprise: an undistinguished line
did not bear you from ordinary stock,
with humble forebears, lacking ancient luster.
Sprung not from knightly blood, fresh to the garb   25
and meager purple stripe which marks that class,
have you come knocking at the inner sanctum
of Rome's majestic Senate as a stranger,
but with a train of relatives who came
ahead of you. As over the broad expanses   30
of Rome's racetrack the crowd awaits a horse,
a handsome thoroughbred from a bloodline
whose glorious victories fill the record books;
the cheers all stir him up, the dusty oval
is glad to recognize him flying by: 35
in just this way the Senate chamber saw
that you, glorious child, were born for it,
and shod your first steps in the kind of slippers
senators wear, fastened with half-moon buckles.
And soon your shoulders recognized the folds   40
of purple-bordered toga and the tunic
worn by the powerful. For you, of course,
your father had prepared a glorious record
to emulate. Indeed, he entered manhood

and right away with warrior zeal attacked   45
Araxes' quivered denizens, a land—
Armenia—hard to teach subjection to
cruel Nero. Relentless war's command
was Corbulo's responsibility,
but that general too was much amazed   50
by such distinguished service from Bolanus,
comrade in arms, partner in toil; to him
would he entrust his keenest worries, share
his fears—which conditions favored ambush
and which were good for pitched battle, which promise   55
made by the fierce Armenians was suspicious
and which retreat was real. Bolanus scouted
the fearsome routes, Bolanus looked for ridges
suited for safe campsites, Bolanus mapped
the country far and wide, opened up torrents   60
and woods which caused harmful delays, fulfilled
the mighty will of his respected leader,
and he alone could carry out commands
so huge. The savage land itself had learned
that hero's face—his was the helmet crest   65
second in battle, closest to the general.
Just so the dumbstruck Trojans, though they saw
the lion skin, although the Nemean bow
pushed back their lines, when Hercules
was fighting them, yet feared Telamon too.   70
Learn, child (of course, you do not have to seek
the handsome love of valor from advisors
outside your own family: let kindred glory
provide you courage. Let the others learn
from legends—Decius, he who charged the foe   75
and died to rally his troops, or Camillus,
whom exile did not keep from saving Rome
against the Gauls), you, learn about your father,
how great his mission to the British shores
which block the waves split by the setting sun,[7]   80
how strong his rule of mighty Asia's cities
during the year assigned, the way he made
his power more tolerable by acting fairly
in judge's robes. Drink in such deeds with ears

cocked forward, let your kin outdo each other 85
commending them to you, and let old men,
your father's comrades, reinforce these lessons.
    So, now you get this journey under way,
and do not drag your feet as you prepare
to go. Not yet have signs of sturdy manhood 90
stolen over your cheeks, your life so far
Is Innocent, nor Is your sIre nearby,
because he died worn out by unfair fate,
and left his twin offspring with no protector;
he did not even get the chance to strip 95
your tender shoulders of their boyhood's purple
and put a man's white toga in its place.
Whom does unbridled adolescence not
corrupt, when that new toga's freedom comes
too soon? Just so, a tree which has not known 100
the pruning hook bears only leaves, and wastes
potential fruit by just producing shade.
But in your heart is love for poetry,
restraint, a character that's schooled in setting
limits, a cheerful sense of decency, 105
a tranquil brow, an elegance which fears
getting too close to excess, and devotion
distributed in every sort of way;
your family's fortunes prompted you to treat
a brother your own age as if he were 110
the elder, to admire your father, pardon
your poor mother. Could she have really been
strong enough to concoct for you herself
that wicked poisoned cup, for you whose voice
could turn aside the serpent's tooth, whose face 115
could win any stepmother's heart and mind?
One would like to harass her ghost, and rob
her pyre of peace with a curse well-deserved,
but you, most worthy child, I see are turning
from what is justified and getting ready 120
to say such words as these: "Please spare her ashes,
that was her destined lot, the baleful wrath
of Fate's to blame, some god's misdeed, who sees
men's hearts too late and does not put a stop

161

right at the start to wicked undertakings 125
and minds planning to do atrocious things.
Let that day be forgotten, not believed
by future ages. Let me, anyhow,
keep silent and allow the evil deeds
of kindred to be buried deep in darkness. 130
She has been made to pay by him who has
concern for all his people, him whose reign
at last permits Devotion to return
and visit earth again, him who is feared
by every wickedness. This vengeance is 135
enough and ought to make us weep. But no,
I wish I were allowed to intercede
and stop the brutal Furies, turn away
Cerberus from your frightened shade, and give
your ghost a quicker drink from Lethe's stream." 140
    Bless you, young man! And yet your mother's evil
seems magnified by what you have just said.
Not just devotion, but the height of valor
has been aroused in you. Lately a friend
of yours blanched at a false adultery charge 145
which made him suffer undeserved disgrace;
the Julian Law was stirring up the court
and rose amid the hundred jurors there,
shaking the thunderbolt of purity;
never before had you experienced 150
the courts and their stern laws, hidden away
while studies sheltered you in peace and quiet,
yet it was you who underwent defending
your anxious friend from fear, and warding off
his foe's assaults while still a fresh recruit. 155
Neither our Founder's statue nor the one
of old Aeneas ever witnessed years
so tender wage bloody civilian warfare
in court. The senators were stunned by what
you tried to do in such a great attempt, 160
and even those not then on trial feared you.[8]
Your body has the same energy too,
your mind has strength enough to carry out
valiant actions and follow huge commands.

I saw you lately where the Tiber seethes   165
beside Rome's training grounds, while you were riding
a fiery horse whose flanks your spurs harassed,
with menace in your look and strong right hand.
If you believe the words I'm telling you,
I was stunned and I thought that you were Mars.   170
Handsome like that astride an Arab horse
and wielding Trojan spears, Ascanius would
go to hunt on "stepmother" Dido's land,
and used to make that wretch †burn for his father†;*
and just the same did Troilus wheel more nimbly   175
and dodge the threatening horses, or at Thebes,
Parthenopaeus, whom the women watched
from lofty towers without a look of fury
in any of their eyes, as he maneuvered
Arcadian squadrons in their city's dust.   180
    So come (our great Leader's support gives you
a boost, your cheerful brother gives your hopes
a sure path to follow), arise with spirit,
take on the valiant cares of life in camp.
    You will be taught about the lines of battle   185
by Mars and Athens' Virgin; wheeling horses,
by Castor; wielding spears, by Romulus,
who let you, as his priest, already clash
the heaven-sent Salian shield which leans against
your tender neck with spears untouched by blood.   190
So then, where in the world, into which part
of all the Emperor's lands will you be going?
Will you swim the choppy stream of the Rhine
up north, or sweat in Libya's sultry fields?
Or make Hungarian peaks, or Slavic nomads,   195
tremble? Or will the Danube, seven-mouthed
and flowing 'round his island spouse, have you?
Will you approach Jerusalem in ashes
and captured groves Judaea planted, palms
producing wealth but not for her own use?   200
What if the lands your great father reined in
should welcome you, how much will wild Araxes
be overjoyed, how much will pride exalt
the plains of Scotland when a denizen,

long-lived, of that fierce land, relates to you: 205
"Here was your father wont to render verdicts,
from this mound, to address his squads; the forts
and lookout posts you see far off from here,*
he built, this wall he girdled with a trench;
these arms, these offerings he dedicated   210
to warrior gods (you still can see the plaques);
he donned this breastplate at the call to arms,
that one he carried off from Britain's king."
In just this way, as Pyrrhus got prepared
to triumph over Troy, Phoenix would tell   215
about Achilles whom he never knew.

     Happy are you, Optatus, who'll rely
upon the sap of youth and will endure
whatever path or palisade you come to,
perhaps yourself commissioned with a sword,   220
to be your friend and soul mate's tireless comrade,
loyal as Pylades, Orestes' friend,
or as Patroclus fighting at Troy. You have
that kind of harmony, that kind of love;
may it endure, I pray. The valiant prime   225
of life escapes me now; henceforth with hopes
and prayers alone will I be any help.
Ah me, if I invite the usual group
and Rome's aristocrats come hear my poems,
you will fail to be there for me, Crispinus,   230
and all throughout the seats my new *Achilles*
will look around for you, the absent one.
But you'll return a better man (predictions
by bards are not in vain), the one who soon
will open up your way to eagle standards   235
and life in camp will let you make it through
the rest of your career until you're ringed
by consul's marshals and you have a chair
that, like your father's once, is made of ivory.

     But, from the lofty hills of Trojan Alba   240
whence the deity closest to us views
the walls of Rome nearby, what message swift as
rumor comes in and fills your house, Crispinus?
Correctly did I say, "The bards' predictions

are not in vain." Behold, the Emperor   245
opens for you the mighty door to office,
commissions you to serve with Roman steel.
Go, child, strive to become good enough for
favors this great, you who happily take
the oath so soon to serve our great protector,   250
and you to whom Germany's Victor divine
entrusts a tribune's saber, your first one.
No less is this than were the very god
of war himself making the valiant eagles
open to you, putting the fearsome helmet   255
upon your head. Go eagerly, and learn
to be deserving of still greater things.

Lament for My Father (*Silvae* 5.3)

    The bitter strength to sing a mournful song
welling up from Elysian springs, and strum
my luckless lyre, bestow on me yourself,
my highly cultured sire. To rouse and prompt
Apollo's Delphic cave the usual way   5
is not right without you. Whatever Phoebus
revealed to me in that cool darkness once,
I have unlearned. Parnassus' fillets fleeing
my hair, and yew, that tree of death, invading
the Bacchic ivy, I've endured, and laurel   10
trembling (uncanny sight!) and drying up.
Certainly I am he who used to go
with inspiration from on high, to praise
great-hearted kings and match their wars with song.
Who rots my barren heart * * * * * * * * * * * * * *   15
* * * * * * * * * * * * Who has condemned my mind
to chilly clouds which keep Apollo blocked?
Around their bard the dumbstruck Muses stand,
not making one sweet sound with instrument
or voice. Their chief herself has propped her head   20
against her silent lyre, just as she stood
beside the Hebrus when son Orpheus died;
and saw the troops of beasts, now deaf, and groves

motionless since music had been destroyed.
    But if, freed from the flesh, you soar and scan   25
bright expanses and basic cosmic questions—
what is the divine, whence comes fire, what track
conducts the Sun, what cause can make the Moon
grow smaller, what restores her when she hides—
and you expand Aratus' famous verse,   30
or if, in some secluded grassy plain
below, with hero bands and blessèd spirits
you live as Homer's neighbor and Hesiod's,
and no more inactive a shade than they,
you make music in turn, blending your songs: 35
bestow great grief with inspiration, father.
The Moon, retraversing the sky three times,
and three times revealing her face, sees me
just sit and not, with any Muse, console
sad cares; for since your burning pyre's red light   40
shone in my face and I drank in the sight
of your ashes with moist eyes, my old pursuits
have little value. Scarcely for this tribute
do I unblock my mind for the first time
and start to drive the rot from silent strings   45
with hand unsteady still, and eyes not dry,
leaning against the mound in which you lie
gently at rest and occupy my land,
where once after Aeneas died, his son,
star-bright, piled Alba on the Latin hills,   50
though he despised plains rich with Trojan blood,
the kingdom his hapless stepmother dowered.
Here I lament for you with funeral gifts
and eulogy—alas—that's Muse-inspired
(no sweeter scent comes from Sicilian saffron,   55
nor rich Sabaeans' special cinnamon
picked just †for you†, nor would the Arabs' crop,
their fragrant frankincense); accept—<behold>—
the groaning of your son, his hurt and tears,
which only special parents ever got.   60
Would that my fortune also let me give
an altar like a temple to your spirit,
and rear a massive structure in the air

beyond the boulder walls of Cyclopes,
or daring stone of Pyramids, and screen   65
the monument with a great grove of trees.
And there would I surpass Anchises' tomb
in Sicily, Opheltes' Nemean grove,
Olympic rites for mutilated Pelops.
But there no Greeks' nude strength would split the air   70
with Spartan discus, nor would horses' sweat
soak in the ground, nor would their hooves resound
on rutted dust; there'd be a single choir,
and I would praise you, sire, and duly tie
upon your brow the leafy prize for bards.   75
Moist-eyed, would I, priest of your shade and soul,
lead the groaning, from which †you'd be distracted†[9]
neither by Cerberus with all three mouths,
nor by the rule that Orpheus once broke.
And as I sang about your ways and deeds,   80
your devotion perhaps would not have ranked
my style second to Homer's epic grandeur,
would even aim to match me with stern Virgil.
    Why should the gods and the Fates' threads of steel
be more abused by her who sits bereft   85
upon a son's warm mound, or her who sees
a young husband's fire and then overcomes
the hands that block, the crowd that holds her back,
from death, were it allowed, upon that blaze.
More resentment from them, perhaps, would smite   90
the gods and Underworld; even for those
outside the family would the bier go by
a pitiful sight; yet, not only were
Nature and Duty there to serve my grief
in what was due:[10] right on the threshold, father,   95
of your fated span, as if taken off
from life still full of sap, do you come near
harsh Tartarus. That girl from Marathon
did not weep for father Icarius
with less abandon than, when Astyanax   100
fell from that Trojan tower, his mother did;
why no, the former choked her final groans
by hanging, but after great Hector's death,

your shame was being a Greek husband's slave.
    Not with the funeral tribute which a swan, 105
sure of its fate, makes with its dying song,
nor what the Siren flock so sweetly threatens
sailors from their dark cliff, will I supply
my father's pyre, nor what with mutilated
mumble Philomela complained and groaned 110
to her soon ruthless sister: these are known
too well by bards. Who has not mentioned branches
and amber tears Phaethon's sisters grew
after his death, Niobe's fate as flint,
and Marsyas, he who dared songs against Phoebus 115
and made Minerva glad the flute betrayed him?[11]
Let Righteousness, mindful of men no more,
and Lady Justice summoned back to heaven,
lament, and Eloquence in Greek and Latin,
Minerva, too, and cultured Phoebus' troop 120
from Helicon, and those who toil †deploying†
Thebes' battlefield in epic lines,[12] and those
who deal out song with lyres of tortoiseshell
whence comes their name and what they take pains on,
and those throughout the world whom lofty Wisdom 125
puts on the famous list of Seven Sages,
or who, in awesome tragic buskins, thundered
Furies, palaces, stars routed from heaven,
and those who thought it pleasant to reduce
their strength to suit the playful comic Muse, 130
or maim their epic flow by just a foot.[13]
Your mind embraced all subjects, you employed*
all forms in which the latent power of speech
is clear, whether it pleased you to enchain
what you began within poetic measures, 135
or shower it in prose and match cloudbursts
(as Homer said)[14] with utterance unbridled.
    Stretch out the face which sudden dust and ash
half-covered, Naples, and put a lock of hair
volcanic blasts had buried on the mound 140
and last remains of your great protégé;
Athens did not give birth to anything
that was more outstanding than him, nor did

cultured Cyrene, or Sparta the brave.
If you lay in ruins, devoid of offspring,   145
your fame obscured, with nothing native left,
by that citizen only could you prove
your Greek descent from old Euboean blood:
that man so often set upon his brow
your prize, a crown of wheat, when he would sing,   150
at your regular four-year festival,
praise-winning verse, with which he went beyond
Nestor's sweetness, Ulysses' powerful force,[15]
and wore prize garlands for both prose and verse.
Yours was no shameful birth from blood obscure   155
and lacking luster, though your parents' fortune
tightened their budget. Yes, in wealthy style
Childhood chose you to wear the purple toga
and golden amulet allowed your rank.
Helicon's sisters smiled on you at birth   160
and Phoebus, fond of you already then
while still a boy, baptized your lyre and gave
your lips their first taste of the sacred stream.
No single homeland claims to share your glory,
your birthplace is uncertain, indecisive   165
the claims with which a pair of lands compete.
That you are hers by birth, Hyele says,
a Greek town adopted by Latin settlers,
where Palinurus fell, that Trojan helmsman,
and woke, poor man, adrift amid the waves.   170
And yet, a greater city proves you're hers
for living there a whole long row of years,
<Naples * * * * * * * * * * * * * * * * *>
so different cities scramble to claim Homer
and offer proof they are his place of birth;   175
not all their claims are true, and yet a fame
immense, though spurious, sustains the losers.
And there, while you advanced your years and hailed
your life, you rushed right off to competition
in hometown festivals, which full-grown men   180
scarcely get through, but you were in a hurry
for fame, and bold in talent. Youthful songs
of yours astonished Naples' folk, and parents

pointed you out to sons to be their model.
Henceforth a constant battler was your voice,   185
not lacking fame at any festal contest.
Not so often did lush Sparta promote
her native sons, the Twins, for victories,
one at the races, one with boxing gloves.
But if winning at home is effortless,   190
what about earning prizes there in Greece,
your brow wreathed now with Phoebus' Delphic bay,
and now with Lerna's wild Nemean celery,
now at the Isthmus with Palaemon's pine,
when often wearied, Victory never strayed   195
and stole the leaves or touched another's locks?
      To you were then entrusted fathers' prayers,
and wellborn youths were steered by your instruction,
and learned the ways and deeds of earlier men,
what was the fall of Troy, how slow Ulysses,   200
how great was Homer running through in verse
battles of horse and men, how much enriched
were righteous rustics with the lore in verse
by old Ascraean and Sicilian poets,
the rule by which the convoluted voice   205
of Pindar's lyre repeats, and Ibycus
who once called down a plague of cranes, and Alcman
whom stern Sparta recites, Stesichorus
the fierce, and she who took masculine leaps,
Sappho, recklessly unafraid of Chalcis,[16]   210
and other worthy lyrists. You made known
cultured Callimachus' song, and the riddles
of Lycophron, Sophron's involved exchanges
in dialogue, dainty Corinna's private thoughts.
Why speak of minor things? You used to bear   215
a yoke like Homer's, matching his six feet
in prose but never left with shorter lines.
What wonder then, if people left their homes
and sought you out, those whom Lucania sent,
and stern Daunus' acres, Pompeii, the home   220
Venus bewails, and Herculaneum,
the land Hercules failed, or those Minerva
dispatched, Virgin who scouts the Tuscan Sea

down from Sorrento's cliffs, or nearer by,
the Cape marked by Misenus' oar and bugle,   225
and Cumae, long ago a stranger here
to her Italian hearth, and those dispatched
by Pozzuoli's port and Baiae's shores,
where fiery lava, spreading deep below,
pants and puffs steam at sea, while homes are safe   230
because the conflagration's underground.
That is how people came from everywhere
to Sibyl's gloomy cave near Lake Avernus
to pose their questions; she would chant the threats
of gods and acts of Fate, and her predictions   235
came true although she broke Apollo's bargain.
Soon too, future leaders of Roman stock
are trained by you as well, and you persist
in leading them into their fathers' footsteps.
With you the great high priest of Vesta's flame,   240
who keeps concealed inside her inner shrine
the image Diomedes stole, grew up
and learned the rites in boyhood; you approved
the Salian priests and showed their shields to them,
and to unerring augurs, what the sky   245
foretells; to him who may unroll the Books
of Sibyl's Revelations, why the priest
of Cybele, and others, must wear skullcaps;
Luperci who, when girt in goatskin loincloths,
will strike young matrons, greatly feared your blows.   250
And now from that flock one perhaps gives laws
to Eastern nations, one keeps Spain in check,
another shuts the Persian out at Zeugma,
and these rein in the wealthy Asian peoples,
and these the Pontus; these in civil posts   255
improve the courts, while those garrison camps
with loyal troops: from you their merit springs.
At molding young men's hearts, Mentor could not
compete with you, nor Phoenix, he who steered
an untamed charge, nor Chiron who would break   260
that same Achilles, when he wished to hear
the bugles blare, with other kinds of music.
      While you were busy with such tasks, a Fury

suddenly waved the torch of civil war
down from the Traitor's Rock, and so stirred up   265
a battle like the Giants' famous one
with Jove. His temple there was shining bright
with wicked firebrands, and Roman squads
resorted to Gallic invaders' madness.
Scarcely was there a respite from the flames,   270
or had that funeral pyre for gods subsided,
when your devoted lips sang consolation
for temples razed, with zeal and much more speed
than those torches had flown, and you bewailed
Thunderer's lightning bolts held captive there.   275
The Roman leaders and the gods' avenger,
the Emperor, were amazed; amid the flames
the gods' own Father nodded his approval.
Already it was also your intent to mourn
with your devoted song, and lavish groans   280
on loss Vesuvius' conflagration caused
your native region when the Father plucked
a mountain, raised it up to heaven and hurled
it down on wretched cities far and wide.

When I too knocked at groves of song, to enter   285
Helicon's lovely vale, after I said
that I came from your stock, the Muses let
me in; for you gave me not just the stars,
and seas, and lands, the usual debt to parents,
but also gave my lyre what charm it has,   290
enabled me to say uncommon things,
and let me hope for fame beyond the tomb.
Such a state you were in each time I used
to charm the Roman upper class with song
and you were there, a happy audience   295
for your own handiwork! Oh, with such weeping
you mingled joy together with your prayers,
your loving fear, and modest happiness!
How much that day belonged to you, how much
the greater share of glory was not mine!¹⁷   300
When an Olympic wrestler's sire attends
a match, he likewise strikes out more himself
and feels the blows more deeply in his heart;

the Greeks are watching closely in the stands
and pay him more attention, while the puffs   305
of dust obstruct his sight, and he is vowing
to die once the victor's crown is in hand.
Too bad that only native leaves, the crown
of wheat for Naples' games, were what I wore
when you were there to see. In such a state   310
would Trojan Alba hardly have contained you
if you had lived to wear, through me, a garland
the Emperor's hand bestowed! What strength that day
could have supplied, how much old age removed!
Because a wreath of Capitoline oak   315
did not combine to rest with Alban olive
upon my head (that hoped-for prize escaped),
how you'd bewail the Capitoline Father's
grudging contests. With your masterful guidance
my *Thebaid* was on the heels of works   320
by ancient bards; you showed me how to spur
my singing on, display the deeds of heroes
and ways of war, and set a scene. My progress
falters along an unclear path without you,
my ship, bereaved, sails on shrouded in gloom.   325
Not only me did your devotion nurture
indulgently: that is the way you were
in marriage, too. You entered wedlock once
and loved but once. Surely I cannot part
Mother from your now icy tomb; she feels   330
and has your presence there, sees you, and pays
your monument a visit morn and night,
as other women nurse with feigned devotion
their grief for lost Osiris and Adonis,
lamenting deaths of no concern to them.   335
　　　Why cite your manner, frank but dignified?
What devotion, such scant regard for gain,
what concern for modesty, such great love
for what is right! Then too, when you were pleased
to take a rest, such charm in what you said,   340
and in your wits, not a trace of old age!
As just deserts, the gods' judicious care
granted you fame, generous praise, no hurt

to ever make you sad. You're taken, father,
neither wanting for years nor with too many,   345
with three more five-year contest cycles joined
to ten. Devoted grief does not let me
count the number, you who deserved to exceed
the finish line of Nestor's life, and match
old Priam's age, and who deserved to see me   350
when I'm your age. But your death's door was not
a sad one, and indeed the cause was light,
no lingering end's infirmities of age
forewarned your body that the tomb was looming;
unconsciousness and death like peaceful rest   355
have stretched you out and borne you down
to Tartarus in the semblance of sleep.
    What groans I then brought forth (my worried band
of comrades saw, my mother also saw,
happy to learn from this how I would mourn   360
for her), and what laments! Grant pardon, spirits,
Father, let it be right to speak this way:
you would not have done more for me.
Blest was Aeneas, who embraced his father
with arms no insubstantial shade could fill,   365
though what he wished to do was steal him off
from his assigned Elysian dwelling place
and carry him again through Greeks in darkness;
* *
when he had dragged his steps while still alive   370
to reach the Underworld, the agèd Sibyl
brought him down to the nether world's Diana.
So too a lesser motive made the lyre
of Orpheus go across stagnant Avernus,
and so Admetus got Alcestis back   375
* * * * * * * * * * * * * * * * * *
If for a day Protesilaus' ghost
returned to his wife, why then, Father, should
neither your lyre nor mine prevail at all
upon the dead? Let it be right to touch   380
my father's face this way, and right to join
our hands, whatever consequence ensues.
    But you, king of the shades, and queen abducted

from near Mount Etna, if my prayers have merit,
banish the Furies' snaky hair and torches,   385
let the shaggy doorman make not a sound
from any of his mouths, let distant vales
keep Centaurs out of sight with flocks of Hydras
and Scyllan monsters, let that final ferry
embark the old man's shade after the crowd   390
has been dispersed from shore, and settle him
gently amid a pile of soft marsh grass.
Go, righteous shades, and swarms of bards from Greece,
shower this brilliant soul with Lethe's garlands,
show him that grove where no Furies burst in,   395
in which there is a seeming light of day,
and atmosphere so very like the heavens.
　　And yet may you come where the better gate
of horn outdoes the spiteful one of ivory,
and as a dream reveal to me the things   400
you used to show. Just so, that gentle nymph
in her Arician grotto told King Numa
the sacred ceremonies he must practice,
so Romans think Scipio's dreams were filled
with Jove, so Sulla always had Apollo.[18]   405

An Insomniac's Prayer (*Silvae* 5.4)

　　What fault or flaw has made me merit this,
O youthful Sleep, most tranquil god of all,
to be the only wretch unblessed by you?
All silent now are herds, and birds, and beasts,
while tipping treetops mimic drowsy sleep.   5
The roar of raging rivers has grown still,
shuddering ocean waves have settled down,
as sea reclines at peace upon the land.
A seventh Moon has come again and seen
my sunken eyes, which Hesperus has seen,   10
and Lucifer, returning seven more times,
and seven times, too, that Trojan's rosy wife
has pitied me, while passing by my sighs,
and sprinkled from her whip a cooling dew.

I've had enough. Oh, for the thousand eyes   15
that Juno's bird-to-be kept open wide—
in shifts, of course, and never all on guard.
But if some lover wants to fight you off,
to stay awake entwined in his girl's arms,
come, Sleep, to me instead. No need to shower   20
my eyes with all your feathers (that's a prayer
for luckier folks). A tap from wand tip's top
is quite enough, as you pass lightly by.

Lament for My Adopted Son (*Silvae* 5.5)

How sad, that I may not begin a work
with all the customary invocations,
hateful now to Castalia's dulcet waters,
loathsome to Phoebus, too. What secret rites
of yours, you sisters of Mount Helicon,   5
what holy altars, could I have defiled?
Speak out, and tell me, if you are allowed,
after the punishment, to state the crime.
Surely I have not set foot in a grove
tabooed? Surely not drunk forbidden springs?   10
What is the fault so great, what the mistake,
for which I now atone? With dying arms
and spirit, lo, a baby grips my heart
and soul, as he is torn away, not mine
by birth, or name and looks; I'm not his sire,   15
but see my tears, my eyes' dark circles, trust
my wails of grief, you who have been bereaved.
Bereaved am I. Let fathers, mothers bare
of breast, assemble here; blacken your eyes
with ash in mourning, †blame the gods above†,[19]   20
any woman who went with shaky steps
to bury a child while her breasts were full,
and beat them as they flowed, and with those drops
of milk has dowsed the pyre's still glowing embers.
Whatever man has plunged in ash a youngster   25
bearing the traces still of tender bloom,
and who has seen flames cruelly snake around

the dead man's down beard, let him be here
and grow exhausted, trading cries with me:
his tears will be outdone by mine and, Nature,   30
you will be put to shame, so fierce, so crazed
is this, my grief for my adopted son.
Even this is a strain, a whole month later,
as I lean on his tomb and turn my wails
to songs with jarring tunes and sobbing words.   35
I strive at this enterprise with my lyre
(my pain and anger brook no keeping silence),
although my head has not its wonted laurel,
my brow, its honored fillets. See, yew leaves
droop in my hair, the grieving cypress' branches   40
block ivy's cheer; and not with ivory pick
do I now strike the strings, but yank them out
from this unsteady lyre, distraught and hesitant
about the fingerings. It helps, alas,
it helps, to pour out song that's worth no praise,   45
and bare in random thoughts my painful sadness.
This is what I deserve, and what the gods
should see, how song and dress reflect my state,
unfit for those above. And let this shame
my Theban work and new Achilles-epic;   50
now nothing tranquil will flow from my lips.
I am that man who could (how many times!)
winningly sooth parents' traumas, sooth pains
still fresh, I am that gentle comforter
of those in mourning, heard by bitter tombs   55
and shades as they were going down below.
I falter and I look for healing hands
with balm, the most effective kind, for wounds
which are my own. Now is the time, my friends,
whose flowing eyes and injured hearts I wiped;   60
bring help in turn, and pay this painful thanks.
No wonder, when I mourned your families' dead,
* *

someone reproached me saying: "You who grieve
others' losses, bad luck will come to you;   65
put tears away, and save sad songs for later."
It was the truth: my strength has been used up,

I have no stock of what to say; my mind
has come on nothing worthy of a shock
so great. Inadequate is all expression, 70
not good enough, all words. Forgive me, child,
you leave me crushed and sunk in gloom. Ah, heartless
was Thracian Orpheus, if he had seen
his dear wife's wound and found himself
something pleasant to sing in consolation, 75
heartless, Apollo, too, if he had clasped
son Linus' early tomb and not been left
in mute silence. I take my pain too far,
perhaps they say, and hoard it, and have gone
beyond the bounds of due restraint for tears. 80
But who, pray tell, weighs my groans of lament?
Too lucky he, too cruel, and with no sense
of Fortune's power, who dares to set the terms
for weeping, or assess the bounds of grief!
He prompts, alas, more wails. Sooner would one 85
hold back rivers as they escape their banks,
or block a raging fire, than ban sad people
from mourning. Let that stern critic of mine,
whoever he is, come and judge these wounds.

  I did not buy and love a chattering pet 90
imported on a slave ship bound from Egypt,
a child schooled in his Nile's proverbial banter,
too quick to speak and make a shameless joke:
my own, he was my own. I saw him born,
my birthday poem pampered his anointing, 95
and as his quavering howls demanded air,
still new and strange to him, I introduced
him into life. What more did his parents give?
But no, I gave you new adoptive birth
and set you free while you were at the breast, 100
my little one; you laughed, still unaware
of what my gifts might mean. Hasty that love
may well have been, but rightly it was hasty,
to keep a freedom so short-lived from losing
a day <at all>.[20] Should I not go unkempt, 105
and smite the gods and unjust Tartarus
with my reproach? Not groan for you, dear boy?

While you were safe, I did not long for sons,
when you had just been born, you curled right up
in my lap, clinging tight, and gazed at me,   110
you to whom I revealed the sounds of words
when I could figure out the unseen hurts
that caused your plaintive cries, and as you crawled
upon the ground, I stooped and picked you up
to kiss, and in my loving lap I †lulled†   115
you eyes now <drooping>,* now, to pleasant dreams.
My name was your first word, my smile, a game
for you, and my expression, your delight.

Appendix 1.

Titles of the Individual Silvae

The order in which the titles are given is the Latin title, a literal translation of it, and my own title.

BOOK 1

1. Ecus Maximus Domitiani Imp.
   The Emperor Domitian's Very Large Horse
   Domitian's Colossal Equestrian Statue
2. Epithalamion in Stellam et Violentillam
   Wedding Poem for Stella and Violentilla
   For the Wedding of Stella and Violentilla
3. Villa Tiburtina Manili Vopisci
   The Tiburtine Villa of Manilius Vopiscus
   Manilius Vopiscus' Villa at Tivoli
4. Soteria Rutili Gallici
   [In Honor of] Rutilius Gallicus' Recovery
   Rutilius Gallicus Has Recovered!
5. Balneum Claudii Etrusci
   The Baths of Claudius Etruscus
   The Baths of Claudius Etruscus
6. Kalendae Decembres
   The First of December
   Domitian's Saturnalia Celebration

BOOK 2

1. Glaucias Atedii Melioris delicatus
   Glaucias, Atedius Melior's Favorite
   Lament for Glaucias, Melior's Favorite
2. Villa Surrentina Pollii Felicis
   The Surrentine Villa of Pollius Felix
   Pollius Felix's Villa at Sorrento
3. Arbor Atedii Melioris
   Atedius Melior's Tree
   Melior's Peculiar Plane Tree

4. Psittacus eiusdem
   The Same Man's Parrot
   Melior's Parrot Is Dead
5. Leo mansuetus
   A Tame Lion
   Death of a Tame Lion
6. Consolatio ad Flavium Ursum de amissione pueri delicati
   Consolation to Flavius Ursus for the Loss of His Favorite Slave
   Consolation to Flavius Ursus for the Loss of His Favorite Slave
7. Genethliacon Lucani ad Pollam
   Lucan's Birthday Poem [Written] for Polla
   On the Anniversary of Lucan's Birth

BOOK 3

1. Hercules Surrentinus Pollii Felicis
   The Surrentine Hercules of Pollius Felix
   Hercules' Temple at Pollius' Sorrentine Villa
2. Propempticon Maecio Celeri
   A Bon Voyage Poem for Maecius Celer
   Bon Voyage, Maecius Celer!
3. Consolatio ad Claudium Etruscum
   Consolation to Claudius Etruscus
   Consolation to Claudius Etruscus
4. Capilli Flavi Earini
   The Locks of Flavius Earinus
   Farewell to Earinus' Lock of Hair
5. <ad uxorem> [note: the title is missing; this is inferred from the preface to book 3]
   To [His] Wife
   To My Wife

BOOK 4

1. Septimus decimus consulatus Imp. Aug. Germanici
   The Seventeenth Consulship of His Majesty the Emperor, Conqueror of Germany
   On Domitian's Inauguration as Consul for the Seventeenth Time (1 January 95 CE)
2. Eucharisticon ad Imp. Aug. Germ. Domitianum
   A Poem of Thanksgiving for His Majesty the Emperor Domitian, Conqueror of Germany
   Thanks to Domitian for a Banquet Invitation
3. Via Domitiana
   Domitian's Road
   Domitian's Highway
4. Epistola ad Vitorium Marcellum
   A Letter to Vitorius Marcellus
   A Letter to Vitorius Marcellus

5. Ode Lyrica ad Septimium Severum
   Lyric Ode to Septimius Severus
   Horatian Ode to Septimius Severus
6. Hercules Epitrapezios Novi Vindicis
   The "Hercules Epitrapezios" of Novius Vindex
   Vindex's Statuette, "Hercules at Table"
7. Ode lyrica ad Vibium Maximum
   Lyric Ode to Vibius Maximus
   Horatian Ode to Vibius Maximus
8. Gratulatio ad Iulium Menecraten
   Congratulations to Julius Menecrates
   Congratulations to Julius Menecrates on the Birth of His Third Child
9. Hendecasyllabi iocosi ad Plotium Grypum
   Joking Hendecasyllables for Plotius Grypus
   Teasing Tetrameters to Plotius Grypus

BOOK 5

1. Epicedion in Priscillam <Abascanti> uxorem
   Lament for Priscilla, the Wife of Abascantus
   Lament for Priscilla, Wife of Abascantus
2. Laudes Crispini Vetti Bolani filii
   Praises for Crispinus, the Son of Vettius Bolanus
   In Praise of Crispinus, Son of Vettius Bolanus
3. Epicedion in patrem suum
   Lament for His Father
   Lament for My Father
4. Somnus
   Sleep
   An Insomniac's Prayer
5. Epicedion in puerum suum
   Lament for His Child
   Lament for My Adopted Son

Appendix 2.
Deviations from Courtney's Oxford Classical Text

Line numbers are those of the Latin text. The names in parentheses are those of editors and other textual critics whose alternatives I have adopted. A discussion of these deviations appears in appendix 3.

1.pref.4	*pro<volassent>* (Klotz)
1.pref.5	*<opus eo tempore hos>* (Saenger; Sandstroem; O. Mueller)
1.pref.29	*<in promptu>* (Slater)
1.pref.32	*<in ipso amphitheatro sedens descripsi et palam recitavi>* (Vollmer)
1.4 after 6	*<curarum pro te partem exceptura capaxque>* (Courtney's App. Crit.)
1.4.13	*<septemplexque>* (Courtney 1984)
1.4.29–30	*in artum / angitur* (Barth; Courtney 1984)
1.4.45	*multum demittere* (Courtney 1966)
1.4.61	*progressus <tandem est e silva maestus opaca / abrumpens>que* (Courtney 1984)
1.4 after 73	*<effusos pelagi tractus terrasque patentes>* (Housman 1906)
1.4.88	*lacera* (Politian, *per* Courtney 1966)
1.6.8	*aparchen* (Phillimore's App. Crit.)
1.6.15	*aestuosa* (Imhof)
1.6 after 96	*<fuso, dux bone, liberalitate>* (Courtney's App. Crit.)
2.1.28	*sed tu* (Vollmer)
2.1.67	*mussat* (Housman 1906)
2.2.147–48	*<praedocta Latinas / parque viro mentem, cui non>* (W. Hardie 1904)
2.5.1	*monstrata* (M)
2.6.6	*at te domat ac* (Courtney 1988)
2.6.70	*cardine* (Gronov)
3.2.30	*remos libramina longos* (Krohn; Courtney 1988)
3.2.138	*quam* (Baehrens)
3.3.78	*fratris* (Courtney 1984)
3.3.80	*permeruisse* (Courtney 1984)
3.4.96	*ipsumque potentius aurum* (Courtney 1968)

4.pref.4	*<eclogas in laudem eius in fronte praepositas; vides igitur te magis honorari non potuis>se* (Coleman, adapting Vollmer)
4.1.9	*rediit* (Markland, *per* Coleman)
	saeptus (Saenger, *per* Coleman)
4.2.6	*dominamque dedit contingere mensam* (Waller, *per* Coleman)
4.2.26	*gravat* (Schwartz, *per* Coleman)
4.4.66	*ingentes* (Coleman's App. Crit.)
4.4.73	*poscit avus* (Politian, *per* Coleman)
4.7.11	*sitit* (Saenger, *per* Coleman)
4.8.17	*lumina* (Markland, *per* Coleman)
4.9.49	*inflatam* (Otto, *per* Coleman)
5.1.19	*questu<que sonant cuncta undique maesto / quae via solandi>* (Courtney 1984)
5.1 after 92	*<victrices monstrant aquilas per proelia fausta>* (Courtney 1984)
5.1.233	*nitens* (Courtney's App. Crit.)
5.2.145	*quas hinc* (Courtney 1968)
5.3.100	*usus* (Wiman)
5.5.84	*<cadentes>* (Baehrens)
5.5.85	*exsopire* (Vollmer)

Appendix 3.

Textual Matters

For the prefaces, I supply Courtney's line numbers only; for the poems,
I give the line number of the translation, followed by the line numbers
in Courtney's edition in brackets.

1.PREF.4

Instead of Courtney's lacuna, I am translating Klotz's supplement *pro<volassent>*. Vollmer ([1898] 1971, 210), writing shortly before Klotz, says that *pro<diissent>* (went forth) has "a great deal of internal probability" (my trans.).

1.PREF.5

Instead of Courtney's lacuna, I translate the supplement *<opus eo tempore hos>*, which his App. Crit. attributes to the combined efforts of Saenger, Sandstroem, and O. Mueller. Vollmer ([1898] 1971, 210) maintains that there is no need for a verb meaning "it is necessary" (*opus* or *oportet*), if one understands the infinitive *onerari* (to burden oneself) as one of exclamation. Courtney's report in his App. Crit. that the lacuna has space for eleven letters favors Vollmer's point.

1.PREF.29

Instead of Courtney's crux †*domonnun*†, I translate Slater's emendation *in promptu*. But that and Saenger's *commodum* (convenient) have, according to Courtney's App. Crit., been endorsed by a number of scholars Shackleton Bailey proposes *donandum* (must be waived).

1.PREF 32

Courtney ends this sentence with an ellipsis to indicate a missing conclusion, but I translate part of Vollmer's suggestion ([1898] 1971, 213) for the sense of what is missing: *in ipso amphitheatro sedens descripsi et palam recitavi*.

1 4.12 [1.4 AFTER LINE 6]

In place of Courtney's lacuna, I have translated his suggestion in the App. Crit. for what the approximate content of the missing line may have been: *<curarum pro te partem exceptura capaxque>*.

🎜 Appendix 3 🎝

1.4.22 [1.4.13]

In place of Courtney's crux †nosteque ex†, I have adopted *septemplexque*, which he tentatively suggested (Courtney 1984, 335) and refers to in his App. Crit. A literal version of *septemplexque ordine collis / confremat* (13–14) with the conjecture would be "let the sevenfold hill resound in turn."

1.4.47–48 [1.4 29–30]

Courtney reads *in artem / frangitur* here. Earlier (Courtney 1984, 335), he conjectured *angitur* and combined it with Barth's *artum*, commenting that this is the "metaphor of equestrian exercise often applied by Statius to his poetry." This is what I have translated.

1 4.70 [1.4.45]

Instead of Courtney's crux †multum sibi demere†, I have adopted his earlier suggestion (Courtney 1966, 98), *multum dimittere*.

1.4.90–91 [1.4.61]

Courtney prints line 61 as two lines, with the lacuna he conjectured earlier (Courtney 1984, 334):

progressus *
* * * * * * *-que moras: 'hinc mecum, Epidauria proles*

Literally, this could be rendered

He started out *
* * * * * * delays, and said, "Hither with me, my son from Epidaurus

Instead, I have translated the supplement he suggested in 1984:

progressus <tandem est e silva maestus opaca
abrumpens>que moras: 'hinc mecum, Epidauria proles,

In each of these versions, note that "said" (*ait*) actually occurs in line 62.

1.4.110 [1.4 AFTER LINE 73]

I have translated the stopgap Housman (1906, 38) suggested—*<effusos pelagi tractus terrasque patentes>*—for the lacuna he proposed between lines 73 and 74, and which Courtney prints.

1.4.136 [1 4.88]

Instead of *laeta* (joyful), I read *lacera* (mutilated). The reading *lacera* does not appear in Courtney's App. Crit. This is puzzling, since he previously (Courtney 1966, 97) had called it the "far superior reading," asserting that "it will cease being perverse to refuse the far superior reading *lacera* . . . and become inexcusable," and even chiding another editor (Marastoni) for "suppress[ing] all mention of it." Phillimore (1905) adopted *lacera* in Oxford's predecessor to Courtney's text; it is one of the annotations Politian based on the exemplar of the *Silvae* (see "The Text of the *Silvae*" in the introduction).

1.6.8 [1.6.8]

Instead of Courtney's crux †*parcen*†, I adopt *aparchen*, the tentative suggestion Phillimore (1905) made in his App. Crit., saying *scripserim* (I might have written). Mozley ([1928] 1982, 64) adopted *aparchen* in his text (as does Shackleton Bailey), explaining it in his App. Crit. as the transliteration of a Greek word meaning originally "first fruits" and then "festival." Several other transliterated Greek words have been suggested: e.g., *narcen* ("numbness" or "stupor") by Damsté (in Courtney's App Crit.) and *heorten* ("festival" or "holiday") by Krohn (in Frère's App. Crit., 1944, 1:46). Vollmer ([1898] 1971, 305) discusses other suggestions of Latin words, including *partem* ("part," i.e., a part of the celebration) by Gronov, and *noctem* (night) by Thomson. Watt's suggestion of *cenam* (banquet) appears in Courtney's App. Crit.

1.6.16 [1.6.15]

Instead of Courtney's crux †*aebosia*†, I read Imhof's *aestuosa*. Vollmer ([1898] 1971) also printed that crux, but with dissatisfaction; following Gevaert and Markland, he discusses (305–306) the suggestion *Ebosia*, an adjective from *Ebusus* (modern-day Ibiza, the largest of the Balearic Islands). Pliny the Elder (*Naturalis Historia* 15.82) praises the figs of Ebusus. Since Caunos in Caria was also famous for its figs, Vollmer (306) renders the phrase "the fig-city of Ebusus" (my trans.). Compare our practice of praising a university other than Harvard by calling it the Harvard of its region.

1.6.109 [1 6 AFTER LINE 96]

Instead of Courtney's lacuna, I have translated the suggestion in his App. Crit. for the gist of what is missing: <*fuso, dux bone, liberalitate*>. The feminine noun *liberalitate* accounts for the adjective *tua* in the preceding line (i.e., "by your generosity").

2 1.36 [2.1.28]

With the phrase "but you" I translate not Courtney's crux †*et diu*†, but Vollmer's *sed tu*. For a discussion of this crux and various solutions, including Vollmer's, see van Dam 1984, 88.

2.1.88 [2.1.67]

"Your house is dumb" renders not Courtney's crux †*fateor*†, but *mussat*, which is what Housman (1906, 40–41) conjectured.

187

❧ Appendix 3 ❧

2.2.189–90 [2.2.147–48]

I have filled Courtney's lacuna with the suggestion of W. Hardie (1904, 158), which van Dam (1984) calls "easily the best suggestion" and what Statius "could very well have written" (275, 276):

> tuque, nurus inter longe <praedocta Latinas
> parque viro mentem, cui non> praecordia curae,
> non frontem vertere minae, sed candida semper
> gaudia . . . .

Literally, this means "and you, by far the most erudite among Latin daughters-in-law, and equal to your husband in intellect, whose heart no worries have changed, whose brow no threats have changed, but who always has shining joy. . . ."

2.5.2 [2.5.1]

Instead of Courtney's *constrata*, I adopt *monstrata* (the reading of the manuscript M). Van Dam (1984, 372–74) discusses the text and concludes that *monstrata . . . ira*, understood as "after you had once displayed your anger," "seems the most attractive solution for this rather elliptic expression" (374).

2.6.9 [2.6.6]

Courtney prints the crux †*ad te tamen at*†, but I have translated the version he suggested earlier (Courtney 1988, 43) but relegated to the App. Crit. of his edition: *at te domat ac*.

2.6.102 [2.6.70]

Instead of the crux †*carmen*† that Courtney prints, I have translated Gronov's emendation *cardine*, although van Dam (1984, 431) maintains that the phrase *cardo vitae* (the hinge of life) means "death." Van Dam also discusses other proposed solutions (431–32), including Markland's *limine* (threshold) and Håkanson's *margine* (edge). Shackleton Bailey adopts the latter.

3.2.36 [3.2.30]

Courtney's text reads *sint quibus explorent* †*primos gravis arte molorchos*†, but earlier (Courtney 1988, 44) he had suggested the following solution for the crux: *remos libramina longos*. The line would then read literally "let there be those for whom balancing tests the long oars." My translation omits *longos* but otherwise substitutes Courtney's earlier suggestion for the OCT crux. In fact, my version—"test and balance oars"—is close to Courtney's own paraphrase—"test the oars by balancing them."

3.2.179 [3.2.138]

Courtney reads *qua*, but here I adopt Baehrens' *quam*. Courtney's text could be translated, in context, as "where thriving Idumaea's groves smell sweet."

3.3.102 [3.3.78]

Courtney prints the crux †*longo*†, but I translate *fratris*, which he "audaciously" suggested earlier (Courtney 1984, 337).

3.3.104 [3 3.80]

Courtney prints *promeruisse* (to have deserved), but previously he suggested (Courtney 1968, 53) that the correct sense (if not the correct tense) could be obtained by reading *permeruisse* (to have been in service). I follow that suggestion and translate it as "to be in service." For the idea that *permeruisse* = *meruisse per* (i.e., "to have served throughout"), Courtney credited Housman (1906, 38), who asserts that *permeruit* has that meaning in *Silvae* 1.4.74. According to *OLD* (s.v. "permereo"), the word means "to serve out one's time in the army"; the only example cited is the line Housman discussed.

3.4.144 [3.4 96]

This line—"the gold itself will thus have more effect"—is my version not of the text Courtney prints, *ipsoque potentius auro* (96; lit., "more effective than gold itself"), but of his suggestion (Courtney 1968, 56) *ipsumque potentius aurum* (the gold itself [sc. "will be"] more effective), which he explains by the paraphrase "the gold of the mirror, *potens* in itself, will be yet *potentius* if Earinus but consents to impart his image to it."

4.PREF.4

For the lacuna in Courtney's text, I have translated the supplement in the commentary of Coleman (1988, 56): *sed hic liber tres habet <eclogas in laudem eius in fronte praepositas; vides igitur te magis honorari non potuis>se quam quod quarta ad honorem tuum pertinet.* This supplement is in turn an adaptation (Coleman calls it an "abbreviation") of the one Vollmer ([1898] 1971, 144) provided in his App. Crit.: *<libellos in honorem eius. tum demum secuntur eclogae ad amicos; vides igitur te magis honorari non potuis>.*

4.1.13 [4 1.9]

Instead of Courtney's crux †*sextus*†, I follow Coleman (1988, 68) in adopting Saenger's emendation *saeptus* ("hedged" or "guarded"). Since *honos* means "honor" (here the "honor" conferred by high office), I have translated the phrase *bis saeptus honos* as "this doubly guarded consulship." Here Statius alludes to the fact that Domitian had double the usual number of lictors for a consul (twenty-four, rather than twelve). Lictors are more like ceremonial marshals than actual bodyguards, so I have translated *novi . . . fasces* (8) as "new marshals' maces." Also, instead of Courtney's participle *rediens* (coming back), I follow Coleman (1988, 68) in adopting Markland's *rediit* (it has come back), which I have translated as "back has come."

4 2.8 [4 2.6]

Instead of Courtney's *dominaque dedit non surgere mensa* (lit., "he has permitted not to rise from the master's table"), I have followed Coleman (1988, 85–86) in adopting Waller's suggestion, *dominamque dedit contingere mensam* (lit., "he has permitted to attain the master's table").

4.2.36 [4.2.26]

Instead of Courtney's *iuvat* (it pleases), the reading in M, which Coleman (1988, 91) calls "weak" coming after *implet* (it fills) in the same line, I follow her endorsement of Schwartz's *gravat*. If I had accepted *iuvat*, I could have translated "and pleases it" instead of "and weighs it down."

4.4.83 [4.4.66]

Coleman (1988, 150) discusses the crux †*tarde*† in line 66. I adopt her suggestion of *ingentes* (mighty), which appears in her App. Crit. (24), not in the commentary itself. Shackleton Bailey (2003) prints *tarde* (not obelized), but the parenthetical question mark in his translation—"arms slow (?) to don a heavy corslet"—indicates a degree of uncertainty.

4.4.93–94 [4.4.73]

The phrase "his great-grandfather demands" translates the Latin *poscit avus* (lit., "his grandfather demands"), a note of Politian's own (i.e., not one based on the exemplar) which Coleman (1988, 26) adopts. The reading of M—*poscit avos* (he demands grandfathers)—which Courtney prints, she calls (151) "meaningless," and she defends her understanding of *avus* as meaning not "grandfather" but "great-grandfather." For the identity of this man as Cn. Hosidius Geta, see her introduction to the poem (136–37).

4.4.110 [4.4.83–84]

The English, "that fields . . . / vanished in floods of lava," is my version of †*totot*† / *rura abisse mari*. For the crux †*totot*† (the "whole" sea), various solutions have been proposed, including *tosto*, by Vollmer (the "burned" sea), and *tanto*, by Marastoni ("so great a" sea); in either case, *mari* is being used metaphorically (a "sea" of lava)—hence my version, "floods of lava."

4.4.135 [4.4.103]

Courtney prints line 103 as two lines

pectus amicitiae * * * * * * *
* * * * * * *cedet tibi gloria fidi*

because of the lacuna Markland suspected and Leo endorsed. The size of the gap suggests that something more is missing than just the verb of which *Tirynthius* (102; "Hercules") is the subject and *pectus* (heart) is the object, but a verb is all that my translation "<will not

outdo>" supplies. Shackleton Bailey (2003) gets rid of Courtney's lacuna and prints 103 as a single line by adopting Slater's *parcus* ("thrifty" or "stingy") for *pectus*; he translates *nec enim Tirynthius almae / parcus amicitiae* as "[f]or neither was the Tirynthian sparing of fostering friendship [i.e., friendship which fosters]" (275).

4.7.11 [4.7.11]

Here I translate Courtney's crux †*maior*† (greater), but instead of his *sitis* (thirst), I follow Coleman (1988, 40, 200–201) and adopt Saenger's *sitit* ("is thirsty," i.e., "runs dry"). Courtney's App. Crit. suggests that what is needed is something like *sedit* (either "has sat" or "has settled") or *sidit* (either "has subsided" or "subsides").

4.8 24 [4.8.17]

Here Courtney reads *liventia pectora* (bruised breast). Following Coleman (1988, 44, 213), I adopt Markland's *lumina*. I then translate *liventia lumina* cross-culturally, drawing on our conception of jealousy as "the green-eyed monster."

4.9.60 [4.9.49]

Following Coleman (1988, 239), I adopt Otto's *inflatam* instead of Courtney's *inlatam* (inflicted).

5 1.26–27 [5.1.19]

Here I have translated the suggestion Courtney (1984, 333) made for the possible content of the lacuna between the two parts of line 19:

nigra domus questu<que sonant cuncta undique maesto,
quae via solandi> miseramque accessus ad aurem

Literally, *questu<que . . . / . . . solandi>* means "and all things everywhere resound with mournful lament, what route to consolation [or 'what way of consoling']."

5.1.126 [5 1 AFTER LINE 92]

In the lacuna, I have translated what Courtney (1984, 334) suggested as illustrative of the missing content: *<victrices monstrant aquilas per proelia fausta>* (lit.,"they show victorious eagles through lucky battles").

5.1.314 [5.1.233]

Instead of the crux †*tholo*† (rotunda) Courtney prints, I adopt *nitens*, which he suggests in his App.Crit., where he also calls attention to line 228, in which *tholo* also appears (the "rotunda" in line 307 of my translation). Shackleton Bailey (2003) adopts Baehrens's *luto* (mud, clay) instead of *tholo*. In that case, Statius is contrasting the media of the various statues—Ceres and Ariadne ("the shining Cretan") in bronze, Maia in terracotta, and Venus in marble.

5.2.174 [5.2.120]

Courtney prints †*patri flagrabat*† as a crux. Vollmer ([1898] 1971, 185) did not, arguing that the transitive use of *flagrabat* was a Statian innovation, by analogy with such compounds as *conflagro* and *deflagro* (518). Nor did Shackleton Bailey (2003) obelize this phrase.

5.2.208 [5.2.145]

Instead of the crux †*vitae*† which Courtney prints in his edition, I adopt the emendation he proposed (1968, 57), *quas hinc,* although he understands *hinc* as "on this side" rather than "from here."

5.3.132 [5.3.100]

Instead of Courtney's crux †*utor*† (I use), I adopt *usus,* Wiman's suggestion (cited in Courtney's App. Crit.), making it parallel to *complexus es* (lit., "you embraced . . . you used").

5.5.115–16 [5.5.84–85]

Courtney's text reads

erexi, blandoque sinu iam iamque * * * * * *
†*exceperet*† *genas dulcesque accersere somnos*

My translation adopts Baehrens' suggestion of *cadentes* (falling) for the lacuna, and Vollmer's suggestion ([1898] 1971, 554) of *exsopire* for the crux. The latter would be a neologism, a compound of *sopire* (to cause to sleep). Literally the line means "cause your cheeks [i.e., 'eyes'] to sleep and induce sweet sleep." This would be typical of Statius' penchant for reduplicatio, but I have conflated the two verbs: thus, "lulled / your eyes . . . to pleasant dreams."

This abrupt ending suggests either that the text has been mutilated or that the poem was not finished.

Glossary

This glossary is based on information found in standard reference works (see the bibliography) and in commentaries on the Silvae; *occasionally I have cited these when it seemed appropriate. Unless otherwise indicated, the line numbers refer to the translation; line numbers followed by "L" refer to the Latin text. For the most part I have used the Roman names for gods. For fuller details about persons addressed or mentioned in the poems, see the introduction.*

Abascantus: Flavius Abascantus, freedman in charge of correspondence for Domitian, widower of Priscilla (addressee of 5.1), addressee of book 5 preface.

Acca: the foster mother of Romulus (see below).

Acheron: one of the rivers of the Underworld.

Achilles: the preeminent Greek warrior at Troy. Son of Peleus, king of Phthia in Thessaly, and the sea-goddess Thetis; his mother disguised him as a girl and hid him on the island of Scyrus in an attempt to prevent him from fighting at Troy. After killing Hector, he mutilated the corpse by dragging it behind his chariot to avenge the death of his friend Patroclus; he healed Telephus with rust from the weapon with which he had wounded him; he pursued and killed Troilus, a son of Apollo; and he was shot and killed by Paris. Achilles is also the subject of an unfinished epic by Statius.

Acir: a river in Lucania, where Flavius Ursus, the addressee of 2.6, owned property.

Acoetes: the squire of King Evander's son Pallas.

Actaeon: a young hunter who accidentally saw Diana bathing; she turned him into a stag, and he was torn to pieces by his own hounds.

Actium: the naval battle of 31 BCE during which the fleet of Octavian (the future Emperor Augustus) defeated Anthony and Cleopatra. The Actian Games were founded in 27 BCE and celebrated every four years on 2 September.

Admetus: the king of Pherae in Thessaly, to whom Apollo granted the right to let someone else die in his place; his wife Alcestis offered to do so, but was saved when Hercules wrested her away from Death.

Adonis: the young consort of Venus, gored to death by a wild boar he was hunting. In an annual festival mourning his death, women planted seeds in shallow dishes; after the short-lived plants died, they lamented the dead Adonis.

Adriatic: the sea between Italy and the Balkan Peninsula; part of Maecius Celer's route from Naples to Syria.

Aegean: the sea between Greece and Asia Minor.

Aegiale: the wife of Diomedes (see below).

Aemilian (Basilica): one of the great public halls in the Roman Forum, on one side of Domitian's equestrian statue; it was rebuilt by Lucius Aemilius Paullus (a nephew of the triumvir Lepidus) and his son Lucius Aemilius Lepidus Paullus. However, the reference to "warrior Paullus" (1.1.45) suggests that Statius confused these men with the more famous member of their family, Lucius Aemilius Paullus Macedonicus, who, as consul in 168 BCE, ended the Third Macedonian War and settled Greece.

Aeneas: the Trojan warrior, son of Venus, who fled with his father Anchises and son Ascanius after the city fell, wandered in search of a new home, and eventually landed in Italy to found the Roman nation; the subject of Virgil's *Aeneid*. Among the events to which Statius alludes are his shipwreck at Carthage, where he met Queen Dido; his consultation with the Cumaean Sibyl; his visit to his father in the Underworld; and his alliance with King Evander and his son Pallas.

Aeneid: Virgil's masterpiece, the Roman national epic (written 26–19 BCE).

Aeolus: the king of the island of Aeolia; Jupiter gave him control of the winds, which blow when he releases them from their cave prison.

Africa / African: this usually translates the noun *Libya* or related adjectives; the Greeks and Romans both loosely referred to North Africa as "Libya."
The "African shoals" (4.5.30) are the famous Syrtes.

Agamemnon: the king of Mycenae, leader of the Greek forces against Troy.

Alba / Alban / Alban Hills: Alba Longa was built by Ascanius after the death of his father, Aeneas. Domitian had a villa in the Alban Hills, where he held the Alban Games in honor of Minerva and awarded the prize of a golden olive wreath; the emperor also gave Statius an estate in the Alban Hills and supplied it with water for him.

Albula: a mineral lake out of which a stream flowed into the Anio at Tivoli.

Alcinous: Homer's mythical king of the Phaeacians, who hosted Ulysses near the end of his wanderings.

Alcman: Spartan lyric poet (7th c. BCE).

Alexander: the great Macedonian general (356–323 BCE).

Algidus: one of the Alban Hills near Tusculo; cool and wooded, it was a popular summer retreat.

Almo: a stream which flowed into the Tiber south of Rome, in which the image of Cybele, the Great Mother, was ritually bathed every year in March.

Alpheus: the largest river in the Peloponnese, which flows into the Ionian Sea through the district of Pisa where the Olympic Games were held; according to myth, the god of the river pursued the nymph Arethusa under the sea all the way to Sicily, where she is a spring.

Alps / Alpine: in *Silvae* 1.4 the phrase "Alpine peaks" (88) alludes to Turin, the birthplace of Rutilius Gallicus, and "the Alps" (134) refers to Hannibal's route into Italy from the north.

Amazons: in myth, a race of women warriors living on the shores of the Black Sea

Ammon: the god Zeus Ammon had an oracle in the Libyan desert which Alexander (see above) visited in 331 BCE and where he claimed to have learned that he was the god's son.

Amphion: a son of Jupiter who built the walls of Thebes by charming the stones into place with the lyre Mercury had given him.

Amphitryon: the mortal father of Hercules; his wife Alcmena was impregnated by Jupiter while they were living at Thebes.

Anchises: the father of Aeneas; he was carried out of burning Troy on his son's shoulders, buried on Sicily, and visited by Aeneas in the Underworld.

Anio: the river at Tivoli on both sides of which Vopiscus' villa was built.

Anthedon: a harbor town on the coast of Boeotia; the birthplace of Glaucus (see below).

Anubis: the Egyptian jackal-headed god, whom Statius identifies with Cerberus (see below).

Anzio: the modern name for Antium, where Vopiscus apparently had a winter place.

Apelles: the most famous ancient Greek painter (4th c. BCE).

Aphrodite: the Greek goddess of sexuality, identified by the Romans with Venus.
"Roman Aphrodite's temple" (1.1.129; *Latiae . . . templa Diones,* 1.1.84L) is the temple, built by Julius Caesar, of Venus Genetrix (i.e., Venus as the mother, through Aeneas, of the Roman people).

Apis: the sacred bull of Memphis; when it had reached a certain age, priests drowned it, embalmed it, and carried it in procession, and then with lamentation looked for its successor.

Apollo: the archer god of music, oracles, and healing; associated with the Muses. He was the father of Asclepius, the god of medicine; when Jupiter killed Asclepius with a thunderbolt for resurrecting a dead man, Apollo took vengeance by killing the Cyclopes (makers of Jupiter's thunderbolts) and was punished by having to serve the mortal Admetus as a herder. His bird was the raven.

Appian Way / Appian Highway: the principal route from Rome to southern Italy. The first leg, from Rome to Capua, was built by Appius Claudius Caecus ("the Blind"), censor in 312 BCE; later it was extended to Brundisium (Brindisi).

Apulian: of Apulia (modern Puglia), a region in southeastern Italy.

Aqua Marcia: the Marcian Aqueduct, famous for its cool drinking water; it was piped under the Anio near Vopiscus' villa (1.3.94) and supplied Claudius Etruscus' baths (1.5.35).

Aqua Virgo: the Virgin Aqueduct, famous for the purity of its water; it supplied Claudius Etruscus' baths (1.5.33) and several baths at Rome, including Agrippa's.

Arab / Arabian / Arabs: Arabia was famous for the myrrh and incense it exported.
The "Arab horse" (5.2.171) is actually "Gaetulian" (5.2.118L; here, loosely, from the interior of Africa), but my translation is meant to convey the modern connotations of "Arabian horses."

Aratus: Greek poet (ca. 315–ca. 240 BCE), best known for his poem about astronomy, the *Phaenomena.*

Araxes: a river in Armenia.

Arcadia / Arcadian: a mountainous area in the Peloponnese, the home of Pan and Mercury ("Arcadia's wingèd god," 1.5.6).
"[T]hat young Arcadian warrior . . . at Thebes" (2.6.63) is Parthenopaeus (see below).

the Archives: I have used this phrase (4.6.9) for a place were old records are stored, although Statius actually refers to *perpetuis . . . fastis* (4.6.7L; lit., "continuous calendars"). Various kinds of calendars were called *fasti,* including the *fasti consulares,* which listed the two consuls for each year.

Arethusa: the nymph of a spring in Syracuse; see Alpheus.

Argive: of the Greek city Argos or its people.
"[A] cow in Argive stables" (3.2.130) is Io, who was given the name Isis (see below) by the Egyptians.
"[W]hat tombs I gave the vanquished Argives" (3.2.184) refers to the Seven against Thebes, and to Statius' own *Thebaid.*

Argo: the ship of Jason and the Argonauts, which Athena helped build.
The author "who charted *Argo*'s course" (2.7.94) is Varro of Atax (b. 82 BCE), whose lost *Argonautica* predated the extant one by Valerius Flaccus (d. ca. 92 CE).

Ariadne: daughter of King Minos of Crete. After she helped Theseus kill the Minotaur and escape the Labyrinth, she fled with him to Naxos, was abandoned there by him, but was rescued by Bacchus, who made her his wife; when she died, Bacchus honored her by turning her wedding garland into a constellation, "Ariadne's Crown."

Arician: Aricia was a city at the foot of the Alban Hills famous for Lake Nemi and the temple of Diana Nemorensis; associated with Diana was the nymph Egeria, who according to legend advised the Roman king Numa (see below).

Arion: a divine horse, the offspring of Poseidon and Demeter; his original owner gave him to Hercules, who in turn gave him to Adrastus, one of the Seven against Thebes, whose life the horse saved.

Armenia / Armenians: the region in eastern Anatolia north of Syria and Mesopotamia; it became a Roman protectorate in Pompey's settlement in Asia Minor and was the object of a tug-of-war between Rome and the Parthians. Vespasian made it part of the province of Cappadocia.

Arruntius Stella: a young senatorial aristocrat in the early stages of a public career, and an elegiac love poet, to whom Statius addresses the preface of book 1 and whose wedding he celebrates in 1.2.

Ascanius: the son of Aeneas, stepson of Lavinia, and founder of Alba Longa.

Asclepius: the god of medicine, son of Apollo, with a temple and healing shrine at Pergamum and another at Epidaurus, to whom Earinus dedicates a lock of his hair in 3.4.

Ascraean: of Ascra, the Boeotian birthplace of Hesiod (see below). The phrase "old Ascraean . . . poe[t]" (5.3.204) refers to Hesiod as the author of *Works and Days,* a sort of farmers' almanac.

Asia / Asian: the Roman province of Asia, i.e., Asia Minor, where both Rutilius Gallicus (1.4.121–22) and Vettius Bolanus (5.2.81–82) served as governor. However, "Asian cardamom" (2.6.128) is actually "Assyrian" (2.6.88L), so there I am using "Asian" loosely to mean "Eastern."

Astyanax: the son of Hector and Andromache, thrown to his death from a tower by Ulysses.

Aswan: the modern name for Syene, in southern Egypt; stone from there was red granite.

Atalanta: in myth, a fleet-footed huntress; she promised to marry the man who successfully ran a race against her but killed the suitors who lost. Hippomenes, with Venus' help, finally defeated her.

Atedius Melior: the dedicatee of book 2, which also contains poems about his late beloved Glaucias (2.1), his villa with an odd plane tree (2.3), and his dead parrot (2.4).

Athamas: the husband of Ino (one of the daughters of Cadmus), who killed his son Learchus when he was driven mad by Juno for raising Bacchus.

Athena: the patron goddess of Athens and deity of strategy, wisdom, weaving, and the olive; identified with the Roman Minerva.
Athena's "Victory" is the figure of Nike in the right hand of Phidias' statue of Athena in the Parthenon.
"Athena's priestess": see Auge.

Athens' Virgin: Athena/Minerva.

(Mount) Athos: the Persian king Xerxes cut a canal through it, because an earlier Persian fleet that had attempted to sail around it had been destroyed in a storm.

Atlas: the Titan who held up the sky on his shoulders; also identified with the Atlas Mountains in North Africa.

Atreus: the father of Agamemnon and Menelaus, brother of Thyestes. Thyestes became the lover of his sister-in-law Aerope and got from her the golden ram on which Atreus' rule over Mycenae depended.

Attis: Cybele's consort, who died when he was driven to castrate himself.

Auge: a princess of Tegea and priestess of Athena; she was raped by a drunken Hercules and gave birth to Telephus.

Augustus: Gaius Octavius (63 BCE–14 CE), first emperor of Rome.

Aventine: one of the seven hills of Rome.

Avernus: a lake in southern Italy near Pozzuoli, believed to be an entrance to the Underworld. Sometimes the name is used to refer to the Underworld itself: e.g., "Avernus' realm" (4.3.167) and "Avernal nymphs" (2.6.146).

Babylon: one of the greatest cities of the ancient world, proverbial for wealth; it was one of Alexander's conquests and the place where he died.

Bacchus: the god of wine, son of Jupiter and Semele; his name is also used to refer to wine itself.

Bactra: one of Alexander's conquests; it became capital of the Parthian satrapy of Bactria.

Baetis: a river near Corduba (modern Cordova), the modern Guadalquivir.

Bagrada: a sluggish river near Carthage.

Baiae: a fashionable seaside resort on the Bay of Naples, noted for hot springs.

Balkan: "Balkan mountains" at 4.3.174 refers to the Thracian Mount Haemus; at 4.7.14 the phrase refers to Dalmatian mountains.

(Monte) Barbaro: Mons Gaurus, northwest of Pozzuoli, a noted wine district, visible from Pollius' villa. It marks the southern end of Domitian's highway, as Monte Massico, near Sinuessa, marks the northern end.

Battle of the Frogs: a mock-epic poem, also called *Battle of the Mice and Frogs,* once attributed to Homer.

Bauli: a suburb of Baiae (see above).

Berber: used to translate either *Nomadae* or *Numidae;* Numidian marble, the type referred to as *giallo antico,* was yellow with red veins.

Black Sea: used to translate several Latin words: *Tomis,* where Ovid was exiled; *Pontus,* location of hazelnut groves; *Phasis,* home of Amazons and a source of pheasants; and *Scythia,* another reference to Amazons.

Blaesus: a friend of Melior who predeceased Glaucias, and for whom Melior established a fund for the Poets' Society to commemorate his birthday annually.

Bolanus: Vettius Bolanus, father of Crispinus

Briseis: the captive woman taken from Achilles by Agamemnon.

Britain: the Roman imperial province of Britannia, where Claudius Etruscus' father went with Caligula, whence Abascantus receives military reports, and where Crispinus' father Bolanus served. Sometimes (5.1.91L, 5.2.55L) Statius refers to Britain as *Thule.*

Brontes: one of the Cyclopes, who make lightning bolts for Jupiter.

Brutus: 1. Lucius Junius Brutus, traditional founder of the Roman Republic (1.4.65); according to Livy 2.7, the women of Rome mourned his death for a year, as they would a father, because he had avenged the honor of a woman (i.e., Lucretia, who had been raped by the son of Rome's last king).
2. Marcus Junius Brutus (ca. 85–42 BCE), one of Caesar's assassins and the author of works derided by Statius as boring (probably speeches), contained in a volume he received from Grypus as a Saturnalia present (4.9.26).

Cacus: the monster killed by Hercules when he came to Rome, an account of which Virgil has King Evander tell Aeneas; Virgil locates his lair on the Aventine Hill.

Cadiz: modern name of Gades; the Greek geographer Strabo mentions a shrine to Hercules there.

Caelian: one of the seven hills of Rome, where Melior's house was located.

Caesar: synonymous with the emperor, as when Melior's parrot hails "great Caesar's name" (2.4.36).

Caligula: Gaius Caesar, the third Roman emperor (12–41 CE); "an *as* issued / by Caligula" (4.9.28–29) alludes to the fact that apparently the bronze *as* coins issued by Caligula were not legal tender after his reign as a result of his *damnatio memoriae,* when all references to him (in inscriptions, on coins, etc.) were eliminated.

Callimachus: a Greek scholar and poet (ca. 305–ca. 240 BCE); he was the first to catalogue the library at Alexandria; his poetry, characterized by learning and refinement, was very influential on Roman poetry.

Calliope: the chief Muse and mother of Orpheus; in 2.7 Statius has her prophesy at Lucan's birth.

Camillus: Marcus Furius Camillus, who came out of exile to save Rome from the Gallic invasion in 387 BCE.

Campania: the region of Italy from Latium to Sorrento between the Apennines and the Tyrrhenian Sea; a fertile volcanic plain with a mild climate.

Cannae: the site in southern Italy where a Roman army suffered a great defeat at the hands of Hannibal in 216 BCE.

Canopus: a proverbially luxurious bathing resort in Egypt, named for Menelaus' Spartan helmsman who was supposedly buried there.

the Cape: see Cape Misenum.

Cape Bonvoyage: this is my version (2.2.101) of *Euploea* (2.2.79L). *Euploea* refers to the temple of Aphrodite Euploia on a promontory visible from Pollius' villa at Sorrento; the Greek word *euploia* means "a fair voyage."

Cape Misenum: a promontory north of Naples, visible from Pollius' villa at Sorrento, that is supposedly the burial place of Misenus (see below). Agrippa made its harbor the main Roman naval base.

Capitoline: used to refer to one of the seven hills of Rome, to the temple of Jupiter located there (which Domitian rebuilt after a fire in 80 CE), and to the games established by Domitian in honor of Capitoline Jupiter, for which the prize was an oak wreath.

Capri: the island near Naples, site of a lighthouse; called "wealthy" (3.1.180; 128L) because of the buildings of Tiberius there (Vollmer [1898] 1971, 390).

Capua: a city in Campania, supposedly founded by Capys, one of the companions of Aeneas (*Aeneid* 10.145).

Carrara: the site of famous quarries from which Michelangelo got his marble; it is near Luna, the home of Marcellus' friend Gallus.

Carthage: a city in North Africa, a Phoenician colony, which fought three wars against Rome and was annihilated at the end of the third; during the Second Punic War, Hannibal crossed the Alps and invaded Italy. In myth, it is the kingdom Dido was founding when Aeneas was shipwrecked on her shores.

Carystos: the source of Carystian marble, the kind called *cipollino verde ondato*, with wavy green veins.

Caspian Gates: a narrow pass in the mountains between Media and Parthia.

Castalia: a spring at Delphi, associated with Apollo and the Muses.

Castor: one of the Twins, the horseman; he is sometimes associated with the Evening Star, as his brother Pollux is with the Morning Star.

Cathay: an archaic/poetic name for China (see below).

Catillus: the legendary founder of Tibur/Tivoli.

Cato: Marcus Porcius Cato (95–46 BCE), the staunch opponent of Julius Caesar. Allied with Pompey in the civil war, he committed suicide after Caesar's victory at Thapsus; he was proverbial as a personification of republicanism.

Caunos: a city in Asia Minor (southeast Caria near Lycia) famous for its figs.

Celer: see Maecius Celer.

Censor: one of two officials, elected every five years for an eighteen-month term to conduct the *census*, the official list of citizens, and, more generally, to supervise morals; their moral authority derived in part from their ability to strike names from the list. Domitian appointed himself censor for life (*censor perpetuus*) without a colleague.

Centaurs: beings who are half-man and half-horse; Statius follows Virgil (*Aeneid* 6.286) in conceiving of them as denizens of the Underworld.

Cerberus: the three-headed watchdog of Hades.

Ceres: the goddess of grain, identified by the Romans with the Greek Demeter; she is called "Athenian" (4.8.69) because Demeter's Mysteries were celebrated at Eleusis, near Athens.
"The agent sent by Ceres / with grain for all mankind" (4.2.50–51) is Triptolemus.

Chalcis: the chief city in Euboea, or perhaps a place on or near Lesbos (for a full discussion, see the note on 5.3.210).

Charon: the boatman who ferries the souls of the dead across the Styx.

Charybdis: a whirlpool that was one of the mythical menaces at the straits between Reggio and Messina (the other was the sea monster Scylla; see below).

Chatti: a powerful German tribe constantly a menace to Rome; Domitian pushed them back across the Taunus River in 83 and 89 CE, and established a permanently defended frontier there.

China / Chinese: the Romans called the Chinese *Seres* and knew them as a source for silk.

Chios / Chian: a variegated marble from the island of Chios, probably dark with light streaks.

Chiron: the kindly Centaur, knowledgeable about medicinal herbs, who helped Theseus woo Thetis and served as a tutor for Jason and Achilles.

Cilicia / Cilician: a region of southern Asia Minor; it produced the best saffron.

Circe: the enchantress who turned some of Ulysses' companions into animals—pigs, according to Homer, but wolves in Statius' account; the promontory of Circeii was supposedly hers.

Cithaeron: a mountain near Thebes; the highest in Boeotia, it was sacred to Bacchus.

Clashing Rocks: the Symplegades, one of the obstacles overcome by the Argonauts.

Claudia: 1. a Vestal accused of unchastity; to prove her innocence, she single-handedly towed the ship that was bringing the Great Mother Cybele to Rome in 204 BCE from where it had gotten stuck on its way up the Tiber.
2. the name of Statius' wife.

Claudius: the fourth Roman emperor (10 BCE–54 CE), one of those under whom Claudius Etruscus' father served.

Claudius Etruscus: son of the freedman Claudius who became Domitian's freedman in charge of finances; addressee of 1.5 (about the baths he built) and 3.3 (a consolation for the death of his father).

Cleopatra: the famous queen of Egypt (69–32 BCE), lover of Julius Caesar and Mark Antony; with the latter, she was defeated at the naval battle of Actium.

Clio. Muse of history.

Clotho: one of the three Fates, she spins the thread of life.

Colchis: the home of the witch Medea, who, when her husband Jason was about to re-marry, killed their two children.

Concord: the personification of harmony within the state; she had a temple on the slope of the Capitoline overlooking the Roman Forum, behind Domitian's colossal equestrian statue.

Corbulo: Gnaeus Domitius Corbulo, a general who served under Claudius and Nero in Germany and in the East; he was the commander under whom Crispinus' father Bolanus served. Nero forced him to commit suicide in 67 CE, but his daughter became Domitian's wife.

Cordova: the modern name for Corduba, birthplace of Lucan (see below).

Corinna: a female Boeotian lyric poet, perhaps an older contemporary of Pindar (see below).

Corinth: the city at the Isthmus, where the Isthmian Games honored Palaemon, who was said to have arrived there with his mother Ino after escaping Thebes and murderous Athamas. Statius alludes to a covered portico leading up to a temple of Bacchus there; Venus's temple on Acrocorinth (the acropolis of Corinth), famous for temple prosti-tution; the valuable alloy known as Corinthian bronze, which supposedly came into existence accidentally when all the metal in the city melted in the fire of 146 BCE; and Nero's attempt (unsuccessful, as were many others') to cut a canal through the Isth-mus.

Corycian: Corycia was a place in Cilicia.

Cos: one of the Sporades islands, home of the poets Philetas and Theocritus, and the place where Hippocrates laid the foundations of medical science.

Crete / Cretan: the home of Ariadne (see above), whom Statius calls "the clever Cretan" (2.6.39) and "the shining Cretan" (5.1.314, unless that refers to the goddess Dic-tynna/Diana). In historical times, Crete was an important source of grain for the Romans; it was also a place where Flavius Ursus, the addressee of 2.6, apparently owned property.
The "Cretan ivy crown" (1.2.303) is the one Bacchus wore in mourning for Ariadne. The "primal Cretan smith" (4.6.60) is one of the Dactyli, inventors of metallurgy, who tend Jupiter's forges under Mount Ida; Statius identifies them with the Telchines ("the Telchines in Idaean caves," 4.6.47L), the first to work iron and bronze, who are usu-ally associated with Rhodes.

Crimean: my "bare Crimean steppes" (3.2.118) translates *Cimmeriumque chaos* (3.2.92L; lit., "Cimmerian darkness"); the Cimmerians migrated from southern Russia across the Caucasus to Asia Minor.

Crispinus: son of Vettius Bolanus and addressee of 5.2, which celebrates his commission as military tribune by Domitian.

Croesus: the last king of Lydia (d. 546 BCE), proverbial for his wealth.

Cumae / Cumaean: the earliest Greek colony in Italy, founded on the coast of Naples by settlers from Chalcis in Euboea; the location of Apollo's oracle, the Sibyl, Aeneas' guide to the Underworld. Cumae was also famous for pottery, including a common, inexpensive type.

Cupid: the god of love (*Amor*), son of Venus, sometimes conceived as a group of "Cupids" (*Amores*).

Cures: a Sabine town important in early Roman history.

Curtius: Manlius Curtius, who is said to have jumped armed and on horseback into a chasm in the Roman Forum, to fulfill an oracle about saving his country; he thereby gave his name to the resulting *Lacus Curtius* (Curtius Lake).

Cybele: the Phrygian Great Mother, whose young consort Attis died from self-castration; her worship was imported to Rome as a response to the crisis of the Second Punic War.

Cyclopes: mythical one-eyed builders and craftsmen, who forge thunderbolts under Mount Etna; they are credited with ancient masonry fortifications at places such as Tiryns and Mycenae.

Cyprus: an island with two famous sanctuaries of Venus, at Paphos and Amathus, and another at Idalium. Much of Venus' mythology (e.g., the story of Pygmalion) is connected with Cyprus, and historically the Greek Aphrodite was likely influenced by contact on Cyprus with Phoenicians and their goddess Astarte.

Cyrene: a city in North Africa, the birthplace of the Hellenistic scholar and poet Callimachus (see above). In Roman times, it was part of the province of Crete and Cyrenaica, an important grain-producing region, where Flavius Ursus, the addressee of 2.6, owned property.

Cythera: an island off the southern tip of the Peloponnese; in myth, near the place where Venus was born from the sea.

Dacians: agricultural tribes living across the Danube; when first united ca. 60 BCE, they expanded into southern Russian, Hungary, and the Balkan Peninsula to the Roman border. Reunited again later, they posed a threat, in response to which Domitian mounted campaigns in 86 and 89 CE; the second of these "Dacian Wars" was the subject of the lost poem with which Statius won the Alban Games in 90 CE.

Dalmatia / Dalmatian: an imperial Roman province and important source of gold

Damascus: a city in Syria, which Statius calls "devout" (1.6.15; *pia*, 1.6.14L) because native, Greek, and Persian gods were all worshiped there (Vollmer [1898] 1971, 305); a source of plums.

Danube: the name either for the whole river or for the upper Danube (the lower Danube was the Ister).

Daphne: the nymph pursued by Apollo who was turned into a laurel tree to save her from his assault; hence, the laurel (in Greek, *daphnē*) is Apollo's tree.

Daunus: legendary king of Apulia.

Dawn: the goddess of the sunrise, whose mortal husband Tithonus suffered from having been granted immortality without accompanying eternal youth.

Decius: Publius Decius Mus, the name shared by three men—father, son, and grandson (mid-4th–early 3rd c. BCE)—each of whom is said to have ensured a Roman victory by "devoting" himself, that is, formally sacrificing himself by charging into the enemy to his death.

Delos: an Aegean island, the birthplace of Apollo.

Delphi / Delphic: the site of Apollo's temple and most famous oracle, where the Pythian Games were held at which the prize was a laurel wreath; attacked by Galatians (a Celtic people in Asia Minor) in 279 BCE.

Devotion: one of my translations (5.2.133) for personified *Pietas* (5.2 92L).

Diana: the goddess of the hunt, identified with the Greek Artemis; as "the nether world's Diana" (5.3.372) she is identified with Hecate. Diana had a temple and grove at Aricia on Lake Nemi at the foot of the Alban Hills, where the priest was a runaway slave who had killed his predecessor; at her festival on 13 August, the priest ran with torches to the grove and the lake. Statius invents a myth in which Diana rescues the nymph Pholoe from rape by Pan and turns her into the plane tree in Melior's garden (2.3).

Dictys: the fisherman who found the baby Perseus (see below) and raised him.

Dido: in Virgil's *Aeneid*, the legendary queen of Carthage who hosts Aeneas when he is shipwrecked there, and falls in love with him through the machinations of Juno and Venus.

Dindymon: a mountain in Phrygia, sacred to Cybele.

Diomedes: a Greek warrior at Troy; on the night the city fell, he stole a statue of Minerva (the Palladium) from her temple there; Romans believed it was kept in the shrine of Vesta.

Dionysus: the god of wine, also called Bacchus.

Dirce: a spring at Thebes.

(the) Dog / Dog Star: Sirius (see Icarius).

Domitian: the last emperor of the Flavian dynasty (51–96 CE), during whose reign Statius composed the *Silvae* and all the rest of his extant work.

Doris: the mother of the Nereids (see below); synonymous with the sea.

Duty: one of my translations (5.3.94) for the personified *Pietas* (5.3.72L).

Earinus: Flavius Earinus, Domitian's eunuch freedman wine steward, at whose request Statius wrote 3.4 to accompany the lock of hair he was dedicating to Asclepius at Pergamum.

Egeria: a nymph associated with Diana at Nemi, believed to have been consulted by King Numa (see below).

Egypt / Egyptian: the imperial Roman province, important supplier of grain to Rome. Egypt was also an exporter of cinnamon, granite (Syenite), and notoriously quick-witted slaves; the home of the phoenix; and the first stage of Maecius Celer's trip to his post in Syria. In myth, Hercules killed the sacrilegious Egyptian king Busiris, who perversely sacrificed guests to the patron of guests, Jupiter; historically, it was the site of Pompey's murder.

Elis: region in northwest Peloponnese in the valley of the Alpheus River in which Olympia is located. The Eleans presided over the Olympic Games.

Elysium: the part of the Underworld which is the realm of the blessed.

Emperor(s): used to translate *Caesar* and *dux* (leader).

Ennius: Quintus Ennius, an early Roman poet (239–169 BCE), whose works included dramas, satires, and the epic *Annales,* which established the Greek hexameter as the meter of Roman epic.

Envy: envy personified (*Invidia*).

Epicurus: an Athenian philosopher (341–270 BCE), whose school was located in his home and famous garden; he espoused detachment and avoidance of disturbance as the source of "pleasure." Statius describes at least two of his addressees, Vopiscus and especially Pollius, as living in accordance with Epicurean tenets.

Epidaurus: the site on the Saronic Gulf of a sanctuary of Asclepius.

Erato: the Muse of love poetry, whom Statius invokes at the beginning of one of his two odes (4.7), identifying her also as the Muse of his epic poem.

Erymanthus: a mountain in Arcadia; capturing the Erymanthian boar was one of Hercules' Labors.

Eryx: a Sicilian mountain, the site of a famous temple of Venus.

Ethiopians: in Homer, a far-off people whom the gods occasionally visit.

(Mount) Etna: the volcano in Sicily, under which Vulcan had his forge, and near which Proserpina was abducted by Hades.

"Étoile": my French version of *Asteris,* Arruntius Stella's Greek pseudonym for Violentilla in his elegiac love poems.

Etrusca: Claudius Etruscus' mother (3.3.145).

Etruscus: see Claudius Etruscus.

Euboea: a long island off the coast of Boeotia; Euboeans from Chalcis colonized Cumae, and hence the Cumaean Sibyl has "Euboean laurels" (4.3.147).

Eumaeus: Ulysses' faithful swineherd.

Eumelus: the hero, prominent citizen, or god represented by a statue at Naples which had on its shoulder the dove Apollo sent to guide the Siren Parthenope to Naples (4.8.67; see also the note on line 68).

Euphrates: a river in Mesopotamia, usually crossed by Roman armies by a bridge at Zeugma; the eastern boundary of the Empire.
 The "rogue Euphrates" (5.1.120; *vagus Euphrates,* 5.1.89L) is more literally the "wandering Euphrates," so called because of its annual floods.

Euripus: the narrow arm of the sea separating Euboea from the Greek mainland.

Europa: the daughter of the king of Tyre; she was abducted by Jupiter in the guise of a bull.

Eurotas: a river in Sparta.

Eursytheus: the king of the Argolid for whom Hercules performed his Labors.

Eurydice: Orpheus' wife, whom he would have rescued from the Underworld had he not looked back before reaching the upper world. The "rule Orpheus once broke" (5.3.79) is more literally "conditions for Orpheus" (*Orpheae* .. *leges,* 5.3.60L), i.e., the terms on which Hades agreed to release her.

(King) Evander: a legendary king at Rome with a palace on the Palatine, who became Aeneas' ally and whose son Pallas was killed by Turnus.

Evening Star: identified with Castor, as the Morning Star was identified with his twin, Pollux.

Falerno: the proverbially excellent Falernian wine.

Fate, Fates: the three sisters who spin and ultimately cut the thread of a person's destiny. Statius uses the Latin terms *Fatum* and *Fata,* as well as *Parca* and *Parcae*—the Latin equivalent of the Greek *Moirai;* he also refers to them as the Sisters (*sorores*), or uses the specific names Lachesis, Clotho, and Atropos.
"Fate's white thread" (4.8.27) is a lucky one.

Father: "his country's Father," i.e., the emperor's title *pater patriae.*

Felix: see Pollius Felix.

Flaminian Way: the Roman road which crossed to the Tiber's right bank over the Mulvian Bridge (the route to Glaucias' pyre, by law outside the city limits).

Flavian: the dynasty consisting of Vespasian, Titus, and Domitian.
"Flavian heaven" (4.3.25) is the *Templum Gentis Flaviae* (the Temple of the Flavian Family).

Flavius Ursus: addressee of 2.6, about whom nothing is known other than what Statius tells us.

Formiae: the place in Italy identified as the home of the cannibal Laestrygonians of the *Odyssey* (1.3.123–23); literally, "the shore of bloody Antiphates" (1.3.84–85L; Antiphates was their king).

Fortune: the Roman goddess of luck, Fortuna.

Forum: Statius not only refers to the Roman Forum (e.g., 1.1.2–3), the original main square in Rome (where the colossal equestrian statue of Domitian was erected), but also to the Forum Iulium dedicated by Julius Caesar in 46 BCE, in which the Temple of Venus Genetrix was located (1.1.130), and the Forum Transitorium built by Domitian ("the newest Forum," 4.1.22).

Founder: Romulus, the mythical founder of Rome (5.2.156).

Fury, Furies: spirit(s) of vengeance for spilled blood, depicted as inhabiting the Underworld, brandishing torches, and having snakes for hair; sometimes Statius uses the Latin word *Furiae,* and sometimes the Greek *Erinys* (singular) or *Eumenides* (plural).

Galatia: the territory in Asia Minor settled by Celtic people, who attacked Delphi in 279 BCE; also, a Roman province since 25 BCE, where Rutilius Gallicus served.

Gallic: having to do with Gaul, the territory roughly equivalent to modern France and Belgium that was made a Roman province by Julius Caesar.
"Gallic invaders' madness" (5.3.269) is literally "the Senones' madness" (*Senonum furias*, 5.3.198L); the Senones led the Gauls who captured Rome in 390 BCE.

Gallicus: see Rutilius Gallicus.

Gallio: one of Lucan's paternal uncles.

Gallus: a mutual friend of Statius and Marcellus.

Ganges: the river in India to which Bacchus traveled before returning to Greece.

Ganymede: the Trojan prince who was abducted from Mount Ida by Jupiter, and became cupbearer to the gods.

Gates of War: this phrase (4.3.12) translates *limina bellicosa Iani* (4.3.9L, lit., "the warlike threshold of Janus"); although it refers to Domitian's new temple of Janus Quadrifons, it conjures up the earlier Janus Geminus, which was left open in time of war and shut in peace.

Gauls: enemies of Rome, who attacked the city on several occasions, including in 390 BCE, when they captured the city, and in 387 BCE, when Camillus saved it.

Gemini: the Twins, Castor and Pollux, whose temple was located in the Roman Forum.

German: the phrase "your German lines" (4.2.95) refers to Domitian's second campaign against the Chatti in January 89, one of the subjects of the lost poem with which Statius won the Alban Games of 90 (a four-line fragment is thought to have survived).

Germany's Victor: *Germanicus,* the honorific title Domitian received for his victory against the Chatti in 83 CE.

Geta: Vitorius Marcellus' son (4.4.92), for whose education Quintilian wrote the *Institutio Oratoria* (ca. 96 CE), dedicating it to Marcellus.

Getes: the Getae, a Thracian tribe on the lower Danube.

Giants: mythical beings who laid siege to Olympus by piling up mountains to reach it; they were defeated by Jupiter and the other Olympians in the Gigantomachy (battle of the Giants). According to one version, that battle took place in the volcanic Phlegraean Fields in the Bay of Naples.

Gilead: "balm of Gilead" is my translation for several different phrases; at 2.1.223 it is the equivalent of *Palaestini . . . liquores* (2.1.161L); at 3.2.183, *opobalsama* (3.2.141L); and at 5.1.288–89, *Hebraei . . . liquores* (5.1.213L).

Glaucias: the slave boy whom Atedius Melior adopted, and in consolation for whose death Statius addressed 2.1 to Melior.

Glaucus: a Greek fisherman who ate an herb which he had seen bring his catch back to life and was turned into a fish-tailed minor sea deity.

Gnat: a poem (*Culex*) whose traditional attribution as an early work of Virgil is rejected by modern scholars

Goat: the constellation Capella, whose rising signals the beginning of stormy weather

Good Luck: Fortuna.

Grace: one of the three Graces, minor goddesses often represented in association with Aphrodite.

Grypus: see Plotius Grypus.

Guinea: the "fowl in humid southern Guinea hunted" (2.4.35) are more literally "[birds] which Numidians catch in the humid south" (2.4.28L), which are the kind we call "guinea fowl."

Hades: the ruler of the Underworld, whose queen is Proserpina, whose watchdog is Cerberus, and one of whose judges is Aeacus.

Hamadryad: a tree nymph.

Hannibal: the great Carthaginian general (247–183 BCE).

Healer: Asclepeius, son of Apollo, whom Jupiter once blasted with a thunderbolt for bringing Hippolytus back to life (see Theseus).

Hebe: the wife of Hercules on Olympus, and a cupbearer to the gods; her name means "youth."

Hebrus: the river in Thrace down which Orpheus' head floated as it continued to sing after the Maenads tore him to pieces.

Hector: a son of Priam, the preeminent Trojan warrior, and the father of Astyanax; Achilles killed Hector to avenge the death of Patroclus and then dragged the corpse behind his chariot.

Helen: daughter of Leda, sister of the Twins, and wife of Menelaus; her abduction by the Trojan Paris precipitated the Trojan War. Her "star" (really an electrical discharge similar to Saint Elmo's fire) was considered unlucky for sailors, as her brothers the Twins (in the form of Saint Elmo's fire) were thought to be lucky. A single such "star" was thought to be Helen's; a pair, her brothers'.

Helicon: the tallest mountain in Boeotia, home of the Muses.

Helle: she and her brother Phrixus escaped their stepmother Ino on the ram with the golden fleece, but she fell off into the body of water which now bears her name (Hellespont literally means "Helle's sea").

Hellespont: the Dardenelles, the narrow strait dividing Europe from Asia; the narrowest point, between Sestos and Abydos, across which Leander swam nightly to be with his love, Hero.

Hera: the Greek goddess whom the Romans identified with Juno; the sister and wife of Zeus, and persecutor of Heracles.

Herculaneum: the town named after Hercules and buried, like Pompeii, by the eruption of Vesuvius in 79 CE; hence Statius calls it "the land Hercules failed" (5.3.222).

Hercules: the hero known to the Greeks as Heracles, son of Alcmena and Jupiter, who prolonged the night of his conception; he was persecuted by Juno and compelled to perform the Twelve Labors (including killing the Nemean lion and capturing the Erymanthian boar) for King Eurystheus; during the Labors, Hercules killed the wicked Egyptian king Busiris, who sacrificed guests to Jupiter. When King Laomedon of Troy reneged on a bargain, Hercules fought a campaign against him, allied with Telamon, brother of Peleus; after his beloved squire Hylas was abducted by nymphs, Hercules left the Argonauts to search for him. Pollius Felix built him a larger shrine on his property at Sorrento; he had a famous temple in Cadiz, and one at Tivoli where oracles were given.

Hermes: the Greek god whom the Romans identified with Mercury, born on Mount Cyllene in Arcadia; he was the messenger of Zeus and the guide of souls to the Underworld. Statius invokes *proles Cyllenia* (2.1.189L) in the context of reporting about the dead Glaucias; hence my translation "Hermes, Guide of Souls" (2.1.261).

Hermus: the gold-bearing river in Lydia where Bacchus supposedly gilds his horns.

Hernican: the Hernici were an ancient Latin tribe whose territory included a heavily wooded part of the Apennines.

Hesiod: the Greek poet (fl. ca. 700 BCE) from Ascra in Boeotia who composed the *Theogony* (a sort of hymn to Zeus which treats his rise to power after several previous generations of gods) and *Works and Days* (a didactic work that is something of a farmers' almanac).

Hesperus: the Evening Star.

Hippomenes: the young man who, with the assistance of Venus, successfully ran a footrace against Atalanta to win her hand in marriage.

Homer: the Greek poet (8th c. BCE?) of the *Iliad* and the *Odyssey*, to whom a mock epic (*Battle of the Frogs,* also known as *Battle of the Mice and Frogs*) was once also attributed.

Hungarian: the phrase "Hungarian peaks" (5.2.195) is my version of *iuga Pannoniae* ("the ridges of Pannonia," 5.2.135L; Pannonia is a Roman province south and west of the Danube).

Hyacinthus: the Spartan youth whom Apollo loved but accidentally killed with a discus, and commemorated with the hyacinth flower.

Hydra: the many-headed water snake in Lerna's swamp, whose killing was one of Hercules' Labors; extrapolating from Virgil's Centaurs and Scyllas (*Aeneid* 6.286), Statius adds Hydras to the monstrous denizens of the Underworld (5.3.388).

Hyele: a Greek name for Velia on the Lucanian coast, where Aeneas' helmsman Palinurus washed ashore; also the birthplace of Statius' father. Its better-known Greek name is Elea, home of the Eleatic philosophers Zeno and Parmenides.

Hylas: Hercules' beloved squire.

Ibycus: a Greek lyric poet (6th c. BCE) from Sicily, who supposedly invoked a flock of cranes to avenge his murder by a band of robbers.

Icarius: the first mortal Bacchus taught to make wine; the farmers to whom he gave it to drink thought he had poisoned them, and killed him. After his dog Sirius led his daughter Erigone to his corpse, she hung herself from grief.

(Mount) Ida: mountain near Troy, site of Ganymede's abduction by Jupiter; also a mountain on Crete.

Idumaea: a region to the south of Judaea, made part of that Roman province in 6 CE; the name was used loosely to refer to Judaea or Palestine.

"Idumaea's groves" (3.2.179) are "sweet" because they contain balsam trees from whose gum is derived *opsobalsama,* one of the aromatics I have translated as "balm of Gilead" (see Gilead).

Ilia: also known as Rhea Silvia, the daughter of Numitor, king of Alba Longa, whose brother Amulius usurped the throne and made Ilia a Vestal Virgin to prevent her from bearing legal heirs to the throne. Impregnated by Mars, she became the mother of Romulus and Remus; when Amulius threw her and her baby sons into the Tiber, she became the river's bride.

Ilium: synonymous with Troy.

Indian: "Indian tusks" (3.3.124) are the elephant ivory for which India was famous; "Indian maenads" (4.2.69) are the followers Bacchus acquired during his travels there, as are "Indian captives" (4.6.86).

Indies: archaic for "India."

Ino: daughter of Cadmus, sister of Semele, and aunt of Bacchus; Juno persecuted her and her husband Athamas for protecting Bacchus; she and her son Melicertes escaped from Thebes, diving into the sea at the Isthmus at Corinth, and became sea deities named Leucothea and Palaemon, respectively.

Ionian: the Ionian Sea was another name for the Adriatic, between the Balkan Peninsula and Italy, or even Sicily; hence, Alpheus pursues Arethusa from Elis to Sicily "under Ionian waves" (1.3.98).

Iris: the rainbow; Juno's messenger (as Mercury is Jupiter's).

Ischia: the modern name for Inarime, the largest island near Naples, which is visible from Pollius' villa.

Isis: the Egyptian goddess whom the Greeks identified with Io, daughter of the Argive river-god Inachus; after Jupiter had changed her into a heifer to hide her from his wife, Juno sent a gadfly which drove her all the way to Egypt.

Ismarus: a city in Thrace, famous for its wine.

Istanbul: the modern name for ancient Byzantium, where an abundance of mackerel were caught and shipped to Italy (4.9.17).

Ister: the lower Danube.

Isthmian: the Isthmian Games were held at Corinth in honor of Poseidon (said originally to honor Palaemon; see below).

Ithacan: Ulysses was king of Ithaca; hence "Ithacan 'wolves'" (1.3.125) are members of his crew transformed by Circe, and "those Ithacan suitors" (5.1.77) are the ones who beleaguered Penelope in her husband's long absence.

Janus: the two-faced god of January who addresses Domitian on inauguration day, and whom Domitian has "linked to Peace, / who's close to him" (4.1.19–20) by building a new temple in the Forum Transitorium, not far from the Temple of Peace. From Janus' temple at the foot of the Capitoline ("martial Janus' grove," 2.3.14), the nymph Pholoe begins to flee Pan (Janus is "martial" because his temple was open in wartime, closed in peace).

Jason: the leader of the Argonauts, and Medea's unfaithful husband.

Jerusalem: the capital of Palestine, it was destroyed by Titus in 70 CE.

Jove: see Jupiter.
"[O]ur Italian 'Jove'" (3.4.27) is Domitian.
"Jove's Games" are the Capitoline Games.
"Tarpeian Jove's temple" (3.4.158) is the temple of Capitoline Jupiter (it is "Tarpeian" because the Tarpeian Rock was near the Capitoline temple).

Jubilee: the New Age Jubilee (literally, the Secular Games) were held by Domitian in 88 CE (see also the introduction).

Judaea / Judaean: the Roman province
"[G]roves Judaea planted" (5.2.199) translates *silvas ponentis Idumes* (5.2.139L; lit., "of Idume planting groves"; see Idumaea).
The "Judaean triumph" (3.3.182) is the one celebrated in 71 CE by Titus and Vespasian for the capture of Jerusalem.

Judge: Aeacus is "the Judge below" (3.3.20).

Julian Basilica: the Basilica built in the Roman Forum by Julius Caesar; it and the Aemilian Basilica flanked Domitian's equestrian statue.

Julian Law: the *lex Iulia de adulteriis*, a law dating from the reign of Augustus, which introduced severe penalties for adultery.

Julius Menecrates: the son-in-law of Pollius, addressee of 4.8.

Juno: the sister and wife of Jupiter, the goddess of marriage, identified with the Greek Hera; she brought about the incineration of Semele by tricking Semele into asking Jupiter to come to her as he did to his wife. Juno had a temple near Pollius' villa at Sorrento.
"Juno's bird-to-be" (5.4.16) is the hundred-eyed Argus, whom Juno posted to guard Io-as-heifer, and whose many eyes became those in the peacock's tail.
"Juno's handmaid" (5.1.137) is Iris.
The "nether Juno" (2.1.200) is Proserpina.
"Rome's own 'Juno'" (3.4.27) is Domitian's wife, Domitia.

Jupiter: the chief deity of the Roman pantheon, identified with the Greek Zeus; the temple of Jupiter Optimus Maximus was on the Capitoline. Roman imperial ideology identified the emperor with Jupiter as his deputy on earth (see also the introduction). In myth, Zeus/Jupiter is notorious for disguising himself to seduce mortal women: as a swan for Leda; a bull, for Europa; a shower of gold, for Danaë; and her own husband Amphitryon, for Alcmena.
"'[B]egin with Jupiter'" (1.pref.) echoes Virgil *Eclogue* 3.60; the proverb that one should start with Jupiter appears in the first line of both Callimachus' *Hymn* 1 (to Zeus) and Aratus' *Phaenomena*.

Labyrinth: the maze King Minos of Crete built to cage the Minotaur; after Theseus killed the monster there, he found his way out by using the thread Ariadne had given him.

Laconian: a green marble, *verde antico*, from near the Eurotas River in Sparta.

Lady Luck: Fortuna.

Laestrygonians: a race of cannibals Ulysses encountered; Formiae (see above) was identified as their home.

Latium / Latin: the area of Italy in which Rome lay.
The "Latin Road" (4.4.7, the Via Latina) ran southeast from Rome until it merged with the Via Appia at Casilinum in Campania.

Laurentian: the "Laurentian" acres of Turnus (1.3.120–21) is a reference to Ardea.

Lausus: in the *Aeneid*, the son of the tyrant Mezentius who dies defending his father.

Lavinia: daughter of King Latinus of Lavinium, first betrothed to Turnus, but then promised to Aeneas; the simile of her blush (1.2.326–27; 244–45L) recalls *Aeneid* 12.65–67, in which her blush inflames Turnus to continue fighting the Trojans.

Leader: my translation of *dux*, one of the terms with which Statius refers to the emperor.

Leander: the young man who swam across the Hellespont at its narrowest point every night to be with his beloved Hero.

Leda: the Spartan queen whom Jupiter raped while he was in the form of a swan; she became the mother of Helen and her brothers, the Twins—Castor and Pollux—as well as of Clytemnestra, Agamemnon's wife.

Lemnos / Lemnian: an Aegean island, supposedly the site of Vulcan's forge.
Venus' "Lemnian husband" (1.2.80) is Vulcan, who once trapped her and her lover Mars with a virtually invisible net.

Leo: the constellation, originally the Nemean lion slain and skinned by Hercules.

Lepcis: Lepcis Magna, port city in North Africa and birthplace of Septimius Severus (see below), addressee of 4.5.

Lerna: the swamp where Hercules killed the Hydra; also where the little boy Opheltes was killed by a snake and then honored with the Nemean Games, for which the prize was a wreath of wild celery.

Lethe: the River of Forgetfulness in the Underworld.

Leto: the mother of Apollo and Diana; called Latona by the Romans.

Libya / Libyan: used loosely by Greeks and Romans to mean North Africa.
"[T]hat Libyan giant" (3.1.227) is Antaeus, whom Hercules wrestled.

Linus: son of Apollo; according to one story, when he was killed by dogs after his mother exposed him, Apollo sent a plague until the king (the boy's grandfather) agreed to an annual dirge in his memory.

Liris: largest river near the Volturnus, flowing into the sea north of Sinuessa; the calmness of its lower reaches was proverbial.

Liternum: a swampy region on the Campanian coast.

Locri: city in the toe of Italy, where Flavius Ursus had property.

Lord Who Holds the Bow: Apollo (4.4.123–24); more literally, *arcitenens . . . pater* (4.4.95L) means "the bow-holding father."

Love: *Amor* in Latin, *Eros* in Greek; the god of love, son of Venus/Aphrodite.

Loves: *Amores,* the arrow-shooting band of Cupids associated with Venus.

Lucan: Marcus Annaeus Lucanus, a Spanish-born Roman poet (39–65 CE), forced by Nero to commit suicide; the nephew of the younger Seneca (see below) and Gallio, he wrote an epic about the civil war between Caesar and Pompey. The anniversary of his birth is celebrated in 2.7.

Lucania: a mountainous region in southern Italy.

Lucifer: the Morning Star.

Lucina: the goddess of childbirth, who attends and assists the delivery.

Lucretius: Titus Lucretius Carus, a Roman poet (ca. 94–ca. 55 BCE), author of *De rerum natura,* a didactic treatment of Epicurean philosophy.

Lucrine Lake: a coastal lagoon between Baiae and Naples, famous for its fisheries, especially its oyster beds.

Luna: an Italian source of pure white marble, near Carrara, the source of Michelangelo's marble.

Luperci: at the festival of Lupercalia, these young men, naked except for a goatskin belt, ran and struck bystanders, especially women, with strips of goatskin; this rite was intended to promote fertility.

Lycian: of Lycia in Asia Minor, where Apollo had many cult sites; an epithet of Apollo.

Lycophron: a Greek poet (early 3rd c. BCE) whose *Alexandra,* about the prophecies of Cassandra, is notoriously obscure in content and expression.

Lydian: of Lydia, in Asia Minor. Historically, the Lydian king Croesus was proverbially wealthy; in myth, Hercules atoned for a murder by serving as the slave of the Lydian queen Omphale, who exchanged clothes with him and made him do woman's work.

Lysippus: a Greek sculptor (4th c. BCE); his works included an equestrian statue of Alexander which stood, with Caesar's head replacing the original, in his Forum; a colossus of Zeus at Taranto; and the Hercules statuette which is the subject of 4.6.

Macedon: the region between the Balkan Peninsula and Greece; its most famous king was the great general Alexander (see above), whose conquests became the basis for the Hellenistic kingdoms.

Machaon: the physician and son of Asclepius who tends Menelaus after Paris wounds him in *Iliad* 4.

Maecius Celer: the addressee of 3.2, a bon voyage for his trip to a post in Syria.

Maenad: an ecstatic female follower of Bacchus.

Maia: the mother of Mercury/Hermes.

Manilius Vopiscus: the owner of a villa at Tivoli, subject of 1.3.

Mantua: a town in northern Italy, the birthplace of Virgil (see below).

Marathon: a plain in Attica, home of Icarius (see above) and his daughter Erigone, "[t]hat girl from Marathon" (5.3.98).

Marcellus: see Vitorius Marcellus.

Marcian Aqueduct: see Aqua Marcia.

Marcomani: German tribe against whom Domitian waged war unsuccessfully in 88 CE.

Mars: the Roman god identified with the Greek Ares, lover of Venus; he fathered on Rhea Silvia (also known as Ilia; see above) the twins Romulus and Remus.

Marsian: the Marsi inhabited mountains in central Italy; the snow from those mountains (1.5.36) fed the Marcian Aqueduct.

Marsyas: the flute-playing satyr who challenged Apollo to a music contest and was skinned alive by him after losing.

(Monte) Massico: mountain near Sinuessa at the northern end of Domitian's highway, and the center of the Falernian wine district.

Maximus: see Vibius Maximus.

"Meadowlands": Pollius' estate at Posillipo (2.2.104; *Limon,* 2.2.82L).

Medusa: the Gorgon whom Perseus beheaded.

Megalia Isle: a small island near Naples, the modern Castel dell' Uovo, visible from Pollius' villa at Sorrento.

Meles: a small river near Smyrna, one of the places claiming to be the birthplace of Homer.

Meliboea: the wife of a Greek hero at Troy (Philoctetes, according to Vollmer [1898] 1971, 432).

Melior: see Atedius Melior.

Memphis: a city in lower Egypt.

Menander: a Greek author (ca. 342–292 BCE) of New Comedy, influential on Roman comedy, to whose realism the quip of the scholar Aristophanes of Byzantium attests· "Menander and life, who imitated whom?"

Menecrates: see Julius Menecrates.

Menelaus: the king of Sparta, brother of Agamemnon, and husband of Helen.

Mentor: the old friend whom Ulysses left in charge of his household and whose form Athena assumed to advise Ulysses' son, Telemachus.

Mercury: identified by the Romans with the Greek Hermes; winged Arcadian god, son of Maia, messenger of the gods, and inventor of the lyre.

Messina: a city in Sicily (modern Messana) across the Strait of Messina from Rhegium (Reggio di Calabria) on the toe of Italy.

Midas: a legendary king of Phrygia, famous for his "golden touch" and proverbial for wealth.

Minerva: the goddess of war, weaving, and wisdom, identified with the Greek Pallas Athena; she had a temple on a promontory near Pollius' villa at Sorrento. She was important for the Flavian dynasty, especially to Domitian, who built two temples for her in Rome, used her image on his coinage, named a new legion after her, and celebrated the Alban Games in her honor.

Misenus: Hector's squire and Aeneas' bugler, supposedly buried at Cape Misenum.

Molorchus: the peasant who entertained Hercules before he killed the Nemean lion.

Molossians: a people of Epirus in northwest Greece; they raised a famous breed of dog, the Molossian hound.

Moon: "the Moon's belovèd" (3.4.61; lit., "the Latmian," 3.4.40L) is Endymion, a beautiful young man whose grave was said to be on Latmos, a mountain northeast of Miletus.

Moorish: "Moorish citrus wood" (1.3.52, 3.3123) was imported from Mauretania.

the Mother: the Magna Mater (Great Mother), whose worship was imported to Rome in response to the crisis of the Second Punic War. When the ship bearing her image got stuck on a sandbar in the Tiber, the Vestal Claudia pulled it free, thereby disproving the charge that she had violated her vow of chastity.

Mulvian Bridge: the bridge by which the Flaminian Way crossed to the right bank of the Tiber.

Muses: the nine sisters, daughters of Jupiter and Memory (Mnemosyne), associated with the arts, Apollo, and Mount Helicon in Boeotia; besides the Muses as a group, Statius refers individually to Clio (Muse of history), Thalia (Muse of comedy), Calliope (chief Muse, Muse of epic, and mother of Orpheus), and Erato (Muse of love poetry). The native Roman equivalent of the Muses are the Camenae.

Myron: a Greek sculptor (5th c. BCE) famous for his bronze animals.

Naiad: a water nymph.

Naples: the modern name for Neapolis, Statius' hometown, formerly called "Parthenope" after the Siren whom Apollo guided there; the site of the Augustalia, games held every four years, in which both Statius and his father achieved victories.

Narcissus: the youth who fell in love with his own reflection in a clear pool.

Naval Basin: the *stagnum navale* (4.4.6L) built by Augustus in 2 BCE on the right bank of the Tiber for mock naval battles.

Naxos: the island where Theseus abandoned Ariadne after escaping Crete.

Nemea: the place where Hercules slew the lion, a cape of whose hide is his trademark; at the games held there, the prize was a wreath of wild celery.

Nemesis: a spirit of retribution (*Rhamnusia*, 3.5.5L, because the best-known shrine of Nemesis was at Rhamnus in Attica).

Nemi: the lake sacred to Diana, where runaway slaves were the "kings" at the grove of Aricia.

Neptune: the god of the sea, identified with the Greek Poseidon.

Nereids: sea nymphs, the daughters of Nereus.

Nereus: a Greek sea god, father of sea nymphs.

Nero: the last of the Julio-Claudian emperors (54–68 CE), who murdered his mother Agrippina; the subject of a lost poem by Lucan. Nero's "Baths" (1.5.86) were on the Campus Martius.

Nestor: the king of Pylos and participant in the Trojan War, proverbial for his long life and wise counsel (Quintilian 12.10.64 contrasts the sweetness of his oratory with the force of Ulysses').

Nile: river in Egypt.

Niobe: a mythical queen of Thebes, who boasted that she was more fertile than the goddess Latona/Leto. The goddess's twin children, Apollo and Diana, punished her by killing all her many children; from grief she turned to stone, a rock that continues to trickle "tears."

Nisida: the modern name for Nesis, an island visible from Pollius' villa at Sorrento.

Nisus: a legendary king of Megara, whose life and the welfare of whose kingdom depended on a lock of purple hair, which his daughter cut to betray the city to Minos of Crete.

North Africa: often this is my translation of *Libye*.

Novius Vindex: an art connoisseur and collector; addressee of 4.6, about his Hercules statuette

Numa: Numa Pompilius, second king of Rome (traditionally 715–673 BCE), who supposedly consulted the nymph Egeria at Aricia.

Numidian: "Numidian marble" (1.2.197; *Libycus*, 148L) is the kind called *giallo antico*, which occurs in a variety of shades between golden yellow and red.

Nysa: Jupiter entrusted the rearing of the infant Bacchus to the nymphs of Nysa, a mythical mountain variously located (in, e.g., Thrace, India, Ethiopia).

Ocean: in Greek myth, the river which surrounds the flat circular earth; I also use this to translate *Doris* (see above).

Oenomaus: the father of Hippodamia, whose suitors had to defeat him in a chariot race to win her, and faced death if they lost.

Oenone: a nymph of Mount Ida, whom Paris abandoned for Helen; he died when she withheld the remedy for the wound he received from Philoctetes, and she killed herself from grief after relenting too late.

Oeta: the mountain in Thessaly where Hercules built the pyre that burned away his mortal parts, crazed from the pain caused by the poisoned robe his wife unwittingly had given him.

Olympiad: the four-year interval between one celebration of the Olympics and the next.

Olympian: of Mount Olympus, or, of Olympia in Greece.
    The "Olympian father" (3.1.153, 267) is Zeus.
    "Olympian Zeus" (2.2.83) is the sculptor Phidias' masterpiece, the cult statue of the god in his temple at Olympia.

Olympic(s): games in honor of Zeus, which supposedly also commemorate the victory of Pelops (see below) in the chariot race against Oenomaus (see above).

Olympus: a mountain in northern Greece, thought to be the home of the gods.

One Who Loosens Cares: Lyaeus, an epithet of Bacchus (4.2.52–53).

Opheltes: the child of a king of Nemea, killed by a snake at Lerna and commemorated in the Nemean Games

Optatus: a comrade of Crispinus (5.2 217).

Orestes: the son of Agamemnon and Clytemnestra; his friendship with his comrade Pylades was proverbial for loyalty.

Orion: the great hunter who became a constellation associated with stormy weather.

Orpheus: the famous mythical singer from Thrace, son of the Muse Calliope, whose songs could charm animals, trees, and even stones; he went to the Underworld and almost succeeded in winning back his dead wife Eurydice. Orpheus was the subject of a lost work by Lucan.

Osiris: the husband of Isis, whose death and resurrection were celebrated annually, especially by women.

Ossa: one of the two mountains the Giants piled on Olympus in their attempted assault on the Olympian gods.

Ovid: Publius Ovidius Naso, a Roman poet (43 BCE–17 CE), whose works include love poetry in elegiac meter (like that of Arruntius Stella); his masterpiece, the *Metamorphoses*, a collection of Greek and Roman myths and legends organized chronologically and thematically; and mournful poetic letters from his place of exile on the Black Sea.

Padua: the northern Italian city where the historian Livy (59 BCE–17 CE) was born.

Palaemon: the son of Athamas and Ino, who drifted with her to Corinth after they escaped the madness Juno had inspired in Athamas; he and his mother both became sea deities. He is commemorated in the Isthmian Games, for which the prize was a pine wreath.

Palatine: one of Rome's seven hills, the site of King Evander's city of Pallanteum (*Aeneid* 8) and of the emperor's palace.

Palestine: the land of the Jews, and later a Roman province; Statius refers to it as a source of imported dates and incense.

Palestrina: modern name for Praeneste, where a famous temple of Fortune was located.

Palinurus: the helmsman of Aeneas, who fell overboard just before the Trojans reached Cumae and was murdered when he was washed ashore; in *Aeneid* 6 his unburied shade asks Aeneas to go back to the port of Velii to find and bury his corpse (365–66).

Pallas: another name for Minerva/Athena.

Pamphylia: coastal plain enclosed by the mountains of eastern Lycia, Pisidia, and western Cilicia; in 133 BCE it became part of the province of Asia, and later was attached to various other provinces. In Statius' time it was a joint province with Lycia, and was one of the places Rutilius Gallicus served (1.4.116).

Pan: the goatish Arcadian god, identified with the Roman Faunus; the pursuer of the nymph Pholoe in 2.3.

Pangaea: a mountain in Thrace associated with Bacchus.

Pannonians: the people of Pannonia, the Roman province south and west of the Danube. Pannonia was one of the places Rutilius Gallicus served (1.4.117).

Paphos: a city on Cyprus near which Venus supposedly arose from the sea, and where a famous temple of hers was located.

Paris: a son of King Priam of Troy, recruited while herding sheep on Mount Ida to serve as judge in the beauty contest between Juno, Minerva, and Venus; Venus' bribe was Helen, whose subsequent abduction triggered the Trojan War. An archer, Paris wounded Menelaus and killed Achilles by striking his only vulnerable point—his heel.

Parnassus: the mountain at Delphi associated with Apollo and the Muses.

Parthenopaeus: an Arcadian warrior, one of the Seven against Thebes.

Parthenope: an earlier name for Naples, from the name of the Siren whom Apollo guided there.

Parthian: of the Eastern peoples whose mounted archers could shoot while retreating; the Parthians' victory at the battle of Carrhae in 53 BCE—they captured Roman standards and Roman prisoners, and they beheaded the Roman general Crassus and his son—made them feared enemies.

Patroclus: Achilles' comrade, who died fighting the Trojans while wearing Achilles' armor because the latter had refused to fight after Agamemnon seized his concubine, Briseis (see above), from him.

Paullus: Lucius Aemilius Paullus, nephew of the triumvir Lepidus and consul in 50 BCE; in 55 he began rebuilding the Basilica Aemilia, which was completed by his son. Statius refers to "warrior Paullus" (1.1.45), so he may be thinking of the famous general Paullus, consul in 168 BCE, who ended the Third Macedonian War and settled Greece.

Peace: the temple of Peace built by Vespasian and renovated by Domitian, in the Forum Transitorium near a temple of Janus.

Peleus: the Thessalian king who married the sea-nymph Thetis and fathered the hero Achilles.

Pelion: one of the two mountains the Giants piled on Olympus in their attempted assault on the Olympian gods.

Pelops: the son of Tantalus, who served him up as a meal for the gods. Only Ceres, distracted by grief for her missing daughter Proserpina, actually ate (the gods revived Tantalus and replaced his missing shoulder with an ivory one).

Penelope: Ulysses' wife, who waited twenty years for his return from Troy; therefore, a proverbially faithful wife.

the Pens: the Saepta Iulia in the Campus Martius originally were voting enclosures; later they were used for displays such as gladiator fights. Destroyed by a fire in 80 CE, they were rebuilt as markets and became a popular spot for strolling.

Pergamum: an important Hellenistic city in Asia Minor, Earinus' birthplace, and the site of a temple and healing shrine of Asclepius. When Statius refers to Troy as "Pergamum," I usually translate it as "Troy."

Perseus: the son of Jupiter and Danaë, raised by the fisherman Dictys who found him afloat in the chest which his grandfather had thrown into the sea. Perseus was the hero who killed the Gorgon Medusa.

Persian / Persians: the kings of Persia were proverbial for wealth; Roman poets also used "Persian" loosely to refer to the Parthians (see above).

Phaeacian: belonging to Alcinous, king of the Phaeacians on the island of Scheria, who entertained Ulysses on his last stop before finally arriving home.

Phaethon: the son of Helios who persuaded his father to let him drive the sun chariot for a day; after he crashed and died, his sisters, the Heliades, became trees weeping "tears" of amber.

Pharos: the famous lighthouse at Alexandria.

Pharsalus: the city in Thessaly near which Caesar defeated Pompey in 48 BCE.

Phasis: a river on the Black Sea, from whose coast in Colchis pheasants were imported.

Phidias: the Athenian sculptor (5th c. BCE) who designed the sculptures of the Parthenon; he made the colossal gold and ivory cult statues of Athena Parthenos and of Zeus at Olympia, the latter of which was one of the Seven Wonders of the ancient world.

Philetas: a Greek scholar and poet (early 3rd c. BCE) from Cos. The author of a variety of work in verse and prose, he was best known as an elegist.

Philetos: Flavius Ursus' beloved slave.

Philippi: the Thracian city near which Antony defeated Brutus and Cassius in 42 BCE.

Philomela: the sister of Procne, whose husband Tereus raped her and cut out her tongue to prevent her from revealing his deed; after the sisters took their vengeance on him by serving him a meal of his young son Itys, she became the nightingale.

Phoebus: an epithet which means "shining"; it can refer to Apollo or to Helios, the sun god represented by the famous Colossus at Rhodes.

Phoenix: Achilles' tutor, who went with him to the Trojan War.

Pholoe: the nymph whom Pan pursued around Rome until she reached Melior's garden, where she became a plane tree.

Phrygian: of Phrygia in Asia Minor. The Great Mother goddess Cybele and her consort Attis are both Phrygian; Phrygian marble, the kind called *pavonazzeto*, quarried at Synnas, was white with purple spots (supposedly the blood of Attis).

Pimpla: a spring in Pieria associated with the Muses and poetic inspiration.

Pindar: a Greek lyric poet (518–438 BCE) from Thebes.

Pirene: the spring at Corinth where Bellerophon captured the flying horse Pegasus; at 2.7.4–5 (2.7.2–4L) Statius seems to associate it with Hippocrene ("Horse Spring"), the Boeotian spring of poetic inspiration supposedly formed when Pegasus stamped his hoof on the ground.

Pleiades: a constellation whose rising is associated with rainy weather.

Plotius Grypus: the addressee of 4.9 jokingly criticized for his choice of Saturnalia present.

Polenza: the modern name for Pollentia, famous in antiquity for black wool, where Flavius Ursus had property.

Polla: the wife of Pollius Felix; perhaps the same woman as Lucan's widow, Polla Argentaria, who commissioned 2.7

Pollius Felix: the owner of a villa at Sorrento (2.2), who enlarged the shrine to Hercules on that property (3.1); he is also the dedicatee of book 3.

218

Pollux: one of the Twins, a boxer, sometimes associated with the Morning Star as his brother Castor was with the Evening Star.

Polyclitus: a Greek sculptor (later 5th c. BCE) who worked in various media, but mainly in bronze; because he was very popular during and after his lifetime, many Hellenistic and Roman copies of his work survive.

Pompeii: one of the cities near Naples buried by the eruption of Vesuvius in 79 CE; its patron goddess was Venus.

Pompey: Gnaeus Pompeius Magnus (ca. 67–36 BCE), Caesar's enemy in the civil war; after his defeat at Pharsalus he fled to Egypt but was murdered as he landed. Statius refers to Lucan's sympathetic portrayal of him in the *Bellum Civile* by saying "you'll loyally mourn / and give Pompey a monument" (2.7.86–87).

Pontus: an area of northern Asia Minor that includes the southern coast of the Black Sea, between Paphlagonia and Colchis south to Cappadocia. Pompey organized part of it into a province in 63 BCE, but most of it reverted to native rulers; it was recovered in the early Empire.

Pozzuoli: the modern name for Puteoli in the Bay of Naples; an important harbor and commercial center, and the birthplace of Pollius.

Praeneste: the modern Palestrina; site of the Temple of Fortuna, and a popular resort because of its cool, elevated location.

Praxiteles: an Athenian sculptor (4th c. BCE), regarded in antiquity as most successful in marble. Among his works is the famous Aphrodite of Cnidus, which allegedly induced Aphrodite herself to ask, "When did you see me naked, Praxiteles?"

Priam: the king of Troy, proverbial for long life and great wealth; his sons included Paris and Hector, whose mutilated corpse he had to ransom from Achilles.

Priscilla: the addressee of 5.1, late wife of Abascantus and friend of Statius' wife.

Probate Court: more literally, the Centumviral Court, whose jurisdiction included but was not limited to lawsuits about wills.

Procida: the modern name for Prochyta, an island visible from Pollius' villa at Sorrento.

Procne: the wife of Tereus, who killed her son Itys as vengeance against her husband Tereus for raping and mutilating her sister Philomela; sometimes she, instead of Philomela, is identified with the nightingale (but usually she is said to have been turned into a swallow).

Propertius: Sextus Propertius (ca. 50–ca. 15 BCE), a love elegist of the Augustan Age. On "Propertius, famed / for his poetic Tuscan grotto" (1.2.341–42), see Tuscan.

the Protector: the emperor.

Protesilaus: the first Greek to die at Troy, killed when his ship landed. His shade was permitted to return to his wife Laodamia for a few hours; after that she spent so much time with a likeness of him that her father burned it, and she committed suicide.

Proteus: a shape-shifting sea god.

Punic: Carthaginian.

Pygmies: in Greek myth, a race of dwarfs famous for waging war against the cranes.

Pylades: comrade of Orestes; the closeness of their friendship was proverbial.

Pyrrhus: another name for Neoptolemus, the son of Achilles.

Pythia: Apollo's oracle at Delphi.

Pythian: the Pythian Games were held at Delphi in honor of Apollo.

Queen of Battles: my translation (4.5.23) of *regina bellorum virago* (4.5.23L), more literally the "manly queen of wars," i.e., Minerva, in whose honor Domitian gave the Alban Games.

Quirinal: one of the seven hills of Rome.

Realm Below: the Underworld. At 2.7.69 this phrase translates *sedes . . . inferorum,* more literally, "the residence of those below" (2.7.57L); at 4.7.15 it refers to the god Dis (4.7.14L).

Red Sea: broadly, the sea between Suez and Sri Lanka, but probably the Persian Gulf; it was a source of pearls (Coleman 1988, 180).

Reggio: Reggio di Calabria, the modern name for Rhegium, on the toe of Italy across the Strait of Messina from Messina (Messana) in Sicily.

Regulus: Marcus Atilius Regulus, general during the First Punic War. Captured after a disastrous defeat in North Africa in 255 BCE, he was sent to Rome to urge the Senate to make peace; he recommended against peace and then, according to legend, returned to Carthage, knowing he would face torture and death.

Rhine: a river in Germany, the Empire's northeastern frontier.

Rhodes: the island location of the famous Colossus .

Rhodope: a mountain in Thrace.

Righteousness: one of my translations (5.3.117) for *Pietas* (5.3.89L).

Romulus: the mythical founder of Rome; son of Ilia/Rhea Silvia by Mars, and the foster son of Acca.

Rumor: my translation (5.1.139) of *Fama* (5.1.106L).

Russian: the phrase "from Russian steppes" (2.5.33) translates *Scythicas* (2.5.28L); the Scythians were a nomadic people, the bulk of whom stayed in southern Russia.

Rutilius Gallicus: Domitian's urban prefect, the addressee of 1.4, which celebrates his recovery from a serious illness.

Sabaean: the Sabaeans were a people of southwest Arabia who made their living from the spice trade.

Sabine: the Sabines were a people northeast of Rome, proverbial for old-fashioned morality.

Saguntum: a Spanish city supposedly founded by Hercules. Its siege and capture by Hannibal (219 BCE) precipitated the Second Punic War; the residents committed mass suicide rather than surrender.

Saharan: "Saharan dunes" (2.5.33) are more literally "Libyan," and "Sahara's sands" (4.3.173) are more literally "Libya's."

Salian: of the Salian ("leaping") priests, associated with Mars. Their sacred shields were copied by Numa from the original, which floated down from the sky.

Sallust: Gaius Sallustius Crispus (ca. 86–35 BCE), late Republican Roman historian, whose style was famous for its brevity.

Salmacis: a spring whose water supposedly emasculated men; in myth, Hermaphroditus acquired his ambiguous sexual nature after the nymph Salmacis lured him into her waters and merged with him.

Sappho: the famous female lyric poet (b. 612 BCE) from Lesbos.

Sarmatian: the Sarmatians were a nomadic tribe related to the Scythians; they became clients of Rome and served as a buffer between the Dacians and the province of Pannonia.

Sarno: modern name for the Sarnus, a river flowing into the Bay of Naples whose course once went right past Pompeii.

Saturn: a god identified with the Greek Cronus, youngest of the Titans, whom his son Zeus and other Olympians defeated and then kept enchained in Tartarus; also, the king during a Golden Age in Italy.

Saturnalia: festival of Saturn celebrated in December, during which roles were reversed and presents exchanged; the subject of 1.6 and occasion of 4.9.

Saturninus: Lucius Antonius Saturninus, governor of Upper Germany, who led a short-lived mutiny, declaring himself emperor in January 89 CE

Satyrs: creatures similar to Pan in goatish appearance and behavior.

Savo: the river now called the Savone, which flowed into the sea a few miles from the Volturnus; swift upstream, it was slowed at its mouth by the coastal marshes.

Scipio: P. Cornelius Scipio Africanus, who supposedly saved his father's life at the battle of the Ticinus River in 218 BCE, and was said to have consulted with Jupiter Capitolinus late at night in his temple's inner sanctum.

Scotland: "the plains of Scotland" (5.2.204) are literally "Caledonian"; this is the northern part of Britain, where Vettius Bolanus served between 69 and 71 CE.

Scylla: the famous many-headed sea monster who menaced the straits between Reggio and Messina; Statius follows Virgil (*Aeneid* 6.286) in including a group of Scyllas in the Underworld.

Sebethus: a stream flowing past Naples.

Semele: the daughter of Cadmus, king of Thebes, and the mother of Bacchus. She was incinerated by Jupiter after Juno tricked her into asking him to come to her as he did to his wife.

Seneca: Lucius Annaeus Seneca the Younger (ca. 4 BCE–65 CE), a Stoic philosopher and author of tragedies; he was Lucan's paternal uncle and, like him, compelled by Nero to commit suicide.

Septimius Severus: the addressee of 4.5, born at Lepcis Magna; he was possibly related to the emperor of the same name (Coleman 1988, 158–59).

the Seven Sages: a canonical list of wise men, including such figures as Thales and Solon.

Severus: see Septimius Severus.

Sibyl: an oracle of Apollo, who gave responses in a cave at Cumae near his temple. She made a bargain with Apollo, promising to trade her virginity in exchange for living as many years as the grains in a handful of sand, and when she reneged on her part of the deal, Apollo kept his without adding equally long youth; she was Aeneas' guide to the Underworld. Her "Books" (the Sibylline Books) were a collection of oracles which a board of Roman priests consulted in times of crisis.

Sicily: the large island off the toe of Italy; Venus had a famous temple there on Mount Eryx, and it also contains the volcano Etna. Saffron was grown there.
The "old . . . Sicilian poe[t]" (5.3.204; *Siculusque senex,* 5.3.151L) refers to Epicharmus (5th c. BCE), an author from Syracuse; best known for his comedies, he also wrote about veterinary medicine.

Sidon: a Phoenician city famous for its purple dye.

Silvia: in *Aeneid* 7, the daughter of king Latinus' herdsman; her pet stag was killed by Ascanius (see above), triggering the Latins to join battle against the Trojans.

Siren, Sirens: in the *Odyssey* they are creatures, half-woman and half-bird, whose songs lure sailors to their death; later, they are associated with music almost as strongly as the Muses are. Naples was originally named Parthenope, after a Siren whom Apollo supposedly guided there, and Sorrento was named for them.

Sisters: sometimes Statius refers to the Fates as the "Sisters" (e.g., "the gloomy Sisters," 3.3.26).

Slav / Slavic: I occasionally translate "Sarmatian" this way (e.g., "nomad Slavs," 4.7.51; "Slavic winters," 5.1.172).

Smyrna: modern Izmir, the birthplace of Claudius Etruscus' father.

Sophron: a Syracusan writer (5th c. BCE) of mimes, admired by Plato.

(Villa) Sorrentina: Pollius' villa at Sorrento.

Sorrento: the modern name for Surrentum, the location of Pollius' villa. Its wine was prized despite its tartness.

Spain / Spaniard / Spanish: the two provinces of Republican times were reorganized into three by Augustus; Spain was a source of gold for the emperor.
"Spain's cattle baron" (4.6.134) refers to the triple-bodied monster Geryon, the capture of whose cattle was Hercules' tenth Labor.
"[T]hose other Spaniards" (2.7.38) are Seneca and Gallio.

Sparta / Spartan: region in the southern Peloponnese.
The Twins' "place / of birth in Sparta" (4.8.72–73) traditionally was Mount Taygetos; the Twins "most important Spartan shrine" (4.8.74) was at Therapnae.
Boxing is "Spartan" (4.2.67) because it is associated with Pollux, one of the Twins.
The discus is "Spartan" (5.3.71) because Apollo killed the young Spartan Hyacinthus with an errant discus.
The "Spartan love" of Paris (2.6.41) is Helen, who was married to the king of Sparta, Menelaus.
"[T]hat chilly Spartan mountain" (1 3.111) is Taygetos.

The "Spartan namesake" (3.2.142) of Egyptian Canopus is Menelaus' Spartan helmsman Canopus, who was supposedly buried there.

"Spartan porphyry" (1.2.201) is literally *purpura . . . / Oebalis* (1.2 150–51L).

The "Spartan stream" (2.6.67), literally "Leda's stream" (*Ledaeo gurgite*, 2.6 45L), is the Eurotas.

"Spartan stripes of green" (1.5.54) refers to the marble called *verde antico*.

The phrase "mother Leda's Spartan wrestling bouts" (4.8.42) alludes to the fact that Spartan girls also participated at the palaestra.

Spinner: the "fatal Spinner's inauspicious hand" (2.1.162) refers to Lachesis, one of the Fates.

Stabiae: a fashionable resort on the Bay of Naples destroyed by Vesuvius, and rebuilt in a new location.

Stella: see Arruntius Stella.

Stesichorus: the author (6th c. BCE) of choral lyrics with a strong narrative element, on various epic subjects; legend has it that he went blind after composing a *Helen*, but recovered after writing a recantation (his *Palinode*) which claimed that Helen never went to Troy.

Strymon: a river in Thrace.

Stymphalus: a region of Arcadia that included a lake infested by monstrous birds; one of Hercules' Labors required that he drive them away.

Styx / Stygian: the river in the Underworld by which the gods swear.

Sulla: Lucius Cornelius Sulla (ca. 138–78 BCE), the Roman general and dictator who became extremely wealthy from campaigns in the East, and who once supposedly possessed the Hercules statuette by Lysippus. He believed himself to be specially favored by Fortune—hence his cognomen Felix—and to be under Apollo's special protection.

Sun: my translation (2.7.31) of Hyperion (2.7.25L).

Syenite: Syene is modern Aswan, the stone "Egyptian Syenite" (2.2.111) was a reddish granite.

Synnadite: the purple-spotted white marble, *pavonazetto*, quarried at Synnas in Phrygia.

Synnas: the place in Phrygia where a purple-spotted white marble was quarried.

Syrian: Pompey made Syria a province in 64–63 BCE. Under the early emperors it was an important military command with four legions; in 70 CE Judaea became a separate province, held by one of the legions originally based in Syria.

Tages: the founder of the Etruscan science of divination.

Tagus: a river in Spain proverbial for the abundance of its gold.

Taranto: the modern name for Tarentum, a city in southern Italy, whose importance as a port was eclipsed by Brundisium (Brindisi). It had a colossal Zeus by Lysippus, and Pollius owned vineyards there; it was also famous for the herds grazed on the nearby Galaesus River (referred to as "Tarentine streams," 3.3.122).

Tarpeian: "Tarpeian Jove's temple" (3.4.158) is the temple of Capitoline Jupiter, near the Tarpeian Rock (see Traitor's Rock).

Tarracina: the modern name for Anxur, the former Volscian stronghold (hence "the high / and mighty citadel of Tarracina," 1.3.125–26).

Tartarus: the area of the Underworld devoted to punishing the wicked.

Telamon: the brother of Peleus and father of Ajax; he helped Hercules fight to force King Laomedon of Troy to keep his part of a bargain.

Teleboean: inhabitants of islands off Acarnania, who supposedly settled Capri.

Telegonus: the son of Circe and Ulysses; he founded Tusculum.

Telephus: the son of Auge and Hercules, accidentally wounded by Achilles on his way to Troy; he was later healed by Achilles with rust from the same spear, thereby fulfilling an oracle that the wounder would be the healer.

Temese: a town in Bruttii (modern Calabria, the heel of Italy), famous for its copper mines.

Tempe: a valley in northern Thessaly where the Peneus River flows between Mounts Olympus and Ossa.

Tereus: see Procne.

Thasos: an island in the north Aegean; the marble quarried there, called *greco livido,* was white with glittering spots.

Thaumas: a sea god, son of Gaea and Pontus and the father of Iris.

Thebaid: Statius' epic poem about the Seven against Thebes, the mythic Greek champions who aided Polynices in his war against his brother Eteocles to gain the rule of Thebes.

Thebes / Theban: city in Boeotia; its walls were built by Amphion playing the lyre Hermes had given him. It was the home of Semele, the mother of Bacchus, and of Ino, who escaped with her son Palaemon to Corinth, as well as the birthplace of Hercules and one of Alexander's conquests.

Theseus: the Athenian hero who killed the Minotaur; he escaped from Crete with the princess Ariadne, whose thread had guided him back out of the Labyrinth and whom he abandoned on the island of Naxos, where Bacchus found her and made her his wife. Because Theseus forgot to change his black sails to white on his return home, his father Aegeus mistakenly thought he had died on Crete, and Aegeus jumped into the sea from a cliff to his death. Theseus and Pirithous had a proverbially strong friendship; Theseus' son Hippolytus, dragged to death by his horses, was resurrected by Asclepius and hidden at Nemi by Diana.

Thespius: a king in Boeotia; he got Hercules drunk and the hero impregnated all fifty of his daughters, either in one night or over the course of fifty nights.

Thessaly / Thessalian: an area in northern Greece, the land of Peleus and Achilles. Thessaly was noted in antiquity for horses and cattle (because of its grassy plains), for medicinal herbs, and for witchcraft; it was also the home of Admetus and his wife Alcestis (see Admetus).

Thetis: the sea-nymph wife of Peleus and mother of Achilles, whom she hid disguised as a girl on the island of Scyros in an unsuccessful attempt to keep him from being recruited to fight at Troy.

Thrace / Thracian: the eastern half of the Balkan Peninsula, the home of Mars, of Orpheus (see above), and of Tereus (see Procne).
The "royal hous[e] / of . . Thrace" (4.6.131–32) alludes to Hercules' Labor involving the capture of Diomedes' man-eating horses.
The "caves where Thracian mares ate human flesh" (3.1.49) are the ones belonging to Diomedes, king of the Bistonians; their capture was one of Hercules' Labors.
A "Thracian winter crane" (4.6.11) is either a great rarity or an impossibility, since cranes were famous for migrating south in the winter (Coleman 1988, 178).
"Philomel, with Thracian woe forlorn" (2.4.27) refers to the nightingale (see Philomela).

Thule: the far northern ends of the earth, sometimes identified with Britain—e.g., as a possible future post for Marcellus (4.4.79), or the place where Vettius Bolanus served (5.2.79).

Thunderer: an epithet of Jupiter.

Thymbra: the location in the Troad of a famous temple of Apollo.

Tiber: the river flowing through Rome.

Tiberius: the second emperor (42 BCE–37 CE), under whom Claudius Etruscus' father began his career.

Tibullus: Albius Tibullus (d. 19 BCE), a Roman elegiac poet roughly contemporary with Propertius; "Tibullus, whom a glowing hearth made rich" (1.2.344; 255L) alludes to Tibullus' lines "let my poverty expose me to scorn for an idle life, / provided that my hearth is bright with a constant fire" (*me mea paupertas vita traducat inerti, / dum meus assiduo luceat igne focus,* 1.1.5–6).

Tiburnus: the legendary founder of Tivoli (Tibur); usually called "Tiburtus."

Tiryns: the location on the Argive plain of a Mycenaean palace; in myth, Jupiter had intended Hercules to become its king (hence he is often called "the Tirynthian"), but Juno connived so that the rule went to Eurystheus instead.

Tithonus: the son of the Trojan king Laomedon; he became Dawn's husband and, given immortality without eternal youth, became proverbial for old age.

Tivoli: modern name for Tibur; the location of Vopiscus' villa and of a shrine of Hercules.

Traitor's Rock: my translation (5.3.265) of *Tarpeio . . . monte* (5.3.196L), the cliff from which traitors were thrown. According to Roman legend, a girl named Tarpeia once betrayed the route up the Capitoline to Gallic invaders.

(Lake) Trasimene: a lake in Tuscany between Perugia and Cortona, the site of a battle in 217 BCE in which Hannibal destroyed two Roman legions almost entirely.

Triton / Tritons: one of a group of creatures, human above and fish below, often shown playing a conch-shell horn.

Troilus: young son of Apollo, chased and killed by Achilles; in most accounts, this pursuit happens in or near a temple of Apollo, but Statius' version (2.6.48, 5.2.175) has Achilles chasing him around the walls of Troy, just as he did Hector (van Dam 1984, 411).

Troy / Trojan: the city whose walls were built by Apollo and Poseidon in a bargain with King Laomedon. It was besieged for ten years by the Greeks after the Trojan Paris abducted or seduced Helen, until it finally fell at night through the strategy of the Trojan Horse.

"Troy's first Greek widow" (2.7.155) was Laodamia (see Protesilaus)

The "royal hous[e] / of Troy" (4.6.131–32) refer to Hercules' adventures with Laomedon, whose daughter Hercules rescued from a sea monster but who tried to renege on the reward he had promised.

Venus' "Trojan mate" (1.2.253) was Anchises (see above).

"[T]hat Trojan's gentle nursemaid" (1.3.127) is Caieta, Aeneas' nurse, supposedly buried at the place named for her.

The "Trojan oar" (3.5.138) is that of Misenus (see above).

"[T]hat Trojan's rosy wife" (5.4.12) is Dawn, whom Statius refers to as *Tithonia* (5.4.9L), i.e., the wife of Tithonus (see above)

Tuore Grande: one of two hills on Capri which might be Taurubulae (3.1.180, 129L; see Vollmer [1898] 1971, 39).

Turin: the birthplace of Gallicus.

Turnus: the Rutulian prince betrothed to Lavinia (see above).

Tuscan: having to do with Etruria.

Why "Tuscan boar" (4.6.12) is superior to Umbrian (a known gourmet item) is one of the topics Novius Vindex and his guest *don't* discuss.

"Propertius, famed / for his poetic Tuscan grotto" (1.2.341–42) alludes to Propertius 3.1.5: "tell in which cave together did you finely spin your song" (*dicite, quo pariter carmen tenuastis in antro*), addressed to the shades of Callimachus (see above) and Philetas (see above):

The "Tuscan Sea" (2.2.2, 3.2.30) is the one west of Italy.

The "Tuscan side" (4.4.7) of the Tiber is the fashionable right bank.

Tusculo / Tusculan: the modern name for Tusculum, a wooded spot in the Alban Hills, a favorite location for villas (e.g., Cicero's).

Twins: the Dioscuri, Castor and Pollux; as Saint Elmo's fire, they were a welcome sign for sailors (3.2.12).

Tyre: a Phoenician city, famous for purple dye.

Ulysses: the Latin name for Odysseus, king of Ithaca, who fought in the Trojan War, put Hector's son Astyanax to death, and was hosted by Alcinous toward the end of his ten years of wandering on the way home to his wife Penelope and son Telemachus.

Umbria: a region of Italy east of Etrutria, extending to the Adriatic.

"Umbria's [boar]" (4.6.13) was a noted delicacy.

"Umbria's vales" (1.4.190) are those on the Clitumnus River, famous for its white cattle.

Underworld: my translation (5.3.91) for *Tartara* (5.3.69L).

Ursus: see Flavius Ursus.

Veii: an Etruscan town, nine miles north of Rome; it was a constant threat in the early days of the Republic, until its defeat by Camillus in 396 BCE. Septimius Severus' father owned an estate there.

Veleda: a German prophetess (1.4.140; 1.4.90L) during the reign of Vespasian; Tacitus refers to her at *Germania* 8 and *Histories* 4.61, 5.22.

Venus: the Roman goddess identified with Aphrodite; as the mother of Aeneas, the founder of the Roman nation, she had a special interest in the city.

Vespasian: the first of the Flavian emperors (9–79 CE); father of Titus and Domitian, the second and third of that dynasty.

Vesta: the goddess of the hearth; in her shrine at Rome an eternal flame burned on which Rome's survival depended, and which the Vestal Virgins kept going
 The "great high priest of Vesta's flame" (5.3.240) is the pontifex maximus.

Vestinus: a late friend of Novius Vindex.

Vesuvius: the volcano near Naples. Its eruption in 79 CE buried Pompeii and Herculaneum, and was the planned subject of a poem by Statius' father (5.3.281; 205L).

Vibius Maximus: the addressee of 4.7, congratulating him on the birth of a son; author of a brief history of the world. His father-in-law apparently fought with Domitian against the Sarmatians.

Vindex: see Novius Vindex.

Violentilla: a widow, the bride of Arruntius Stella and the subject of some of his elegiac love poetry.

Virgil: Publius Vergilius Maro (70–19 BCE), Roman poet, author of the *Aeneid*; the *Culex* (the *Gnat*) was also attributed to him in antiquity.
 "Virgil's monument" (4.4.69) is the tomb, about two miles outside of Naples, which the poet Silius Italicus restored and treated like a shrine

Vitorius Marcellus: the dedicatee of book 4 and addressee of 4.4; also the dedicatee of Quintilian's *Institutio Oratoria,* intended for the education of Marcellus' son Geta.

Vopiscus: see Manilius Vopiscus.

Vulcan: the Roman god identified with Hephaestus, god of smiths and husband of Aphrodite.

Vulturnus: a river in southern Italy, dredged and bridged as part of Domitian's construction project.

West Wind: the wind that blows in the correct direction to get Maecius Celer to Egypt (3.2.57).

Western isle: island of the Hesperides, from which Hercules, as one of his Labors, took the golden apples.

Xerxes: Persian king who invaded Greece in 480 BCE, after having bridged the Hellespont with pontoons and dug a canal through the Athos promontory to avoid sailing around Mount Athos.

Zeugma: literally "the Junction," the chief crossing point of the Euphrates; a frontier post and hub of trade routes, it was added to the province of Syria in 58 CE.

Zeus: "Olympian Zeus" (2.2.83) was the sculptor Phidias' masterpiece (see Phidias).

Notes

INTRODUCTION ·

1. Clinton 1972.

2. Archias of Antioch, whose right to Roman citizenship was defended by Cicero, is the extemporaneous poet best known to us; see Cicero's *Pro Archia,* cited by A. Hardie (1983, 82).

3. Nauta (2002, 201 and n. 29) disputes this identification.

Citations of the *Silvae* in this introduction give first the line numbers of the Latin text, then the lines of my translation.

4. Newlands 2002, 191, 196; she also describes Naples as "an alternative Rome" (37).

5. Griffith (1969, 137–38) regards Juvenal's Fourth Satire as a parody of Statius' *Bellum Germanicum,* based on the evidence of the surviving four lines, and observes (142) that in those four lines are three of the names of the eleven advisers listed in Juvenal 4.72–118 who were summoned by Domitian for a consultation.

6. Newlands (2002) titles one section of her introduction "Poetry of Praise" (18–27).

7. Van Dam 1984, 453.

8. A. Hardie 1983, 220 n. 54.

9. Bright (1980, 20–49) provides a thorough discussion of the title's significance.

10. Newlands 2002, 222–23, 236.

11. On this possible connection between the *Eclogues* and the *Silvae,* see Bright 1980, 37–39. Tanner (1986, 3042) proposes that some of the *Silvae* emulate the *Eclogues* both in their contents (e.g., he compares 4.8 with *Eclogue* 4; both treat the birth of a child) and in their nature as *eclogae* (selections), while their arrangement into four books imitates the *Georgics;* he then suggests that the *Silvae* are thus in a sense making "an amends" for publishing the *Thebaid* (i.e., Statius' *Aeneid*) without having first published minor works as Virgil did. Newlands (2002, 36) regards the poems as "a new version of pastoral," and calls *Silvae* 1.3 on Vopiscus' villa "a bold rewriting of pastoral" (127).

12. Feeney 1996, 1439.

13. Newlands 2002, 38–43, esp. 38 (in the section titled "Ecphrasis").

14. Newlands 1988, 2002, 119–20 and n. 8; see also van Dam 1984, 187.

15. A. Hardie (1983, 132) calls a poem on a bath "a relatively new departure in Latin literature." Newlands (2002) asserts that *Silvae* 1.5 may be the first full-length poem on baths (200) and calls road building a new subject for poetry (285).

16. Newlands 2002, 222.

17. Pavlovskis 1973, 1. For a recent discussion of Statius' attitude toward wealth and luxury, see Connors 2001, esp. 215–17, 228–29, 231; in her discussion she treats the *Silvae* as part of a "literature of leisure" which "encourages its audience to imagine the world as a storehouse for treasures to be transported to and consumed by Romans" (229).

18. A. Hardie 1983; Vollmer ([1898] 1971) had stressed epideixis almost a century ear-lier in his commentary. Hardie adopted the approach of Cairns (1972), who overzealously applied the prescriptions of rhetoric to all of Greek and Latin poetry. Van Dam's review (1988) of Hardie is quite critical, as are his remarks (1984, 64) in the introduction to his commentary on *Silvae* 2.1. I have long been critical of this generic approach; see my review of Cairns (Nagle 1977).

19. Vollmer [1898] 1971, 373, in his introduction to 2.7; cited by Newmyer 1979, 75 and n. 22.

20. Van Dam (1984, 334 on 2.3.73–77) says this Poet's Society was the *collegium scrib-arum*. The full name of this group is the *collegium scribarum histrionumque* (association of writers and actors); it is also sometimes referred to as the *collegium poetarum* (the poets' as-sociation).

21. Bright 1980, 7.

22. Bright 1980, 10.

23. Bright 1980, 6. In 4.4 Statius also owes the personification of the epistle to Horace, probably by way of Ovid; Coleman (1988, 138, on 4.4.1–11) cites the relevant passages, but neither she nor Vollmer ([1898] 1971) makes this point explicitly.

24. Newlands 2002, 228.

25. Newlands 2002, 130–38, on *Silvae* 1.3; "Luxury Redeemed" (127–38) also treats 1.3, and "Rewriting Horace" (160–63) is one section of her treatment of 2.2. Nauta (2002, 202), however, observes that Statius can also present life on his Alban estate as one of content-ment amid modest circumstances akin to Horace's experiences on his Sabine farm (see *Silvae* 4.5.1–22; 4.8.39).

26. A. Hardie 1983, 86–87.

27. Vessey 1986, 2761.

28. Newlands 2002, 253–54.

29. On Elizabethan wit and the *Silvae*, see Vessey 1986, 2759.

30. Slater 1908, 4.

31. See van Dam's introduction to *Silvae* 2.1 (1984, 68); the quotation is from his gen-eral introduction (8). Less hyperbolically and more persuasively, he observes that Statius "often has one central idea in his poems, preferably one that gives room for ambiguity and paradox" (68). Included among what he calls "half-way situations" (7) are those which hover (he uses the German term *Schwebesituationen*) "between light and shadow, death and life, boy and girl, son and slave" and feature such juxtapositions as life/myth and nature/cul-ture (8).

32. Nisbet (1978) argues in favor of identifying the two Pollas, based in part on those putative puns on her name; in making his argument, he gives a full list (8) of other exam-ples of such puns.

33. Van Dam (1984, 218, on *Silvae* 2.2.36–42) gives these and other examples of bilin-gual wordplay. Vollmer ([1898] 1971) 288 gives *lethargos* as the Greek word, and the Greek lexicon confirms that this is a specialized medical term (meaning "lethargic fever"), while *lethargia* is the lay term for "drowsiness" or "lethargy"; despite Statius' Greek her-itage, I wonder how knowledgeable he was about medical terminology. Van Dam mentions (218) a third type of etymology, the "allusive," which is "based on association": e.g., *taciti . . . mystae* (4.8.51/71; lit., "silent initiates," because those initiated into the Eleusinian Mys-teries were forbidden to reveal what they had seen and heard). Vollmer ([1898] 1971, 216, on *Silvae* 1.1.6) also collects examples.

34. For example, Mozley ([1928] 1982, ix) characterizes 1.1, 3.4, 4.1, and 4.2 as "all marked by the flattery that the subservience of the times was eager to bestow"; Vessey (1986, 2798) views such poems as faithfully reflecting an ideology developed, self-protectively, by Domitian.

35. Ahl (1984) uses the term "figured speech" for language operating through such figures as irony and ambiguity, with both a surface and an implied meaning; with reference specifically to *Silvae* 3.4 he comments on earlier critics' "failure to understand that 'flattery' of the emperor is not necessarily either flattering or sincere" (205). Newlands (2002, 19–21) cites ancient evidence to support her claim that panegyric could not only praise but also advise and warn; she borrows the concept of "faultlines" from Sinfield (1992), saying that such writings "do not subvert, but . . . disturb," and characterizes the *Silvae* as "neither works of flattery nor subversion but rather poems of anxiety as well as celebration" (Newlands 2002, 23, 24).

36. Dewar 1994, 209, 206 (quotation); he also refers to the "extravagance" of Latin panegyrical writing, "with the high value it placed on sheer outrageousness of idea and expression alike" (209).

37. Coleman 1988, xxv.

38. Cancik 1965, 45 (my trans.).

39. *OLD*, s.v. "nitor" 4, "nitidus" 6.

40. Such contrasts are what van Dam (1984, 7–8) calls "half-way situations."

41. Pavlovskis 1973, 2.

42. Coleman 1988, 113, on lines 41–42; 114, on line 45; 117, on line 52, and 125, on lines 88–89.

43. Coleman 1988, 108, on line 14.

44. Van Dam (1984, 9) remarks briefly on Statius' semantic inventiveness, and comments on specific examples in the poems of book 2 (20 nn. 85–91). Vessey (1971, 273–74) interprets Statius' phrase "the boldness of my style" (*audaciam stili nostri*) in the preface to book 3 as a reference to this feature, but Coleman (1988, xxvi) maintains that he was referring to his speed of composition. Vessey (1986, 2758) claims that "Each word . . . is pressed up to, and then beyond, the limit of meaning," and in a section titled "Words under Stress" (2765–69) he supports this assertion with an examination of the first thirteen lines of *Silvae* 2.1.

45. Filangieri and Sbordone 1958, esp 52–53.

46. Arens 1950, 243; cited by van Dam 1984, 118, on 2.1.95.

47. Szelest 1972, esp. 315–17. For a more recent and more thorough treatment of this topic, see Coleman 1999.

48. Nauta 2002, 235, 206.

49. Nauta 2002, 207; A. Hardie (1983, 183) had previously used the term "career review."

50 Wallace-Hadrill 1996, 297–99.

51. Wallace-Hadrill 1996, 298 and n. 88; see also 307 and n. 128.

52. For Etruscus' age at recall, see Martial 7.40.6.

53. Cf. A. Hardie 1983, 183 (and n. 2): "With one exception (the equestrian procurator Vibius Maximus), no appointment, prospective or confirmed, and no career, actual or potential, is mentioned without reference to the Emperor's indulgence."

54. Coleman 1988, 135–36.

55. Nauta 2002, 217–18; but see Coleman 1988, 222–24, for a different interpretation of his assignment. Because Statius uses poetic language in naming the various public ap-

pointments and offices, sometimes the particular referent is subject to interpretation, as here.

56. Van Dam 1984, 189 (citing Cancik 1968), 190–91.

57. Van Dam (1984, 331) comments on the oxymoron *secrete palam,* paraphrasing it "you live alone, but openly in the midst of all," and "you live apart in the middle of others." The idea of withdrawal, retirement, is the essence of Epicureanism.

58. Men who fathered three children earned a privileged status, with exemption from certain obligations and priority in seeking public office; those who did not actually have three children could acquire this status by a special grant from the emperor.

59. "Through Polla, Statius offers us a glimpse of the imperial woman, like Violentilla an economic power in her own right and an authority within her household" (Newlands 2002, 188).

60. White 1978.

61. Vollmer ([1898] 1971, 213) infers that the performance is mentioned in the damaged portion of the text.

62. Coleman (1988, 83–84) speculates that Statius had prepared 4.2 before attending the banquet.

63. "Circulation," "communication," and "presentation" are all terms used by White (1974, 55 and 56, 40, 56). Nauta (2002) employs "communication" in his subtitle.

64. White 1974, 40 and passim.

65. To support his claim that epic poetry is not, however, profitable, Juvenal declares (7 86–87) that Statius had to sell a pantomime libretto or starve.

66. White (1975) concludes from his survey of the evidence that Martial and Statius share only six patrons, noting that Martial addressed a far greater number of individuals. See Nauta 2002 for a treatment of the two poets in tandem.

67. Nauta 2002, 203

68. See Griffin 2000, 76 and n. 384, where she cites Syme (1958), Jones (1992), and Waters (1964) The quotation is from Newlands (2002, 10).

69. Griffin 2000, 59–76.

70. Newlands 2002, 8–9; she also cites (8 n. 31) the rejection by Coleman (1998) of the idea that 93 was significantly more dangerous than other years.

71. Scott (1933) collects and discusses instances of the religious aspect of the imperial cult under Domitian in the *Silvae.* Vessey (1986, 2798) observes that "[t]he 'Silvae' give us valuable, if poetical, clues as to Domitian's exalted vision of his office," and asserts that "Statius' poems to the Emperor mirror faithfully an ideology developed, self-protectively, by Domitian." Writing elsewhere on the banquet in 4.2, Vessey claims that the *Silvae* "contain . . . an accurate and authentic statement of attitudes purposefully disseminated and encouraged by Domitian himself" (1983, 211).

72. Griffin 2000, 63–64.

73. Griffin 2000, 63; Vollmer [1898] 1971, 384.

74. Scott 1933, 255.

75. Griffin 2002, 81. Jones (1992, 108–109) draws slightly different conclusions from his review of the evidence.

76. Vessey 1983, 210.

77. Scott 1933, 252. Vespasian's coins depict him wearing the radiate crown, which previously had been limited to deceased members of the imperial dynasty; according to Vessey (1983, 213), Domitian brought his father's policy to "a logical conclusion." Solar

symbolism is involved in the radiate crown, and in 4.3 the Sibyl asserts that conditions in several parts of the world would be improved if Domitian drove the sun chariot (136–38/ 170–74).

78. Coleman 1988, 97, commenting on the phrase *ore nitebat* (4.2.43/61).

79. Fears 1981, 56–74 ("Jupiter in Augustan Religious Policy"), 74–80 ("Role of Domitian").

80. Slater 1908, 3.

81. Reeve 1983, 398.

82. Reeve 1983, 397–99; Reeve 1977, 202, 205 and n. 17

83. Coleman (1991, 336) calls Courtney's text "sceptical," and speaks of his refusal to accept the "solecisms, ungrammatical expressions, and plain nonsense" that previous more conservative editors attributed to Statius (334). Verstraete (1992, 381) calls it "a salutary reaction against the generally more conservative editions that have preceded it over the past century." Pucci (1992–93, 158) says that Courtney "has questioned decisions of most of the *Silvae's* modern editors and returned to the earlier traditions of scholarship on these complex poems." Håkanson (1969, 13) criticizes this extremely conservative tendency and states that the purpose of his own book was to oppose it (14).

84. Vessey (1971, 274) argues that Statius' self-proclaimed "*audacia* . . . is a complicating factor in textual criticism of his work. It is difficult to decide just what Statius might have allowed himself to write, just how far he may have strained . . . the normal usages of the Latin tongue for the sake of novel effects." Reeve (1983, 398 n. 12) maintains that Vessey has misinterpreted the word *audacia* and claims that in fact it refers to Statius' extemporization.

85. What follows is based on Coleman (1988, xxviii–xxxii).

86. Slavitt 1997, x.

87. That is, the *Thebaid* (Melville 1992) and the *Achilleid* (Slavitt 1997, 3–37).

88. Boyle and Sullivan (1991, 250–69) include 1.6, 4.2, 4.9, 5.3, and 5.4.

89. Vollmer ([1898] 1971, 265), commenting on 1.3.1, remarks on the importance of beginnings, including but not limited to the first word; he gives *regia* as one of his three examples of an important opening word.

90. Nagle 1995.

91. Courtney 1966, 1968, 1971, 1984, 1988.

BOOK 1

1. An asterisk indicates that the Latin text is discussed in appendix 3.

2. I borrow the phrase "old tradition" as a translation for *fama prior* (1.1.8) from the French version of Izaac (Frère 1944, 1:14), "l'antique Tradition."

3. Statius here alludes to the verse form known as the elegiac couplet. The first line of this couplet is a dactylic hexameter—the meter of epic—while the second line is a pentameter consisting of two units, each containing two and a half hexameters. In Latin as in English the word "foot" has both metrical and anatomical meanings. Because the second line of an elegiac couplet is one "foot" shorter than the first, Latin poets frequently joked about the meter and the personification of Elegy "limping." Here Statius imagines instead that Elegy's second "foot" has grown and therefore she may duly celebrate her poet in higher, epic style.

4. Courtney (1966, 97) finds it implausible that the Muses could be fooled this way; he maintains that *fallit . . . sorores* means something more like "and mixed among the sisters tries to pass."

5. My phrase "water piped" corresponds to the Latin *emissas . . . nymphas* (1.3.37). The word *emissas* is a participle of the verb *emitto,* which means "to dispatch (on a mission)," if applied to a person (*OLD,* s.v. "emitto" 1a), and "to drain off," if applied to a liquid (*OLD,* 5a). The word *nymphas* can mean "water nymphs" or simply "water." Slater (1908, 59) renders it "fountain-fairies," while Mozley ([1928] 1982, 41) calls them "water-nymphs." Shackleton Bailey (2003) capitalizes *Nymphas* in his Latin text (64) but translates the phrase as "water discharged" (65). Although Vollmer ([1898] 1971, 271) notes that Statius frequently uses *nympha* instead of *aqua* to mean "water," I think it is quite possible that Statius has both meanings in mind here—"water drained" and "nymphs let loose."

6. My use of "restful" to translate *pigros* (usually "lazy" or "sluggish") in the phrase *pigros . . . somnos* (1.3.42) is borrowed from Courtney (1984, 332).

7. Vollmer ([1898] 1971, 291), commenting on line 83, cites the testimony of Suetonius (*Vespasian* 16) that Vespasian had reintroduced and increased tribute from the provinces, which his predecessors had partially waived.

8. Vollmer ([1898] 1971, 298) notes, in commenting on line 34, that the use of marble colored red, white (most of all), and green (sparingly) was intended to beautify the bathers' skin tones.

9. Vollmer ([1898] 1971, 310), commenting on line 73, explains that these junkmen also sold toys and did tricks.

BOOK 2

1. The phrase "with too sharp a pencil" corresponds to the Latin *asperiore lima* (2.pref.10; lit., "with too rough file"); perhaps a closer cross-cultural translation would be "with too rough an eraser."

2. The Latin *quem . . . frigidum erat . . . ni statim tradere* (2.pref.17–18) literally means "which [i.e., the actual lion and the lion poem] would have been cold if not delivered immediately." My translation tries to catch the pun in the adjective *frigidum,* which literally means "cold," but figuratively is used of a "lame" or "flat" argument, or a "dull" or "tedious" subject (*OLD,* s.v. "frigidus" 8b, 8c). Perhaps "stale" might also convey this pun.

3. The phrase "reversed my harp" translates *versa . . . / . . . lyra* (2.1.27–28). Both Vollmer ([1898] 1971, 321) and van Dam (1984, 88) discuss this allusion by Statius to the practice of reversing the fasces at the funeral of a Roman magistrate.

4. With "your hope and frequent prayer," I follow Courtney (1971, 96) in interpreting the pronoun *tibi* (2.1.54) as referring to Glaucias. Van Dam (1984, 102–103), however, understands the antecedent as Melior. A translation following that interpretation could read

> Where is the expectation, not remote,
> of manhood yet to come, the hoped-for badge
> of honor on your cheeks, the beard by which
> your master often swore?

5. My neologism "wave-faring" translates Statius' own coinage *fluctivagus* in line 95 (lit., "wave-wandering"); the word also occurs at 3.1.84 (my 122). Van Dam (1984, 118) discusses this neologism and Statius' liking for compound adjectives.

6. In the phrase "hunched for wrestlers' chaining holds," the word "hunched" translates *curvatus* (110). Van Dam (1984, 123) says this adjective "is rather rare before St[atius], and then generally of old age." Perhaps "stooped" would even more effectively catch the paradox of a young athlete as *curvatus*. Shackleton Bailey (2003) omits *curvatus* in his translation of line 110.

7. The phrase "and wore / a charming cloak" renders Courtney's reading *gratus amictu* in line 113 (lit., "charming with a cloak"). Van Dam (1984) prints *Graius amictu* (lit., "Greek in respect to his cloak," or in my context "a Greek-style cloak") and comments on the text and the cultural significance of wearing the *pallium* in imperial Rome "especially by the bookish upper middle class, which thereby symbolized its dedication to Greek culture" (125). Shackleton Bailey (2003) also reads *Graius amictu*.

8. The repetition in "boldly" and "bolder" reflects the repetition of †*magis*† *sequitur . . . magis . . . trahentem* (2.1.198; lit., "he follows more . . . dragging more"). The translation "boldly" (rather than "more") derives from a solution Courtney (1968, 54) suggested for the crux: *audens*.

9. My three lines condense five of Statius' (36–40):

> non, mihi si cunctos Helicon indulgeat amnes
> et superet Piplea sitim largeque volantis
> ungula se det equi reseretque arcana pudicos
> Phemonoe fontes vel quos meus auspice Phoebo
> altius immersa turbavit Pollius urna[.]

Literally, this means "Not if Helicon should lavish on me all its streams [i.e., Aganippe and Hippocrene] and Piplea [a spring on a mountain in Pieria] should overcome my thirst, and the hoof of the flying horse [i.e., Hippocrene] should bestow itself copiously, and the mysterious Phemonoe [the first Pythia] should unlock the chaste spring [i.e , Castalia] or the ones which my Pollius, under Apollo's auspices, has roiled by immersing his urn more deeply."

Van Dam (1984, 218) comments on the several instances of etymological wordplay in these few lines. "Piplea" is derived from the Greek verb *pimplēmi,* which means "to fill," as *superet . . . sitim* (overcome thirst) suggests. The "flying horse's hoof" alludes to Hippocrene ("Horse Spring"), so named for the belief that is sprang forth from where Pegasus' hoof had struck. Phemonoe, whose name is derived from the Greek *phēmēn noeō* (to know prophecy) is appropriately described as "mysterious" (*arcana*). The "chaste spring" which Phemonoe might unlock puns on the similarity of Castalia, a spring at Delphi, to the Latin word *castus* (chaste).

10. I owe my translation of *non talem* (25) as "no match" to Mozley ([1928] 1982, 121), who rendered the synonymous *qualem nec* in line 30 as "outmatching."

11. See note 10.

12. I have translated the phrase *reis . . . raptis* in line 95 of Courtney's text. Van Dam (1984, 444–45) suggests *aliis . . raptis,* which could be translated in context as "to those whom you console / when other people die."

13. This list of works by Lucan in lines 65–88 (54–72 in the original) is roughly chronological; the only one which survives, except for a few fragments of several others, is the epic known as the *Bellum Civile* (*The Civil War*), which was incomplete at the time of the poet's death. Our other source of information about Lucan's corpus is the ancient biography (*vita Lucani*) attributed to Vacca. Among the lost works, Vacca refers to one about Troy (*Iliacon*), one about the Underworld (*Catachthonion*), a panegyric of Nero which won a prize when

it was performed in Pompey's Theater (*laudes in Neronem*), an extemporaneous work of some kind—a mime libretto, a dramatic monologue, or something else—about Orpheus (*Orpheus*), and a work—scholars have debated whether it was in verse or prose—about the famous fire at Rome (*de incendio Urbis*). In Statius' list, the reference to Hector and Priam may correspond to the *Iliacon;* "the realm Below," to the *Catachthonion;* "ungrateful Nero," to the *laudes in Neronem;* "Orpheus," obviously, to *Orpheus;* and the "sinful despot's wicked fire," to *de incendio Urbis.* The "discourse" (*adlocutione*) about Polla does not appear on Vacca's list (unless perhaps it is one of Lucan's *Silvae*), or in any other source; it is conventionally referred to by the word Statius uses here, as the *adlocutio ad Pollam* (address to Polla). Finally, of course, Philippi and Pharsalus refer to the *Bellum Civile.* The above account is indebted to van Dam (1984, 477–83).

BOOK 3

1. The phrase "put back the thwarts" translates the Latin *transtra reponat* in line 28. Courtney (1988, 44 n. 5) cites Casson (1968, 262), who argues that a freighter of this type would not have oars or rowers' benches, and translates *transtra reponat* as "replace the hatch covers." If one accepts Casson's argument, then my translation could read "cover the hatches." Courtney counters, however, that Statius was a poet, and a *poet's* ship does have oars.

2. The phrase "(bad luck to use it twice)" is a gloss, based on Vollmer ([1898] 1971, 398), who comments that the act of throwing the gangplank overboard appears to be a superstition.

3. In translating *armatis seu iura dares* (94) as "or made / rulings in courts martial," I follow the version of Izaac (Frère 1944, 1:109), "rendre la justice à tons bataillons," rather than the more common interpretation of, e.g., Slater (1908, 120), "dispense justice by moral authority to armed tribesman," and Mozley ([1928] 1982, 163), "giving laws to armed peoples " Shackleton Bailey (2003, 195) offers a version which is nicely ambiguous—"gave judgment to men in arms."

4. Here (line 18 of the Latin), and again at my line 115 (81 of the Latin), I follow the paragraphing of Mozley ([1928] 1982) and Shackleton Bailey (2003), who also starts a new paragraph at line 89 (my 126). Courtney prints the poem as an uninterrupted block of 112 lines.

5. In lines 131–32 I translate the crux Courtney prints in line 93 of his Latin text: †*litus libertatemque Menandri†.* Shackleton Bailey (2003) adopts Baehrens's emendation of *lusus* for *litus,* and Markland's reading of *iocandi* for *Menandri,* and then translates this as "the shows, the freedom of jest."

BOOK 4

1. My phrase "at both a sparring match and bayonet practice" translates the Latin *et sphaeromachia . . . palaris lusio* (30–31 in Courtney's edition). I follow the *OLD* definition of *sphaeromachia* as a boxing match with padded fists; hence my notion of "a sparring match." Coleman (1988, 61) understands *sphaeromachia* as a different kind of training with safety precautions, namely, fencing with foils. The phrase *palaris lusio* literally means "play involving wooden stakes." According to Coleman, soldiers and gladiators practiced with

wooden swords against a stake, i.e., a dummy target; hence my cross-cultural "bayonet practice."

2. Coleman (1988, 69–71) concludes that Statius is referring to the temple of Janus which Domitian completed in 95, and which was located in the Forum Transitorium (*novique / . . . fori*, 14–15 = "the newest Forum's," 22) near the Temple of Peace. Janus is traditionally associated with peace, inasmuch as his gates are open in time of war and closed in time of peace; thus Peace is both physically and spiritually "close" to Janus. In order to convey the double meaning in *vicina*, I have translated the Latin phrase *vicina Pace ligatum* (13; lit., "bound to neighboring Peace") as "whom you have linked to Peace, / who's close to him."

3. The Latin in line 38, *et tibi longaevi renovabitur ara Tarenti*, literally means "and the altar of agèd Tarentum will be renewed by you." My version of this cryptically allusive line, "you will repeat the New Age Jubilee," glosses it as a reference to the ceremonies of the Ludi Saeculares ("Secular Games" or, to make the meaning somewhat clearer in English, "Centennial Games"). Domitian had held them in 88; they were due in 110 years (the interval Domitian borrowed from Augustus), so Janus is predicting hyperbolically that the emperor will still be ruling in 198 (see the introduction).

4. Coleman (1988, 100) interprets the phrase *templa . . . des* (60; "may you give temples") as referring to "Domitian's entire programme for building temples, not merely those projects honouring the deified Flavians" (i.e., the *rata numina*, "the duly deified," in line 59). If the phrase does refer only to projects for the Flavians, I could translate "and build temples for them" instead of "and build new shrines for gods."

5. See Coleman (1988, 114–16) for an explanation, with illustrations (figure 3, plates 1–2), of the appearance and function of the "blocks" (*umbonibus*, 47) and "posts" (*gonfis*, 48).

6. I owe my rendering of *impeditus* (68) as "tangled" to Coleman (1988, 17), who translates it as "entangled."

7. I owe my rendering of *dubias* (77) as "hesitant" to Coleman (1988, 17).

8. The literal meaning of line 156, *ultra sidera flammeumque solem*, is "beyond the stars and fiery sun." Coleman (1988, 134) cites Housman (1906, 44–45), who interprets this line as "south of the zodiac and the ecliptic." The words "ecliptic" and even "zodiac" (or "equator") sound too prosaic and scientific for Statius' epic tone here, especially since this phrase echoes Virgil *Aeneid* 6.795–805.

9. I owe my translation of *stagnum navale* (6) as "Naval Basin" to Mozley ([1928] 1982, 229). Slater (1908, 153) called it "Sea-fight Lake," since it was used for mock naval battles.

10. The phrase "garden homes" translates *suburbanis . . . hortis* (7). Mozley ([1928] 1982, 229) uses the phrase "suburban pleasure-gardens," while Coleman (1988, 23) renders it "the gardens on the outskirts of the city." Shackleton Bailey (2003, 267 and n. 3) calls them "suburban villas" and insists that *horti* are not "gardens" but "a suburban residence (villa)," citing Martial 5.62. In that epigram Martial does speak of having purchased *horti* which are in need of furnishing, and that does sound more like a residence than a park. Nonetheless, *OLD* (s.v. "hortus" 2) defines the word (usually plural in this sense) as "Pleasure-grounds or gardens," citing as an example Cornelius Nepos *Atticus* 14.3, *nullos habuit [hort]os, nullam suburbanam . . . villam* ("he had no *horti*, no suburban villa"), which seems to contrast rather than equate the two things. The *Thesaurus Linguae Latinae* VI 3016.76–79 cites a longer version of the passage from Nepos, along with ones from Cicero *Pro Milone* 74 and Pliny *Historiae Naturales* 36.123, which seem to group *horti* along with

other types of property that include both land and a residence. As an alternative to "garden homes," either "estates" or "mansions" might better convey the socioeconomic nuances of Statius' phrase *suburbanis . . . hortis.*

11. Literally, *sonus circumit* (26) means "sound goes around." See Coleman (1988, 143), who comments that the idea of ears "buzzing" as a sign that one was being talked about corresponds to our concept of them "burning."

12. The Latin which I have rendered as "the Probate Court's presiding spear" (*centeni moderatrix iudicis hasta,* 43) literally means "the presiding spear of the hundred jurors." I call this court "Probate" rather than the traditional "Centumviral" (which refers to the jury pool of one hundred men) because it served as a court for cases relating to wills (among other kinds of important civil suits) and influenced the development of the Roman law of succession (Berger [1949] 1966). A spear (*hasta*) was planted in front of the tribunal in the Basilica Julia; so here, as Coleman (1988, 146) observes, Statius personifies the spear as the jury itself.

13. The verb I have translated as "he is stitching" is *subtexit* (59). *OLD* (s.v. "subtexo" 3b) cites this passage to illustrate the definition "follow up with something additional." This is a metaphorical extension of the meaning of weaving something inside or under another piece of fabric (for which *OLD,* 1, includes *Silvae* 1.2.99 among the illustrative passages: "and weave your myrtle in your laurel wreath," 1.2 130). Coleman (1988, 35–36) determines that Marcellus' "current post" is the office of *praetor,* which he held in 95 CE, and "another task" refers to his appointment as *curator Viae Latinae* (superintendent of the Latin Highway) for the following year.

14. My translation of *obliquae* (60) as "slanting" is borrowed from Coleman (1988, 149), who argues that *obliquae* refers to the diagonal southeast direction of the Latin Road across Italy. Vollmer ([1898] 1971, 464), on the other hand, understands it as a reference to the hilly terrain through which the road passed; *obliquae* in that case could be translated as "sloping." Coleman refutes Vollmer by insisting that *obliquae* refers only to direction, never to elevation.

15. The Latin *in omni vertice Romuli* (33) literally means "on every peak of Romulus," but my version, "Rome's septuple hills," tries to capture the hint of a pun on Septimius' name that Coleman (1988, 166) notes in this line.

16. My version of lines 47–48, *sunt Urbe Romanisque turmis / qui Libyam deceant alumni* (lit., "there are foster sons in the City and the Roman squadrons who would befit Libya"), is based on the interpretation of Coleman (1988, 169) that Severus is one of those knights at Rome who are a credit to Africa. Previous translations by Slater (1908, 158), Mozley ([1928] 1982, 241), and Izaac (Frère 1944, 2.156) were apparently influenced by Vollmer's notion ([1898] 1971, 472) that in contrast to Septimius, some native Romans behave as badly as Africans. That interpretation could be rendered as follows: "But ranked as knights are sons of Rome / whose actions suit an African." Shackleton Bailey (2003) translates these two lines as "In the City and Rome's squadrons there are some worthy to be fosterlings of Libya" and argues against Coleman's version (279 and n. 5).

17. Whether or not the title (*Hercules Epitrapezios Novi Vindicis*) is Statius' own, he appears to be alluding to the name of this statuette with a repeated bilingual pun, a leitmotif in the poem. He repeats forms of the word *mensa* ("table"; in the plural, also "meal") six times (in the translation, lines 21, 43, 58, 73, 79, 96; in the Latin, lines 16, 32, 45, 56, 60, 74). Every time but once it is prominently placed at the end of a line, and the last appearance is expressly the "last" (the phrase *supremis . . . mensis* refers to Alexander's last meal).

18. Lines 15–16 of the original, *donec ab Elysiis prospexit sedibus alter / Castor,* literally mean "until the other Castor looked forth from his Elysian home." Castor's twin is Pollux (together they are the constellation Gemini). Vollmer ([1898] 1971, 477) discusses their association with the Morning and Evening Stars; Coleman (1988, 150) comments on the more familiar tradition associating them with the Underworld, and the idea that they alternated days "on earth and beneath it."

19. In line 70 the Latin *fertur Thebanos tantum excusasse triumphos* literally means "he is said only to have justified his Theban victory." I have made explicit Statius' imputation of a reason for Alexander's regrets about Thebes. For the idea that Alexander felt guilty only for the destruction of Thebes, Coleman (1988, 189) cites Plutarch *Alexander* 13.

20. The phrase in line 84 of the Latin, *furias immisit honestas,* literally means "loosed honorable frenzy." According to Florus 1.22.6, cited by Vollmer ([1898] 1971, 482), the Saguntines built a pyre in the middle of their forum on which they destroyed, by fire and the sword, their possessions, their families, and themselves.

21. Coleman (1988, 200) points out the pun on the addressee's name, so typical of Statius; to catch it in translation, one might say "For the Greatest, I try a slimmer song." Coleman further maintains (204) that *alter Maximus* (32; "another [or 'a second'] Maximus") is another such pun, since there cannot be more than one "greatest"; I find this somewhat unconvincing, since a Latin superlative need not be exclusive, and thus *maximus* can mean "very great" instead of "greatest."

22. The phrase "nomad Slavs" renders *refugis . . . / Sarmatis* (50–51), which more literally means "fugitive [or 'runaway'] Sarmatians." In this interpretation of *refugis* as "nomad," I follow Coleman (1988, 207).

23. I owe my translation of *socii portus* (7) as "fellow-harbor" to that of Mozley ([1928] 1982, 257), "fellow-haven."

24. The "grandfather" here is Pollius Felix, and the seaside villa is the one in *Silvae* 2.2 and 3.1.

25. This evidently refers to a statue; see Vollmer [1898] 1971, 490; Coleman 1988, 217. Before Housman (1906, 46) emended the feminine *Eumelis* to the masculine *Eumelus,* Eumelis was identified with Parthenope, the Siren for whom Naples was originally named (line 3 of this poem addresses Naples as Parthenope; for an allusion to the myth, see 3.5.79–80/112–14). There is inscriptional evidence for Eumelus as a local god, but Coleman objects that a god should be receiving worship, not bestowing it, and suggests he is a hero or prominent citizen. She also observes that the phrase *felix Eumelus* may be one of Statius' characteristic bilingual puns, since *eumēlos* in Greek means "rich in sheep."

26. The line break after "before" seems awkward, but oddly Statius himself ends line 16 with the conjunction *priusquam.*

27. Coleman (1988, 51) translates *nec lenes halicae nec asperum far* (31) as "No smooth-tasting groats or rough flour," but her note (233) interprets this pair as "two types of *puls* with contrasting flavours." My translation is meant to convey the idea that these two grains are used for porridge, as well the interpretation of Newmyer (1987, 71) that the contrast between *lenes* and *asperum* is one of texture rather than taste.

BOOK 5

1. The word "mane-brushed" renders the crux †*iubatis*† (83; lit., "maned"). Shackleton Bailey (2003) emends to *gravatis,* which he translates as "burdened."

2. For Domitian's temperate habits, see Suetonius *Domitian* 21.

3. According to Suetonius *Domitian* 13, the emperor permitted statues of himself to be erected on the Capitoline only if they were of gold or silver, and of specific weight.

4. Here Statius alludes to the *lavatio Magnae Matris* on 27 March; Vollmer ([1898] 1971, 507) notes that technically Cybele ends her mourning for Attis on 25 March.

5. Vollmer ([1898] 1971, 508) cites Tacitus *Annales* 16.6 as evidence that the Egyptian practice of embalming apparently was first introduced to Rome by Nero for his wife Poppaea in 65 CE.

6. This refers to an appointment as military tribune, the first step not only for those intending to pursue a military career but for any who wished to be a senator. In this poem, Statius praises Crispinus for his appointment to this post at age sixteen, two years earlier than usual. The poet's point of departure is an actual trip by Crispinus. Statius then speculates about his addressee's travel when the youth is appointed in the future. By the poem's end, the emperor has already made the appointment.

7. My translation "the British shores / which block the waves split by the setting sun" corresponds to the Latin *negantem / fluctibus occiduo fissis Hyperione Thulen* (54–55). The underlined Latin phrase corresponds to my "split by the setting." I have adapted my translation from that of Courtney (1986, 45), whose emendation it is: "Britain which resists the waves cleft by the setting sun."

8. Courtney (1986) adopts Leo's reading *tunc* and prints *nec tunc reus ipse timebat* (lit., "and the one not then the defendant himself was afraid"). Vollmer ([1898] 1971) printed the reading of M, *nec te reus ipse timebat;* paraphrased it as "et ipse is, qui non erat reus, te timebat" ("and the one who was not the defendant himself feared you"); and explained it as meaning that Crispinus' brilliant defense put the prosecutor in an awkward or even dangerous position (184, 518). Mozley based his translation on Vollmer's interpretation: "and even the innocent feared thee" ([1928] 1982, 296–97 and note c).

I have translated Courtney's text—"and even those not then [*tunc*] on trial feared you" —adding "you" for clarity, and translating "those" rather than "the one" to generalize (not just the prosecutor but everyone else in the court). Shackleton Bailey (2003) reads *et te reus ipse timebat*, translates this as "even the accused himself was in fear of you," and asserts that his emendation produces a "logical climax. The statues have never heard anything like this . . . , the Senators are dumbfounded, and the defendant himself is frightened by his advocate's demonic eloquence" (340–41, 397).

9. With the phrase "you'd be distracted" I have translated the crux †*averteret*†, which Courtney prints in line 60; but his App. Crit. cites *hau cedere* as his own earlier suggestion (Courtney 1966, 99–100). If I adopted that suggestion, I could translate the passage this way:

> lead the groaning myself, to whom you could
> not fail to be returned by Cerberus
> with all his mouths nor rules Orpheus broke.

10. My translation of *se . . . / . . . in iusta dedit mihi* in lines 71–72 follows the interpretation of Courtney (1984, 339), "presented themselves to me for performance of the due obsequies."

11. Minerva invented the flute, but then she threw it away because of how it made her look when she played, cursing anyone who picked it up; Marsyas did so, and hence her delight at his being flayed alive after Apollo defeated him (Vollmer [1898] 1971, 531).

12. In lines 121–22, "those who toil †deploying† / Thebes' battlefields in epic lines," I translate Courtney's *quis labor Aonios seno pede †duceret† campos* (92; lit. "those whose toil it is to lead [or, 'arrange'] Aonian [i.e., Boeotian] fields by means of six feet at a time [i.e., in hexameter lines]"). Vollmer ([1898] 1971, 532) prints *ducere* unobelized and comments on the multiple meanings both in the verb *ducere*—"to be a leader on the battlefield" and "to be a leader in the art of representation/description"—and in the phrase *Aonios. . . campos:* "Boeotian" fields are both those around Thebes, i.e., an allusion to the Seven against Thebes and literary treatments including Statius' own *Thebaid,* and those associated with the Muses on Helicon. Mozley ([1928] 1982, 310, 311) adopts *cantus* (songs) and translates "those . . . whose toil it is to guide Aonian song in six-foot measures." Shackleton Bailey (2003, 354, 355) likewise reads *cantus,* but omits *Aonios* in his translation: "they whose toil it is to make song in six-foot measures." Leaving the adjective out is reasonable, since it does not add anything really meaningful—an argument in favor of reading *campos.*

13. Those who "maim their epic flow by just a foot" (131; *heroos gressu truncare tenores,* 99) are writers of elegy. On the elegiac couplet, which alternates hexameter (i.e., epic) and pentameter lines, see note 3 on 1.2.11–12; 1.2.9L.

14. The parenthetical gloss "(as Homer said)" alludes to *Iliad* 3.222 ("words like snowflakes in a winter storm"), which Vollmer ([1898] 1971, 533) cites as the origin of the simile in line 103: *et effreno nimbos aequare profatu* ("and match cloudbursts / . . . with utterance unbridled").

15. In lines 114–15 (*ora . . . Pylii ducis oraque regis / Dulichii*), Statius literally refers to "the mouth of the Pylian leader and the mouth of the Dulichian king." Vollmer ([1898] 1971, 535) cites Quintilian 12.10.64 for the different oratorical styles with which Homer endowed these two characters.

16. The reference to Chalcis has provoked scholarly discussion, since the place has no immediately obvious connection with Sappho. Based on Politian's marginal note *quidam leucade,* scholars have debated whether the text in line 155 should read *Leucade* rather than *Chalcide,* since there was a tradition that Sappho jumped to her death from the cliffs of Leucas (see Ovid's *Heroides* 15, the Letter from Sappho). Vollmer ([1898] 1971, 539) quotes from Buecheler's letter to him, suggesting that someone connected it with the Chalcis on or near the island of Lesbos (otherwise unknown except for the reference in Stephanus Byzantius which he cites); Buecheler also notes a possible pun between *Chalcis* and the Greek word for bronze, *calchos,* appropriate in a context of "masculine leaps" and being "recklessly unafraid." Frère (1944, 2:199 n. 5) suggests that "Chalcis" here is a metonym for contests between two poets, since a tradition associates a contest between Homer and Hesiod at the funeral for Amphidamus of Chalcis; here it would mean that Sappho would have been unafraid of a contest with Alcaeus, her male contemporary lyric poet from Lesbos. Shackleton Bailey (2003) adopts the reading *Leucade* (360), but suggests that if *Chalcide* is the correct reading, it is "a mistake . . . a possibility not to be excluded, especially in a poem published posthumously" (402).

17. My translation of *quam non mihi gloria maior* in line 219 is indebted to the paraphrase of Vollmer ([1898] 1971, 543).

18. Frère (1944, 2:160 n. 4), commenting on 4.6.86, quotes Valerius Maximus 1.2 ext. 3 on Sulla's Apollo statuette; before a battle, in front of his troops Sulla would embrace and pray to a statuette of Apollo taken from Delphi.

19. I retain Courtney's crux †*et crimina fertet*† (and bring accusations) in line 14, but my translation follows the interpretation of Vollmer ([1898] 1971), who prints these words without the obeli (199) and explains these *crimina* as "accusations against the gods" (549). Like Mozley ([1928] 1982), Shackleton Bailey (2003) adopts Politian's *ferto* and translates *cineremque oculis et crimina ferto* as "let her endure with her eyes the ashes and the crime" (374, 375). Mozley's version, "let her endure to behold these ashes and this crime" (333), is somewhat clearer and certainly more idiomatic.

20. Courtney reads <*ullum*> / . . . *diem* (76–77; lit., "any day"); Vollmer ([1898] 1971, 201, 553) adopts Baehrens's suggestion *unum*, which could be rendered here as "a single day."

Works Cited

Ahl, Frederick M. 1984. "The Art of Safe Criticism in Greek and Rome." *American Journal of Philology* 105: 174–208.

Arens, J. C. 1950. "-Fer and -Ger: Their Extraordinary Preponderance among Compounds in Roman Poetry." *Mnemosyne*, 4th ser., 3: 241–62.

Berger, Adolf. [1949] 1966. "Centumviri." In *The Oxford Classical Dictionary* [1949] 1966, 180.

Boyle, A. J., and J. P Sullivan, eds. 1991. *Roman Poets of the Early Empire*. London.

Bright, David F. 1980. *Elaborate Disarray: The Nature of Statius' "Silvae."* Meisenheim am Glan.

Cairns, Francis. 1972. *Generic Composition in Greek and Roman Poetry* Edinburgh.

Cancik, Hubert. 1965. *Untersuchungen zur lyrischen Kunst des P. Papinius Statius* Spudasmata 13. Hildesheim

———. 1968. "Eine epikureische Villa: Statius, Silv. II.2: Villa Surrentina." *Altsprachliche Unterricht* 11.1: 62–75.

Casson, Lionel. 1968. "Maecius Celer's Ship." *Classical Review* 18: 261–62.

Clinton, Kevin. 1972. "Publius Papinius ST[——] at Eleusis " *Transactions of the American Philological Association* 103: 79–82.

Coleman, K. M , ed and trans. 1988. *Silvae IV*. By Statius. Oxford.

———. 1991. "A Forest Transformed." Review of Courtney 1990. *Classical Review*, n.s., 41: 334–36.

———. 1998. "Martial Book 8 and the Politics of 93 AD " In *Greek Poetry, Drama, Prose, Roman Poetry*, edited by Francis Cairns and Malcolm Heath, 337–57. Papers of the Leeds International Latin Seminar, 1996. Leeds.

———. 1999 "Mythological Figures as Spokespersons in Statius' *Silvae*." In *Im Spiegel des Mythos: Bilderwelt und Lebenswelt / Lo specchio del mito· Immaginario e realtà*, edited by Francesoco de Angelis and Susanne Muth, 67–80. Wiesbaden.

Connors, Catherine. 2001. "Imperial Space and Time. The Literature of Leisure." In *Literature in the Roman World*, edited by Oliver Taplin, 208–34. Oxford

Courtney, E. 1966. "On the *Silvae* of Statius." *Bulletin of the Institute of Classical Studies* 13: 94–100.

———. 1968 "Emendations of Statius' *Silvae*." *Bulletin of the Institute of Classical Studies* 15: 51–57.

———. 1971. "Further Remarks on the *Silvae* of Statius." *Bulletin of the Institute of Classical Studies* 18: 95–97.

———. 1984. "Criticisms and Elucidations of the *Silvae* of Statius." *Transactions of the American Philological Association* 114: 327–41.

———. 1988. "Problems in the *Silvae* of Statius." *Classical Philology* 83: 43–45.

———, ed. [1990] 1992. *P. Papini Stati Silvae*. Oxford.

Dewar, Michael. 1994 "Laying It On with a Trowel: The Proem to Lucan and Related Texts." *Classical Quarterly* 44· 199–211.

Fears, J. Rufus. 1981. "The Cult of Jupiter and Roman Imperial Ideology." *Aufstieg und Niedergang der römischen Welt* 2.17.1: 3–141.

Feeney, Denis. 1996. "Statius, Publius Papinius." In *The Oxford Classical Dictionary* 1996, 1439.

Filangieri, R., and F. Sbordone. 1958. "Neologismi nelle 'Selve' di Publio Papinio Stazio." *Atti della Accademia Pontaniana* 6: 35–56.

Frère, Henri, ed. 1944. *Silves*. By Statius. Translated by H. J. Izaac. 2 vols. Paris.

Geyssen, John W. 1996. *Imperial Panegyric in Statius: A Literary Commentary on "Silvae" 1.1*. New York.

Griffin, Miriam. 2000. "Domitian." In *Cambridge Ancient History*, edited by John Boardman et al., 11:54–83. 2nd ed. 1984–2000. Cambridge.

Griffith, John G. 1969. "Juvenal, Statius, and the Flavian Establishment." *Greece and Rome* 16. 134–50

Håkanson, Lennart. 1969. *Statius' "Silvae": Critical and Exegetical Remarks with Some Notes on the "Thebaid."* Lund.

Hardie, Alex. 1983. *Statius and the "Silvae": Poets, Patrons, and Epideixis in the Greco-Roman World*. Liverpool.

Hardie, W R. 1904. "Notes on the *Silvae* of Statius." *Classical Review* 18: 156–58.

Henderson, John 1998. *A Roman Life: Rutilius Gallicus on Paper and in Stone* Exeter.

Housman, A. E. 1906. "The *Silvae* of Statius." 20: 37–47.

Jones, Brian W. 1992. *The Emperor Domitian* London.

Melville, A. D., trans. 1992. *Thebaid*. By Statius. Oxford.

Mozley, J. H., trans. [1928] 1982. *Statius*. Vol. 1. Cambridge, Mass.

Nagle, Betty Rose. 1977. Review of Cairns 1972. *Helios*, n.s., 11: 78–87.

———. 1995. *Ovid's "Fasti": Roman Holidays* Bloomington, Ind.

Nauta, Ruurd. 2002. *Poetry for Patrons: Literary Communication in the Age of Domitian*. Mnemosyne, suppl. 206. Leiden

Newlands, Carole 1988. "Statius' Villa Poems and Ben Jonson's *To Penshurst:* The Shaping of a Tradition." *Classical and Modern Literature* 8: 291–300.

———. 2002. *Statius' "Silvae" and the Poetics of Empire*. Cambridge.

Newmyer, Stephen Thomas. 1979. *The "Silvae" of Statius: Structure and Theme* Mnemosyne, suppl. 53. Leiden.

———, comm. 1987. *Silvae* By Statius. Bryn Mawr Latin Commentaries. Bryn Mawr, Pa.

Nisbet, R. G. M. 1978. "*Felicitas* at Surrentum (Statius, *Silvae* II.2)." *Journal of Roman Studies* 68: 1–11.

OLD. See *Oxford Latin Dictionary* 1982.

The Oxford Classical Dictionary. [1949] 1966. Edited by M. Cary, J. D. Denniston, et al. Oxford.

The Oxford Classical Dictionary. 1996. Edited by Simon Hornblower and Anthony Spaworth. 3rd ed. Oxford.

Oxford Latin Dictionary. 1982. Edited by P. G. W. Glare. Oxford

Pavlovskis, Zoja. 1973. *Man in an Artificial Landscape: The Marvels of Civilization in Imperial Roman Literature*. Mnemonsyne, suppl. 25. Leiden.

Phillimore, John S., ed. [1905] 1962. *P. Papini Stati Silvae*. Oxford.

Pucci, Joseph. 1992–93. Review of Courtney 1990. *Classical World* 86: 157–58.

Reeve, M. D. 1977. "Statius' *Silvae* in the Fifteenth Century." *Classical Quarterly*, n.s., 27: 202–25

———. 1983. "Statius." In *Texts and Transmission: A Survey of the Latin Classics,* edited by L. D. Reynolds, 394–99. Oxford.

Scott, Kenneth. 1933. "Statius' Adulation of Domitian." *American Journal of Philology* 54: 247–59.

Shackleton Bailey, D. R., ed. and trans. 2003. *Silvae.* By Statius. Cambridge, Mass.

Sinfield, Alan. 1992. *Faultlines: Cultural Materialism and the Politics of Dissident Reading.* Berkeley.

Slater, D. A., trans. 1908. *The "Silvae" of Statius.* Oxford.

Slavitt, David R., trans. 1997. *Broken Columns: Two Roman Epic Fragments.* Philadelphia.

Syme, Ronald. 1958. *Tacitus.* Oxford.

Szelest, Hanna. 1972. "Mythologie und ihre Rolle in den 'Silvae' des Statius." *Eos* 60: 309–17.

Tanner, R. G. 1986. "Epic Tradition and Epigram in Statius." *Aufstieg und Niedergang der römischen Welt* 2.32.5: 3020–46.

van Dam, Harm-Jan. 1984. *P. Papinius Statius Silvae Book II: A Commentary.* Mnemosyne, suppl. 82. Leiden.

———. 1988. Review of A. Hardie 1983. *Gnomon* 60: 704–12.

Verstraete, Beert. 1992. Review of Courtney 1990. *Phoenix* 46: 380–82.

Vessey, D. W. T. C. 1971. Review of Håkanson 1969. *Classical Philology* 66: 273–76.

———. 1983. "*Mediis Discumbere in Astris:* Statius, *Silvae,* IV, 2." *L'Antiquité classique* 52: 206–20.

———. 1986. "Transience Preserved: Style and Theme in Statius 'Silvae.'" *Aufstieg und Niedergang der römischen Welt* 2.32.5: 2754–802.

Vollmer, Friedrich, ed. and trans. [1898] 1971. *Publius Papinius Statius Silvarum Libri.* Hildesheim.

Wallace-Hadrill, Andrew. 1996. "The Imperial Court." In *Cambridge Ancient History,* edited by John Boardman et al., 10:283–308. 2nd ed. 1984–2000. Cambridge.

Waters, K. H. 1964. "The Character of Domitian." *Phoenix* 18: 49–77.

White, Peter. 1974. "The Presentation and Dedication of the *Silvae* and the *Epigrams.*" *Journal of Roman Studies* 64: 40–61.

———. 1975. "The Friends of Martial, Statius, and Pliny, and the Dispersal of Patronage." *Harvard Studies in Classical Philology* 79: 265–300.

———. 1978. "*Amicitia* and the Profession of Poetry in Early Imperial Rome." *Journal of Roman Studies* 68: 72–92.

BETTY ROSE NAGLE, Associate Professor of Classical Studies at Indiana University, is the author of *The Poetics of Exile: Program and Polemic in the* Tristia *and* Epistulae ex Ponto *of Ovid* and the translator of *Ovid's* Fasti: *Roman Holidays,* also published by Indiana University Press.